THE SIEGE
OF ISFAHAN

Also by Jean-Christophe Rufin

THE ABYSSINIAN

THE SIEGE
OF ISFAHAN

Jean-Christophe Rufin

Translated from the French

by Willard Wood

W · W · Norton & Company

New York · London

Copyright © Editions GALLIMARD, Paris, 1998
English translation copyright © 2001 by W. W. Norton & Company, Inc.
Originally published in French as *Sauver Ispahan*

First published as a Norton paperback 2002

For information about permission to reproduce selections
from this book, write to Permissions,
W. W. Norton & Company, Inc.,
500 Fifth Avenue, New York, NY 10110

The text of this book is composed in 11.5/13.5 Granjon
with the display set in Granjon and Arabesque Ornaments Two
Composition by Gina Webster
Manufacturing by Quebecor Fairfield
Book design by Margaret M. Wagner
Production manager: Leelo Märjamaa-Reintal
Manuscript editor: Amy Robbins

Library of Congress Cataloging-in-Publication Data
Rufin, Jean-Christophe, 1952–
[Sauver Isfahan. English]
The siege of Isfahan / Jean-Christophe Rufin ; translated by Willard Wood.
    p.   cm.
ISBN 0-393-04988-4
I. Wood, Willard. II. Title.

PQ2678.U357 S2813 2001
843'.914—dc21   00-048953

ISBN 0-393-32339-0 pbk.

W. W. Norton & Company, Inc., 500 Fifth Avenue, New York, N.Y. 10110
www.wwnorton.com

W. W. Norton & Company Ltd., Castle House, 75/76 Wells Street, London W1T 3QT

1 2 3 4 5 6 7 8 9 0

THE SIEGE
OF ISFAHAN

I
THE BIRTH
OF A LIE

1

There was nothing to suggest that a scandal was brewing. The royal caravanserai in Kashan was still in those days the most beautiful of the enormous inns where travelers and their servants and horses could find safety and rest along the hard roads of the Orient. It had been built one hundred years earlier at the instigation of the great Shah Abbas, the liberator of Persia. According to tradition, when that king visited the caravanserai's kitchens, the lids on the bubbling pots over the fire rose two inches in the air as he passed, to show him that all inanimate objects came under his sway, as well as all men. From that time on, the inn had never failed to strike those who stayed there with its splendor. A great sense of peace reigned over it, and there was no sign that it was about to be abruptly shattered.

True, everyone had smiled on the previous evening to see a wretched and peculiar-looking Frankish traveler arrive. It would be hard to imagine a more pitiful retinue: other than himself, the traveler had only one servant, a tiny, doddering Mongol, to care for his ancient mule. The Mongol's flat face, hideous to the Persians in that it reminded them of Tamerlane and the tribes from the Asian steppes, was deeply wrinkled, and his chin was adorned with three or four thick gray hairs, twisted like strands of sisal. His calves were encased in rags held in place by ratty strips of cowhide. The master was hardly more presentable. On the first night, he had been seen only by candlelight and had managed not to show his face much. A high collar was drawn up around his ears, and a wide-brimmed hat shaded his features. His clothes were worn and very dirty, but he seemed in no hurry to shed them. To judge from the extreme modesty of his luggage, he most likely had nothing to change into. Toward ten o'clock, with no one yet having heard the sound of his voice, he silently crossed the courtyard. To reach his apartment, he deliberately avoided the main stairs, called *muhtabi* in Persian, or "place of moonlight," where Persians generally congregate at night to admire the cool reflection of the nocturnal orb. The idlers lounging there commented mildly on this strange figure, for the Frank seemed to carry considerable weight at the hips, and his trousers, which the Franks generally wear tight, were baggy. But Persians are for the most part resigned to the peculiarities of foreigners. Their deformities are proof of the corrupting effect of eating impure meats; the Prophet in his wisdom had declared them unlawful, but foreigners gorged on them vilely.

Everyone had also seen two Persian merchants arrive the same night on their way back to the capital driving a mule train heavily loaded with bulky packs. These two were known by sight to the regulars at the caravanserai, especially the younger one, who bore the sacred name of Ali. This strapping young man had crisscrossed Persia in every direction, to Kandahar and Herat among the Afghans, to the khanate of Khiva, where slaves were bought and sold, as well as west to Basra on the Euphrates, and east as far as India and the lands of the Great Moghul. He had very nearly reached Mecca and, zealous Muslim that he was, promised himself to go there soon.

Ali and his older companion had eaten dinner quietly, from time to time glancing at the stranger, who sat apart. Nothing would happen until the next day, however, and things stood there until the siesta hour, when a favorable opportunity offered.

In the large square courtyard ringed with a double row of pointed arches, the sun caused the dazzling reflection of the white porphyry to shimmer over the ground. At this point in the afternoon, both men and beasts lay steeped in torpor. Stretched out on rugs laid directly on the stone floor in the shade of their paneled front rooms, sleepy travelers listened endlessly to the pure sound of the water lapping at the edges of four pink marble fountains in the corners of the courtyard. The sky, without a cloud or a bird, was no longer in league with the furnace outdoors but had become a distant and delicious lid of cool ceramic tile.

It was at this moment that the stranger, relaxing his caution, came out onto the upper balcony to take the air, bareheaded and in shirtsleeves. He rested his elbows on the columned balustrade and lifted his face voluptuously to the sun.

Ali, lying on the Ardabil rug that always accompanied him on his travels, propped himself on one elbow and laid his hand on his friend's arm to wake him.

"Look!"

The traveler wore his hair long, gathered at the back with a ribbon in the style of the periwigs of the day. Yet it did not seem to be a wig but rather his own hair, which grew thickly and without receding. Was this the detail that caught Ali's attention, or had he spied despite the distance the plump hands and slender wrists?

"I've been telling you this for two days," whispered Ali to his drowsy companion.

The foreigner, his gaze roving over the courtyard and its arcades, noticed Ali's eyes brightly trained on him from the shadows. He started and drew back from the parapet, disappearing into his rooms.

Ali, convinced by this sudden withdrawal of the justice of his suspicions, jumped to his feet and told his friend to wait for him. He slunk along the wall, climbed to the upper story, and halted at the stranger's door. As usual in a caravanserai, the door was not shut, and anyone could proceed into the antichamber, a ten-foot-square portico covered by a half dome. In a corner was heaped the mule's meager pack harness. A fetid odor emanated from the saddle padding and hung in the confined space, the concentrated smell of an animal so old and dry that he sweats nothing but blood and the juices of his entrails. The Mongol manservant, seemingly overcome by the exhalations, sat on a burlap sack. Before he could react, Ali strode to the second door and opened it. At the rear of the large vaulted room, the stranger leaned against the chimneypiece with his back to the light.

The Mongol had by now grabbed Ali's arm, showing surprising strength for his slight frame, but he backed away at a signal from his master.

The merchant stepped forward into the room. The Mongol, once more obeying a signal from his master, withdrew, closing the door behind him. The traveler gestured at a stone bench along the wall, inviting the Persian to sit down. Ali waved off the suggestion, keeping his burning eyes on the stranger, and asked him in Farsi:

"Do you understand our language?"

The traveler shook his head.

"Turkish?"

"Very little," the foreigner answered in that language, his pronunciation poor.

He added that he understood Arabic better.

His voice was unsteady, as though queered by emotion, or else it had been deliberately forced from its natural register.

"Very well then," said Ali, "we'll speak Arabic."

He continued to look at the traveler with shining eyes. The silence prolonged itself as the two examined each other.

"What do you want?" asked the Frank finally.

"What I want?" Ali repeated with a frightening smile. "I simply want . . . to invite you to the hammam with me."

The foreigner flinched.

"The bath at this caravanserai is one of the most pleasant in the country. We can talk comfortably there, while a slave kneads our sore muscles and women rub our bodies with rose milk."

"Thank you for your kind invitation," the visitor finally answered, clearly distressed. "I am deeply touched by it, and you have put me in your debt. However . . ."

"However?"

Ali's smile grew increasingly menacing and sinister as he slowly drew near, gazing steadily and unblinkingly at the traveler, who spluttered.

"However, I cannot accept. In the first place, I confess my poverty. Custom requires that in return for so gracious an invitation I honor its issuer with a present . . . Alas, I am in no position to do so."

"Never mind. You will be my guest. All the pleasure and honor will be mine. If anyone is indebted, it is the person on whom a stranger lavishes his presence."

"No, no, I cannot. I . . . have taken a vow."

"A vow not to wash?" asked Ali softly, his smile never wavering.

He was now standing very close to the foreigner. Examining the stranger's slender nose at his leisure, the delicate bloom of his skin, on which the numerous fine wrinkles of age had left their tracery, and his silky cheeks, Ali grew increasingly strong in his conviction, and the stranger grew increasingly distressed.

"Come now, sir," said the traveler, making a final attempt to recover his composure, his voice sliding out of control, "why are you so intent on dragging me off to the hammam?"

"Why?" rumbled Ali, taking a last step. "Why?"

Pale and petrified, the traveler watched as the merchant raised his two hands and grasped the collar of his batiste shirt. Anyone watching might have expected the man to tighten his grip around the other's throat, but the foreigner had a different premonition and simply closed his eyes, thinking: All is lost.

"Why?" asked Ali once more, his face close to the other's.

Then, with a great sound of ripping fabric, he tore the edges of the traveler's shirt apart, exposing an ample bosom tipped with large nipples.

"Just to be certain," he shouted in a voice calculated to rouse the entire caravanserai, "that you are a woman."

European cities are first of all spaces, which may be green or not: streets, squares, and sidewalks from which the mass of more or less grouped buildings emerges. A city in the Orient, by contrast, is a compact weave of constructions so dense and continuous that one barely sees the narrow cut made by its alleys. At rare intervals, this fabric is holed and a garden or a square appears, encircled and circumscribed, planted with tall trees. Isfahan, which was at that time the capital of Persia, seemed to draw equally on both traditions. The center of town was occupied by the Chahar Bagh, an enormous green space reminiscent of European design. The Persians imagine paradise as a garden: such was the Chahar Bagh, a paradise on earth for those who were virtuous enough for God to have made them rich. In the heavenly paradise two cool streams are said to meet at a central pool, defining four gardens that represent the four corners of the earth. Similarly, the Chahar Bagh was divided into four parts by the Zayande River and an avenue that crosses the river at right angles over a bridge of thirty-three arches. All that can be seen of the Chahar Bagh from the vantage of this bridge is a harmony in green, as dense as in the parks of Europe, a tracery of gardens and tree groves dominated by poplars and lindens. The handsomest palaces built by the Safavid kings of the previous century were hidden along it, not as in Paris with a courtyard on one side and a garden on the other but with a garden on either side, in the most charming way. The whole gave an impression of elegant disorder and simplicity. Nothing could match this naturalness, unless it was the unremitting daily efforts of the gardeners to create and maintain it.

Other than this interior lake of greenery, the city conformed to the Oriental tradition. Handsome structures, palaces and mosques, dating for the most part from the periods of Turkish or Mongol rule, were still scattered throughout it, equipped with vast courts and in some cases with veritable inner gardens. But squeezed as they were into tortuous alleys, they turned a scornful back on passersby, exhibiting only a windowless brick wall. A few rare houses situated in the immediate vicinity of the Chahar Bagh took part in both worlds, the world of open parks and that of interweaving walls. One of these, which was neither the handsomest nor the largest, nor the most richly furnished, was famous largely for its esoteric garden and its parties. The Persians called it the house of Mirza Poncet. The man who lived there was a Frank who enjoyed general respect and affection for the eminent services he performed. Everyone in the capital knew that this Jean-Baptiste Poncet, an honorable apothecary and doctor, had arrived fifteen years before on horseback, practically penniless, after crossing Palestine and the Valley of the Euphrates. And everyone knew that he brought his wife with him, or at least the woman he presented as such, named Alix.

At one time a rumor made the rounds that the doctor had abducted the young woman, and that she had even taken part in her own capture, killing a man. But in their early years in Isfahan, neither Poncet nor his wife offered any clarification on these points, and they had avoided any contact with the Frankish diplomatic colony. Owing to the great number of foreigners in Isfahan, the majority English and Dutch, there was no lack of fodder for the rumor mill. The Persians therefore never learned anything more about it. Their lingering suspicions only increased their sympathy for a man who had perhaps been guilty of showing too much ardor in love. In the East, passion, with its tears, its mad gestures, even its murders, is accounted the most beautiful thing in the world.

The doctor's reputation, along with the gaiety and hospitality of his household, gradually swept away the last traces of mistrust.

Alix had played a significant role in gaining the community's acceptance. In a country where women are confined to the harem, she was privileged to go about freely, and at home she maintained an open house.

Not long after arriving in Isfahan, she had given birth to a baby girl. Her pregnancy did not seem to have changed her, however. She affected the same graceful and deliberate figure that she had had at twenty, and the same clear blue eyes. She was as elegant in the flowing veils of her Eastern dress as in the hoops and panniers of her European fashions. Most of the time, she went about in hunting clothes—a short jacket, boots, and corduroy pants—in which she rode horseback like a man.

In this country where all the coinage of the world—ducats, thalers, écus—was melted down at the border and stamped with the image of the king of Persia, Alix's house in Isfahan operated a contrary alchemy: gold dissolved on entering it and was transformed into delicious foods, precious plate, entertainments, and fireworks. Nothing could have disposed the Persians more favorably toward Alix and Jean-Baptiste than to see them live in step with this country, which, at the height of its refinement, was being threatened on all sides and seemed to take its increasing decadence as a spur to enjoy the pleasures of the moment.

Their serene existence was thrown into turmoil by a sudden dramatic turn of events. At the death of Louis XIV, all Isfahan was stunned to learn that the regent of France was in personal correspondence with Jean-Baptiste Poncet. The French ambassador discovered this when he opened—as was his prerogative—the official mail addressed to those under his administrative care. Thus it became known that Poncet had received an invitation to Versailles to supply the regent with information about Abyssinia, where he had once traveled as ambassador. Twenty years before, when Poncet returned from this embassy, the regent—then known as the duc de Chartres—had not had the opportunity to meet him, but he had read Poncet's memoirs and admired them greatly. The Persians were pricked by a lively curiosity on learning that this apothecary, who was so familiar a figure to them, had penetrated to the heart of a legendary kingdom in Africa and subsequently met Louis XIV. Furthermore, they were flattered that Poncet, in a position to make comparisons, had all the same chosen to live in Isfahan.

The Frankish colony, for its part, had finally grasped that the Poncet living in Persia and the Poncet who had brutally affronted the diplomatic world by abducting the daughter of the French consul in Cairo were one and the same. Fortunately, the crime was old, and Monsieur de Maillet, against whom this crime had been committed, was no longer in the foreign service. A few years after the lamentable abduction of his daughter, the French consul of Cairo had published a book of philosophy. Strange, and even incomprehensible to men of reason, it so scandalized the church authorities that they gave it their official condemnation. The poor man was recalled by the king, and none knew what had become of him since, or whether he was still alive. Poncet suffered no ill consequence from the discovery of his past, unless it was being beset with invitations from all over town to tell the story of the fabulous events that for a time had made him an Abyssinian.

Alix and Jean-Baptiste had plunged into this reexamination of the past with good will. The stories brought back memories of their vanished youth. Reviving those times, even for the benefit of others, allowed them to feel again the heat of the embers buried there. Aside from themselves, all the actors in those long-ago stories had disappeared and perhaps died. This was the only shadow that oppressed them in telling these tales. They felt their good fortune at being together, at having shared those happy times, and at being able to relive their joy. Yet they were sad to have lost sight of the others who had taken part in those marvelous moments.

Around this time, they took into their house an English boy of about thirteen whose parents had died while exploring Central Asia. Jean-Baptiste had long been in correspondence with them on botanical subjects, as they were members of a scientific society in Liverpool. When it became absolutely clear from the testimony of several travelers that the parents had been massacred, George officially became a son in the Poncet household.

Life resumed its course after these events. Alix and Jean-Baptiste were suddenly terrified, though they never admitted it to each other, at seeing an unlimited expanse of tranquillity open before them. They did not go so far as to think that happiness was not making them happy. But their joys, their sufferings, their hopes—their entire life, in short—were now veiled, despite every effort, in a persistent nostalgia.

Things might have stood there if, on a peaceful day that started off like any other, a strange and troubling bit of news had not reached Jean-Baptiste.

2

Among his eminent clients, Jean-Baptiste Poncet counted a Persian dignitary called the nazir, a title that corresponded more or less to that of high chamberlain in a Western court and raised him to the rank of prince. He was responsible for all that belonged to the king, which was considerable. In his care, for example, were some three hundred houses in the capital which the sovereign owned personally, and which he dispensed as favors to one or another of his courtiers; the nazir collected the royal levy and saw to it that all that was owed to the crown in terms of rents, fines, and commercial obligations was duly paid. Naturally, the nazir took his share of these funds whenever he could do so without drawing too much comment. Only his respect for the king kept him from misappropriating funds on a truly colossal scale. Nonetheless, he was already very rich and powerful.

Poncet went to see the nazir on foot that morning, for he liked nothing better than to walk across the Chahar Bagh at sunrise. The shadow of the great maples along the avenue turned the water in the narrow canal running down its center green. At intervals, where the water flowed into dark, shimmering pools, he could hear the murmur of little falls. At this early hour of the morning, with the birds cheeping and the blinds, pushed by sleepy arms, clattering open, it seemed that both a town and a forest were rousing themselves from sleep after mingling in the soft night.

At his side the doctor still swung the same leather case full of medicine vials that he had kept with him since Cairo. His hair, which he still wore long, curled as it had and was hardly less black than before. A long acquaintance with Eastern countries had taught him outward politeness, though this in no way lessened his freedom of manner or thought.

As he approached the entrance to the palace, he smelled the fragile, plaintive odors of jasmine rising from the garden in the air already warmed by the rising sun. A resplendent carriage was drawn up in front of the stables, and a dozen richly attired servants bustled about it quietly.

"The prime minister is in session with the nazir my master," said the guard who greeted Jean-Baptiste at the gate.

"Very well. I'll come back tomorrow."

He envisioned a pleasant stretch of free time ahead and a long walk.

"No, no, he left instructions for you to come in."

Without waiting for an answer, the servant led the medical man to a small pavilion off by itself in the garden, surrounded almost entirely by a reflecting pool bordered with pebbles and hyacinths. Jean-Baptiste spent the better part of an hour there, supplied with tea and biscuits, watching the black-backed carp undulate in the green water of the pool.

Finally, he was led into a low room, almost at ground level, where the nazir sat waiting for him on a silk carpet. The man's cheeks and chin were covered by a short beard, whereas his mustache, in the style of Persians from Georgia, was allowed to grow so long that he might easily have tucked it behind his ears. His large embroidered tunic failed to hide his corpulence, which seemed due as much to muscle as to fat, distributed over a mountaineer's robust frame. His enormous hands, with their thick wrists, rested on his knees like tools left idle at the side of a field. Among the peasantry there were many who rose in society only through the successive efforts of several generations. But some managed to ascend to the heights using no more than the same attributes that would have made it possible for them to subdue a bull or help a cow to calve. In every royal court in every period of history there have been examples of such mixtures of roughness and flattery, coarseness and refinement. Behind this melding of opposites there is generally cunning, and the nazir, had he ever needed to sell his possessions, could have turned his own store of cunning into ready coin all his life without fear of ever running short.

"Dear friend," began the nazir as soon as Jean-Baptiste was settled, "the prime minister has just left me, and we have been discussing an extremely singular piece of news."

Jean-Baptiste was not unduly surprised that the nazir should consult him on a political issue. Since becoming his doctor and gaining his confidence, he had found that this dignitary often opened up to him on personal subjects as well as questions affecting the state.

"Quite simply, it is about you, dear Mirza Poncet."

"About me! But in what way could I possibly interest the grand vizier?"

The morning was already well along, and the sun was now high in the sky, yet there was still an exquisite freshness in the shade of the garden; the blue and red tiling on the walls was lit by the reflections from the pool. The nazir signaled to one of the servants, who brought in two glasses of Shiraz wine on a chased platter. During this pause in the conversation, the Persian appeared to be searching for an appropriate opening.

"You undoubtedly know," he said, "that many foreigners now enter our land, and that we reserve the warmest welcome for them. The king himself has ordered that not a hair on the head of a foreigner be touched. Although they worship at different altars and their customs are reprehensible to us, they are our sacred guests."

Jean-Baptiste mistrusted this beginning. Had he, who had been a foreigner in this country for more than fifteen years, in any way breached the laws of hospitality?

"Most travelers come here for the purpose of trade; others, though they may really belong to this first group, pretend to have an official embassy to our court, and we try to sort out the truth or falsehood of their claims. And still others are men of religion, in which quality I maintain that they may visit this country, though theirs is not our faith. In a word, we welcome everything except lying and shameless debauchery."

The nazir sipped his wine and then, revolving his glass gently, watched with visible enjoyment as the golden liquid sheeted down the sides of the crystal.

"Here is what happened," he continued. "A young merchant of our nation, an extremely pious man well versed in the ways of foreigners, grew suspicious of a Frankish traveler. He followed him for two stages, to the caravanserai of Kashan."

Jean-Baptiste, though somewhat nonplussed by this introduction, nodded politely.

"Having decided to verify his suspicions, the young merchant discovered that the traveler was in fact . . . a woman."

"A woman!"

"So it would seem," said the nazir with some embarrassment, his nose reddening.

"It should be easy enough to determine one way or the other."

"No doubt, but don't forget that we are speaking of a foreign woman. Even under the circumstances and in the face of such treachery, our people showed honorable restraint . . . All that they know is that she has large breasts. They didn't proceed any further with their investigation."

"So a traveler with large breasts has been arrested in Kashan," continued Jean-Baptiste, making an effort to repress his hilarity.

"Yes, and this woman—unless we are dealing with a monster such as we sometimes find among our eunuchs, made by nature to confuse our good sense and our modesty—this woman, I was saying, is now in our hands."

"Here in Isfahan?"

"No, in Kashan, at the barracks of the royal guard. She has been given a cell of her own, or what really amounts to a suite, for I understand that she lacks for nothing. They have not even separated her from her horrible Mongolian manservant."

"A Mongolian manservant! The devil!" said Jean-Baptiste. "And what are you going to do with this admittedly unusual equipage?"

"To tell the truth, we are in an awkward position. The merchant who provoked the arrest, while showing admirable vigilance, was not as discreet as we could have wished. The rumor has spread even here, in the bazaars of Isfahan, that a female spy dressed as a man has tried to take advantage of our indulgent ways—you know the state our country is now in."

The nazir glanced around him as though to make sure that none of the servants were close enough to hear. Leaning toward the doctor, he whispered:

"Last year, rebel Kurds almost reached Isfahan. Now the Afghan dogs have captured Herat and nothing can dislodge them. Another of their tribes is stirring in Kandahar; people say they are ready to march on us. In the meantime, the Turks have taken Erevan in Armenia and are considering, along with the Russians, what part of our empire to gobble up next. One meets many people here, particularly among the more pious Shi'i, who argue that we should expel all the foreigners who live on our soil and who act as accomplices for our neighbors."

Then, in an even lower voice:

"It is easier to do battle with others than to recognize one's own weaknesses . . ."

Poncet carried his glass to his lips to avoid having to produce the slightest expression. He knew just how full of dangers the Persian court was, and none was more treacherous than being told a thing in confidence.

"The prime minister, with whom I have just met," the nazir continued, "is not entirely displeased at the incident. You know that since his pilgrimage to Mecca there hasn't been a more zealous servant of the faith. He finds the king much too weak and would be glad to force his hand. The minister's idea is very simple: he wants to try and convict this woman as a spy. The beheading will be held in public. By spilling these few drops of blood, the prime minister hopes to frighten many foreigners and make a number of them leave, while placating the Muslims who are muttering against the government and accusing it of weakness."

The stout nazir shifted his weight painfully, his two huge fists planted on the marble floor, to relieve the pressure on his backside. With certain builds, thought Jean-Baptiste, it is far better to be born into a civilization that has adopted the armchair . . .

"How may I be of service in all this?" he asked.

"It's very simple. Clearly, we must be certain of two things before we convict this woman of spying: first, that she is really a woman, since her offense consists of lying on that score; and second, that she is not an actual spy. We are ready to make an example of her, but not at the cost of quarreling with any of the nations that we trade with."

Poncet recognized this way of thinking as the dominant one at court, where subtlety was carried to such an extreme that it went beyond compromise and shaded into weakness, with the disastrous results that were plainly visible.

"Now," said the nazir, stretching one side of his mustache almost to arm's length, "I suggested your name to the prime minister. Your fame has already brought you to his attention, and he accepted readily. You will therefore leave as soon as possible for Kashan, a voyage of less than three days. Your official mission will be to visit this traveler and penetrate the veil of intimacy to determine the question of his or her gender. You belong to the same nation, so there can be no offense."

Jean-Baptiste bowed his head.

"As it is Your Excellency's wish, I shall certainly carry it out."

"Good," said the nazir, and he undertook in the same breath to rise to his feet, which he accomplished by heaving himself up on the railing.

Once standing, he led Jean-Baptiste into the garden and walked with him toward the entrance. After a few steps, he stopped in the shade of a palm tree, squeezed Jean-Baptiste's arm as though to make him hold still, and went on in a low voice:

"The prime minister is unaware of this, but I quite believe that you will be able to tell us a great deal about this woman—for I am convinced that it is a woman. I expect to learn all about her plans from you, and whether she is on a mission, and of what sort and for whom. But this is something you will not breathe a word of to anyone but myself. I must draw some advantage from the favor I am doing you."

Poncet took it that his assignment would be amply recompensed and that the nazir would help himself in passing.

"I am grateful to Your Excellency for having suggested me to the prime minister for this mission. But kindly tell me why you believe I will be able to penetrate this woman's plans when I don't know her at all?"

"Listen, Poncet, the favor I am doing is not what you think. You won't receive a penny for your part in this. But because you have been my doctor for ten years and I value you in that capacity, I have chosen to render you a great service. That service does not consist in my having mentioned you to the grand vizier, but rather in having hidden something else that concerns you—something I believe is compromising."

There was a bustle behind them as the servants tidied up the pavilion. The nazir looked back, then, drawing even closer to Jean-Baptiste until the black hairs of his mustache tickled the Frenchman's nose, he whispered these words:

"When I sent a slave to question her, the woman gave your name. She claims to know you. For the moment, I am the only person who is aware of this. It would be best for me to find out quickly who she is and whether her arrest might compromise you."

3

Every time Jean-Baptiste left Isfahan to ride on horseback in the surrounding countryside, he experienced physically all over again the reasons why he loved this country. The resemblance between the landscapes of Persia and Abyssinia was so clear, they had such a similar attraction for him, that they must have promoted some hidden harmony in his soul. This region of Iran, like the Ethiopia he had discovered long ago, was formed of high plateaux bordered all around with snowcapped mountains, set in latitudes where the sun rules, lights, and warms without troubling the limpid air of the highlands. Because the mountains are at no great distance from the sea, there are no hot winds like the sirocco to make the atmosphere stifling and unhealthy. In Isfahan, the climate is so healthy that the shiniest metal can be left exposed to the air and not rust.

On this land, superbly set off by its high altitude, a race of proud men had maintained millennial dynasties that, while constantly under threat and often brought down, were never obliterated, for they were the heart and the raison d'être of these peoples. In Abyssinia, as in Iran, the desire to meld with a universal religion has been tempered by an unwillingness to give up the particularity of the native gods. This no doubt accounts for why these solitary countries are also heretical ones. The Persians are Muslims, but of the Shi'i sect, just as the Abyssinians are Christians, but Copts: it is their way of being neither completely outside of the world nor entirely within it. One has to have felt how familiar these high plateaux are with the heavens in order to understand.

Jean-Baptiste was galloping on a Turkoman horse the nazir had lent him, having commandeered it from the royal stables for the occasion. By nightfall on the second day he was already entering Kashan.

The town was one he knew well, as he had often been called there because of the scorpions. The great abundance of these creatures in Kashan is a fact well known throughout the country. The locals claim that a talisman prepared in former times by the astrologers has mitigated the curse somewhat and made the scorpions more scarce. Aside from the general conjurations, there were special formulas such as the one used by foreigners. Every morning at the gates to the city one might see a line of foreigners declaiming in a loud voice to the invisible poisoners: "Scorpions, I am a stranger and you are not to touch me!" This formula was supposed to safeguard them.

Despite the precautions people took, Jean-Baptiste was summoned to Kashan two or three times a year to attend to a particularly serious scorpion bite or a particularly eminent victim.

When he arrived at the royal palace where the man or woman he was to examine was being detained, Jean-Baptiste was met by a dignified old man whom he knew well, having treated both his daughters, bitten the same night by a scorpion in their bedroom. The man was an akhund, which is to say a reader and a chanter of the praises of Muhammad at Friday prayer. His great age, piety, and near total blindness had qualified him to guard the embarrassing stranger whose sex was an issue of interest to the Persian court.

"Ah! Poncet," exclaimed the old man on hearing the doctor announced by his young slave. "I am delighted that they chose you for this task. At least we know that you'll do it without triggering a scandal. In truth, this person is anything but accommodating. Man or woman, I wouldn't want him in my house. He won't eat, presumably for fear of being poisoned, and other than the nazir's emissary, no one has managed to get even a word of explanation out of him."

"Does anyone know at least what country this person is from?" asked Jean-Baptiste, who had been pondering the question during his ride.

"A book was found in his saddlebags that looks like a Bible and that one of the doctors at the *madrasa* recognized as being written in the language of the French."

"A Frenchman, then," said Poncet thoughtfully.

"And one who speaks to us in Arabic straight from Egypt."

Then it must be someone I knew in Cairo, thought Jean-Baptiste, still perplexed. In the five years he had lived in that city, he had met so many people that it was useless to review them all in memory.

"It would be best for me to see the prisoner straightaway," he said.

"Careful," admonished the akhund. "Keep in mind that this traveler is not yet a prisoner. Officially, he is being held here to protect him from any who might take vengeance on his person. Hence I particularly advise you to avoid using violence."

"I'm not in the habit of manhandling those who are put into my care."

"Yes," said the old man shrewdly, "but what if he refuses to be examined?"

"We'll see. My task is to convince him that it's in his best interest. May I begin?"

"I see no reason not to," said the old man. "Unfortunately, it is late and the sun has set."

"Well, you do have lamps, don't you?"

"But the creature won't allow any into his apartment! This monster, who is neither a man nor a woman—God's curse on him—lights himself solely by the light of the moon, which leads me to suspect some form of sorcery. I wouldn't want anything terrible to happen to you."

"Have no fear. Lead me to this person, and I'll answer for the rest."

Reluctantly, the akhund clapped his hands for his slave. The boy appeared instantly.

"Daryush, take a lamp and lead this aga to the traveler." Then, turning to Poncet, he asked, "Do you need any instruments?"

At the suggestion of a physical examination, two red spots appeared through the thinning white beard on the old man's cheeks. People credit the Persians with having freer morals than they in fact do, simply because they may take more than one wife and even contract temporary marriages. But the number and frequency of one's liaisons take none of the mystery away from sex. When a man shuts his wives up behind doors, he becomes the most complete stranger to their world and the least able to take part in any of their secrets.

Jean-Baptiste tapped the case he had set down beside him and, with a gesture to indicate that it should all be left to him, asked to be shown the way immediately.

The old man allowed him to go, guided by the slave. They crossed several courtyards and climbed two staircases—one of them a monumental stair leading to the king's apartments, the other a narrow and unobtrusive passage to the second floor over the stables. A row of heavy doors, all of them shut, stretched away down a long corridor.

The wing was deserted. At last, the slave stopped in front of two doors that faced each other across the hallway.

"The servant is on that side," he said.

"Take me straight to the traveler."

"Certainly. Here we are."

The slave struggled with a heavy lock and pulled back a long bolt.

The well-oiled door swung silently open onto the cool freshness of a large, entirely dark room.

"Give me the lamp and wait outside," said Poncet.

Holding the heavy metal lamp, he advanced a few feet into the enormous room. The lively light of the flame found nothing in the darkness to strike against, and the lamp, rather than rewarding his sight, blinded Jean-Baptiste, though he held it high in front of him. He heard the sound of the door closing and the slave thrusting the bolt home.

"Where are you then?" he asked in French, turning to look on all sides.

From the darkest corner of the room a voice whispered: "Put out the light if you want to see me and let your eyes grow accustomed to the darkness."

Poncet blew out the flame. Within a few moments the moon, clearly visible through a small round window, had filled the space with a soft blue light that brought the furniture and the traveler's outline into view.

"Sit down here."

Jean-Baptiste saw that the akhund had had the good taste to furnish the apartment in the European style. He took a chair, and the traveler sat down across the table from him.

"Are you French?" asked the stranger in a normal voice, and Jean-Baptiste started at the sound.

"Yes."

"I am too."

By God, was it possible? In these inflections Jean-Baptiste had the impression that he recognized, across the chasm of the years . . .

"And do you know," the stranger continued, "Docteur Poncet?"

Jean-Baptiste bounded to his feet. He was pale and pierced by a sudden emotion.

"But," Jean-Baptiste hesitated, "it's me!"

Then the stranger, also standing, experienced a gust of emotion and threw her arms around him, crying:

"Oh, how happy I am!"

"Françoise! Françoise!" murmured Jean-Baptiste holding her tight against him.

Françoise from Cairo, Françoise the faithful servant who had comforted Alix during Jean-Baptiste's long voyage to Abyssinia. Françoise who had helped the lovers flee and shared the dangers and discomforts of their rebellion. Françoise, finally, who had set off for France with Maître

Juremi, his great friend, whose absence Jean-Baptiste felt inconsolably. And here she was back again after fifteen years of silence, fifteen years of the most complete absence.

During this time, the slave had returned to the akhund, as his master had ordered. After a half hour, the old man sent him back to see how the doctor was getting on. The boy pulled back the bolt and called into the darkness: "Mirza!"

"Yes?" said Poncet with a certain asperity.

He was seated and, still holding Françoise's hands in his, had embarked on a passionate conversation.

"My master sends me to ask whether the operation has been performed," the slave boy whispered.

"Operation?"

"That was his term . . ."

"Ah! Yes," said Jean-Baptiste laughing. "Well, I am making headway. Just tell him that: I am making headway."

The slave left to bring this enigmatic message back to the old man, who was pacing in his office.

"What a miracle it is to have finally found you," said Françoise once they were alone again.

"To have found me! So you were looking for me . . . It wasn't by accident that you fetched up here?"

"Yes and no. It was certainly by accident that I discovered a few months ago that you were in Isfahan, but I have had only one thought since, which was to join you there as quickly as possible. By the way," she added with a sudden note of trepidation, "Alix?"

"She is with me, as beautiful as when you knew her. Be careful you don't make her collapse with joy when she sees you."

"Oh, how happy I am, Jean-Baptiste, and how eager I am to see her!"

"And . . . Juremi?"

"It's a long story . . ."

"But tell me at least, is he . . . still alive?"

"Still alive, yes, at least when I last saw him, which was at the beginning of the year. But that's what I have come to tell you, Jean-Baptiste, that he is in great danger and only you can save him."

"In danger! How do you mean? Where? Oh! Françoise, tell me the whole thing right from the start."

Françoise started to tell the story, but a thousand questions about Alix and Jean-Baptiste crowded into her mind as she narrated it. Fifteen years of their four lives, fifteen years of adventures and joy, of trials and contentment, could not be brought out in a collected way. The secrets of the two friends melded together. They answered one question with another, and punctuated their accounts with tears, while nothing very clear emerged.

Almost an hour had gone by. The akhund received the same answer every time he sent the slave for news.

"He is making headway. Headway! All very well," the old man groaned more and more ill-temperedly each time. "And you say they are in the dark. Hmm! I had no misgivings about Poncet, who seems to me an honest man, but who knows what kind of spell that jinn may have cast on him! We are trying to find out whether it's a man or a woman, but I wouldn't be surprised if it had several sexes with which to lure away even the purest souls . . . Daryush! Now listen to me: you're going to go back there, but this time you're going to pull back the bolt as quietly as possible and enter the room, do you understand? Be careful not to succumb to any temptation—it could cost you your life! But let your eyes grow adjusted to the dark and look around. I want to know what they are doing."

Trembling, the slave performed the task. Owing to his master's influence, he was terribly afraid of magic, and the situation seemed to him full of sorcery. He glided into the cell invoking Ali and Imam Reza. He was still trembling when he returned to the akhund.

"Well?"

"Well . . . Oh, my master! Be assured that no one could report to you more faithfully what he saw."

"Out with it!"

"All right . . . they are holding hands . . . and they are crying."

"So that," said the old man, "is what he calls making headway! They are crying! The poor doctor has fallen under the creature's spell, that's for certain. His mind was unable to resist. The monster is dangerous, Daryush, I am telling you, and the prime minister was right: we will have peace only when we have beheaded it properly."

4

Riding at a fast gallop along the road to Isfahan, Poncet was no longer
the same man. Though in the fullness of maturity, he was suddenly reex-
periencing the exaltation of his youth. Françoise had returned. She was a
prisoner, in danger, perhaps even condemned to death. And Juremi was
alive, lost somewhere, and in need of his help.

Jean-Baptiste was sure that Alix would, like himself, become passionately concerned on hearing the news. He even worried that she might
undertake some desperate action on learning that Françoise was a prisoner
so close by. He decided to go directly to the nazir's when he reached Isfahan,
without resting or changing his clothes. Jean-Baptiste presented himself at
the gate, his sweat-streaked horse dancing in place as though unable to stop
galloping. Mud-spattered, his face framed by a three-day growth of beard,
the traveler was led to the drawing room, where he let himself fall onto a
rug furnished with pink pillows. The nazir soon appeared.

He lowered one knee slowly to the ground, then the other, before collapsing cross-legged with a groan.

"Well?" he said. "What have you discovered? Is it a woman?"

"Your Lordship, there can be no doubt on that score."

"Excellent! The prime minister will be happy to know that we can
expect a public torture. The poor man really needs one at this stage."

"Alas! there are circumstances that I believe will make this execution
impossible."

"Impossible! Who is this woman?"

"But first, are you sure that no one can hear us?"

The two men were seated next to one of the columns that supported
the arcades of the patio. Servants came and went barefoot on the terra-
cotta tiles. The nazir had a vivid memory of one of the king's favorites
being executed for conspiracy after being betrayed by one of his slaves.
Despite the effort it cost him to move, he rose and brought Jean-Baptiste
near the spurting fountain at the center of the garden. Seated on its mar-

ble rim, they could keep watch in all directions, and their voices were covered by the clapping of the water.

"You can speak freely. And I order you to leave nothing out, Poncet."

Jean-Baptiste had prepared himself en route for this delicate task. He knew that it was impossible to reveal Françoise's true identity without condemning her to death. A penniless former servant and moreover the wife of an outlaw, she would weigh little in the balance, particularly when reasons of state militated for her execution. The doctor's recommendation by itself would not suffice to spare her, and the unfortunate woman, defenseless as she was, would make an ideal public example. He had to find something else. But what? Françoise could not be made into an official representative of France or some other European nation: the ambassadors of these nations would be questioned, and the lie would soon be discovered. What, then? Jean-Baptiste had turned the matter in every direction while on the road without finding a solution. Luckily, at the last moment, entering the gates of Isfahan, he had had an idea. At first it had seemed too outrageous. But he told himself that the die was cast. Courageously, he plunged into his story.

"You know me well enough, Your Grace, to know that I would never conceal anything from you. Yet the truth is astonishing, almost unbelievable. In any case, I will tell it to you baldly. What I have learned is . . . that this woman is the concubine of Cardinal Alberoni."

Having uttered these words, for better or for worse, Jean-Baptiste felt a delicious sensation steal over him. A lie! He had not allowed himself the pleasure in a very long time.

"The concubine of Cardinal Alberoni!" repeated the nazir, stiffening as though struck by lightning.

"The very woman," murmured Jean-Baptiste, blinking as though before an apparition.

There was nothing to surprise a Persian in the woman's being the concubine of a cardinal. Chastity was thought to be not so much a virtue as a fantasy, like those mythical beasts one invokes knowing perfectly well they don't exist. But for the cardinal to be Alberoni, that was altogether unusual. Alberoni, the man who had dominated European politics for the last five years! Born in Italy, this skillful prelate had become councilor, then prime minister, to the king of Spain, whose marriage to the daughter of his first master, the duke of Parma, he had arranged. When he was quite sure of his own power, Alberoni had launched all the king's forces against Austria with the intention of freeing Italy from the yoke of the Holy

Roman Empire. On his orders, Spanish troops landed in Sicily. An alliance was then formed between France, England, and Holland to oppose this invasion. In response, the Turks, the Stuart Scots, and the Swedish—all of them hostile to Austria and England—had given their support to the cardinal and, in the end, followed him to defeat. In 1718 the Scots were driven out of England, the Swedes defeated by the Russians and the Turks by Prince Eugene, while the Spaniards were routed from Italy. The fall of Cardinal Alberoni was a foregone conclusion, and the king of Spain had expelled him the following year.

This saga had held the world rapt right up to the denouement. By his audacity Alberoni had held history's stage for five whole years in the void left by the death of Louis XIV. The great man was now an outlaw, hiding somewhere or wandering from place to place, once again the simple son of a gardener that he had been at birth—unless he was preparing his revenge through some extraordinarily bold new stroke. His allies, his protégés, and his servants must also have been reduced to flight and hiding. As to his concubines, if he had any—and how could a man at such a pinnacle of power not—it was hardly surprising that they should seek refuge at the far ends of the world in disguise.

"Did she offer you any proof?" asked the nazir, less to express his disbelief than to strengthen the conviction he had immediately formed.

"Your Excellency is well aware that I have traveled in France and Italy."

Of the business in Abyssinia, when it finally became known in Isfahan, the Persians had mainly absorbed the fact that Jean-Baptiste had gone to Versailles to meet the king of France. This exploit gave him a certain credit, which he had never abused, but he felt the moment had come to draw on it.

"Did you meet the cardinal?"

"Yes, in Parma, when I was traveling through that duchy."

"Was his concubine with him?"

"In truth, Your Grace, we are touching on a sacrosanct topic, as these things were disclosed to me in confidence as a doctor. Yet I find myself obliged to reveal this professional secret in order to protect a secret of state, namely, the presence of this person in the kingdom. I will tell you then that it was precisely in order to attend to this concubine that I was summoned by Cardinal Alberoni. At the time she was not trying to hide her sex but only her condition."

"Don't tell me, Poncet, that you made yourself guilty of that most heinous act against God, abortion."

"Then I will say nothing, and leave Your Grace to follow his imagination."

Every people designates what it finds to be touching or disgusting as it sees fit. The Persians were not shocked by infanticide, as long as it was discreet, but they took grave exception to using any means to end a pregnancy. Presumably the order of the world was less threatened by the disappearance of a child after its birth—a relatively common occurrence, after all—than by man's sacrilegious intrusion into the female mystery of generation.

"And you positively recognized her?"

"Was it not Your Grace who honored me with the confidence that this person had made use of my name? Yes, she recognized me and I recognized her."

The nazir, to mask his perplexity, raised one thick arm and started scratching the nape of his neck. His long nails traveled across his skin with the sharp sound of a saw biting into a log. This gesture, which no doubt quickened his thinking when he was called on for an apt response, also had the virtue of directing his attention to the spot where the ax would fall if, in this delicate and risky business, he made a decision that led to his disgrace.

Jean-Baptiste, who now saw his lie take on a life of its own, was already frightened at the extent to which he was committed to it. This was no time to back out, however. He had simply to anticipate the nazir's thoughts in order to set them rolling down an appropriate incline.

"Of course," said Jean-Baptiste suddenly, "it would be unfortunate if anyone took it into his head to broadcast the poor woman's identity."

"Yet the French ambassador would be very interested in such a prisoner, and God knows what price he might pay to have her returned to him," suggested the nazir shrewdly.

"Forgive me if I express an opinion different from Your Grace's. It seems to me that the French no longer attach any importance to this business. The crux was Alberoni, and he is defeated. They will take no vengeance on his concubine, unless they want to draw the world's mockery. On the contrary, once you officially disclose the presence of this woman here, it is your neighbors who are likely to put the fact to nefarious use."

"In what way?"

"It seems to me that given Persia's delicate position, the Russians and the Turks are both looking for any pretext to attack you. The Russians will ask that this woman be delivered to them. If you refuse, they will take it as a hostile act and say that you are fomenting a plot against them, since Alberoni was the ally of their Swedish enemies."

"And if we hand her over?"

"Then the Turks will claim that you are taking sides with Austria and Russia. They have just suffered reverses in Europe. Ibrahim Pasha would be happy to regild his escutcheon at your expense. The prime minister's prudent politics of neutrality would all be jeopardized at one stroke. Instead of having to fight only the Afghans, you would be caught in the crossfire between two or three nations."

The nazir's powerful hand, leaving the back of his neck, clapped down on Poncet's shoulder, and Jean-Baptiste was almost thrown bodily into the fountain.

"Your reasoning is excellent and agrees with my own on all points," he said.

Yet in the silence that ensued, Jean-Baptiste sensed too much melancholy in the nazir's mood to feel confident. The Persian could not bring himself to halt a development in which his interest was not directly involved. He would not free Françoise unless some future profit could be suggested to him.

"They say that Alberoni did not leave Spain empty-handed," Jean-Baptiste insinuated softly.

"Ah! Really?"

"The king of Spain only resolved to disgrace him because the victors insisted on it, but he loved his minister and certainly didn't strip him of his possessions."

"And where would Alberoni have put all this gold if he were in flight?"

"The banking and credit systems hold no secrets for an Italian. Alberoni can travel in nothing but a tunic to any place on earth, and the Florentine money changers will count out for him whatever sum he requests."

The nazir knew this system well. All along the road to India and even in Isfahan these privileged auxiliaries to commerce—Jews and Italians— were well established. One sometimes had to go to them to fill the holes in the state treasury.

"All right. Alberoni is still rich, but what then?"

"Why then, Your Grace," said Jean-Baptiste spiritedly, "show them the true and adorable face of your country and its ruler: grant the poor woman her freedom and respect her anonymity. Authorize her to live in Persia, forbidding her only to leave the country without your agreement. I am sure that she knows where her lover is. She will give an account of these kind deeds and inform him to whom she owes them: he will know how to reward them justly. If perchance he is in any position to call her to him, wherever he is living, you will be well placed to negotiate the terms of her departure."

The nazir was quiet for a moment, then, with a vivacity that was exceptional in so large a body, he grabbed hold of Jean-Baptiste and trotted with him down the graveled alley.

"Tell me, Poncet, tell me in all honesty," he whispered in his ear, "I know the question is delicate because you are an acquaintance, practically a friend, of this woman . . ."

Poncet protested vehemently. The nazir drew him back to his side by making clucking sounds.

"All right, not a friend, just as you like, it doesn't matter. But tell me honestly. Is she still . . . desirable? Do you think that Alberoni will make an effort, a genuine effort, to recover her?"

Jean-Baptiste was delighted. The hook had been solidly taken. All that remained was not to pull too hard on the line. The nazir would surely see Françoise himself. She was over sixty, and though Jean-Baptiste still found her beautiful, with a beauty that came from her inner goodness, he feared that the Persian might judge her cruelly.

"All I can say is that Alberoni was very attached to her when I saw them together and she in no way led me to understand that she had quarreled with him."

"Yes, yes, that's all perfectly well understood, but tell me: is she still a desirable woman?"

Jean-Baptiste did not hesitate for long. An idea offered itself and he seized it:

"Desirable?" he asked. "How can I explain, you know . . . for a cardinal . . ."

"Yes," said the nazir, nodding his large head in conviction, "you are right. It's true that those men have no common sense."

He straightened up, let go of Jean-Baptiste, and resumed the solemn aspect that he normally wore. He had made up his mind.

"Return home," he said to Poncet, whose grime and fatigue he only now appeared to notice. "I will try to bring the prime minister around to this way of seeing things."

As they reached the door of the stables where Jean-Baptiste's horse was waiting, the nazir expressed a final worry:

"I was forgetting one crucial point: all these mullahs who wanted us to make an example of this woman, what will they say when we let her go? We can't broadcast the reasons for our clemency."

Jean-Baptiste, who had relaxed his attention, searched for an answer in vain. It was the nazir who came up with one.

"Bah!" he exclaimed over his shoulder as he turned away, "we'll certainly find someone else to behead."

5

Françoise arrived at the end of the afternoon, to the clamor of thousands of birds chirruping in the foliage of a large sycamore. The whole family, with Alix in front, was assembled in the courtyard. The two women looked at each other a moment in silence, each quitting her dreams and regaining her foothold on the hard ground of the present. When they had recognized each other—despite time, its hardships, and its marks on the flesh—they embraced tearfully. Several long minutes filled with tears of joy, laughter, and emotional outbursts passed. Everyone pressed around the new arrival.

Françoise, wearied by her trip, soon needed to sit down. They installed her on a rattan chaise longue in the cool of a terrace that opened onto the garden and was shaded by a trellis of wisteria. Alix immediately wanted to introduce her daughter:

"Her name is Saba, in memory of Abyssinia. Tell me, Françoise, if she isn't the image of me at sixteen."

It took a mother's blindness to believe it, and Françoise smiled indulgently. It was true that there might possibly be some resemblance between the features of the mother and the daughter. But any likeness in line had been well hidden when the drawing was colored in. Alix's hair was blond with a few darker reflections, but Saba was a redhead, her hair an unabashed red that trumpeted its color and displayed a full range of hues. Pulled back into a ponytail, the red flames framed Saba's face like anger. The girl, by character grave, calm, and reserved, had her father's coal-black eyes and, with her blazing mane that cast embers onto her skin in small spots, the sort of beauty that commands respectful silence. Françoise hugged her and felt a great current of tenderness pass between herself and this reserved girl-child.

Alix went off to find George, their adopted child, who had been in the courtyard only minutes ago. On the point of being introduced to Françoise, he had run away to the bottom of the garden. Jean-Baptiste found him there and brought him back, flushed red to his forehead and trembling. The poor boy made an awkward bow, unsure whether to kneel as well. Françoise examined him indulgently, this handsome, timid boy, whose eighteen years sat on him with the disorderliness of a body divided between different ages. His tall stature and wide frame were already those of a man. But at the prow of this long hull was a small, narrow face framed by light blond hair, delicate as a child's, that quivered at the slightest alarm. After introductions had been made all around, Françoise called the Mongol servant who had accompanied her and, taking him by the hand, brought him into the center of the circle.

"And this is Küyük, who does not speak our language, though he speaks many others. He is a man of great worth, and I owe him my life."

Küyük bowed at the end of this presentation without showing the least expression. His lifeless face was engraved with fine wrinkles, as deep and straight as gashes. At this point, servants carried in three large round majolica plates full of pilau, rice braised with mutton or chicken. One of the platters was flavored with pomegranate juice, a second with lemon, and the third with saffron. Jean-Baptiste served a sparkling wine from Fars that was in every respect like champagne.

Much later, in the main drawing room, seated around a fire that tempered the cool night air, they listened to Françoise calmly tell the story of her adventures and what had happened to Juremi.

"When we parted company at Acre, after leaving Egypt, and after Alix's abduction, do you remember that Juremi and I were headed for France?"

"To join forces with the camisards," said Jean-Baptiste.

"That was Juremi's plan. He couldn't stand being an outlaw. He went back to his Protestant brothers, and I followed him. Someday I may have time to tell you about those terrible years . . . But that is all so far in the past, and I'll go straight to the end: the camisards were crushed. We were nearly killed. Someone warned us in time and we fled to Spain, then England. Juremi knew the country and could speak the language. We soon found work, he as a woodcutter, I as a seamstress."

"In London?" George had the courage to ask, blushing to his ears.

"No, child. But England is your country, isn't it? In Surrey. The place was green and tranquil; we might be there still. Except that Juremi, after so many years of adventure, couldn't stand the peace and quiet for more than six months. He became melancholy. You know him: he needs to put his energy to work. And he has the same energy he always did. And the same bearish appearance. He hasn't lost a hair from his head or his beard, though now his hair is all gray. But in the midst of these ashes, his eyes still burn."

At this description, two small tears flowed silently down Françoise's face, catching at the sides of her nose, from where she wiped them away on one side and the other with the tip of her index finger.

"Anyway," she continued, "I was telling you that in England he gave me a good scare. He stopped eating, grew listless, started talking of his past life—Juremi, who never looked back. He missed you a great deal, Jean-Baptiste, which I could well understand since I too would have liked to have news of you. But his memories made him brood. I was sure the big softhearted brute was plotting some desperate action."

"Why didn't you write me?" Jean-Baptiste interrupted.

"Write you where? We had no idea where you were. The inquiries I made in France turned up nothing. You were certainly no longer among the Turks, but then where? In Russia? China? India? How were we to know? No, we had to struggle on by ourselves. At that point, I had an unfortunate idea. One of my clients was the wife of a Swedish financier. The woman told me at length about the misfortunes of her poor country. You know that under Charles XII Sweden was extremely prosperous, a conquering nation. As long as they attacked their small neighbors— Poland, Denmark, Courland—the Swedes were always victorious. But one day they attacked Russia and wore themselves out against her. When Charles XII died, everyone fell on the defeated country. I mentioned this to Juremi just to interest him in something other than his own despair. I told him that soon there might be no Sweden. All of a sudden he got carried away. The plight of these Protestants in distress moved him deeply. Not because they were Protestants particularly—though it reassured him that they wouldn't just dismiss him if he flew to their rescue. No, what concerned him was that they were in distress. He loves desperate causes. That's just the way he is. And I don't understand why he takes such pleasure in fighting because, though he never accepts being defeated, he also can't stand to see himself among the victors . . ."

"So you left for Sweden," said Alix. "What madness. Couldn't you find a way to stop him?"

"Dear Alix," said Françoise sadly, "you know perfectly well that we women must refrain from voicing our dark forebodings. It rarely serves to ward off tragedy, but it always makes people blame us afterward for provoking the mishap with our fears. Besides, how could I have objected to

Juremi's plans when I saw that he was now happy, completely revitalized at the idea of exchanging the company of sheep for brotherhood and action? No sooner had we arrived in Stockholm than the Swedes, whose army was shattered, put him in command of a regiment."

"But he didn't speak their language," Jean-Baptiste objected.

"Not a word, and it's a tongue that you can't learn unless your parents have given you the right shape of throat at birth. But apparently there is no need to express yourself in great detail in order to make war. He shouted his orders in Arabic for the attack, in Turkish for maneuvers, and in Italian for standing down. The soldiers adored him."

They laughed, but softly, so as not to awaken Küyük, who had dozed off by the fire.

"For my part, I stayed in Stockholm," Françoise continued, "where I had never seen so much blackness. The sky was dark twenty hours a day, just like the water of the port that I saw from my window. And the news I received was just as black because the war was being fought on all sides against a multitude of enemies. The darkness everywhere started to seep into my soul, so that I was almost relieved when the news came . . ."

"That he was wounded?" asked Jean-Baptiste, deeply troubled.

"No, I don't think so. Here's what I learned. Juremi was told to lead his regiment against the Russians. His ill temper, which the others called bravery, had singled him out for duty on the most desperate front, where battles were fought at ten-to-one odds. In December they came in contact with the Russians, and on the fifth of January—"

"Of this year?"

"Yes. Eight months ago, on the fifth of January, he was driven back with his troops into a snowy basin. At the bottom of this valley was the flat expanse formed by a frozen lake. The cold was terrible. Behind every pine in the surrounding forest, the Russians had placed a skirmisher. It was impossible to light a fire on the lake for fear of casting the men into the freezing waters. There was no way out. As it happens, this was fortunate, since had there been the slightest opening Juremi would have thrown himself into it and met his death. On the second night he surrendered to a Russian general who spoke French. In this absurd war where he understood his enemies better than his own troops, he was finally able to hold a real conversation. I learned all this from two Swedish couriers. The Russians allowed them to bring the bad news back from the front so as to further soften the resistance of the last combatants."

"So he fell into the hands of the Russians," said Jean-Baptiste, who was starting to draw simple conclusions about the course of action ahead.

"That's the one certainty."

"They didn't . . ."

"Execute him?" said Françoise, showing that she had the courage to pronounce the word that had stuck in Jean-Baptiste's throat. "No, that's not how the Russians operate. I am sure of it, having talked to dozens of witnesses."

"So what did they do with him?"

"He must be a prisoner, but where and under what conditions I have no idea. I told myself that I would learn nothing further in Stockholm and that's why I set off on my journey. Our life didn't allow us to set any money aside—I took everything we had, which wasn't much, and bought the necessities for the voyage, mostly the mule you saw, actually a perfectly serviceable animal."

"And Küyük?" asked Saba, who had followed Françoise's account with passionate interest.

"Küyük?" she asked, smiling at the young girl. "Chance put him in my path. You have to imagine what Stockholm was like when the armies were routed. There were all sorts of refugees, wounded soldiers, lost children. This Mongol slept in a shed at the foot of the building where I lived. During the day, he built a small fire on the snow and used it to cook whatever the kitchen help tossed his way. I suppose he had been conscripted into the tsar's army and captured by the Swedish during an earlier campaign. He spoke a bit of Swedish, but more Russian and also the languages of the Asiatic hordes. People called him the shaman and seemed wary of him. I thought he might prove useful to me, and anyway it would be a good deed to return him to his own land. He followed me when I set off at the beginning of February."

"You were dressed as a man?" asked Alix.

"Yes, it was a strange idea, wasn't it? I often regretted it afterward, especially when I reached countries where men and women look radically different from one another. In northern Europe, in wartime, it was a precaution that was easy to take—men shave and wear their hair long."

"Only faint reports of that war have reached us here," said Jean-Baptiste, "but am I not right in thinking that it is not yet over? The Russians have not signed a peace with the Swedes. How were you able to leave the country?"

"Through Poland. I adopted the disguise of a Catholic pilgrim and directed my steps toward Częstochowa to visit the Black Virgin. And I was desperate enough, if you can believe it," she said, laughing, "to actually go and pray to the Holy Mother, though I am not particularly given to ritual devotion. She must have heard me because she granted my prayer!"

"Granted your prayer! In what way?" asked Saba.

"Well, first of all, in questioning the pilgrims from the East, I discovered that it would be extremely dangerous for me to enter Russia without a clear purpose or valid papers. At another time this news might not have stopped me, but . . . how can I put it? . . . I didn't feel strong enough to face such difficulties all on my own. Then there was another miracle. A man whose legs had been broken when his coach lost a wheel came to Częstochowa to try and regain the use of his limbs. He was carried in a litter and had five servants to look after him. One of them spoke French and told me that his master, who was very rich, had made his fortune in Persia during the last twenty years trading watches and precious jewelry. The poor man was constantly bemoaning the fact that he couldn't return there, because that's where the only doctor who could cure him lived. I asked him the doctor's name. It was you."

Everyone wondered at the coincidence. Alix ordered another round of sparkling wine. The conversation broke up into commentary and questions, with all present wanting to give their own opinion. Jean-Baptiste alone remained silent, absorbed by the thought of all he would have to do, starting the very next day.

6

Jean-Baptiste had never met the ambassador from Muscovy, henceforth the Russian Empire, but the man was widely known to be incapable of doing anything simply. In every respect like the government whose mission to Persia he headed, he affected Western manners while being ignorant of Western tradition, as were his servants. The diplomat was in consequence a dreaded host, at whose house it was always a danger to be served.

Poncet discovered this firsthand. He had barely settled on a couch when a Russian servant, a giant from the forests, absurdly dressed in tight red livery and still wearing his sheepskin-lined boots despite the heat, tripped over the carpet and distributed the contents of a cup of tea and a bowl of sherbet over Jean-Baptiste.

"What an ass!" howled Israël Orii the ambassador, raining blows from his cane on the unfortunate muzhik.

Jean-Baptiste dabbed at his blue suit of clothes with the somewhat murky water that another Muscovite held out to him in a silver basin. Peace was eventually restored, and the ambassador, after his shameless display of anger, resumed the satisfied and benevolent expression he generally affected, his head against the high back of his carved chair, framed by two wooden eagles.

"I was just getting to the point, Your Excellency," said Jean-Baptiste hurriedly, afraid that another dish was on its way to coat his knees. "It concerns one of my very good friends, the friend dearest to my own heart and my wife's. He was my partner in Cairo in the art of healing with plants. His skill at concocting remedies is unequaled, and without him my own doctoring is not half what it should be."

Israël Orii blinked to signal his approval. This show of serenity no doubt struck him as in keeping with his own idea of his majesty. Unable to contain his natural disposition, however, he tapped his foot impatiently.

"This dear friend whom life has separated from us, I have just learned, is even now in your country, in the land of your emperor."

"What excellent news," said the ambassador in his nasal, singsong French. "My heart always rejoices to learn that the best practitioners of the arts of man—craftsmen, scholars, and artists—are converging on our great country."

"That is to say," Jean-Baptiste added with some hesitation, "he is converging but . . . more because he is converged."

Israël Orii grimaced to express his surprise. His face was clean-shaven, in keeping with the fashion newly imposed by Peter the Great, who wanted his people to have a modern appearance. His mobile features and large bright eyes exaggerated his expressions as though he were a mime.

"What I mean," said Jean-Baptiste, "is that the honor of being in Russia, which he undoubtedly feels, is not the product of his own choice. He was made prisoner in the most unfortunate circumstances. In brief— and it is the subject of my visit—the man is the victim of a terrible misunderstanding."

He then undertook to recast the saga of Maître Juremi in a favorable light for the benefit of the ambassador, who once again rested his head against his eagle's nest and kept his eyes half shut. In brief, the Protestant had simply wanted to rejoin his friends peacefully in Persia. The Swedes had conscripted him against his will. He had willingly allowed himself to be captured by the Russians, knowing that in the vicinity of the tsar he would find a merciful civilization and the chance to resume his own path.

"And what may I do for you?" asked Israël Orii finally with a shrewd smile.

Jean-Baptiste was well aware of this man's skill—all Isfahan had had the chance to observe it and at times feel its effects. He was the first ambassador worthy of the name that the Russians had sent. Previously there had been a series of more or less picturesque merchants who assumed the title for the privilege it conferred on them and occasionally consented to send messages. The Persians welcomed them as ambassadors out of kindness but looked on them as men of no account. The limit had been reached some twenty years earlier, when one of these diplomats had made himself famous at a banquet given by the king. Not wanting to lag behind the Persians in drinking but not accustomed to the sweet alcohols of the East, the poor man was overcome by nausea and heaved the contents of his stomach into his astrakhan hat. The king noticed and pointed a finger at him. Desperate at appearing bareheaded before the shah, a breach of etiquette, the so-called ambassador clapped his hat back on his head, forgetting what it now contained . . .

In sending Israël Orii to Isfahan with all the necessary pomp, Peter the Great had wanted to break with this ridiculous past. But no one doubted that a man of this caliber in a place such as this would not only represent his nation but be charged with advancing its interests. Russia coveted parts of northern Persia, perhaps even Persia as a whole, which would give it access to the warm-water ports of the Persian Gulf. The French looked on anxiously as the Russians placed their pawns in the area. After Israël Orii's arrival, the French ambassador had had a brainstorm when, after several sleepless nights, he noticed that the name of this Georgian diplomat was an anagram for *il sera roi,* or "he will be king." Radiant, the Frenchman visited the court to point out this troubling coincidence and excite suspicion against the tsar's envoy. Unfortunately, he managed only to provoke smiles and actually increased Israël Orii's prestige, the Persians proving perfectly willing to believe the man destined to become king. "After all," they remarked serenely, "there are many other places on earth where he might become one."

There was nothing a man of such mettle could not do, as long as he saw it as being in his interest. Jean-Baptiste took a deep breath and steeled himself to make his request.

"I thought Your Excellency might transmit a petition to the court of the tsar concerning my friend, exposing his innocence and the injustice of withholding his freedom from him."

"My dear sir," replied the ambassador levelly after a period of internal deliberation, "I have only one wish and that is to please you. Alas, what you have asked is impossible. The huge victories of my master, Peter the Great, have brought his glorious armies thousands—what am I saying?—millions of captives. In his benevolence, the emperor has no wish to deprive them of their liberty. He therefore has them led to neglected portions of our vast country, where they may busy themselves, while earning a livelihood, in increasing the general prosperity. There is no department of government, I assure you, that keeps records of these foreigners. They pass through, and there is an end to it. No one judges them, no one condemns them. The state takes no further interest in them than to designate a place for them to live in and to see to it that they get there. In consequence of the freedom we give them, we have no notion of their subsequent fate."

Israël Orii could see that this answer was disappointing to Jean-

Baptiste. As a well-informed man who maintained a number of spies at court, the Russian had learned immediately of the business of Alberoni's concubine and knew that Poncet had received her in his house. There was a clue here that should be kept sight of, as it might lead to the conspiracy Alberoni was undoubtedly hatching from his hideaway. The man whose freedom Jean-Baptiste had come to ask for was probably mixed up in it. The ambassador should leave the door ajar.

"I can see how much my powerlessness displeases you," he continued, "and how painful you find this business. Please believe that I would most like to help. Let me consider. Yes, I do see a way that I might help you along."

The ambassador, distilling his words in the calmest manner, hoped to build tension and thus give all the greater weight to his conclusion. Unfortunately, one of the giant servants bustling about the room without apparent motive chose that delicate moment to knock into a statue. Craftily set in the half-light, it had every appearance of marble but proved, on crumping dully on the floor, to be of plaster. The incident ruined the diplomat's effect and left him impatient to upbraid his staff once and for all. He finished quickly:

"There is only one solution, as I was saying: it is for you to go to Russia personally and seek news of your friend, find him, and bring him back yourself."

"But do you think that I would be allowed to go?"

"I can . . . give you a letter of recommendation to our court. It would allow you an interview with a high official, perhaps even the minister himself, if he is available. The one thing I cannot guarantee, of course, is your safety. To reach our country you would have to cross lands that are anything but peaceful . . ."

Jean-Baptiste had not expected this proposal. Yet it was logical and foreseeable. He had imagined having to move heaven and earth from Persia, sending couriers, winning over diplomats and ministers. But to go himself in search of Juremi . . . During the past sedentary years, he had gradually eliminated all thoughts of travel, risk, and adventure from his mind. The ambassador's words made him slightly light-headed, a not disagreeable sensation.

"Well," he said hesitantly, "why not in fact, if it's the only solution . . ."

"The only one," Israël Orii confirmed. "Though not without its risks."

Jean-Baptiste felt his heart thumping strongly, and the knocking of this ghost within him spoke clearly enough of what he secretly wanted to do.

"Your Excellency, if you would prepare the letter I will see what arrangements I can make . . ."

"Right away," said the ambassador advancing toward the desk.

"No!" cried Jean-Baptiste, so impatient that he could not spend another ten minutes in that chair. "I cannot wait . . . patients . . . urgent care . . ."

"I understand. In that case, send someone to fetch the letter in a short while, or tomorrow—whenever it's convenient."

Jean-Baptiste thanked him profusely, and this time it was he, striding toward the door, who tripped over the carpet.

Pleased with his craftiness, Israël Orii returned to his office whistling a fisherman's ditty from the Black Sea. He chose a pen and, in the heat of his inspiration, wrote two letters. The first was the safe-conduct Poncet had asked for, describing him as a doctor from Isfahan. The second, longer letter described Poncet's past history, his life in Isfahan, and the Alberoni affair. He sealed it, addressed it to M., chief of the tsar's police, and tossed it into the case containing the secret correspondence for Moscow.

Jean-Baptiste went directly home, head down, his hands jammed into the pockets of his coat, fiddling with some dried seeds, his keys, and some bits of paper he was in the habit of forgetting there.

He crossed the garden, oblivious to Françoise, who was reclining in the shade with Saba beside her. The girl had silently and discreetly taken to looking after Françoise and in a few days had assumed the place of confidante once held by her mother in Cairo. Seeing Jean-Baptiste obviously preoccupied, they knew better than to interrupt his somber ruminations and let him pass without a word.

First he went to his laboratory. George was there working on a distillation. The boy had learned the rudiments of botany from his first parents and was now deepening his knowledge with Jean-Baptiste's equipment. He showed real talent. But he was so serious, so full of naive confidence in the progress of rational thought, that Jean-Baptiste made a point of holding up to him an opposing, poetic concept of the world of plants and its secret relations to the world of humans. In any case, today Jean-Baptiste was in no mood for George's company. He shut the laboratory door and went out instead into the garden behind the house. Simples had been planted on one side, while the rose garden stood on the other. Jean-Baptiste took a pair of garden shears hanging by the door and went into the plot for medicinal herbs. It was planted in narrow bands crowded with scented tufts, some leafy, others twiglike. He passed the little army of plants in review without finding anything suspect to cut back, rip out, or divide. And anyway, the little garden had never done anyone harm. After a few minutes he threw the shears down beside a cold frame and went to sit on a stone marker used to set buckets on. He was sitting there, his arms crossed and a furious expression on his face, when Alix entered the garden plot.

"I was looking for you," she said.

She was wearing a blue twill dress, loose from the waist down, which she pressed to her legs as she passed through the narrow alley.

"Well?" she asked, drawing near, "what did the ambassador say?"

"He can't do anything."

"You're going yourself."

Alix's tone was perfectly neutral. It held no trace of any question, doubt, or reproach. Perhaps it was simply an intuition. Jean-Baptiste looked over at her briefly, surprised and curious.

"A shame," he muttered. "Juremi is an old man by now. He wouldn't want anyone to go to any great trouble over him. I tried. It didn't work. That's just the way things are."

Alix looked at him, her lips forming a faint smile, but he avoided her gaze. She took his hand and, overcoming a slight resistance, led him behind her out of the medicinal garden to a stone bench in the rose garden where they could sit side by side. She continued to hold Jean-Baptiste's hands in hers. He maintained his brooding expression.

"Listen to me for a moment," she said softly. "You know perfectly well, Jean-Baptiste, that events dictate our lives in most things. On the rare occasions when we are free to make a decision, we have no right to choose anything except happiness. Well, we will never be happy if you stay. You will reproach yourself every moment of your life for not having gone to Juremi's rescue, and you'll reproach us for having kept you from it. I hate the idea of your leaving, Jean-Baptiste, but you will go."

The rose garden, planted in the Persian style, had no alley. Instead, a thick lawn, trimmed with scissors by the servants, covered the ground right to the base of the flowers. Against this verdant background, the pale features and bare arms of Alix, her swelling breasts under the gathers of her low neckline, floated between the worlds of earth and heaven, of man and plants. Jean-Baptiste looked at her and, overcome by a gust of emotion, pressed her to him. Usually he was the first to reject any melancholy, the way a person avoids a color that doesn't suit him. This time Alix had been more vigilant than he. Reminding him of the very essence of their love, she had restored his optimism and his will. Of course it was indecent to show too much joy at the thought of leaving. But it was no less ridiculous to hide that he had already decided to go, which she knew perfectly well. He would set forth and bring back Juremi, and in addition to the joy of saving his friend he would have the happiness of a homecoming to Isfahan.

Already he felt all the benefits of arriving at this decision. First in looking at Alix, inhaling her scent, grazing the back of her neck with his lips, he found that his memory was working, as it does in those who are about to leave, to fill his mind with the most insignificant things, which tomorrow would be the most precious.

In a different spirit now, he pointed out the thousand inconveniences his absence would cause. Some were practical: would Alix be short of money? what would she do if the political situation worsened? Alix answered all this seriously. She would continue to deliver medicines to the clients for whom Jean-Baptiste left prescriptions; she would trim household expenses, and with him gone, they would spend nothing on parties and extraordinary celebrations. If there was turmoil in Persia? And why else, she asked cheekily, did she continue to practice riding and fencing?

Then he raised a final objection, which he put to her tenderly: wouldn't she suffer too much from their separation? She answered that she would suffer more from holding him back.

Reflecting on the conversation later, she realized she might not have admitted the entire truth, having not yet seen it clearly herself. Of course she had first steeled herself to the decision by thinking about Jean-Baptiste, his nostalgia for Abyssinia and travel, his friendship for Juremi, and his freedom. But later, little by little, she had sensed that this return of turbulent, uncertain, and adventurous times answered a secret and unacknowledged need of her own. With Françoise at Saba's side and Jean-Baptiste gone, she felt suddenly freed as a mother and a wife. What woman, having embarked as young as she on a happy and uninterrupted love, does not dream of recovering—even to a slight extent—the emotions of a still unfinished first youth, when freedom does not yet consist solely in making another happy.

7

At the far end of the large dark space formed by the Chahar Bagh gardens, the thirty-three arches of the bridge over the Zayande were lit by the moon's reflection on the river. Most of the houses on the bridge, used as shops during the day, were closed, and only a few stalls still kept their handsome fruits gleaming in the light of hanging oil lamps. It was after ten o'clock when a shadow crossed the bridge silently, bounding along, keeping to its darkest parts. From its height, the figure seemed that of a man, a foreigner by his soft boots. Nothing else about the passerby was visible, wrapped as he was in a felt cape that covered even his head. The Persian merchants paid no attention to him. Once across the bridge, the figure turned right and advanced into a maze of narrow streets, the Armenian suburb of Julfa.

The man picked his way through the neighborhood with ease, despite the darkness, walking for almost ten minutes without seeing anyone. Finally he stopped at a high wall, above which towered the branches of a large mulberry tree. There was a small nail-studded door in the wall, which the man struck three times with the hilt of his sword. Through the grille of a garden, a voice asked him in a trembling whisper:

"Are you sure you were not followed?"

"Quite certain, Monsignor."

"Shh! Not that word, please!"

The door opened a crack and the stranger entered an entirely dark space, at whose far end a pale rectangle appeared. The host and his visitor crossed toward this opening and came out onto a large terrace planted with four lemon trees. Around the terrace on all sides were rooms in which shadows moved and children wailed. Only one room was lit: the dull glow of an oil lamp feebly pushed back the darkness. On the floor were a red rug and a copper tray. The visitor was invited to sit down. His host, who sat cross-legged facing him, was well along in years, practically an old man. He wore a cheap cassock of blue cotton. His hair was braided into a crown around his head, and his face was punctuated by a short, pointed beard. He had the fragile features of a bird—long, pointed nose and darting, fearful, hungry eyes.

"Believe me," he said, "if it were anyone but you, Poncet, who have saved my life twice already with your medicines, I wouldn't take the risk."

Jean-Baptiste, who had uncovered his face on entering by removing his felt shawl, bowed his head momentarily in respect:

"Thank you, Monsignor."

"Shh! Stop calling me that."

"Are you no longer Nerses, the Armenian patriarch?"

"Hush, I say! Of course I am, and that's just why I have to hide like a rabbit."

"As long as I have known you, Mon . . . Monsieur, I never thought to find you in such a state. What has happened?"

"What has happened, my friend, and you are probably the last to hear of it," said the old man, pinching the bridge of his nose nervously, "what has happened is that our poor church is paying the price for being isolated in a sea of peoples plotting to destroy it. The Turks in Istanbul insist on our giving them money. As we are unable to, the Persians have decided to repay the debt themselves and tax the members of our faith accordingly. But the monsters pocket ten gold pieces for every one they credit to us, which makes everyone unhappy: the Turks, because we owe them a large sum of money; the Persians, because we have incurred debts toward the Turks; and our own brothers, because it's they who are really being cheated. You can't imagine the threats that have been made against me, forcing me to hide in this way."

Poncet assumed an expression of dismay, all the while repressing a smile. He was well aware of the source of these misfortunes. The Armenian church of Persia was in an unusual situation. The patriarch owed his office to Persia's Muslim ruler, paying him a large sum of money for it. He then obtained reimbursement by selling lesser offices, from the *vertabiet,* corresponding approximately to our rank of bishop, to the *derder,* a cleric who filled the functions of a secular priest. At the end of the chain were the faithful, who ultimately footed the bill, buying indulgences and prayers from this burdensome clergy. No church practiced simony more unashamedly. Everything was for sale: holy relics, blessings, sacraments, and even the arrangement of marriages or, for that matter, adulterous liaisons. Of all the accessories to faith, the most lucrative was holy oil, which the people used to make amulets and medicine, and which the priests sold at a high price.

"I beg your pardon," said Jean-Baptiste, "but did I not hear that perhaps you precipitated your own downfall by approaching the Turks to—"

"Yes," the patriarch interrupted, "and where was the harm in that? I went to the Grand Signor to ask for justice. My brother—the dog would devour his own mother, yet I must still call him my brother—my brother, the Armenian patriarch of Jerusalem, was brazenly competing with us by blessing holy oil at half price. I went to the Turks to demand that they uphold our traditional rights as Armenians residing in Persia. We have always had responsibility for the great shrines of Armenia, and on this ground alone we hold the exclusive right to sell oils of unrivaled spiritual quality to all the members of our church, wherever they may live. Naturally these cost a bit more."

Jean-Baptiste had already encountered the traffic in holy oil among the Copts in Cairo and was in no way shocked by it. What did stun him was the prelate's frank admission of impelling greed.

"And you met with bankruptcy in trying to get a judgment to this effect?"

"You have to understand, Poncet, that I considered it an investment. With the monopoly on holy oil I could have repaid the entire sum in less than six months."

The patriarch paused for a moment, as though following in the shadows the treasure-laden convoy he had dreamed of. Then he roused himself, and his face assumed an expression of extreme displeasure.

"How was I to know that the Turks, agreeing to all my demands, would take my gold and then, the moment I left, listen to my false brother from Jerusalem and annul the *firman* I had received?"

This surge of anger was followed by despondency, and the old man collapsed on his cushion.

"What is to be done, Poncet? What is to be done?" he panted.

"I wouldn't know. Perhaps prayer would help?"

"Please, this is a serious discussion . . ."

The lamp sputtered and the small, liquid noise reminded Jean-Baptiste that he was thirsty. He regretted that the old man's bankruptcy, coming on top of his natural avarice, prevented him from offering his guests something to drink.

"How hot it is!" said Jean-Baptiste, taking off his coat and opening the collar of his shirt. "And how dry!"

But the devilish old man, who was himself dry as a stick, seemed unwilling to take the cue.

"Your Catholic priests, in truth, are the only ones to have given me any support at all," he went on somberly.

On the strength of his earlier experiences with Jesuits and Capuchins, Jean-Baptiste had kept his distance from all religious orders. In Persia there were two main ones: the Italian Capuchins and the Portuguese Augustinians.

"Were they really acting disinterestedly?" asked Jean-Baptiste.

"You mean, are they hoping to convert us? Hah! You make me laugh! No, they have given that up. We managed to discourage them. A hundred times they've succeeded in converting us, and a hundred times we have returned to our own beliefs. It goes like this: they bring us to Rome, we prostrate ourselves before the pope, we put water in our communion wine, and we intone the credo. They think we've swallowed the hook. But it's just that we Armenians are polite to the very bottom of our hearts: we would never contradict another person in his own home. But no sooner are we here once more than we send the pope to the devil, forget the credo, and drink our holy wine as pure and as red as the blood of our Lord. No, trust me, the Catholics have no faith at all in an Armenian's conversion. They prefer to take us as we are."

"Then why do they support you?"

"No doubt they are simply making common cause with the other Christians in this country of Muslims. Perhaps they hope that our troubles will serve their own ends, which are unknown to me. Some of them have recently been counseling me to appeal to the king of France to threaten intervention against Persia and the Grand Signor of the Turks unless they stop trying to quash us."

"Wretched man! Do nothing of the sort!" cried Jean-Baptiste.

"It's true that you were once charged with a mission of this kind on behalf of the Abyssinians," said the old man, suddenly remembering the business at hand.

"Believe me," said Jean-Baptiste, shaking his head, "I have seen enough to know that the king of France will do nothing. If he should decide to take some action against Persia, it would never be enough to protect you and is far more likely to cause you grave harm."

"Yes, that's what the Augustinians say. I thought they were jealous of the Capuchins' proposal. My God! oh my God!" moaned the patriarch, less by way of invoking the heavens than to relieve his anxious mind, "you are my last chance, Poncet. What hope can I give my compatriots? They no longer want to pay and are ready to take revenge on me for the hardships the Persians inflict on them."

Jean-Baptiste had not yet come to the object of his visit. He had preferred to listen to the old man, knowing what he wanted to ask for but still uncertain as to how he might repay the service. Hearing the patriarch moan, he had an idea.

"Monsignor . . ." he began.

"Shh," said the patriarch weakly, unable to invest much energy in this token show of caution.

"The king of France will not help you in any way, nor will the tsar of Russia, nor the emperor of Austria. But there is a man in Europe who may find it in his interest to rescue you, a powerful man, though at the moment he is in a delicate position . . ."

"Who is it? Tell me, Poncet," panted the patriarch, whom this glimmer of hope had for a moment revived.

"This man was the prime minister of Spain but left his country temporarily, planning to return more powerful than ever."

"The prime minister of Spain, you don't mean . . . Alberoni?"

"Himself."

"Was not the coalition that he led against Austria defeated?"

"Precisely, Monsignor, he needs allies—especially in the East, whence, as I happen to know, he plans to effect his return to power."

The patriarch sat fully upright on his seat. He felt the sudden urge to see clearly.

"Ho there!" he cried, clapping his hands to summon an invisible servantry. "Someone tend to this lamp, which is dying. Quickly! And bring tea to wake us up a bit."

Figures started busying themselves in the darkness of the courtyard.

"But tell me, Poncet," he went on, leaning toward the doctor, "this cardinal, this Alberoni, is he rich?"

"Is he? More than you can imagine. All of his holdings are with the Medicis, and he is still the covert master of Spain."

An unkempt servant in gypsy dress, her fingers dirty and fat as sausages, was already setting two small glasses before them, which she filled with dregs of tea. Jean-Baptiste was so overcome by thirst that he tried to drink too quickly and burned himself. The old man sipped a mouthful noisily and, to Poncet's great admiration, swallowed it without apparent discomfort. His insides were apparently as leathery as his outsides.

The bitterness of the drink made the patriarch grimace, and he once more looked downcast.

"Yes," he said sluggishly, "we still have to find a way to approach this gentleman."

This time it was Jean-Baptiste who looked around him worriedly and spoke in a low voice:

"No one must know this, Monsignor, but I will tell you: the cardinal's concubine is staying at my house."

"His concubine!" cried the patriarch indignantly.

He was not surprised, of course, that the Catholic prelate entertained relations with a woman, but he disapproved of the cardinal's not taking her formally before God, as he had done. He quickly perceived that this moral notion had no place in the conversation and chased it from his mind.

"So you think that through this woman . . . ?"

"Precisely, Monsignor, which is why I made such an urgent request for an interview."

The patriarch, whose mind was filled with his own affairs, had entirely forgotten that it was Jean-Baptiste who had called for their meeting.

"I must soon travel to Europe," Poncet continued, "to convey a message to the cardinal."

"You?"

"Yes, because his concubine, whom I treated in former times, trusts no one but myself to carry a letter to so important a man."

"Then you know where he is?"

"I know how to reach him. Yet to do that I will need help."

After a time he continued:

"I will need your help, Monsignor."

"Mine!" said the patriarch, drawing back.

Yes, yours. But have no fear, it is very simple. I would like to be baptized in your church."

"Are you mad? And am I also to circumcise you at your age?"

"No, no, there is no question of my becoming a real member of your church. All I need is a declaration written in your hand and authenticated with your seal."

"And what use will you make of this?" asked the patriarch, suddenly suspicious. "You are a free man, you can travel wherever you like without having to assume a false identity."

"In Persia, certainly, but I must travel a great deal farther, across the whole Turkish Empire, where my name, for all the time that has elapsed, is still linked to a disturbing incident."

"I understand," said the patriarch, and it was true that he had just gathered the terms of the bargain that the doctor was proposing. "Then if I were to write out these documents, you would agree to carry a request from me to the cardinal, is that right?"

Jean-Baptiste was not so low as to agree to the patriarch's proposal out loud. He simply blinked in a knowing way, which the patriarch took for a sign of assent. The silence sealed their bargain wordlessly.

"Write your letter, Monsignor, and prepare my certificate," said Jean-Baptiste in conclusion. "I will drop by tomorrow to pick them up."

"Certainly not! Come back here in full daylight? A sure way to have me found out! No, no, I'll have this paper delivered to you myself by a confidential messenger."

Having reached this agreement, they parted, each of them happy. Jean-Baptiste had never doubted that in coming to see the patriarch he would get what he wanted. He had thought he might have to pay a more exorbitant price, however, and suffer delays that would only drive up the price further. As it was, things could hardly have gone better. Now everything was ready. He had just arranged for the safe-conduct that would protect him from the Turks; the Mongol servant, who would accompany him on his travels, had seen to their horses. He gave himself another week to put everything in order for his departure, to be sure of reaching Russia before winter. He felt relief and whistled gaily under his breath as he strode through the deserted streets.

The patriarch, meanwhile, ordered all the lamps extinguished as soon as his visitor had left and climbed to the roof terrace to lie down. There, looking up at the starry night over Isfahan, he dreamed of a great man arrayed in purple robes, who smiled at him.

8

Françoise's audience with the king of Persia was set for the following day. The nazir would accompany her, to see that his good offices were properly acknowledged, and only the prime minister would be present otherwise, since the identity of the famous concubine was to be kept a secret. Yet when the nazir's two officers arrived the next morning at Poncet's house, their orders were to bring not only Françoise to the palace but her host, the Frankish doctor, as the king wanted to meet him also. This last-minute change created turmoil in the house. First, Jean-Baptiste had to be roused from bed. He had returned late from his visit to the patriarch and was still asleep in his pavilion behind heavy, wild silk curtains. When the party finally reached the nazir's, they found him extremely annoyed at the delay. This was not a function of any general regard on the part of Persians for punctuality. Time is not a commodity in that country, and no one is concerned about its thrifty use. But in the present circumstances, a late arrival at the palace could have grave consequences. The nazir ill-humoredly explained the situation to them along the way.

"The whole thing will hinge," he said in a low voice, "on whether the sovereign has been drinking. With the weather dry and clear, and with it now being almost eleven o'clock in the morning, thanks to your tardiness, I am afraid he will already have started in."

"Are you concerned that it will make him sleepy?" asked Jean-Baptiste cautiously.

"Make him sleepy! That's the last thing it will do! On the contrary," said the nazir, pointing a thick finger threateningly at Jean-Baptiste's chest, "he is never so enraged as when inebriated, and in direct proportion to how much he has drunk. The danger is that he will set upon the prime minister. Poor Hutfi Ali Khan is an exceedingly pious man, as you know, and he has sworn never to touch a drop of alcohol. The king values him and, when in possession of his senses, recognizes the man's extraordinary qualities. But when he isn't, he cannot stand to see his prime minister stay sober."

Thus enlightened as to the inner workings of power, the visitors were announced at the palace. Jean-Baptiste had been there a number of times already, as the king of Persia did not hide himself from public sight but offered many occasions on which he might be viewed. On previous visits, though, Jean-Baptiste had always been an anonymous presence at a large reception.

Experience had taught Jean-Baptiste to maintain a prudent distance from great men, a practice he had followed with few exceptions since arriving in Isfahan. He had particularly hoped that he would never have to treat the king himself, whose excesses made him unpredictable in meting out both favors and punishments. Poncet knew two musicians who, for having played tunes in the king's hearing that displeased him, had had their hands cut off.

The approach to the royal palace was unimpressive. The Persians do not conceive majesty in the vertical dimension, and their buildings rarely rise skyward, keeping instead to a modest height. On the other hand, they recognize power by the space it occupies: their palaces must be vast, and the greater the surface they cover, the greater the power of the king who lives there. Thus they are composed of enclosures and gardens, with each enclosure containing other smaller enclosures, until one comes to the residence of the king. The architects seem to have taken the plan from nature, borrowing from the onion or, more poetically, from the rose, whose precious heart is protected by concentric layers of petals. In the palace, actually, the extreme, most inaccessible, and best-protected core is made up of women, since the very bosom of the royal residence still encloses the concentric circles of the harem.

Jean-Baptiste and Françoise had no wish to penetrate the palace so deeply. At each new enclosure that they passed, they felt an added twinge of anxiety.

The refinement of the galleries and gardens increased as they advanced. The last of these, abutting on the king's apartments, was planted almost entirely with roses. Isfahan's climate is so favorable to these flowers, and its gardeners so numerous and of such formidable skill, that the roses were triumphant in size, variety, and splendor. They were of all sorts: they climbed, formed arches, stood as bushes, carpeted the ground, fell in cascades. Some were dense and silky like pompoms, others large and fleshy, opening onto satiny intimacies. Their perfume in the walled garden was so heady that a more temperate monarch would have found intoxication in their scent alone.

Since the Safavids had driven the Turks out of Persia one hundred years before, the original race of hardy warriors had gradually given way to a more delicate breed of royals. Only one conquest preoccupied it: the conquest of ever-renewed pleasures and still untasted delights. The kings had concentrated in their palaces all the most beautiful instances of jewelry, silks, tapestries, and music produced in the neighboring countries and in Iran itself. Just the sight of these temples to taste was reassuring to the rulers—it seemed unlikely that barbarians could ever penetrate these walls without falling to their knees in admiration before they reached the last one. Yet the Afghan tribes were starting to come down from their mountains . . .

"Oh no!" said the nazir, gnashing his teeth in Jean-Baptiste's ear, "they're taking us to the wine pavilion."

Most palaces, and those of the king in particular, had a special pavilion reserved for the delectation of alcohol, though this in no way precluded its consumption in the other rooms. Persia produced much excellent wine, and the Persians drank a great deal of it despite the prohibitions of their religion. This they justified by citing their love of poetry, saying that it was there they found the inspiration to taste the mystic wines of Hafez and Sa'di.

On reaching the entrance to the pavilion, the visitors were announced by the captain of the king's personal guard, a young officer with a grave and noble expression, impeccably turned out in his gold-braided white uniform. The king was waiting for them in the large room, alone except for the prime minister. This worthy elder had a broad, thick beard and a short mustache in the style of the most conservative mullahs and was seated on a rug below the royal dais. He looked distraught, his eyes gazing off into space. On the floor around him, amidst a disorderly scattering of pillows, were the remains of a drinking party: half-full glasses, colored flagons, bowls of fruit. A gathering of courtiers and dancers had clearly been ushered out only moments before to preserve the privacy of the audience. But there could be no doubt that the nazir's fears were well founded: the king was not abstaining, and this was obvious at first glance.

Shah Huseyn, ruler of the millennial kingdom of Persia, had no recognizable resemblance to a descendant of Cyrus the Great. Standing on his dais, he looked at his visitors with displeasure. But his short stature failed to impress, nor did his elongated face, consumed by two large green eyes and framed by a weedy beard. On this inadequate figure hung a tunic of extraordinarily rich brocade, faced on the front with a quintuple band of silk frogging, inlaid with pearls. A cunningly knotted turban, beige with black leopard spots, doubled the volume of his head and raised skyward, like the arm of a drowning man, a plume of iridescent blue. This elegance was to no avail. On the contrary, the disparity between the rich stuffs and the poor physiognomy they enveloped was painful to see. The monarch, indeed, seemed aware of this and wore his splendid clothes with sloppy abandon. There was something almost touching in the man's desperate efforts to assert his freedom in the only way allowed him: by staining the front of his tunic and wiping his greasy hands on the tail of his turban.

Before this spectacle, the nazir was obliged to set the example, reminding the visitors that this was no time for pity but rather for prosternation.

"Your Majesty," said the nazir with the mastery of an accomplished courtier, "allow the basest of your slaves to kneel before you. As Your Majesty was kind enough to remember his servant by honoring him with the revelation of one of his precious desires, it is my pleasure to present, in a fitting posture of prosternation, two foreigners who give echo to Your Majesty's immense glory as it spreads each day across the universe."

Jean-Baptiste glanced admiringly at the nazir. The speech was sober and well spoken. Most amazing was that these gracious nothings, recited with unction, were uttered by an individual more easily imagined deep in the mountains chopping firewood.

The king nodded and the nazir accepted this as a sign to continue:

"Here giving thanks and paying homage to Your Majesty is the begum Françoise, the very adorable favorite of His Holiness Cardinal Alberoni, prime minister of Spain, currently outside his country, who testifies everywhere he travels of his submission and faithfulness to Your Majesty."

Out of breath after this declamation, the nazir noisily sucked in air. Françoise, who spoke no Persian, had less trouble than Jean-Baptiste in keeping a straight face. She curtsied with all the grace she could muster. Jean-Baptiste was touched to notice that despite her age she had taken considerable pains to please. He even thought he could see a certain voluptuous pleasure in her face at wearing the beautiful taffeta dress Alix had lent to her and that she had altered herself in the preceding days.

"And here, O venerable lieutenant of the true Prophet who is in paradise, daring to appear before you is Seigneur Poncet, a European doctor, and in truth the flower of doctors and of Europeans, who throws himself at your sublime feet in the hope of approaching their magnificence."

Turning back to Poncet, he whispered:

"Well, what are you waiting for?"

Jean-Baptiste considered the aforementioned sublime feet, squeezed into slippers that were spotted with jam and spilled drink. He wondered for a moment whether he should go so far as to apply his lips to them. He knew from his long sojourn in the Orient that these social gymnastics, while humiliating in Europe, were actually wholly compatible with the maintenance of one's dignity here. However bizarre or awkward they might seem, they were arbitrary conventions like wearing a hat or a mustache. In Persia, as long as the king remained king, everyone cheerfully agreed to lick his feet if that was the rule. The same people could as respectfully slit his throat the following day.

Fortunately the monarch, guessing Jean-Baptiste's internal deliberations, took a small step backward as though to avoid being bitten. The situation resolved itself with a prudent but sincere genuflection.

"Take your places," said the king amiably enough.

His ill humor was clearly directed at the prime minister, not at his visitors. He clapped his hands and ordered his guests to be served.

Two remarkably tall, bare-chested black slaves brought in a tray lined with goblets of fine Venetian glass and carafes of cut crystal filled with pale yellow, amber, and bright red liquid.

Françoise was served first, then the nazir, and finally Poncet, each accepting a taste from this assortment of the wines of Fars and Georgia. The king followed the decanting of the liquids with a tender gaze. When the slaves arrived before the prime minister, the man tried to decline discreetly, but the king noticed and grew indignant:

"What!" he cried. "I understand your refusal to drink alone with me. I will even allow that you do not have to drink with my friends, as it would spoil their mood. But with foreigners, honestly!"

"Your Majesty," whimpered the old man, bowing, "ever since going on the pilgrimage—"

"And what about it? What about this pilgrimage? Will you never stop hammering at our eardrums with the same old story? And what do you think he learned over there?" asked the king, turning to his audience. "That they don't drink wine in Mecca! Some news! They have none. The poor wretches make nothing but an execrable date juice. No wonder the Prophet in his wisdom forbade them to drink it."

He signaled to the slaves to renew their assault on the prime minister. "What will you have, red or white?"

"Your Majesty!"

The elderly man raised both his hands in supplication. The others felt horribly uncomfortable. Yet even while being thus humiliated, the minister retained such a venomous expression and showed such hatred of the world in general and of foreigners in particular that it was difficult to see him being teased in this way without taking some pleasure in it.

"A man who doesn't drink is dreary," said the king sententiously. "Do you think God created dreary men? Do you think he takes pleasure in having to countenance, as I do, this sanctimonious face day after day? No, I can tell you. Drink did not appear on this earth for us to neglect it."

So saying, he raised his beautiful glass to eye level and admired its pure reflections. Then, combining the pleasures of taste with those of sight, he took a sip.

Before long the monarch was completely beside himself, and the onlookers, dumbstruck, refrained from making the slightest movement. After a few last bursts of invective at the prime minister, Huseyn fortunately gave in to a languid torpor. He settled back on his pillow and declared:

"Once again my good nature has prevailed, you sober dog, whom I appointed minister only to plague me. I will again listen patiently while you trouble my exalted thoughts with your pinch-faced maunderings. Come! What are you waiting for?"

The prime minister, judging that the storm had passed, slowly started to speak. He described how Françoise's identity had been discovered, casting himself in the most favorable light possible, and repeated the decision to grant her hospitality in Persia on condition that she not try to leave the country.

The sovereign nodded during this speech, seeming two or three times to address a polite bow to Françoise. The nazir tried to assert his worthy part in the affair by interjecting a few highly wrought sentences.

"Enough!" said the king with a show of weariness. "I understand. You have both served me very well and will be rewarded."

Jean-Baptiste, who was studying him intently, could not help feeling a great compassion for this little king. No man was ever less fitted for the role. This ruler felt toward those around him none of the desires—hatred, possessiveness, envy—that are the necessary fuel to turn the wheel of power. He was weak and disinterested, whereas he needed to be strong and avid in order to impose his will and make decisions. Wine, unfurling its gauzy mists around him, offered the sole means of relaxing the tension. His face now grew calm again thanks to this antidote and wore, under the turban that had slid down over one ear, the unloved and doleful look it must have had in childhood.

Jean-Baptiste had reached this stage of his pitying assessment when the conversation turned to him. In response to a question from the king, the nazir answered that Poncet was a doctor. He had at one point traveled to Africa to treat the negus of Abyssinia, and thence to Europe, where his clients had included Cardinal Alberoni.

"And why has he never treated me?" asked the king, drawing himself up.

"But, Your Majesty," the nazir mumbled, "the royal doctors—"

"are asses! And all on this man's payroll," he added, throwing a pillow at the prime minister's face.

Rising, he addressed Poncet:

"Step aside with me for a moment, as there is no need for these two to hear of my weaknesses—I had rather they discovered them by themselves. It will give me a little time before they use their knowledge to kill me altogether."

He led Jean-Baptiste by the arm to one of the pavilion's openwork walls, where a white mock orange exhaled a sweet smell. The consultation lasted five long minutes. The king disclosed his attacks of bile and the pains that sharply lanced his insides before meals.

"Can you relieve me of this pain?"

"Your Majesty, I believe I can."

"With plants?"

"Exactly."

The king turned back toward the others and exclaimed:

"And those pigs let me go on suffering!"

He then addressed Poncet again:

"How long will it take you to prepare the remedies to cure me?"

"That is . . . perhaps two days."

"And how long does this treatment last?"

"Ordinarily I advise continuing the treatment for three months."

"So be it," said the king, making a face. "As long as it isn't too bitter! Just one more thing: to your way of thinking, is wine . . ."

"Dangerous to your health?"

"Yes," said the king quickly.

His face was so beseeching that once again Jean-Baptiste was moved.

"Be moderate in your drinking, Sire, if that is possible. But it would be even more dangerous suddenly to stop drinking altogether."

An expression of infinite gratitude spread over the features of the unhappy monarch. In returning to the others, followed by Jean-Baptiste, he was radiant with joy.

"This doctor is a genius," he said. "You will receive a reward of five hundred tomans for bringing him to me, nazir. And twenty lashes in punishment for having taken so long to do so. And as to you, dear Doctor, I will expect you in two days with my medicines. For the next three months you will live at the palace. Bring all your belongings and cancel any other clients. You will not step beyond the palace walls, as I want you on hand night and day. If your treatment agrees with me, I will appoint you my physician for life and cover you with gold. If not . . ."

9

On the roof of Jean-Baptiste's house was a triangular structure traditionally found on Isfahani houses called a *badgir,* or "wind grabber." Thanks to this chimney in reverse, the least breath of air from any direction is brought into the house to cool it on summer days. The silent gathering seated pensively that night around Jean-Baptiste's enormous study listened to the northeast wind puffing in the *badgir,* weary after crossing the deserts of Khorasan.

On the doctor's worktable were two letters covered with stamps and wax seals. One was from the Russian ambassador, brought as promised by a special messenger during the afternoon. The other was a birth certificate made out in Jean-Baptiste's name by the Armenian patriarch.

Jean-Baptiste rocked back on the legs of a small armchair, never lifting his eyes from the two documents.

"It's all there," he said disgustedly, rising to his feet and pacing around the room, "yet I'm unable to leave."

Françoise and Alix, sharing a narrow sofa, each leaned an elbow on one of the armrests, chin in hand.

"I am coming around to the Persian way of thinking," said Jean-Baptiste. "Maybe it's a sign. Something in the heavens is guiding us and doesn't want Juremi rescued."

"Have you now turned to superstition too?" asked Françoise, more surprised than reproving.

Her long association with the Protestant Juremi had armed her against superstitions. Yet though she never admitted it to her stern companion, she occasionally found comfort during times of danger and distress in reading the omens.

"Ah!" cried Jean-Baptiste, taking the remark as a reproach, "you're right, Françoise, I can just hear how Juremi would laugh if he ever learned that he was to die because the stars had made discouraging signals at us . . ."

He sat back down at the table.

"Still, I don't see how I am supposed to go against the king's wishes. He's weak, yes, and cannot even defend his country against foreigners. But the little power he has left is more than enough to crush me, who have no one to help me, and to track me down however far I might go."

The room was once again filled with the dull roar of the wind.

"So . . . flight?" said Jean-Baptiste, as though speaking to himself. "It takes two or three weeks for a traveler with baggage to reach the borders of the Persian Empire, which is more than enough time for them to catch me."

Saba was seated in an armchair near the front door, looking silently at the floor. Jean-Baptiste smiled gently as he walked by her, then turned back to his thoughts.

In the silence, a sober, somewhat trembling voice spoke up:

"You would have to die . . ."

They all looked around, stunned to see who had spoken. George was standing near the door, and despite the shadow in which he hid, they could see him blush as all eyes turned to him.

"George, what do you mean?" asked Alix angrily.

The young Englishman, so shy that he shrank from even mild expressions of tenderness, never let Alix's natural love for him develop. She found it extremely difficult to communicate with this skittish youth.

"Nothing . . ." said the boy, who had spoken without considering that it would lead to his being questioned.

"Yes, yes, develop your idea," exclaimed Jean-Baptiste, who had leaped to his feet and was walking toward the young man with happy excitement.

He turned to the others and added in a loud voice:

"An excellent idea. I must die! He's right. He's right."

"Come, Jean-Baptiste, explain what you mean!" said Alix, turning pale.

"That is to say, you must only appear to," George mumbled.

"I did understand you to mean that," said Jean-Baptiste, giving him an affectionate pat on the arm as he went by.

George, sensitive to the least physical contact, smiled and stiffened. Jean-Baptiste returned to the center of the room, near the torch set on the leather desktop.

"George's plan is excellent. We couldn't possibly think up a better one: in the excitement of my audience with the king, do you see, not being as young as I once was, my heart . . . I've made up my mind: I'll die tonight!"

The women emitted a cry of dismay.

"What a horrid thought!" said Saba.

"No, don't take it so tragically. As soon as I am dead, I'll be reborn. I'll be transformed into . . . a poor Armenian pilgrim who returns to the land of the Turks to visit his family."

Jean-Baptiste laughed. He felt a sudden relief.

"All the same," said Alix gravely after a long moment, "don't you think that makes a few too many lies? First Françoise and Alberoni; then the Armenian patriarch and your false identity; now your death . . . Someday you will return. How will we set all this to rights?"

"Alberoni will never come here to confront Françoise; the Armenian patriarch won't take offense at one lie more or less—they are his stock-in-trade. And as to my death, there will be time enough to decide about that when I return. My intuition tells me that this king, if he goes on at his present rate, will not survive me for long, and whoever succeeds him won't care one way or the other whether I am alive or dead."

"And if he does live?" said Alix.

"So many questions! Sufficient unto the day is the evil thereof. Let me die in peace tonight; we'll deal later with how to bring me back to life."

Whatever her forebodings about the plan, Alix could tell that she would never dissuade Jean-Baptiste from it. He clung to the idea, although he did agree, since he only had to present himself to the king the day after next, that he would stay in this world twenty-four hours more. His demise would occur the following night.

All that day, they made discreet preparations. His family walked about, handkerchiefs in hand, overwhelmed by grief. The man for whom they were weeping, meanwhile, had to restrain himself from singing with joy.

At a very late hour of the first night, Jean-Baptiste was still at his desk, putting his papers in order. The window was wide open on the garden, whose plants were visible in the dark only from the reflection of the starlight off their glossy leaves.

Jean-Baptiste's excitement had more or less subsided. He experienced a mood of quiet joy, which he savored dreamily before going to bed.

He started suddenly. George was standing stiffly in front of him, tense at his own audacity.

"You scared me, George, I didn't hear you come in."

"Please, I'd like to talk to you."

The young man never called his adopted father by name. Calling him "Father" would have been a betrayal of his true parents, whom he still felt tenderness toward and was unable to believe were actually dead. But calling him "Jean-Baptiste" would have been taking too great a liberty, and it didn't agree with George's grave respect for authority. In point of fact, neither one had found the right tone. The young man responded to Jean-Baptiste's familiarity with the stiffness of a soldier at present arms. In addressing his father, he never used any other form than "Please."

"Well, sit down and talk," said Jean-Baptiste as affectionately as he could.

George remained standing.

"Will you go alone tomorrow?" he asked.

"No, I am taking Küyük, Françoise's servant, who speaks many languages and may be useful to me."

George had calculated how best to use his meager resources of courage. He now threw them all into a single sentence, which he spoke in a blank voice:

"Tomorrow I will go with you."

Jean-Baptiste examined the young man, who stared straight before him with wide eyes, as though looking past the walls into the darkness to an imaginary horizon. What a strange character! Jean-Baptiste rose and, leaving George to his silent vigil, ambled around the room with his hands behind his back.

Jean-Baptiste liked the tone: "I will go," not "Let me go . . ." He himself had taken a long time to understand the value of such words—he had had to make the detour through Abyssinia to realize that one doesn't ask for freedom, one takes it. This extraordinary boy had discovered the right direction instinctively. One sensed a violent passion inside him, which he held in check behind his shyness. He was certainly determined to go whatever happened. If Jean-Baptiste refused, the boy would find another means, perhaps by running away, but he would never give up . . . That in itself made one want to agree.

All the same, thought Jean-Baptiste, traveling with a person as hard as this to say two words to! Just as I'm gathering momentum, it seems an awfully heavy ball to clamp to my leg.

As he walked around the room, he looked at George from behind, still standing motionless. The poor boy! His parents had been two obsessed and quite fanatical scientists, who had dragged him along in their craze to explore. He probably felt some need to follow in their footsteps and even meet the same fate. Better for him to discover the world with a man who could teach him how to put it to use and wasn't looking for a way to leave it behind.

It's true, thought Jean-Baptiste, and the idea put him in a good mood, there's no dead man more alive than myself! Come, we'll find a way to get past the stiffness of this new leather. The trip will break him in, and if we find Juremi, the old so-and-so will do the rest.

He made his circuit and came back to stand before George.

"You aren't on the patriarch's passport," he said severely.

The young man proved more comfortable on this subject, where feelings played no part. As it turned out, he had prepared his answers.

"All we have to do is shave my hair to form a cross. We'll say that I am a novice waiting for ordination. I'll look so much like a priest that no one will ask me anything—Armenian passports are for the laity."

"You don't speak Armenian," said Jean-Baptiste severely.

"My parents made me learn the basics of it in preparation for our voyage, along with some Turkish and Persian. I can write it, and as to speaking . . . we'll just say I'm mute."

Then, lowering his eyes, the reply dangerously resembling an attack, he added:

"Besides, I believe you don't speak Armenian either . . ."

Jean-Baptiste's mood of contentment drained away. For a moment he was sorry he had agreed to take this boy, whose sharp intelligence often irritated him. His questions, always pertinent, demonstrated a rigor and logic that often caught Jean-Baptiste out.

"No, I don't speak Armenian," said Jean-Baptiste. "But in contrast to you, I speak Persian like a native. Some of the Christians in the eastern part of Persia are Armenians who have forgotten their own language. I'll just say I'm from there."

George's remark had put him in a bad mood and at the same time, because it was penetrating, made him realize how useful it would be to have the fellow along.

"Well," he said sharply, "what are you waiting for to run to Julfa and buy some cloth of the kind Armenian pilgrims wear? No one in that part of the city knows you. Just tell the tailors it's for a costume party."

George did not move, afraid he had not entirely understood.

"Have two habits made, and let yours be simple like a novice's," said Jean-Baptiste, turning toward the window so as to cut short the conversation.

Jean-Baptiste died the following night. His moans and cries began to alarm the servants toward the end of the afternoon, as he lay stretched out on a rug in the cool shade of a terrace. To establish a somber association of ideas in the minds of the onlookers, he lay under a flowering fuchsia that rained down purple droplets on him like poisoned blood. The dying man clutched his chest and spat into a long-necked pot.

Between cries of pain, he pointed to some albarellos on a shelf, and Alix gravely reached down the medicines for him to drink. What the servants did not know was that these jars contained only herbal teas and that the dying man was quenching his thirst with appealing mixes of chamomile and verbena. When the whole household had witnessed these scenes, Alix asked to be left alone with her daughter and Françoise in the invalid's company. Kitchen maids, footmen, and stable boys were all given errands in town, in the firm expectation that they would indiscreetly spread the sad news across the capital.

That night the mistress of the house, pale and dry-eyed, announced that Jean-Baptiste was on the point of death. Meanwhile, in a pavilion off to one side, hidden by an arbor, Saba was cutting her brother's hair with trembling fingers so as to leave only four locks in the shape of a cross. Wearing the robes made for him that afternoon, a rough, long-sleeved habit, George slipped out by a garden door and had himself announced at the main gate, hidden by his ample hood, as a father confessor. Alix welcomed him gravely and led him to the dying man's bedside. In the meantime, Saba braided Jean-Baptiste's black hair into a crown around his head in the Armenian style. No one would have recognized him with his hair like that. Everything then happened very fast. After all the household had retired to bed except for an old guard, the family group performed a little ceremony at the rear of the property in the rose garden. The liturgy consisted of nothing more than turning the earth in a rectangle at the center of the lawn and raising a wooden cross over it.

No Persian would be surprised the following day to learn that Alix, who had lived so long in Isfahan, had followed the Muslim custom of burying her husband immediately, the very same night, as the Prophet's companions had buried Muhammad. No one ever knew that the father confessor, who had arrived alone, left before dawn in the company of another Armenian, who hid his face.

On the following day, everything was in order; the house was officially declared to be in mourning. The appearance of a death was all the more accurately maintained in that the survivors' grief was very real.

II
TO THE
CASPIAN

10

Françoise's Mongol servant had brought two mules loaded with the travelers' meager necessities to the gates of Isfahan. All three travelers had hidden enough gold under their tunics to meet traveling expenses and, if necessary, to supplement their little caravan. As to the medicine case, Jean-Baptiste had spent the night preparing it. He tied it in a bundle of sacking on his animal's croup.

The wretched convoy set off in the small hours of the morning. The first town along their road was Kashan, where Jean-Baptiste had gone to meet Françoise. The speed of the horse on which he had ridden there was still strong in his memory, as fleet as Alexander's Bucephalus, from whom, according to the nazir, Persian horses are descended. In contrast, the mules' plodding seemed desperately slow. Freedom, whose light and joyous music he had been hearing for the past several days, now resumed its true aspect, one he had forgotten: that of a long, arid effort in a vast space.

Thousands of streams flowed down from the mountains, watering the fertile plain overspread with vineyards and houses. Shah Abbas had long ago built a gigantic wall between two escarpments to impound the waters. The travelers climbed slowly to the peaceful banks of this lake. From below, the ravine-furrowed mountains had seemed to match the heavy hearts of the travelers with their tears. But when they reached the lake's green waters, reflecting the cloudless sky and the purple heather and this-tles that carpeted the mountain meadows, the travelers felt pure elation. Jean-Baptiste, already reacclimated to slowness, was moved and delighted to renew his acquaintance with the earth, its unexpected wonders, and the slow unfolding of surprises it reserves for those who love it.

George had only traveled outside of England that once, with his par-ents, on their harsh trip to Persia, clad in a redingote—a rather sinister garment only enlivened by its name, the French mispronunciation of the English "riding coat," afterward accepted back across the Channel by the English. Was it the emotions stirred in him by wearing a disguise for the first time? or the elation of leaving human habitations behind, some few of which were still visible in the valleys below, to reach the abode of the winds and the azure sky? or was it simply his pride at being alone with Jean-Baptiste as his equal? At any rate the young man felt an emotion that another person, less on his guard against it, might have called happiness.

At Qum, on their tenth day out, they made some purchases. This holy city, where Musa in former times had brought the teachings of Ali, hosted innumerable shrines where everyone—from humble merchants to doctors of the Shi'i sect, from kings of Persia to simple pilgrims—took part in celebrating the Prophet and his son-in-law. Despite these observances, which were doubtless inadequate, the city had been destroyed innumerable times by invasions, floods, and earthquakes.

At the time of their visit, Qum had been magnificently rebuilt and was renowned for its industries, particularly the manufacturing of excellent soaps and white pottery. The travelers bought a stock of these articles to make their identity as Armenians more credible, as no Armenian has ever been known to pass up a chance to engage in trade. And finding locally made sword blades, the strongest in all Persia, they chose three good ones, light and finely sharpened, which they secreted in their bundles to use in case they fell in with bad company.

This precaution had as yet no basis in fact, for the people they had met on the roads and in the villages were all honest folk. The real danger, as long as they remained so close to the capital, lay in their being recognized. Several times they thought they were being stared at with unnatural insistence.

"Our Mongol footman," said George one day, "has passed through here once already, when he was traveling with Françoise. He's the one who is arousing suspicions."

This explanation was probably correct. Küyük had the sort of face one doesn't forget. As long as nothing was discovered in Isfahan, they were probably safe, but if someone actually tried to track them down, their disguises would not protect them in the company of so distinctive a figure. As a precaution, they decided to travel at night. The next town they reached was Qazvin. They slept in the enormous caves where the natives go to fetch water after it has flowed down from the surrounding mountains through long subterranean canals.

They crossed uneventfully into the land of the Medes with its garish green pastures and frequent streams. The last place where the Persian king's authority was still strong enough to put them in danger was the city of Tabriz, known to the Franks as Tauris.

To get there they first had to cross a large river, then climb a mountain where the mud made passage in winter so difficult that large stone causeways had been built, the only ones in the whole country, to help travelers negotiate the sheer slopes. In these mountains and in the forests ringing their lower elevations, they saw many deer and grouse, which the Persians do not hunt; they also saw several pairs of eagles, which the local inhabitants do capture using trained sparrow hawks. Made breathless by the steep path, the travelers hardly found time to talk. Jean-Baptiste was sorry about this at first, but on the rare occasions when he wanted to share his feelings he was abruptly reminded of the distance separating him from his all-too-serious son. As they reached the saddle of the last pass, they could see the flat roofs and minarets of Tabriz and far off in a green mist the pure line of Lake Urmia. Jean-Baptiste uttered an exclamation of delight, while George's only comment, discouragingly, was spoken with a blush:

"If only I had an anemometer, I could measure the wind speed."

After spending many long days outdoors or, like night birds, in the crannies of cities, they felt the need for a more human shelter. In Tabriz they decided to ask for hospitality from some Portuguese monks. This seemed a less dangerous stopping place than a caravanserai full of Armenians. It was common enough for Armenian pilgrims to avoid their fractious countrymen and the quarrels and contentions of the merchants by seeking out another community in which to stay. The Portuguese welcomed the travelers soberly but with warmth. That night they served their guests a copious meal of eggs, cheeses, an excellent lake fish, and a lamb dish whose succulent meat was scented with the flowers and aromatic herbs the animal had grazed on during its short and tender life. With the meal came a concentrated and delicious wine, perhaps the most intense in the world, made with the small golden *shahani,* or "royal," grape.

When they had finished, three large Augustinians with grave faces came to sit with them and eat pistachios.

"Did you enjoy the dinner?" asked the elder of the monks politely.

"We certainly did, by our patriarch Nerses!" Jean-Baptiste started in, somewhat flushed with wine and only too happy to show George that he had not been caught out of character. "If Saint Gregory in his pit had fed on such food, by the grace of God, he would still be among us today."

"Certainly," said the monks, shaking their heads. "Yet if that great saint were still practicing the religion you impute to him, he would most likely not have eaten with you tonight."

"And why is that?" asked Jean-Baptiste, looking around him as though to draw support from his two companions, one ostensibly a mute, the other unequivocally a Mongol, and thus both incapable of replying.

"Our Lady of August!" blurted out the oldest of the Portuguese monks, pointing at a Madonna hanging on the wall above them.

"Our Lady of August?" repeated Jean-Baptiste, suddenly afraid.

Then he remembered Murad, the Armenian cook he had brought back from Ethiopia and on whom he secretly modeled himself in playing his role. Murad had observed his religion's fasts simply by whimpering that damnation was upon him. Thus, on the days when he was supposed to abstain from flesh and wine, foods his appetite never allowed him to forgo, he could be heard moaning piteously. It came back to Jean-Baptiste that he sighed thus every Wednesday and Friday of every week of the year, as well as on ten other liturgical occasions: Christmas, Trinity, the Feast of the Transfiguration, etc. One of Murad's ten weeks of whining was Our Lady of August.

"My God!" cried Jean-Baptiste, pretending to the most extreme confusion. "Is it already Our Lady of August? What a catastrophe! See how easily travelers become strangers to themselves, my brothers, and sin through unawareness."

"You were not unaware of it," said the leader of the Augustinians calmly. "When you arrived here I said to you myself: 'Welcome and may the Feast of Our Lady transfigure you!'"

"Yes, you did say that!" said Jean-Baptiste, opening his eyes wide and looking in all directions.

George stared at his knees and the Mongol absently tugged on one of the strings that served him as a beard, disgustingly raising a small cone of swarthy skin.

"Listen," said the monk, pulling his bench closer, and it seemed to Jean-Baptiste that the other two were also drawing the circle tighter, "I don't wish you to commit the sin of lying, which would be as horrible for us as for you. Simply admit the obvious."

To be caught so near the start, and hardly out of Persia! thought Jean-Baptiste, foreseeing the unfortunate consequences of his return to Isfahan, his punishment at the hands of the king, and his family's ruin.

"Come, we ask you straight out: confess."

What could they possibly want from him, these three austere old men, their curly beards so matted as to look like felt scarves pulled over the lower part of their faces? Jean-Baptiste was on the verge of throwing himself at their feet, confessing everything, and pleading for mercy when the monk in charge spoke up:

"Since you are unwilling to say anything, I'll say it for you: you have stopped observing the fasts. Allow me to say that what you are doing is right."

So that's all it was, thought Jean-Baptiste, looking at the monk and hardly daring to believe it.

"Yes, what you are doing is right," the Augustinian repeated, "because these innumerable penitences are no more than usurpations, imposed on you by men who would divert you from Jesus Christ's true message."

A conversion! There was no more to it than that, and Jean-Baptiste suddenly felt an enormous flood of relief, which, thanks to the wine, immediately rose to his cheeks. These Roman Catholics had perhaps given up trying to convert Armenians, as the patriarch claimed, but when Providence dropped three poor, shaky members of the Armenian church into their laps, travelers from a distant province who were weak enough to disobey their tradition, the temptation was simply too great for these disciples of the true faith.

The Portuguese, working in turn for the next two hours, offered spirited arguments in favor of papism.

Jean-Baptiste, nibbling pistachios and accepting the sweet wine the monks were now liberally pouring out for him, happily agreed to everything. At midnight, his face burning and his steps wobbly, he led his friends to their night's rest in the strictest orthodoxy, blessing Innocent XIII, Our Lady of August, and Vasco da Gama.

The following morning, the two false pilgrims and their Mongol groom asked earnestly for the governor's name and place of residence, telling the monks they planned to go immediately to the Muslim authorities to declare their change of religion, as the law required them to do.

Unfortunately, they lost their way en route. Though the poor Portuguese retraced the path between their convent and the governor's palace a hundred times before nightfall, they saw themselves forced to accept the premature loss of these three new converts.

While the Augustinian chapel echoed with inconsolable complines, the three damned souls were hurrying across the mountains to the north as fast as their mules could trot. They wanted to leave Azerbaijan as soon as possible, a province the Persians consider the land of fire, and where fire-tending peoples known as the Gabars still show travelers a place from which the underground fire that they worship erupts. For Jean-Baptiste, these flames nearly became the flames of hell, and he was glad to reach the safety of the cool waters of the Araks River, which was not too impetuous at this time of year. They crossed it by ferry and landed on the opposite shore, where the king of Persia's authority was no longer recognized.

With a conqueror's wisdom, Shah Abbas, again, had known that it would be difficult to keep the province of Armenia. He had therefore made sure to ruin all the villages along the border between it and the rest of Persia. In this way, if the Turks sometimes managed to seize Erevan and the surrounding area, as they had just done, their advance would not directly threaten Persia, protected as it was by this broad band of desolation.

Jean-Baptiste's little company advanced over tracts of dark, swirling dust, the funereal remnants of dead volcanoes. They met ruined villages that also bore the marks of fire, though in this case set by the hand of man. To add to the terror of the scene, heavy, moisture-laden clouds from the Black Sea darkened the sky, loosing a few large drops of rain that pierced the ash as though it were the flesh of a corpse.

Jean-Baptiste was so deeply penetrated by the melancholy scene that he almost decided to turn back. After all, it wasn't too late. He thought of Alix and Saba with deep tenderness and missed them painfully.

As they were crossing a rubble field that had once been a village, a delegation of bearded locals approached them. Now that Armenia was back in Turkish hands and war was again likely, travelers on the roads were rare, and Armenian deacons even rarer. The poor peasants had come to ask Jean-Baptiste if he might bless the oils they commonly used to invoke happiness and prosperity, states one might have thought beyond reach in this locality. George was surprised to see his worthy father comply with the request. After all, Jean-Baptiste had suffered a great deal from the forces of obscurantism himself and took pride in having once helped stop their spread to Abyssinia, yet he now started muttering made-up liturgical formulas with an ease that surprised even himself. The poor folk accepted the holy unctions with a transfiguring gratitude. And they insisted on paying for the service. Jean-Baptiste refused, but they explained that the efficacy of the operation was in direct proportion to their sacrifice in having it performed. In the end the sham pilgrims pocketed the offering and were allowed to resume their path.

Jean-Baptiste felt vaguely ashamed at having taken part in such traffic, and he was further annoyed to feel George's silent disapproval weighing on him.

Finding no words to justify himself, he nursed his anger in silence, which had the benefit of completely dispelling his melancholy. By the time Mount Ararat appeared above the horizon, Jean-Baptiste had once again concentrated all his thoughts on reaching Erevan as quickly as possible and drawing closer to Juremi.

11

In Isfahan, far from the storms provoked by the landscape in the travelers' minds, things were perfectly quiet. The nazir, the prime minister, and the king himself had learned on the day following it of Jean-Baptiste Poncet's demise. Not one of them dared to imagine, or even idly speculate, that this tragedy might reflect anything but the authentic hand of fate.

The king stopped drinking entirely for all of one short week, having resolved one morning to do so, as he at first proclaimed, for good. He cried copious tears in the days that followed and was extremely demoralized. There were touching scenes, which his *qulam-shahs,* or slaves of the king (who correspond approximately to our gentlemen-in-waiting), kept concealed as much as possible. The story spread nonetheless. Sultan Huseyn asked his prime minister for forgiveness by kissing his feet and solemnly vowed to stave in a thousand barrels of wine in the capital. On the second day his faith wavered, and the king discreetly informed the head of his personal guard to puncture the barrels at the top only and not at the bottom. The holocaust was thus limited to spreading the wine's bouquet to the four winds while preserving the liquid itself.

As time wore on, the king's abstention from drink made him increasingly irritable, and the monarch began to mete out the death penalty liberally without experiencing any relief. He consulted his astrologers and holy men ten times a day. His favorite, a magus named Yahya Beg, seized the opportunity to take revenge on the general-in-chief of the armies, who was his hated brother-in-law. He convinced the king that this loyal officer had actually been hatching a plot, the evidence of which was clearly visible in the stars. The king sent couriers to bring the traitor back to the capital and put him to death.

In the following days the king passed from abject fury to total demoralization. The prime minister decided that the king was ripe for signing a decree expelling all Christian clerics and limiting the freedom of foreigners, an ordinance he had long been contemplating. Alas, on entering the

palace with the text in hand, the prime minister was unpleasantly surprised to hear the beat of tambourines and the bells of dancing girls, by
which he understood that he had arrived too late. Wine was flowing in
torrents, and the king, his face flushed, his eyes dancing, threw a slipper at
his prime minister, setting off a volley of laughter among the courtiers.

The evening was so delightful that no one dared inform the king of
two items of news that were circulating in the capital that night: that the
king's orders had been executed and his best, not to say only, general had
been relieved of his head; and that Mahmud, the leader of the Afghan
rebels, had crossed the eastern border with forty thousand men.

Alix in the meantime was bravely fulfilling the duties of a young
widow. She had not found it difficult in the first days to wear a funeral
face. Jean-Baptiste's abrupt departure had shattered her. More painful
even than her husband's absence was the feeling that she had not laid in a
sufficient provision of those last avowals and long, murmured goodbyes
that sustain one's memory.

The tears she shed with her innumerable visitors were therefore perfectly sincere. In her anteroom there gathered women of the world, veiled
and unveiled, foreign diplomats, and a whole string of Persians of varying
origins and religions. This parade of well-wishers joined its feigned tears
to the authentic tears of the false widow, whom Françoise and Saba took
turns attending.

After the first week, the weather turned hot again, as it so often does
in Isfahan, and the desert wind dried everything, even Alix's tears. The
nights were so stifling that cots were brought out into the garden. These
vigils under the starry sky of the high Persian plateau took such a happy
turn that the weeping in this company of women soon gave way entirely
to ringing laughter.

Mornings, by contrast, were unbearable. Alix would return to her
doleful role like a galley slave to his oar. She let it be known that she would
receive visitors for two more days before going into seclusion. On the
evening of the second day, weary of condolences, she had already removed
her widow's uniform when a last and impromptu visitor was announced.

Alix ill-humoredly consented to see her visitor, and a small woman
entered, enveloped in two veils that hid her to the ankles. She could view
the world only through a lacework lattice that was almost as close-knit as
ordinary fabric. Even when they wore veils, Persian women generally

allowed as much as possible of their hands, ankles, and beautiful eyes to show. This woman must have been quite remarkably modest.

"Are we alone?" asked the visitor, her voice muffled by the veils that covered her.

The sound made Alix feel hot.

Alix signaled to the servants to withdraw: "There, now no one will disturb us."

She then saw the little ghost shimmy and shake the two sheaths off over her head one after another. The sight that greeted Alix was charming and entirely unexpected. From the severe silhouette came a very young woman, as fine and graceful as a miniature. Her two enormous eyes, which were absolutely black, smiled all by themselves, and her unusual manner of darting her glance, somewhat sideways and from below, gave her a look of mischief and complicity. She wore her long black hair woven in a complicated braid and held by a sort of pearl diadem. Her dress, simply cut with a deep neckline, was of red silk, ornamented with golden birds whose eyes and beak were made of balas rubies and first-run emeralds. Alix exclaimed in surprise.

"Don't be afraid," said the young woman, advancing toward her hostess and taking her hands.

She had long, thin fingers, on only one of which, her left ring finger, did she wear a ring, but a ring so heavy it pulled her finger toward her palm so that it was visible only by the band of white gold.

"I have wanted to visit you for several weeks," she continued, "but unfortunately this . . . mourning . . ."

Her eyes crinkled as she said this, until she seemed to be laughing outright.

"Well, you are too kind," said Alix, regaining her composure, "do sit down."

She herself chose to sit on a sofa in the middle of the room. It was a narrow piece of furniture that seated two, built in the new style of the Regency according to a design by Jean-Baptiste. Instead of settling across from her as every other visitor had done, the young woman came and sat next to Alix, gathering her silk dress with a pretty gesture, its starched lining squeaking as it creased.

"Now," she said, turning to her hostess, who blushed to feel her so close, "my name is Nur al-Huda."

"What! Then you're . . ." cried Alix starting to rise.

But the young woman stopped her with a firm gesture.

"Yes, the wife of the prime minister. His fourth and last. You probably have heard news of our wedding, which was celebrated three months ago," the young woman went on with a little look of concern. "It's true I'm his wife. My contract with him is entirely regular: I have a ninety-nine-year *muta,* or 'lease,' as I think you call it. When it runs out, we'll see about a renewal."

Imagining the old man with his long beard, his cruelty, and his air of falseness, and seeing the delicate child at her side, Alix felt a staggering wave of disgust.

Nur al-Huda burst out laughing at Alix's astonishment, revealing a set of even and perfectly white teeth.

"Come, I know what you are thinking," she said, leaning toward Alix. "The grand vizier, that mean and sinister old man with . . . me."

"No . . . not at all . . ." spluttered Alix.

"What do you mean 'no'? Ah! I'm going to think that you wish me harm. Can you for a moment imagine his bony fingers with their grubby nails touching me here?"

She mimed a caress of her smooth breasts, plumped even higher by her dress now that she was seated. She laughed, with the silvery laugh of a child.

"Don't worry," she said simply and as though to move on rapidly to another subject, "I resisted his advances for a long time, as befits a person of interest. I finally allowed him to possess me only in the most total darkness. The poor man derives such pleasure from it that he would be sorry to learn that the woman he is clasping is a Nubian servant, one quite expert in love, while I sleep peacefully on the floor above . . ."

"But," said Alix, so fascinated she forgot to marvel that a stranger would make her such a revealing confidence, "aren't you afraid of being discovered?"

"No, not really," said the girl lightly. "If he ever saw the woman in his arms, I can tell you he wouldn't think of marrying her. And if he learned that I had tricked him, he would only desire me the more. The poor man loves me, you see."

Truly, no one who saw that charming face and the impish grace of that smile could help loving their owner instantly.

After this strange introduction, Nur al-Huda leaped to her little feet and made a circuit of the room, running the tips of her fingers across the blood-red curtains and a large bouquet of Hemerocallis. Then she came to stand in front of Alix.

"You like the color red, don't you?" she asked.

"Yes. Red . . . and pink," said Alix uneasily.

"They are not the colors of mourning," said Nur al-Huda, looking obliquely but fixedly at Alix, who felt threatened.

Alix was still searching for a reply when the young woman abandoned her posture of severity and lapsed back into her broad smile and look of mischief.

"Come, don't worry, I know everything and it makes no difference to me."

"Everything? What do you mean?"

"Oh, everything," said the young woman distractedly, seeming to give all her attention to a bumblebee attracted by the corollas of the large flowers.

"But . . ."

Nur al-Huda sat back down on the sofa, pouting like a child imitating grown-up anger.

"Come, come," she sighed, "don't make me tell you what we both know. That your Jean-Baptiste is not dead, that his grave is empty (and for good reason), that at this moment he is galloping toward Russia disguised as an Armenian . . . Is there anything else you would like to know?"

Alix was dumbstruck.

"All right, listen, we'll make everything perfectly clear, both of us. I am your friend. Jean-Baptiste Poncet treated me when I was a child and refused to accept any payment from my family, being as we were very poor. We are Circassians, and my grandparents turned their caravan toward Persia half a century ago. Wanderers, musicians, dancers—yes, that is what my parents are, and what I was too until I married my dear husband. You know the rule among Persians: when they marry, their origins are erased—the slave becomes a mistress, the dancing girl a great lady. But you can see that misfortune follows me. Fate has just given me the means to show my gratitude to the doctor who saved me, and he chooses this moment to disappear."

"But how did you know . . . ?" asked Alix, starting to relax.

"Don't trouble your head over that. We bohemians are part magician, part seer. Our brothers sleep in the streets, which allows them to see and hear a great many things. But no one else knows, or will ever know, what I know. You have my word on that."

So saying, she took Alix's hands in hers, and truly it was impossible not to believe her sincerity.

"Dear Alix," she continued gaily, "I did not know you, but you are just as I imagined you, and in truth I love you already. It is my belief that we two shall be able to render each other great services."

Nur al-Huda, lively as a gazelle, had no sooner spoken than she kissed her new friend on both cheeks.

"Yes, great services," she went on. "For instance I can tell you that this famous Cardinal Alberoni, whose name your friend has used, is no longer in hiding. The nuncio sent by the new pope arrived last week. He has confirmed that the cardinal went to Rome to find refuge, as was suspected all along. The nazir will certainly try to draw advantage from Cardinal Alberoni's return to the living."

"My God," said Alix unhappily, "will they never leave Françoise alone with this business?"

"Don't fret, we'll watch and see what they are preparing and you'll be able to ward off any complications. There are a thousand other dangers I will probably learn about before anyone else, and I can tell you if they threaten to come near."

Alix, still surprised and struggling with a last residue of mistrust, thanked her.

"Don't think you are getting off scot-free, though," said Nur al-Huda. "I need you too. Things are no longer so simple now that I am a rich woman. I am watched, followed. You saw the eunuch waiting in the entry? He goes everywhere with me. It is sometimes a great bother. Because marriage doesn't stop a person from loving, wouldn't you agree?"

12

Mount Ararat, shaped like a night bonnet with its white pompom and grayish folds, is so desolate a spot that it is hard to believe, if ever Noah's ark made land there after the Flood, that any of its passengers would have felt like disembarking. Yet the Armenians claim that it is so, and that the ark is still on Ararat's summit intact. God keeps anyone from climbing up to it, according to local lore: as you approach the summit, the ground sinks as though it were liquid.

Jean-Baptiste and his little caravan, wearied from their long road, gave no thought to verifying these claims by climbing the mountain. And while the ark was only a hypothesis, the tigers and wolves who lived in these parts were an established fact. The travelers therefore left Ararat in the distance, on their way around it passing through the village of Nashivan, which was in ruins and horrible to look at. Farther along they passed several villages of Roman Catholic Christians, converted a few centuries before by an Italian Dominican, whose gift of religion held considerable danger: the poor villagers had been persecuted on all sides ever since, by Armenian Christians and Muslims alike. Finally the travelers came in sight of Erevan. Here there were no ruins. They were able to sleep again in the shelter of a caravanserai, this one of stone with enormous walls, but lacking in all comforts. Nonetheless, they were obliged to pay the duty called *sercolfe,* meaning "lock," which had been inflated to an exorbitant amount by the political conditions. Aside from such details, there was hardly any evidence of the war. Could one even call it a war? Two winded empires had once again exchanged this inaccessible province, which was only readily accessible in times of flood. Neither the Persians nor the Turks apparently had much use for this austere landscape, as both had access to hospitable coasts and fertile plateaux. On entering Erevan, the travelers saw no evidence of recent damage to suggest that it had lately been the scene of fighting. The Turkish army seemed rather to have performed a seasonal migration than a military campaign. Everywhere were carts of hay and forage, pulled by oxen with sawed-off horns, look-ing anything but warlike. From the somber faces of the recently arrived troops, it was hard to tell who were the victors. The Persians were proba-bly delighted to leave Erevan for the haven of their own mild land and gladly bequeathed to the new arrivals the icy mists of the city's endless winter and the intolerable Christians who claimed to be at home there. Toward the center of town, around the fortress and the citadel it protect-ed, the activity of the military was more palpable. The fort was surround-ed by three mud-brick walls with battlements, forming a narrow and irregular rampart in the Oriental style. Abandoned by the Persians who had appropriated its eight hundred houses, it now was in the hands of the Turks. All around, the great maze of the bazaar and the poor houses of the Armenians extended evenly as far as a hill where there stood the bishop's palace and the great cathedral, named the Katoghike. From the high ground of the hill, the fort seemed nothing more than the narrow ghetto where the Armenians had confined the Persians and now were confining the Turks, who were childish enough to imagine they had conquered the local population.

The disguised travelers enjoyed perfect anonymity within the city. No one inquired into their activities. The Armenians, frenziedly buying and selling, had no curiosity about a person unless he appeared solvent, not to say rich. The Turks' arrival was no doubt excellent for business, as an army needs a great deal of everything when it is settling in and the Armenians were long accustomed to profiting from defeat as well as victory.

Küyük stayed at the caravanserai to guard the luggage while Jean-Baptiste and George went into town to gather useful information. Which way should they go next? What identities should they choose? and what pretext for traveling? Should they be concerned about war farther north toward the Caucasus Range, which lay between them and the Russian Empire? Unable to ask an Armenian because of their ignorance of the lan-guage, they roamed through the area where the Turks congregated, at the fort and in the teahouses they frequented. George announced that he also understood enough Turkish to overhear useful conversations and pro-posed that he and Jean-Baptiste separate in order to be more discreet and to increase their chances of learning something interesting. They decided to meet up that evening on the steps of the Katoghike.

With his black hair braided in a crown around his head, his beard, unshaven since the start of the trip, shadowing his cheeks, and his com-

plexion dark from the sun in the mountains, Jean-Baptiste could absolutely pass for an Armenian. He sensed not the slightest curiosity on the part
of those around him. Having bought two chickens in the market, which
he held by their feet, wings flapping and heads dangling, he strolled
through the streets of the bazaar offering his noisy wares, though with no
intention of selling them. He reached the fort, saw that merchants were
admitted during the day, and entered. In the narrow streets, Jean-Baptiste
passed a number of Turkish soldiers dressed in quilted blue vests and,
despite the fine weather and absence of any battle, wearing their heavy
pear-shaped helmets with the curtain of chain mail hanging down to the
napes of their necks. As with all the armies of the Ottoman Empire, this
one brought together the most disparate peoples, recruited in the course of
conquests and captures, from Tartars to Slavs, from Asians to Phoenicians,
all of them swaggering as men do when bearing arms.

Jean-Baptiste reached a large square, and there, seated on a stone
bench, he allowed his chickens to set their feet back on the ground and
peck contentedly at the spaces between the cobbles. He saw a heavy cannon pass on a cart, headed for the battlements. During the afternoon, several groups of janissaries, most of them on horseback, paraded their white
bonnets and fierce expressions. Although visibly intent on impressing
with their importance and haste, they seemed as much at loose ends as the
soldiers they commanded.

From the conversations he overheard between his neighbors, Turks
who, like him, were enjoying an idle respite in a warm spot, Jean-Baptiste
learned two things: first, that the military preparations so quietly under
way were not directed at the Persians, whom everyone believed to be
extremely weak. Rather, the Turks expected danger from the Russians to
the north—which was hardly encouraging. The other news was that a
great military leader, sent by the sultan to command operations, had
arrived the previous day. Daoud Pasha, as he was called, was a renegade
Frank who had become a Turk and won many victories on behalf of the
Porte. Pleased with what he had learned, Jean-Baptiste left the citadel at
five o'clock, gave his chickens into the hands of a runny-nosed, barefoot
boy, who took immediately to his heels, and made his way to the cathedral.

He had not gone fifty paces when he saw George. The young man was
walking bareheaded, his hood off, his eyes on the ground. It took Jean-
Baptiste a moment to realize that George's hands were tied behind his
back, and that the two Turks on either side were guarding him—that he
was a prisoner. He followed the group at a distance as far as the Qechi-

qala fort, a forward post of the citadel where the janissaries and their leaders had set up quarters. When he was sure that the guards were leading George inside, Jean-Baptiste ran back to the caravanserai, seized the Armenian patriarch's letter, and returned to the fort on the run. He presented himself at the gate.

"And what do you want?" asked the Turkish sentry roughly, his two giant hands encircling his lance.

"To see my friend, who has just been mistakenly arrested."

"The Russian spy?"

"No, no, he isn't Russian and he's even less a spy. We are poor Armenian pilgrims on our way to Van and I have our papers here . . ."

The big Turk shrugged and stepped aside with bad grace to allow Jean-Baptiste through.

"Go tell it to the janissaries."

Jean-Baptiste entered. The courtyard was badly kept and crowded with horses. Under their brightly colored damask harnesses, the animals were mud-spattered and stood in a sparse layer of bedding that was turning to manure. The officers he passed looked at him suspiciously. Luckily, he did not have to search for long, discovering George chained to a slender stone column. Three men stood beside him and seemed to be questioning him.

"He won't answer," said Jean-Baptiste sharply as he approached.

The three men turned around, and their leader exclaimed:

"What does this one want?"

Jean-Baptiste shuddered to see the man. He was not a large man, in fact rather on the small side, but his beard, which was thin and red, framed a venomous face from which hung a huge and swollen goiter. He was probably one of those mountain peasants captured at a young age by the Turkish army on the skirts of the Alps and raised in a hard school, feeding on turnips in ordinary times and on spoils in time of war, one of those soldiers who, fearing their masters, resenting their parents, and hating peace and happiness, were the very strength of the Turkish Empire—until the empire in turn became their prey.

"Here are his papers, Sire," said Jean-Baptiste handing the brute the letter with the patriarch's seal. "This man is my companion. He is innocent but is incapable of saying so because he has lost the use of speech. And that, furthermore, is why we are on a pilgrimage."

The janissary considered the rolled letter Jean-Baptiste was holding out to him. Believing it to be a parchment, he motioned it away. Because of his religion, he looked on any contact with impure animals, whether dead or alive, as sullying.

"Does this document give you the right to spy on our armies?" he asked with a terrible smile.

"In no way, most noble aga."

"Then why has this dog—whose voice will return to him without benefit of a pilgrimage, I warrant, and a very loud voice too—why has he been following our soldiers, listening to them, nosing into their business? And look at him. Have you ever seen an Armenian with hair or eyes like that?"

So saying, he ripped a tuft of George's blond mop from his head, making the boy wince with pain.

Jean-Baptiste embarked on a detailed refutation, but the janissary wasn't listening. For several moments he had been paying attention to a growing murmur from the direction of the fort's entrance, which soon translated into a flurry of activity in the courtyard. A detachment of horsemen wearing big yellow turbans and coats of mail entered the fort, making its walls echo with the hollow noise of unshod hooves. At the center of the knot of horsemen was a figure to whom the highest deference was being paid. The dignitary drew his feet from his large stirrups, dismounted, and disappeared into the building before Jean-Baptiste could glimpse any more of him than a broad gray beard and a coat of yellow nankeen.

The newcomer's arrival put the three janissaries in a state of high excitement, and they were clearly in a hurry to join him. At a command from their leader, two guards seized Jean-Baptiste, untied George from his column, and led them both to a cell in the basement.

There the prisoners spent a miserable night in almost utter darkness, alone, hungry and thirsty, seated on the dank, uneven ground, the very basalt bedrock on which the fortress had been built. George controlled himself until the middle of the night, then let his tears flow.

"It's my fault," he sobbed, "it's all my fault!"

Jean-Baptiste pitied him sincerely. He told himself that he had been hard on the boy ever since their journey started, that he had shown him little consideration or support. Yet the boy was courageous, hardworking, and generous. And it was hardly his fault if his parents had stuffed his head with scientific notions and a naive faith in progress, which, together with his timid and respectful character, sometimes made him irritating. After all, he was still a child.

He took him in his arms, and under the cover of darkness, the boy relaxed his usual stiffness, allowing himself to sob more bitterly than before. Since they were going to die, George wanted Jean-Baptiste to know how thankful he was to have been taken into his home. He spoke at length of the happy days he had spent in the garden in Isfahan, of the hours in the laboratory, of his games with Saba.

"And look, since it's the end of the road, I have a secret to tell you, Jean-Baptiste."

Never before had he dared to call his father by name. Death was certainly spurring him to make progress.

"An awful secret. Listen to me."

Ten times he was on the point of speaking, and ten times he stumbled over an invisible obstacle. Jean-Baptiste calmed him and told him the confession could wait until morning, after a good night's sleep. What could he possibly have to tell me? he wondered.

The night wore on. After a few frightened starts and a last sob, George fell asleep against Jean-Baptiste's shoulder.

Bah! thought the older man, at that age you feel guilty about everything. He probably broke one of my retorts or something like that.

And as the other's grief had distracted him from his own troubles, he fell into a peaceful sleep.

13

In the Rome of that period, the Piazza Navona, built on the ruins of Domitian's stadium, was given over to the chaos and stench of an enormous food market. Bernini's sculpted figures, with their clasped arms, alarmed eyes, and writhing torsos, seemed to be struggling out of a shipwreck and trying to flee the rising tide of citrus and flayed animals.

Not far from the square, and extending its ignominy, lay the Via Dell' Orso, crowded with the sort of hotel that offers the traveler every pleasure with the possible exception of rest. One of these establishments, rising five lopsided stories, bore the mysterious and ridiculous name of the Inn of the Laughing Bull.

As only mediocrity is hateful, this hotel could pride itself on being superlative in a number of ways: it was the most slovenly, most insalubrious, and most unsavory for its clientele of any hotel in Rome, a city not without its share of claimants for the distinction. Furthermore, it provided the amenity of being almost opposite the Castel Sant' Angelo, that elegant finger the Vatican points at the city and its corruption.

The hotelkeeper, one Paolo, had no doubt considered it prudent not to bring his brains when he left his native Puglia: his curly black hair rested directly on the line of his eyebrows—there was not a finger's breadth between them. His beard, of the same hue, attempted to rejoin the mass of his hair by climbing as high as his lower eyelid. The poor man, in point of fact, was extremely gentle and seemed to suffer from his terrifying physical appearance. Every encounter with himself at the mirror in the morning turned into a street brawl. Paolo would emerge from these bouts with his face horribly cut, yet the blood had not dried before his bristles had already grown back.

So extreme was his hirsuteness that he no longer frightened anyone. His guests never paid their bills, and his barking only made them smile. More than one tenant had felt the impulse to soothe him by patting him on the head. Tonina, the house servant, was the only one who had sometimes given in to the impulse, being young and spry enough to avoid being kicked. Paolo's indulgence toward her had another cause. Some guests were drawn less by the hotel's low rates than by the young girl's charms. Looking in every respect like the Madonna of the Pilgrims, Tonina was only too happy to distribute on earth a bit of the beatitude that Caravaggio had made manifest in his fresco.

Paolo spent his days in a cubby at the foot of the stairs. On the wall behind him were two rows of numbered nails, though none of his roomers would have so far forgotten himself as to leave his key there.

It was still hot on that September morning, and Paolo was sprawled on his little wooden counter when a man entered the hotel furtively.

"Well, Paolo! Gone to bed already?"

"Imbecile! Is that your idea of humor?"

The man walked up to the counter and set his elbows on it. By his accent, he came from the south. But the generations in his home country, after innumerable harvests of blood, had brought forth this pale vintage, with amber skin, a honeyed smile, an acid aftertaste, and, if truth be told, a muddy character.

"Is he upstairs?"

"Most likely."

"Answer me!" said the visitor, slapping his hand down on the counter.

"Listen, Mazucchetti, I'm not your paid informer, do you hear? Yes, he's upstairs. Now leave me alone."

The man went to the foot of the spiral staircase, glanced up the flight of steps, and came rapidly back to Paolo.

"Tell me," he said, in his lowest voice, "do you think he has any left?"

"Ohh! Now that's enough, I—"

Quick as lightning, Mazucchetti grabbed the hotelkeeper by the collar. As the poor victim didn't have the option of raising his eyebrows, he proved his astonishment by opening his mouth.

"I . . . I don't have the slightest idea. It seems that he does . . . Probably not much . . . But last week a letter from France arrived for him. He went to a money changer and afterward paid me what he owed."

"There, you do know," said Mazucchetti, letting his victim go. "So, with a little bad luck we may run into each other a few more times."

"A pleasure," said Paolo darkly as he rearranged his collar.

But the visitor was already in the stairway climbing the steps four at a time to the top floor. He turned down a dark hallway, tripped over a foul-smelling bucket, and knocked on a flimsy door whose cracks admitted daylight.

"Come in. Ah! It's you, Mazucchetti, and about time. My watch says five past ten."

"We said ten o'clock."

"Exactly, not five past ten. At any rate, sit down."

Mazucchetti settled on a small rush chair. His host preferred to stay standing, resting his elbow on the open window ledge, where Tonina's scolding voice floated up to them.

"Mazucchetti, let's get right to the point. A man of my rank does not shy away from the truth, even when it proves painful. Well, we are coming to the end of our search."

The speaker was an old man filled with extraordinary energy, or perhaps rage. He had abandoned the superfluities of fat, muscle, and hair for an essential being composed of much bone and little skin. No vanity survived, only its distant relic in the cut of his long coat and pants, which were frayed by laundering, much mended, worn to the nub, and hardly worthy of a great lord, yet it was precisely the manner of such a lord that was evident in his least gesture.

"Yes, to the end, truly," the old man said. "If I don't obtain justice from the pope this time, I will leave. I have used up my last resources. You know this. Perhaps you indulge some disbelief on this score, but you are wrong. I have nothing left."

A crow landed on the window ledge, looked at the two men in fright, and flew away.

"Well, I am waiting. What is the latest news?"

"Alas! I have little to tell His Excellency the consul," said the Italian, a small smile playing at the corners of his lips. "Only this week I visited three secretaries, one protonotary, and two bishops. That's a lot. Each time I carefully brought up your book, which they knew. They all condemn *Telliamed* . . ."

"But have they read it?" cried Monsieur de Maillet, stamping his feet on the uneven floor tiles.

"In any case, they all cite the same reason. You question the age of the earth as set forth in the Bible, and you deny that all beings were created at the same time."

"Listen, Mazucchetti," the old man howled indignantly, but in a pitifully broken voice. "I have proven it to you a hundred times starting from basic assumptions: my book is no more than the meditations of an honest man. While on a walk in Egypt, I saw a cliff a great distance from any coastline, and I observed that shells were embedded within the rock."

"From which you deduce that the sea has fallen over the course of the ages, I know, I know," said Mazucchetti, tapping his foot impatiently.

"And my entire system springs from this! From an incontrovertible fact. Ask those cardinals to leave their palaces and walk with me along a beach. I am convinced that I will make them see it: the sea is falling."

"I have been engaged in this profession for more than ten years," said Mazucchetti in acid tones, expressing considerable contempt. "You will find no one more well connected than myself when it comes to the Vatican's business: I have arranged for rulers to be divorced and for heretics to be blessed. But as far as taking cardinals to the seaside, you'll have to find someone else."

Monsieur de Maillet appeared to feel the force of these threatening words. He drew back, sat down on a chair, and fumbled nervously in his pocket for an old lace handkerchief, now reduced to a handful of tatters.

"Don't abandon me, Mazucchetti, I know how valuable you are. All the same, you've been promising me an audience with the Holy Father for some time now . . ."

"Is it my fault," asked the Italian, determined to wring the most from his victory, "if there is a new pope this year? if everything had to be started all over again because Innocent XIII is surrounded by a different court and a different set of favorites?"

"No, clearly. But you must understand that I hold it of the utmost importance to have the papal condemnation lifted before I die. I am only waiting for you to tell me whether there is still a chance, a single chance, for me to see the pontiff."

The go-betweens whose chosen territory was the Vatican were probably the most disillusioned and least softhearted adventurers of any on earth. There came to them on the one hand sinners, hardened to their vices and betrayals, and drenched in all the corruptions of the century, yet in whom there survived a sufficient spark of ideality and purity to believe in a merciful heaven. On the other hand they served the ministers of God, elected to divine favor for eternity, who had albeit not renounced the voluptuous pleasures that gorge the bowels of the world and that the go-between endeavored to procure for them with the utmost discretion. The trick was in making both sides part with their very last ounce of gold.

"Yes," said Mazucchetti gravely. "There is still a chance."

"Wounds!" sputtered the old man, already on his feet. "Are you telling me the truth? Mazucchetti, may I then entertain hopes once more?"

"High hopes," said the adventurer with false detachment.

"Speak. Tell me."

"I can't go into details. The matter must remain secret. All you need know is that the new pope has changed everything and that a new person has appeared in his entourage. As he and I have some acquaintance, I am very much counting on him. But . . ."

"But?"

"There is a price."

"How much?" asked the consul, trembling.

"Let us just say about one thousand écus."

"Horrors!" cried Monsieur de Maillet. "Where will I ever find such a sum? I no longer have anything, Mazucchetti, nothing."

The go-between allowed these protestations to go on while he looked calmly out the window, the way you shut the door and wait for an infant to fall asleep. Monsieur de Maillet truly did not have a groat. The money he had recently received had been swallowed up immediately by his debts. Nonetheless, he was still hoping that funds from the sale of a small wood near Metz, once the property of his wife, who died after their return from Cairo, would reach a certain Roman money changer before long. The sum would come close to one thousand écus—the go-between's instinct had been razor-sharp. After that, the old man would have nothing, for good and all. If I ever want to return to France, he told himself, I must not spend this money. But what good would it do him to return to France, another part of him countered, if he would only leave it for the fires of hell? After much groaning, much pacing about the room and internal debate, Monsieur de Maillet stopped and turned toward the Italian.

"Are you certain, and I underline 'certain'—you must give me your absolute word of honor on it—that this man holds sway over the Holy Father?"

"He will be your last but your most solid supporter, Excellency."

"One thousand écus," said Monsieur de Maillet. "And not one more."

By the old man's tone, the expert knew that he had reached bottom. He accepted.

When two guards arrived to take the prisoners from their cell, a fine summer sun was high in the sky. The stones of the fort seemed less black, and a horse's dun coat in the middle of the courtyard shone like a caress of nature, offering a joyful sight. When it came to dying, it was just as well to do it in good weather and to have the last color you saw be blue. Such were Jean-Baptiste's thoughts as he stepped out of the cell, dizzied by the light and rather famished. Beside him, George was still shrouded in sleep. The freckles on his nose, the disheveled cross of hair on his shaven head, and his big blue eyes made him look like a porcelain mannequin.

The guards had tied neither their hands nor their feet, and for a moment, as they passed a gallery leading out of the fort, Jean-Baptiste had the idea of running headlong into it. But the gate was far away, the court-yard full of soldiers, and anyway they were weak. Best to resign them-selves to their fate. They were led to another wing of the building, where the dignitaries had entered the previous day, and which must have housed the officers' corps. The guards first took the wrong door, then made the prisoners retrace their steps and climb a stairway. Everything was in a state of bustle and confusion. Officers and men alike wore busy expres-sions, bellowed orders, and bumped into each other in the corridors. Only the captives seemed immune to the general alarm.

After opening several doors by mistake, the guards finally showed them into a large room lit weakly by windows of green glass and further darkened by a ceiling of smoke-blackened cedar.

Seated in the center of the room was the dignitary they had glimpsed the previous day, visible over the heads of others only by his large white turban. Many groups, mostly consisting of janissaries, argued loudly and heatedly, waiting in disorder for the great man to provide arbitration.

More than an hour passed before the case of the two false Armenians came up. Jean-Baptiste squeezed George's hand to console him and was surprised to see the poor boy smile, resigned to his short and tragic fate. Finally, they were shoved in a flurry of elbows and shoulders into a nar-row clearing in the midst of the many groups. They fell to their knees on the rug at the feet of the elderly man who held their lives in his hands. He wore an ample silk caftan decorated with flowery green mandorlas on a red background. In the space between his gray beard and his white turban, there appeared a broad face with the long, sharp, purple-striped nose of a grenadier, set between two lively, laughing eyes that darted fire.

"What have these two done?" he asked in bad Turkish with a Frankish accent.

Jean-Baptiste boldly raised his head and, in the desperateness of his situation, lashed at his memory as though it were a team of horses.

"They are Russian spies," said a janissary standing next to the old man.

"Execute them! Execute them!" voices yelled.

"Russians, really. Do they have papers?"

"Yes, Effendi," said Jean-Baptiste, who had managed to hold on to the parchment signed by the patriarch.

While the old man examined the writing, Jean-Baptiste inspected him closely. The text was in Persian and the dignitary shook his head to show that he couldn't understand it.

"They were following the soldiers and secretly listening to them talk," went on the janissary. "They're spies."

"What do you have to say?" the old man asked wearily. It was clear that he had already come to a judgment.

Then Jean-Baptiste, on a sudden inspiration, straightened up and, looking the magistrate right in the eyes, said to him in French:

"And how is your gout, Effendi?"

The janissaries, who understood nothing of these words, drew silent, and the old man appeared to be in the grip of a violent curiosity.

"My gout," he answered in the same language, "is acting up horribly. Do you claim to have some remedy for it?"

"It worked quite well for you the last time," said Jean-Baptiste, smiling. Then he added, "In Venice."

"In Venice . . . That goes back . . ."

"Oh! Twenty-five years at least. Time passes. We were both young."

The old man suddenly straightened his entire bulk, grasped Jean-Baptiste's hand, raised him to his feet, and, to the stupefaction of the Turks, wrapped him in a powerful embrace, crying:

"Poncet!"

14

Certain men, while endowed with great good qualities, are fated to be ruined by a venomous enemy in their own mouths that proves as fatal to themselves as to others: their tongues.

The marquis d'Ombreval had paid heavily for the curse of making witticisms. All his life he had instantly drawn the goodwill of his peers, only to yield to the unsurpassable pleasure of turning his epigrammatic wit on them, wounding them all the more irreparably in that they had earlier opened themselves to him without reserve.

The younger son of an excellent family from Lorraine, he had entered the army of King Louis XIV, where he distinguished himself by his bravery and intelligence. Regrettably, he responded to a minister's reproof with such insolence that he earned himself a week's imprisonment. On the day he left prison, he also left France. After a stay in Venice, where Poncet had known him, he offered his valor to Prince Eugene of Savoy, who had earlier felt the force of it from the opposite camp. But his brilliant career with the emperor was brought to a close by a bad pun, which made its way to its subject and caused d'Ombreval to be cashiered. He returned to France, though he had fought in the opposite camp for four years, received a pardon, then sinned again in his usual manner. Pursued by the mortal hatred of friends turned enemies, he soon had no other recourse than to offer his bravery to the Turks, who entrusted him with the organization of their armies. Thus he became Daoud Pasha. His poor command of the Ottoman language at first obliged him to make good use of it. But no sooner had he mastered it sufficiently than he fell back into his old vice and slandered the grand vizier. The sultan had shown him clemency and only exiled him to the East, where he put him in command of the newly conquered province of Armenia.

The appearance of Jean-Baptiste, whom he had considered a friend in Venice, gave d'Ombreval double pleasure: first, it provided him company in this distant province; second and more important, as this friendship

went back more than twenty years, it belied and, as it were, avenged the
marquis's perennial incapacity to entertain cordial relations in any quarter
for more than a fortnight.

Seated on rugs around a copper platter, on the upper floor of the fort
used by Daoud Pasha as his country residence, the men celebrated their
reunion by filling porcelain cups from an opaque flask inscribed "Mineral
Water of Carbonnieux." It was a very dry white Graves that had not suffered in transit.

"One has to be careful here," said d'Ombreval, pointing at the carafe.
"The Turks are not like the Persians, they are not indulgent about this.
Actually, they are only concerned to save appearances."

"So you are now a Muslim?" asked Jean-Baptiste, who hardly remembered the marquis to be a man observant of religious laws.

"I was never much of a Christian, and I am no more of a Muslim. The
seriousness of all this is exaggerated . . . My trade is to serve, and I wear
the livery of my masters. Ah! Poncet, what a shame that we did not meet
in Istanbul: I would have shown you my palace, one of the handsomest in
the Top-Hana. In the early morning, when the sun strikes the waters of
the Golden Horn, with all the minarets rising through the trees across the
way and all the lead domes with their gray reflections, it's worth being
damned eternally for."

He raised his glass and emptied it in one draft, adding:

"Just what I am doing, as it happens."

He asked Jean-Baptiste to recount his adventures in detail and to tell
him the purpose of his trip. D'Ombreval vaguely remembered having met
Juremi in Venice at about the time he joined Poncet as a partner in the
apothecary trade. They remembered those days fondly, Daoud Pasha
often turning to George to repeat "Ah! What a time it was, young man!
What a great thing is Europe!" and to wipe away a tear. Two servants
brought in a plate of steaming kebabs, which they ate with their hands.

"Frankly," said d'Ombreval, a tide of voluptuous pleasure rising in
him as he ate and drank, "life is rather amusing, don't you find? There
you are with your braid around your head looking like an washerwoman,
while this fellow is missing half his hair, and I sit here in a big turban and
a frock commanding in the name of the Ottoman sultan! There are days
when I wonder if I'm not dreaming. In Istanbul, I can delude myself
somewhat: I've furnished my house like a château in Lorraine and sur-
round myself with a society that would make you doubt that
Constantinople ever fell. But here . . . ?"

"Do you think that war will break out soon?" asked Jean-Baptiste, mindful of the realities of his voyage even as the old man waxed on. "We have left our entire family behind in Isfahan."

"War? With the Persians? No, not from this side anyway. We are in Erevan only because someone has to hold this accursed place of Noah's. The Persians are too weak. If we weren't occupying it, the Russians or someone else would. But you know the janissaries, the so-called elite of this army: they are Shi'i. It's an odd fact, but the Beshtashi sect they belong to worships with the descendants of Ali. The Grand Turk, whom they preserve and protect—when they aren't cutting his throat as they did last year—is a Sunni of the first water. Does that make any sense? At all events, the janissaries have little stomach for fighting the king of Persia, who shares their beliefs. No, I can confirm that our army is advancing no farther."

Stretching out his legs, Daoud Pasha grimaced with pain.

"Actually, Poncet, you couldn't have come at a better time. This gout never lets up anymore, and it's truly torturing me in this mountain climate."

"Our medicines are in a caravanserai at the entrance to town, guarded by our manservant."

"I'll give the order to have them fetched and you can move in here. This fort is built of cold, dank stones, but there are better accommodations than the rooms you were first shown to. A month of this regimen and you'll be completely restored, by which time you will have cured me of gout."

"It is a great pleasure, dear Marquis, to have found you again, and we still have many stories from the past to remember. But as we are now free, thanks to you, I believe we will resume our road as soon as possible. I have already mentioned that we must reach Juremi before winter."

"As you wish," said d'Ombreval, disappointed but unwilling to press the point.

This meeting across the years had something rare and precious about it. The marquis was already looking forward to the pleasure of returning to Istanbul and saying: "Do you know, I ran across a friend in the East that I have known for twenty years." Best not to run the risk of ruining the occasion by prolonging it.

"It seems to me that in any case you should abandon your disguise," he said. "Even here it will make you look suspicious, and I cannot host you in that fancy dress for long without having tongues wag."

"The problem is that I was implicated in an unfortunate incident, now some time ago, on Turkish territory . . . in Egypt," said Jean-Baptiste with hesitation. "I killed a janissary."

"No! Can this be?" cried Daoud Pasha.

"It was a rotten business, and I really had no choice. I was abducting my wife . . ."

"Abducting your wife! Wait, don't say another word. Here is a story that is going to liven up our dinner in a bit. Abducting your wife! That's just like you . . . All the more reason for you to jettison that garb, which hardly befits so chivalrous a man . . ."

"I became an Armenian," said Jean-Baptiste, "to avoid problems with the Turks, in case this business—"

"Well, you are no longer an Armenian: everyone here has seen that you are a Frank. But don't worry—the Turkish government hereabouts is me."

"And when we continue our travels?"

"You couldn't have chosen a worse identity. The Armenians are odd birds, and their neighbors detest them. Have you seen their religion? All those saints that no one has ever heard of. Did the names Saint Caiane or Saint Repsime mean anything to you before coming to this country? You have only to go to the Monastery of the Three Churches, a two-hour ride from here, and they will show you the relics of these unfortunate women: the arm of one and the thigh of the other, nothing else is left. There is also, if you care for such things, a rib belonging to Saint James, a finger of Saint Peter's and two belonging to Saint John the Baptist . . . No, really, you can't have any respect for people who parcel out holiness in separate cuts."

"Then what do you advise?"

"Travel as Franks, quite simply. Do you have papers?"

"A letter from the Russian ambassador to his government."

"Take care not to show it before you arrive in Russia! In these parts, you are either an ambassador and therefore respected, as long as you have the proper accreditation, or you are a merchant and allowed to go free. But there is nothing so hated as people who fall between the two. Do you have a little money?"

"Enough."

"In what currency?"

"In Persian tomans."

"Go to the marketplace and change all that for Venetian sequins, which are accepted everywhere. Then go and buy yourselves several lengths of cloth, some fine damask, the sort of thing that Franks like to wear. You'll say that you have come from Persia, where you were selling jewelry. In the same bazaar, you'll find a seamstress who will take only a day to make a doublet exactly like one of my own. The Armenians are extremely skillful at this kind of work. You'll see as soon as you've crossed into Georgia: those fellows respect anyone wearing a fine hat and clothes in the European style. No people are simpler than the Georgians. The highest mark of nobility in that country is to be a hereditary executioner."

"Charming."

"No, no, you'll see, they'll welcome you splendidly. And they have nothing but disdain for money. For one of those necklaces that their wives wrap around their necks in five or six rows, they will give you anything you want."

"They say the women are extremely handsome," hazarded Jean-Baptiste, still looking for a subject that would elicit a positive opinion from d'Ombreval.

"In Isfahan that may be true," the old campaigner replied. "The Georgian women you see there have been abducted expressly for their beauty at the age of five or six. They take the very finest, whose parents are easily talked into it. But you can't look at the ones who are left without damaging your eyesight, and you go near them at your own risk."

"Are they strongly jealous?"

"Not in the least. But these young ladies dab their cheeks with a horrible paste that smells like cow dung."

"And . . . where can we find horses?" asked George, ever practical and eager as well to leave a topic that might injure his modesty.

"As to horseflesh, leave that to me," said Daoud Pasha. "You won't have any complaints. I know that foreigners admire the little horses from these parts, to the point where the Turks think we have none at home since all the Europeans travel here to buy them. Well, I find their trot jerky, and it makes my back hurt. I brought some Bretons from France, which I bred to their little Barbaries. By God, you'll see how it came out: you sit in the saddle as though installed in a cabriolet. I'll tell my groom to prepare two of them for you and a little Turkoman for your valet."

Jean-Baptiste thanked him warmly. He repaid his debt by supplying Daoud Pasha with some extract of colchicum for his gout and by giving the Turkish surgeon instructions for replenishing the remedy as often as needed. They stayed two more days in Erevan and took pleasure in strolling there in the clothing of their native country; the sun seemed the warmer for it, and the town less grim . . .

The marquis d'Ombreval spent two delightful evenings in their company. He regaled them with carp and trout from the river, a food for which Armenia is famous all through the East. Never pausing for a moment, he told them all the nasty stories he knew of the great figures of Europe. Denouncing these absurd figures had cost him so dear, and he invested so much wit in the telling, that his passion for anecdote, to which he had forfeited his life, made him a sort of martyr to caricature, one of those prophets burned at the stake for having had the courage to tell men the full measure of their sorry truth.

Finally, they were ready. Jean-Baptiste had unbraided his long curly hair, and George had shorn his and covered his blond stubble with an elegant felt tricorn, a gift from their host. Come back to life after a detour through their dark dungeon, George seemed to have learned to smile, and without having grown familiar, he had somewhat relaxed his stiffness toward Jean-Baptiste. Their brief death had left them reborn, not as father and son, which they had never really agreed to be, but as two brothers separated by their ages but joined by their experience of a common ordeal. Nonetheless, the young man did not go so far as to tell Jean-Baptiste the secret he had briefly mentioned, and Jean-Baptiste, so as not to embarrass him, did not mention it either.

They prepared for their departure by talking of inconsequential things and by singing. The horses d'Ombreval had found for them were indeed extraordinary animals: as high-spirited as Arabs, and as big and strong as draft horses.

Daoud Pasha accompanied them as far as the gates of the town. A surly detachment of janissaries surrounded them, and a motionless crowd lined the streets to watch them pass. Remarkably, silence greeted the advancing procession. The only sound was the dull clopping of the unshod hooves on the cobbled streets.

"Now this is something I like," said Daoud Pasha. "In our country, they honor you by yawping and clapping, and it's all very disagreeable. Here the greatest mark of respect is to be silent."

When they reached the outskirts of town, the little troop stopped and d'Ombreval embraced his long-lasting friend warmly. The old man could not hide the emotion welling up in him on seeing the three men leave. His tears most likely came at the thought that he had given them a freedom he himself did not have.

As long as they were in sight of the town, Jean-Baptiste held back and kept his mount at a slow trot. But when they had left the sinister folds on Ararat's flanks far behind, they plunged down into the moist valleys of Georgia. In a few hours the landscape around them had changed: cicadas chirped in the tall grasses by the road, the dark blue outline of the horizon followed the rounded form of hills, with their thickets of pale green chestnut trees and black cypresses. The only regiments that met them were lined up immovably in battle rank—countless vine plants, with their varnished leaves and heavy burden of big violet grapes. Walking up the hill to attack them, a song on their lips, came the first harvesters.

Heaped with wealth and honors but always striving to acquire more, the nazir sometimes, walking through Isfahan's warm and starry night, missed the simple life of his native mountains. It was with the intention of abandoning himself to a session of sweet nostalgia that, wrapped in a plain black coat, he let himself out of his palace through a garden door to which he had the only key. The Chahar Bagh was dark and deserted, but when he reached the small streets of the Eastern city he noticed with displeasure that despite the late hour there were many idlers about. He chose the darkest alleys and, drawn from the serenity of the dreamer, returned to his earlier preoccupations.

This devil of a Poncet had chosen the worst moment to die! First he put a treasure in the nazir's hands, then he fled to heaven or to hell—most certainly to hell—taking the key with him. Alberoni had reappeared in Rome, this had been confirmed by none other than the papal nuncio. It was the moment to bring out the concubine, but the vile woman had declined to collaborate. The nazir had gone politely to visit her, but she answered in the sweetest tones that Isfahan was the ideal place for her to stay. She didn't miss her cardinal and had no intention of writing him. No matter how the nazir insisted or what veiled threats he made, she wouldn't budge.

He walked with his head down, his hands clamped meditatively to the ends of his mustaches. Pulled tight in this way, the two corkscrews of hair reached down to his lower abdomen.

Lost in thought, he took a wrong turn, climbed a stairway that made him pant heavily, and found himself walking under a set of stinking archways that covered the street.

He had never been known to give up when there was a large profit in the offing, and this business, as he had felt from the start, was certainly promising. There was the possibility of money, of course, but also the chance to make useful contacts abroad. Who was to say that he would still be in Persia tomorrow, with all the dangers that threatened the country from the outside and with its unpredictable ruler? A reasonable man should be prepared for the worst, that is, for flight. Something of the kind truly had to be at stake for the nazir to consent to visit once more, and in his own home, the vile Leonardo.

Was it this door or the other across the way? The two were equally pitiful, and a small stream of gray water issued from under each to meet in the central gutter, whose milky, sickening water cascaded down the middle of the alleyway.

He tried to open one of the doors. It resisted. Then it must be the other. Leonardo never locked his door, for the simple reason that he had no one to tend it for him and he couldn't open it himself. The nazir climbed to the second floor by a sort of open staircase whose treads were dangerously bowed.

Leonardo was seated in front of a table covered with a rug. A few books floated in the yellow glow of an oil lamp. The nazir recognized Leonardo by his lace bonnet and his shiny, dented nose, sculpted into planes like a monstrous sharp-edged diamond of flesh. Suspended in the same pitch darkness, the nazir recognized with dismay several pairs of cat's eyes—it was not the least of Leonardo's peculiarities that he had made these accursed animals first the lodgers, and now the masters, of his cloaca.

The only certain fact about Leonardo's life, though it now lay in the distant past, concerned his birth on the island of Chios. Everything afterward was wrapped in murk. He claimed to have been a sailor. Had he followed a quiet career in the merchant fleet? Perhaps, but he also claimed to have been a soldier and a corsair. Nothing proved he had not been a galley slave instead. Yet he might have been all of these, and also a buccaneer, an escaped slave, and a castaway. He told stories set on every continent, but so might an innkeeper from Chios who had simply listened to his clients. His early life therefore remained a mystery. When Leonardo appeared in Persia he was already old. The Portuguese had been employing him for several years in their trade stations in the gulf. One day, for no known reason, he had gone to Bandar Abbas and asked to work in Persia. His limbs were quite deformed already but he was not yet entirely crippled. He attached a single condition to his request: that he be allowed to bring his two cats. The Portuguese had been using him as an interpreter, and as he claimed to have knowledge of every language on earth, the Persians used him in the same capacity.

As his rheumatism progressed, Leonardo had moved away from the coast and progressively higher onto the interior plateaus. Finally, he landed in Isfahan. While he was incapable of almost any movement, he still had two extremely agile organs: his insolent tongue and his highly deformed right hand, in which he painfully wedged a pen, running it for hours over sheets of paper that he blackened with a remarkably well-formed script.

His most lucrative work, outside his translations, was making false documents, false receipts, and false bills of exchange, which he sold. Denounced and dragged before the nazir in judgment, Leonardo obtained his release by demonstrating not his innocence but rather his utter, rare, and skillful culpability, requiring the highest level of art and learning, samples of which he readily supplied his judge. It would have been sheer idiocy to deny oneself the use of such talents. The nazir pardoned the forger and discreetly kept him in his employ.

"Sire," Leonardo greeted his benefactor in his nasal voice, "your courier advised me this afternoon that you would visit, and as you can see, I have done my best to make my residence fit to receive you."

This apparently meant that he had cleared the table. In the dark, the nazir stumbled over bundles of rags left on the floor. He took hold of a chair and collapsed into it without saying a word. In fact, the smell of cat urine that met him on entering this house always had the effect of reducing him at first to silence. Leonardo willingly filled the gap:

"How may I assist the master toward whom my grateful thoughts fly each morning when my dazzled eyes open onto what they take to be his image, the new sun in its full glory?"

In fact, the nazir owed a great deal to Leonardo for his eloquence, and his own skill as a courtier had benefited enormously from this athlete of the well-turned compliment.

Filtering the air through his mustaches, the nazir took a deep breath and said:

"I need you to write an extremely important letter for me."

"In what language, Sire, is this missive to be written?"

"In French."

"Ah! Ah!" said Leonardo.

These two little spasms indicated laughter and signified that nothing could be easier.

"Don't snicker. You'll need to put yourself to some trouble. This is no ordinary matter."

Leonardo assumed an expression of extreme interest and deference.

"It's the letter of a woman writing to her lover," said the nazir.

The forger laughed again, much louder this time. According to the nazir's sources, Leonardo had never shown much interest in women, and his tastes rather inclined, so rumor had it, the other way. But boudoir gossip had always fascinated him, especially when it concerned the court. One of the cats, awakened by its master's noisy laugh, stretched and started walking slowly along the table toward the nazir. Leonardo would put up with anything when it came to himself: one could trample all over him without raising a murmur. But he was capable of the most violent furies and of endless caprices if one ever touched his cats. The nazir therefore allowed the animal to walk collectedly back and forth near his face, watching it from the corner of his eye.

"Yes, but it's not just any woman or just any lover," he continued in an authoritative tone. "The man is a cardinal, and the woman is his concubine."

His mouth wide open and his head thrown back, Leonardo was laughing.

"A cardinal! Oh! How happy that makes me. Ooh! Sire, my poor kidneys! Ouch! The concubine of a cardinal!"

"Careful, Leonardo," said the nazir patiently, "it's not going to be easy. There will have to be some manners to it, and some feeling."

"Manners. Ah! Ah!" the forger repeated, howling now with laughter. "Yes, yes, and some feeling . . . A cardinal . . . Oh! Oh!"

The cat looked over at its master and turned its back on the visitor, raising its tail. The nazir patiently closed his eyes to shut out the proffered vision of hell. Finally able to bear it no longer, he slammed his hand down on the table.

The cat jumped away; Leonardo closed his maw over the stumps of his teeth. In the frightened silence, the nazir's cavernous voice resounded:

"Take a paper and a pen, you imbecile. We are going to do this together. And I won't leave until we have produced something good!"

15

The Mongol servant Küyük had always gone on foot, trotting behind the mules, until Daoud Pasha presented his masters with three handsome horses. Jean-Baptiste hadn't even asked himself whether the little Tartar knew how to ride. When he saw him in the saddle, however, he understood that a horse was not simply a familiar mount to Küyük but a complement, a double, without which he was only a crawling larva. Küyük rode to perfection, though not as taught in the academies: he kept his legs straight in the stirrups, spread like rifles stacked at an encampment, and held his hands very high in front of him. The animal obeyed so well that it was impossible to tell through what movements the rider conveyed his instructions.

Küyük's face had never registered the slightest expression at his masters' changes in guise and reversals of fortune. Since being set on horseback, though, he was radiant. His eyes, normally half closed, were now opened wide, and his mouth was ajar when he galloped. It made one think of an old, desiccated field soaking up the waters of a flood.

They stopped for only a night at Tiflis. Despite the many attractions of the capital, their hearts were set on leaving Georgia as soon as possible. An incident occurred there that almost delayed them. On the night of their arrival, in one of the houses that serve coffee and tobacco, George had been curious to try the strong drink made of the resin of the poppy. All night he had visited strange worlds, and after much laughing, much crying out in terror, much moaning with pleasure, he had awoken the next morning extremely ill. Jean-Baptiste had given him an antidote, and by noon they were back on their way.

As they traveled north on the plains of Georgia, the terrain rose ahead of them gently at first in low rolling hills, then became steep and craggy. The mosquitoes that had been pricking their exposed skin every night since Erevan now disappeared because of the altitude. At last, through the heat haze lying heavily on the horizon, they saw the high, bright mass of the Caucasus Mountains appear. They formed a continuous wall with no apparent break. A line of annual snow marked the summit ridges. There was only one road to Muscovy through this rampart; rarely used and poorly maintained, it climbed to a high altitude. In their first three days on it, they didn't cross ten caravans. Arriving at a high spot from where they could see the fearsome crust of ice deposited on the summit, they could still make out below the green clouds of maritime pines the high spikes of cypress, and the comb marks of the vine rows across the closely cropped nape of Georgia's hills.

Everything changed at the first pass. Within a few meters, they left behind the still-warm and scented air of the Mediterranean climate to confront the cold wind from the north, one of those land breezes that, made hungry by its passage over steppes and deserts, bites everything in its path and feeds on clouds down to the last one.

Küyük, straight in the saddle, pointed his flat nose into the wind and inhaled deeply, no doubt to draw distant and familiar particles from it. Tossing its mane, his horse, and therefore he himself, trotted gaily in place, circled, and edged sideways.

George, after their many adventures together, was more natural and friendly toward Jean-Baptiste, even using the familiar "tu" with him. But he had in no way given up his convictions. Just as he expressed his feelings better, he also dared to articulate and put forward his objections.

Poncet looked at the Mongol's metamorphosis with a curiosity tinged with respect:

"Our shaman is finding the spirit of the steppes again," he said.

George shrugged his shoulders and launched into a learned explanation of climate and its influence on the humors and animal fluids that irrigate the nervous tubes. Jean-Baptiste let him talk, counting on Nature to show him one day that she contained not only laws and systems but beauties and mysteries.

The alpine meadows, on these September days, smelled of rotting grass and the leavings of the herds. Night fell early and suddenly, heralded by a frozen breath tumbling from the glaciers. The travelers slept in wooden cabins that they rented from the shepherds for a king's ransom. The dried fruits they had brought from Georgia served as the basis of their ordinary fare, lending a sweet fragrance to the gray and bitter cheeses that they bought locally. As they advanced into the high valleys, they encountered new languages and ever-changing races of people. Each encampment—they couldn't be called villages—was a nation unto itself with its own religion and its own speech. The air was electric with invisible hatreds, and each person lived in fear of all others. It was as though man had been created first on these frozen heights and descended from them bit by bit to take up habitation in the warm, soft corruption of the valleys. Those who had remained so close to the sky seemed still to be near their origins, speaking familiarly with the gods and spending their short lives pursuing the eternal quarrels they attributed to them.

The Caucasus chain is very wide, and at its center, like the keep of a castle to which the other summits are only outward redoubts, rises the enormous mass of Mount Kazbek. Its perpetual ice is broken into gigantic walls and blades, which shine in the daylight and stand out against the black sky at night. Their vitreous mass absorbs the broad warm body of the sun during the daylight hours and after dark spits back its cold and bluish skeleton.

As they approached Kazbek's walls, the encampments grew rarer and the meadows more and more desolate—the monster had emptied the area around itself to provide a place for its sorceries, not for men. The only people to venture there were those who were most intrepid in defying the spirits, and those who were entirely possessed by them.

During the past several stages, Küyük had been showing signs of nervousness. All day he would pick up anything he found in the naked valleys that might feed a fire. At night he lit the campfire in an open place slightly above the path. While his masters slept, rolled up in their furs, the Mongol kept watch, his feet crossed near the embers, his back to the mountain, scanning the dark meadows with slitted eyes.

Despite their vigilance, they were attacked on the third day of their crossing of Mount Kazbek. It was dawn, and Küyük had drifted off to sleep. By the time he heard the horses neigh it was too late. The twelve men who emerged suddenly from the darkness had overpowered the travelers, tied them up, and taken possession of their baggage and animals.

The little band of brigands into whose hands they had fallen spoke a Tartar language that Jean-Baptiste did not understand, and he could not question Küyük about it because there were two men separating them. The thieves were in any case not talkative, and the leader, who walked at the rear of the column, addressed the travelers by cracking a long whip and grunting significantly. They had only a short distance to go as the band's lair was near the road. The nearness, though, offered the prisoners no comfort, as the spot was so deserted they could not expect help.

Day broke as they arrived in the brigands' camp. Four of the outlaws took charge of Jean-Baptiste's and George's horses. Probably never having seen such big ones, they approached them with great caution. Several women, encased in animal skins that made them look exactly like their husbands, emerged from their cave holding children by the hand or in their arms. The travelers, were it not for the way they were led there, might almost have thought they were arriving as they did every night at a shepherds' camp. Though leaving the travelers' hands tied, the bandits invited them to enter the cavern with perfectly civil gestures. Küyük's look of distrust signaled that despite these courtesies the bandits might be planning to cut their throats. Jean-Baptiste began to look uneasily at the large knives that the mountaineers carried at their belts.

They stepped at last past the entrance of the cave and plunged into the darkness beyond, after each had cast a last glance back at the verdant flank of Mount Kazbek, strewn with enormous white boulders looking no bigger than pebbles. They saw that the sky had grown cloudy during the last hours of the night. Weather changes quickly in the mountains. The abrupt barrier of the Caucasus holds in the storms rising off the Black Sea, but as soon as the clouds ascend even a few feet above the crests, a storm spills over them within an hour, like milk on the boil.

The cave was shallow but considerably wider than its entrance. It formed a veritable hall in which the Tartars had arrayed their poor riches. A fire of twigs and dry grasses was supposed to warm, dry, and light this habitation, though in fact it only darkened it with a gray smoke that made the children cough.

When they were all seated around the fire, with their horses hobbled and their baggage piled near the entrance to the cave, a general uneasiness was felt. It seemed to Jean-Baptiste that the bandits were as uncertain as they of what should happen next.

The travelers' appearance no doubt thoroughly confused the bandits. The only people who traveled these roads in such small caravans were usually locals. When the Russians crossed—as they had not done recently—they took care to come armed, strong in numbers, and with scouts and an escort. These two fine gentlemen with their blue and red clothes, their slender boots, and their baggage full of gold, were certainly hiding something. Were they in advance of a larger force? or did they plan to use some sort of weapon or even sorcery? The most familiar-appearing of their captives was Küyük, and the leader curtly addressed him in rapid-fire, guttural speech.

But Küyük did not seem to understand and shook his head, never taking his eyes off the fire. A long silence followed this failed exchange. Through the mouth of the cave they could see that the sky was now black and that a heavy rain was pelting the lush grasses. A flash of lightning whitened the curtain of rain for an instant, and Küyük raised his head and listened as though to determine its distance by the faint thunderclap that followed it.

The storm, with its noises, colors, and smells filling the humid air, provided a welcome spectacle and dispelled the tension that arose from the misalliance of these too-humble captors and their too-gentle captives. Everyone was absorbed in watching the storm when Küyük, with a suddenness that froze his hearers, uttered a loud, piercing cry that rose from the depths of his bowels and resounded off the blackened walls of the cave.

What followed was still more extraordinary. First Küyük modulated his ululation into a long rise and fall, then he collapsed to the floor, curled into a ball and shaken by silent spasms. When he finally raised his head again, the frightened onlookers saw a face contorted into inhuman ecstasy. His eyes bulged, exhibiting through the wide-open slits of his eyelids two blue eyeballs of the pale nacreous hue of freshly spilled sheep entrails. He sprang up in a single bound, his limbs outspread as though his quilted garments had suddenly frozen solid, and began to shiver from head to toe, his teeth chattering.

The storm outside had moved closer. The lightning, now more frequent, came in through the dark opening of the cavern and ricocheted off its walls, making it glow like a giant vial of opal. Violent thunderclaps followed hard on the flashes of lightning, resonating against the rock. At every explosion Küyük literally jumped into the air without apparent effort. The elements seemed to have made him their toy. And in truth he no longer retained the appearance of a human being during these moments. He was the embodiment of celestial ire, the spirit of the lightning and wind, materialized before his dumbstruck audience.

The Tartars drew back from him instinctively and huddled in a close group on the far side of the fire, the children in front. These peoples believed that Nature could sometimes be appeased by the offering of innocent children, on whom she feasted to renew her power, which would otherwise wane as the world aged.

But Küyük ignored the children. As the thunder became less frequent, the Mongol seemed to recover his volition somewhat and, while remaining inhuman, performed recognizable gestures. He neared the fire, held his hands out, and burned the hemp bonds at his wrists over the low flame.

Jean-Baptiste glanced at the brigands to see if this solemn act of liberation sparked any opposition. The poor group were far too terrified. In any case, Küyük went on without giving them time to consider. He deftly removed the sheep's-wool sheaths that served him as boots and jumped barefoot onto the glowing embers. His cries now took on an incantatory modulation, which he accompanied with dancing on the fiery coals. As drawn as his face had been at the beginning of his fit, his features now relaxed as he stood in the fire. His head was slightly thrown back, his eyebrows raised, and he seemed to chew while shooting his lips out, somewhat like Daoud Pasha tasting his burgundy. The fire dance lasted a long time. The strange chant and the sight of the human feet caressing the embers were mesmerizing, a sort of erotic play in which flesh stayed flesh but desire turned to fire. The audience, watching with wide, upturned eyes, seemed to contemplate other scenes of voluptuousness. The whole cavern was filled with the supernatural. Even George was spellbound. Jean-Baptiste smiled with pleasure.

Transfigured, royal, sanctified, Küyük was the absolute master of the world. For long minutes, hours possibly, he strung together invocations and dialogued with mysterious spirits that everyone seemed to see as well as he. At the height of his trance, he grabbed a dagger from the outlaw leader's belt and plunged it into his right forearm, then into his chest, with no other expression than a slight grimace of happiness.

When all this at last came to an end, the morning was far along. The sun once more shone on the alpine meadow and struck the entrance to the cavern, turning its ceiling gold.

Küyük rejoined the world just enough to perceive the Tartars and to give them orders, which they executed with total submission. The truth was that his own language was very similar to theirs, and Jean-Baptiste understood that it was so as to fool them that he had not answered at first.

The shaman directed them to saddle and pack the horses and to prepare a haunch of lamb that hung in a corner of the cavern, wrapping it piece by piece in leather sacks. On his orders, two goatskins of ewe's milk were fastened to the sides of his saddle. Jean-Baptiste and George, freed of their ropes, mounted their horses at a signal from their magician valet. He followed suit and, not giving the kneeling bandits another look, set off at the head of the little column.

They rejoined the road and rode a further league at a trot. After a long bend to the right, they reached a thicket of wild rhododendron, speckled with the purple dabs of its last flowers. In the midst of this cluster of small trees they discovered a grassy clearing where they dismounted. Küyük, who along the way had resumed his wrinkled and sinister aspect, had no sooner dismounted than he sprawled full length on the ground. The others let him sleep until the following day.

16

Across from the Mosque of the Imam, its enormous dome of turquoise tile the aqueous pallor of clear water only lightly veiled with algae, there extended a large esplanade called the Royal Square. Twice a week it filled with markets but stayed empty on the other days. Anyone walking across it drew the curious glances of idlers squatting in the shade of its perimeter walls during the hot hours. Alix dreaded traversing the square, where a foreign woman became more than ever a spectacle and a target. She always hastened her step whenever she started across it. On this afternoon, after leaving the bazaar where she had dressed in her new clothes, she was more troubled than usual as she approached the Royal Square. Her steps squeaked on the river sand that covered the ground. She found herself walking so fast that she almost tripped. She suddenly felt—was it from the momentary fear of losing her balance and her dignity? or was it from the unaccustomed sensation of moist warmth trapped around her head by her veil?—in any case, she suddenly felt a delicious thrill of pleasure at the thought that for the first time in her life she was entirely hidden from the sight of others.

Around her, blurred by the tulle plastered to her face like a soft compress, appeared other darkly veiled figures, also visible only as mysterious drapes of cloth.

Alix slowed down, strolled practically to the far end of the great square, so great was her pleasure in the sensation of her invisibility. She had always taken great pains to vary her appearance but now discovered with joyous surprise the pleasure of having no appearance at all.

In this agreeable mood she approached the prime minister's residence. The grand vizier of course lived tucked away in the greenery of the Chahar Bagh. Next to the ceremonial entrance, barred by a wrought-iron grille, was another more modest one through which she entered. She crossed two courtyards where a numerous cast of footmen and maidservants went about their business, then angled right toward the harem. A simple doorkeeper guarded the first entrance, to which many men had access—servants, officials, palace retainers—as long as they had a valid reason for entering. Before the second door was a nasty old man who held the title of captain of the door. He performed his duties ill-humoredly, assisted by two broad-shouldered servants who looked eager to put their musculature to work. Alix announced her identity in Farsi without removing her veil, and the old man allowed her to pass. She then entered a final gallery formed by a succession of courts lit by openings in the roof and peopled only by the fringed forms of potted palms. The third door, which gave onto the women's apartments, was hidden from view by an angle in the wall. Alix announced herself and was stopped by an obese eunuch with a milky, wrinkled complexion, wearing the customary tall pointed hat tilted slightly forward and held in place by a chin strap. Alix was obliged to unveil herself before him and would have experienced this return to visibility as highly unpleasant had not Nur al-Huda, who had caught sight of her from a distance, hailed her exuberantly. The prime minister's favorite embraced her without ceremony and led her by the hand to her rooms.

The precaution of placing attendants, guards, and eunuchs at the doors cloaked the center of the harem in more mystery than it actually had to those who could enter it freely. The women's court was slightly smaller than the men's but built on the same plan: a large central impluvium surrounded by high-ceilinged rooms with a gallery above them. The ceramic tiles on the walls, the murmuring fountains, and the potted plants were the same there as elsewhere. The absence of weapons, of mustaches, and of deep voices was agreeably compensated for by an abundance of fine fabric and silvery laughter. All in all, one was still in the real world, and as long as one did not look at these things through the dark filters of desire and prohibition, they were simple and ordinary.

The drawing room to which Nur al-Huda led Alix was a high, windowless room, lit by transom windows. The frescoes covering the four walls offered a panorama of flowering gardens where every kind of musician was playing. Just as the Persians allow themselves wine to lend wings to poetry's noble flights, so they have not quite brought themselves to forbid artists to represent the world and even the human figure. The pleasure it affords presents a strong argument against depriving themselves of it, with the explanation that God would not have put such delights on earth unless He intended them as rewards for his servants. In the battle, present in every religion, that pits pleasure against sin, the Persians have had the courage to declare a winner and surrender to it with delectable resignation.

Nur al-Huda seated Alix beside her on a banquette, in front of a small table laden with rosewater pastries and dates.

"I am truly glad you've come," she said, and kissed her friend in a transport of joy. "We barely have an hour to get ready. By the way, have you brought the medicines?"

Alix reached under her veil and removed a package tied with string.

"Perfect!"

Nur called for tea to be served, then dismissed the slave girl and leaned toward Alix:

"First let's get the distressing news out of the way. The situation is bad. Several times my dear husband has again had slippers tossed at his nose. The king is furious at the news that is reaching him. Do you know that the Afghans refuse to be stopped by anything? They have just launched themselves across the Seistan desert with Lord knows how many mercenaries from that area, whom they call the Baluch. Can anyone truly have such an odd name?"

She laughed, and Alix couldn't help being won over by her gaiety.

"That," continued Nur al-Huda, "and the earthquake in Tauris . . ."

"An earthquake!"

"What! You didn't know? There isn't one stone standing on another there. The Blue Mosque has been completely destroyed. Didn't you feel the shocks? I saw this chandelier move with my own eyes."

"When was it?"

"Last week. Oh! Don't be so worried for your Jean-Baptiste," said Nur al-Huda, covering Alix's hand with her own. "He passed through Tauris long ago. By now he must be in Muscovy."

"Let's hope so," said Alix, still not reassured.

"This signal from the heavens has stirred up the palace fortune-tellers, and with my dear husband helping them to blame all our troubles on foreigners, they may get their way. Believe me, you would do well to prepare discreetly the things you would like to take with you. Be ready, that's all. If the danger ever comes to a head, I'll let you know."

Alix was upset by the news.

"Now," said Nur al-Huda gaily, "we are not going to let our thoughts be darkened by these things. The world is perfectly capable of sending us misfortunes all on its own. Let's concentrate on being happy."

Hearing the young woman express the principles that had guided her

own life, Alix looked at her with melancholy attention. She had the feeling that this stranger was actually more her daughter than her own
daughter was: Saba, always so serious and stiff, would never have spoken
such words.

They then went over every aspect of the plan they had afoot, and
when the hour was over Nur al-Huda clapped her hands and called for
her eunuch Ahmad.

They heard his leather slippers scuffing the stone floor of the court
before he entered. He was solidly built, with a narrow face, prominent
cheekbones, and a pointed chin. One long slender hand rested on the
other, and he bowed until both were over his knees.

"Rise, Ahmad," said Nur al-Huda, smiling. "Do you see this
woman?"

Alix held herself straight. She was once more enveloped in the dark
blue veil she had worn to hide herself on the way over, but she lifted the
front to show her face.

"We don't want to overload your memory unnecessarily, dear
Ahmad," said Nur al-Huda, "so when I refer to her, I shall simply say 'the
lady in blue.' "

The eunuch once more slid his two hands down over his knees.

"We are going to accompany this lady in blue to the royal palace
because she has some medications to deliver. This will allow us to take
some air. While she performs her errand, we will walk around the Chahar
Bagh and return to pick her up afterward. You may leave us now. Wait at
the outer door for us to arrive, and please, don't walk too close to me in the
street. I don't want to feel that I am being hurried."

In plain sight across her knees Nur al-Huda held the red veil she
made every pretense of planning to put on. As soon as the eunuch had
disappeared—and she went to the door to make sure that he had left
the courtyard—she grabbed the blue veil, which Alix had removed,
and handed her the red one. Each now wearing the other's color, they
covered their faces and, squeezing hands a final time, directed their
steps toward the three doors, proceeding gravely through each, one
after another, with the eunuch at their heels. Once in the street, the
eunuch dropped back ten paces so as not to overhear their conversation.

"My husband never lets me go out without that clown," said Nur
al-Huda as they walked.

"Is it always the same one?"

"Luckily, it is. And I was allowed to choose him. He's not a bad sort. He only wants to put food on the table for his three children . . ."

"His three children!"

"Yes, though he claims to have been a eunuch since childhood. I don't really know how the operation is done, but it sometimes succeeds only partially. And I can tell you that this particular flower is not as thornless as would appear."

Alix cast a glance back over her shoulder at the man who hid such secrets under his harmless livery.

"It's a little detail that only I am aware of," continued Nur al-Huda, "and it makes us accomplices. As long as I am discreet in my actions, he is perfectly happy to keep quiet."

Walking at an amble, Nur al-Huda had led them as if by accident to a square in the city's oldest quarter. Turkish and Mongol minarets rose above the roofs, and the ogival portal and ultramarine dome of the Friday Mosque could be seen. It was on this parade ground that the day officer of the palace guard traditionally took command of his detachment before leading them to the palace.

The two women arrived on the square just as the ceremony was ending, which Alix guessed to be more than pure coincidence. The troop was mounted and coming in their direction. The two pressed against the wall to let it pass. Though the hoofbeats echoed deafeningly off the walls of the square, the clinking of the curb chains and sword rings could be distinctly heard. In the lead, on a bay horse that nervously raised and lowered its head, came the guard's commanding officer. He wore a white uniform, and his narrow waist was wrapped in six turns of a broad green sash. By custom, his pale blue turban, on which a plume was planted, was also formed of six turns.

He rode past the two women, invisible under their veils, without a glance. Alix, looking up at the officer's face from below, noticed two things: the sharp planes of his shaven jaw, for he wore no beard, and his youth. His face combined the passing features of childhood with the eternal profile of the ancient Parthians, whose image is preserved in the steles of Persepolis. The whole conferred on him an age-old and a thrilling beauty that was at the same time grave and pleasant.

The vision lasted no more than an instant. Its effect on them was still strong, though the square was by then empty and the scent of horsehair and leather hung in the air.

"Did you see him?" asked Nur al-Huda.

Alix understood. She felt happiness for her friend, but also a slight displeasure, which she forbade herself to examine further.

The rest all went off as planned. They made their way slowly to the royal palace, following the horsemen's path. The lady in red conducted the lady in blue to the entrance manned by the royal guard, and a soldier allowed the lady in blue to pass on presentation of a note, her package of medications clutched under one arm.

Then the lady in red, escorted by her eunuch, continued her walk until the muezzin sounded the call to prayer, at which point she turned back toward the palace.

The north-facing flank of the Caucasus trends toward Russia along an interminable slope carved by valleys of pine and larch. So even is the relief that the very mountain torrents dawdle and change direction at every moment; and the paths skirting them, to keep step with this whimsy, make sharp bends along the ridgelines. During the descent, often when the traveler thinks he is already at the bottom, he reaches a bend in the road only to discover a vast panorama of the wild mountain chain with its icy peaks, its desolate gray moraines, and the black, close-ranked pine forests carrying forward their dogged assault.

The travelers pushed on for one long stage after another without meeting a soul. Often they were forced to lead their horses by the bridle as the low branches of the conifers formed an arch at head level over the path. The ground, lit in patches where the pale sun managed to reach it, was carpeted with dry needles and squirrel-gnawed pinecones. Where the canopy thinned, the travelers discovered bushes bearing red currants, bilberries, and wild raspberries. Jean-Baptiste and George, no doubt already missing the sweets of the East, feasted on the berries under Küyük's reproving glance—as a strict carnivore, he didn't touch them.

Since the time when the shaman had revealed his gifts, a certain discomfort had developed among them. The Mongol, for his part, continued to behave as before, as dour and taciturn as ever. Jean-Baptiste would have liked to express his thanks to Küyük and perhaps start a real conversation with him on his beliefs, his history, and on the spirits of the steppe. He never found the opportunity. Besides, what language would they have used? Küyük spoke Mongol and a bit of Swedish and Russian . . . maybe Turkish?

George, while recognizing that the shaman had saved their lives, considered him a skillful prestidigitator and asked Jean-Baptiste to question him about his tricks.

"I noticed," said George, laughing—because now he often laughed—"that he didn't really stab himself with the dagger blade. He held it in his hand, like this, always with the back of his hand toward us. And when he pretended to push it into himself, he was really sliding his hand down the handle as far as the hilt."

Küyük saw these gestures out of the corner of his eye and understood that they were talking about him. Jean-Baptiste used this as an excuse to silence the boy and avoid a discussion that would have been ridiculous and in any case persuaded no one. For although Jean-Baptiste was not going to defend the shaman against the charge of rascality, and although he did not believe in spirits either, what he had experienced in the cavern convinced him that the human mind could bring the supernatural into being. And he didn't think that it could be explained away by sleights of hand.

The best thing would have been to clear the air by bringing their isolation to an end, but the valleys stretched on interminably. Days passed. It rained a bit, then the clear autumn sky returned, accompanied by warm westerly winds. Finally, in early October, the larches became rarer, and they entered a dense birch forest that hugged the contours of a nearly flat, sandy soil carpeted with ferns and broom. Whenever they passed near any of the little ponds that dotted the countryside, they startled teal and other ducks into flight.

One late afternoon, in a hazel thicket, they came across a broad, freshly cleared path, its mud deeply rutted by the passage of heavy carts. After following it for an hour, they reached a small log camp. There, in the smoke of slash fires, Russian peasants with dirty beards, round caps, and vests buttoned up to their chins were digging the ground, rifles slung over their shoulders.

17

The hen, its wing tips red and its breast a shimmering white, pecked at scattered oat grains, unafraid of people. Jean-Baptiste and George, who were sitting on a log bench basking in the weak sun that had just emerged after a shower, held out their hands to her. She came and pecked at them, greedily and a little disappointedly.

The travelers were in their fourth farmyard. Since explaining themselves, with much difficulty, to the first set of peasants, they had been led considerable distances from one izba to another, always without the slightest explanation. The Russians, with a surprising mix of cordiality and suspicion, of orderliness and improvisation, were passing the foreigners around among themselves. At first the strangers were looked on as a threat because they had arrived from the direction of the enemy. It now seemed that they were being held only because they had been held before, though the charges against them were no longer remembered. They had the distinct impression of having even been forgotten, and they started to form plans of escape. Nothing could have been easier, it seemed: at some point during the long hours when they were left alone, they had simply to walk straight ahead and keep walking. But where to? The Russians have invented that strange form of captivity where the prisoner is contained not within cell walls but instead by vast reaches of empty space around him. The travelers' horses had stayed behind at the second stop, presumably confiscated by one of the officials who came to peer into their faces from time to time and give the terrified peasants orders concerning them. For the moment their baggage hadn't disappeared; they couldn't touch it, but they could see it, apparently intact, heaped on a harvest table under a shed. To grab it, run away, set their course to the east using the lichen on the birch trees as a compass, reach the Caspian . . . this was as far as they had reached in their thinking. They were about to explain the plan to Küyük in sign language so as to get his opinion when they heard the sound of galloping hooves approaching from a great distance. At last a troop of Cossacks rode into the clearing of the izba. The men wore long woolen coats and had swords at their sides. Two of them held long, slender lances and wheeled menacingly before the farm carts. The man who appeared to be their leader rode out from the group and dismounted nimbly despite his great size. He walked up to the foreigners and stared at them from two yards away with an air of indignation. As with his companions, his features displayed a mixture of the Tartar and Slav races, whose strong currents combined in a great boiling of blood and temperament. When he had completed his wordless examination, the ataman leapt back into the saddle, not bothering to bring his chafing horse to a standstill, and the whole troop galloped off as fast as they had come.

An hour or so later, the same detachment returned. This time it flanked a young officer wearing a fine red velvet doublet. When he dismounted and walked toward them, the prisoners were pleased to note that he was holding the letter of accreditation that the Russian ambassador in Persia had drawn up for Jean-Baptiste. Seized from them by the peasants on the first day, the document seemed to have gone astray definitively. Now, by an extraordinarily confused route, the Russian Empire was offering them proof of its incomprehensible but very real efficiency.

"Which of you is Monsieur Jean-Baptiste Poncet?" asked the officer as he drew near.

His French was excellent and full of charm, with the broad operatic vowels that Russians plant within each word.

Poncet stood and indicated himself.

"Greatly honored," said the officer, bowing his head. "I am Colonel Saint-Août."

He then went on, in explanation of his French name:

"My family left France in the last century."

Jean-Baptiste returned the soldier's greeting, then introduced George ("my son") and Küyük ("our manservant"). He was almost tempted to introduce the hen, which they had come to know and which had unashamedly joined the circle of their conversation.

On Jean-Baptiste's invitation the officer took a seat on a block of wood while the others resumed their places on the bench.

"You've come from Persia?" the young colonel began.

"Yes," admitted Poncet, "by way of Mount Kazbek."

"That was brave."

"Thank you."

"Did you not know that the whole area is a military zone? Our troops have only just conquered it, and the work is not yet done."

The officer's open face, with his short hair brushed forward on his forehead and temples, elicited natural confidence. Jean-Baptiste answered him without fear or reserve.

"We knew it, but how else were we to reach Muscovy?"

"And what was to be your destination once there?"

"Moscow, I suppose. We want to see our friend receive justice . . ."

"I know," said the colonel, unfolding Israël Orii's safe-conduct. "It is all written here."

He pretended to reread a part of the letter, then went on:

"Moscow is far. The tsar, the court, and the administration have all transferred here because of the military campaigns. Are you quite sure of finding what you are looking for in the capital?"

He smiled in an enigmatic way. Jean-Baptiste responded with a gesture that seemed to say, What else can I do?

The officer left the question unanswered and moved to another topic:

"We are interested in Persia. You must know a great many things about this country. You have just crossed its northern provinces. I have always dreamed of going there, and it would give me great pleasure to hear you talk of it."

Jean-Baptiste had the impression of being in a fencing match. Each had to explore his adversary's weaknesses and cut short his attacks with little counterattacks of his own.

"As one grows older, Colonel," he said with a smile, "one's sight grows dimmer. And my son, for his part, lacks experience. We crossed all those provinces like two blind men and wouldn't know what to tell you about them."

Saint-Août acknowledged the point with a nod of his head, smiling.

"May I ask you a question in turn?" asked Jean-Baptiste. "Are we free?"

"As free as the clouds," said the officer with a great sweep of his arms.

"Without our baggage? and without horses?"

"Those things will be brought to you immediately, and you may go where you like. Yet if I inspire any trust in you at all, you will listen to me: I am returning to the side of someone who would be highly honored to meet you and could very likely help you in your search. As your movements are entirely free, nothing prevents you from following the same road as myself and even accompanying me."

Here, thought Jean-Baptiste, is a jailer with good manners. I like him.

An hour later, mounted on three horses that had been saddled for them and packed with their gear, the travelers were following a dirt road that led flat and straight to the horizon. Saint-Août was in the lead. Jean-Baptiste and George rode on either side talking pleasantly with him.

The imperial army of Russia, with its enormous mass and thousands of bivouacs, appeared before the travelers all of a sudden as they crested a rise. George gave a cry of astonishment, and Jean-Baptiste himself could not help being struck. In all their displacements under the tormented skies of these infinite expanses they had seen no one at all, or very nearly—a few rare houses, occasionally a horse, a colonist's family, or a sparse group of Tartars. And suddenly all humanity was there in its great multiplicity, scattered into human particles, and horses that appeared minuscule at this distance, carts, weapons, and stacks of cannonballs, but actually forming a single entity gathered into the body of a great army; they could make out its trunk, its limbs, its head and wings, settled like a bird of prey over the rough surface of the moors and forests.

They were standing upwind when they caught sight of this apparition, and no noise came to them from this multitude. The silence made the throng even more imposing. Nor did the riders speak as they descended slowly toward the army's outposts.

Their feelings of respect, even fear, evaporated as they came into contact with the first units. The order they had imagined from a distance turned into unimaginable confusion. Composed of all the nations of the empire, this large army's only strength was in the poverty it assembled. Things got done because of invisible but permanent miracles, thanks to which men understood each other though they shared no language, orders were transmitted though no one took responsibility for them, and hunger and disease were avoided though there was no system in place to explain it. One could understand why standards bearing the image of an eagle, banderols with an Orthodox cross, and even sinister flags representing the martyrdom of Christ were constantly being brandished in the air, planted in the ground during halts, and held aloft during marches—for if the divine Providence that watched over this army had faltered even for a moment, the consequences would have been horrible, as only Providence saw to it that this great heartbeat and this substanceless body fought.

It was early afternoon, not the time when the army appeared at its most pitiful—for that you had to come at dawn. At that hour the most heartrending cries arose from the plain on which the army camped, for it was then that the soldiers performed the one order of Peter the Great's that was universally detested: in twos (one seated and the other bending over his victim), they shaved, some with the edge of their sword, others with a fragment of glass, still others with a sliver of malachite or obsidian, but very rarely with a true blade, their facial skin chapped and red from the daily removal of all traces of the beard their emperor had prohibited. To its bravery and anarchy, this army of martyrs thus added the ridicule of being the only army in the world to start on the offensive already covered with self-inflicted gashes.

The presence of Colonel Saint-Août was an open sesame in this chaos. He was known and greeted by all; more extraordinary, he seemed to know his way around. After crossing an entire encampment of cavalry and two regiments of Buriat foot soldiers, they reached a hamlet of stone houses that must have been the only settlement on the plain before the horde invaded it. The roofs of its cottages had no gutters, and the bottom of the walls bore the black mark of past spring rains. Through an open window, they saw a well-kept room with two beds, a plumed brass helmet on each. It must have been the campaign quarters for the officers. Saint-Août invited the three foreigners to sit on the window ledge, ordered their baggage to be unpacked and stacked along the wall, and moved away for a time. He spoke with two high-ranking officers who cast glances in the foreigners' direction. There was a sharp debate, and the sound of raised voices. Then Saint-Août's interlocutors indicated a direction with large gestures, as though throwing apple cores over a wall. In the end, the three saluted each other amiably and Saint-Août returned.

"Leave your things here, they won't be disturbed. I am going on a little walk. You might find it of interest to follow me."

Jean-Baptiste and George accepted the suggestion, leaving Küyük to guard their belongings.

On the outskirts of the hamlet was a wooden fence surrounding a plot of moldy cabbages and bolted lettuces. Beyond was the forest. They entered it, a dense wood of tall chestnuts with every so often a stand of bare-trunked beeches through which the eye could see far. They passed two detachments fanned out in the undergrowth, after which they saw no one. Gradually, through the song of the cuckoos and larks, there penetrated a distant chunking sound that echoed off the thick trunks. Saint-Août went on talking and smiling. Rays of the sun eagerly darted their white shafts into broad slices of the forest. Everything was pure and joyful; yet the slow and regular sound, growing closer, struck them ominously.

They had soon drawn near the sound and entered the clearing where it was coming from. The trees had been logged in a great circle. Huge stumps covered the ground, the felled trunks lying between them, limbed and barked. At the other end of the clearing stood a circle of officers, watching in silence and with folded arms while a giant exerted all his might against an oak. He had made a deep notch in one side to guide the fall of the vast trunk and was now attacking the other side. The ax hummed through the air and struck with accuracy, making the sharp sound the walkers had heard from a long way off.

The man was covered in sweat. Beside the tree his frame looked fragile, as the human condition does when measured against the great forces of nature. But in comparison with the other men, he was an imposing figure. His milky skin was spotted with flecks of bark and moles. His shoulders were roped with muscle that jumped under the exertion. A rather firm layer of fat surrounded his stomach and erased his hips, causing his belt to slide down and reveal his buttocks. After every blow he spat into his hands, hiked up his trousers, and picked up the ax again.

He signaled to the new arrivals to stand alongside the others. It took only five more strokes to make the oak, which was straight-grained and as big at the base as three oxen, to slowly lean from the vertical and, in a heartrending farewell of compressed branches and torn-off leaves, crash to the floor of the clearing with the rumbling sound of a cannonade.

A hearty round of applause, thin-sounding after the preceding fury, went up from the gathering of spectators. The giant kissed the ax handle and sank the ax blade one-handed into the flat of the stump. Someone held out a towel to him and he wiped down his upper body.

Several officers came up to congratulate him and make comments. A man in civilian clothes, looking somewhat like a British Presbyterian minister with his black suit buttoned from top to bottom, approached him and said a word in his ear.

The giant nodded, then looked over at Saint-Août and signaled him to approach.

"Come," said the colonel to his two companions, "I am going to introduce you to the tsar."

18

The ground was littered with broken branches and foliage, making a protocolar approach difficult. Taking large steps, cautiously yet with haste, Jean-Baptiste and George finally reached the lumberjack, who was now back in his clothes and accepting the last compliments from his little court. Saint-Août made the presentations in Russian, and the tsar with a silent smile held out his hand at the end of a long arm. Jean-Baptiste realized it would be ridiculous to kiss it; he shook it respectfully, noting that the tsar's hand was unusually slender and soft to have just cut down such a large tree. George nearly fell over into the brush but managed honorably to deliver this form of greeting, which neither his stay in the East nor his British birth had prepared him for.

There followed a fairly lengthy silence, interspersed with the crackling sounds made on every side by the officers as they walked over the carpet of branches. Peter I stared at the strangers from his great height and searched for something to say. Saint-Août waited. Finally, like a cannonball laboriously loaded, came the explosion of this royal exclamation:

"Bonjour, Messieurs!"

His open hand slicing through an imaginary tree, the tsar indicated that his efforts at French would stop there and burst into booming laughter, interrupted by fits of coughing. At that moment they heard the harness bells of two woodsman's carts, which had come to bring the little company back to camp. In a flurry of good-natured scuffling, everyone climbed aboard the old telegas and squeezed in along the benches. The tsar was somewhere in the middle among the others. Jean-Baptiste couldn't see him as he sat with his back to the direction they were traveling and faced the receding rows of oaks that had so far been spared by the monarch. A porcelain gourd circulated from hand to hand, and soon thirty male voices joined in launching the deep notes of a drinking song into the hushed forest.

Jean-Baptiste wondered anxiously why the tsar had decided to receive them in person. He was afraid the questioning about Persia would start all over again, this time directed by a ruler who would not abide having his authority contravened.

The trip was not a long one. They were soon back at the hamlet where they had left their belongings. The passengers all jumped happily to the ground and walked around to the entrance on the other side of the building. The door was in proportion to the house: low and narrow, with a stone threshold and a worm-eaten lintel. Jean-Baptiste and George followed Saint-Août and joined the little crowd slowly making its way in. The entrance hallway was dark, its plaster falling in flakes. Beyond were two rooms whose ceilings, supported by dangerously bowed beams, were hardly higher than the tsar's head. Each room held a long table with benches around it. The guests took their places gaily. A woman shouted out orders, triggering gusts of male laughter. Jean-Baptiste pointed to the corner of a table in the right-hand room, far from the center of commotion. He and George slid into their seats quietly. But when everyone was more or less settled, they heard the tsar's gigantic voice booming in the next room and understood with terror that he was clamoring for the Fransuskis. Their tablemates denounced them loudly, and they were obliged to take their place at the imperial table across from the tsar. Saint-Août, who had left them in the crush, reappeared at their side.

Before anything else, drink was brought. Large demijohns encased in wicker were handed around the table, the tsar helping himself in turn, deftly using only one hand. At the first toast, Jean-Baptiste recognized that he had probably not yet seen all the trials this journey held in store for him. The glasses fell back noisily to the table and a brief, contented silence followed.

Poorly dressed servant girls bustled around the table and the great fireplace with its cooking smells. Jean-Baptiste noticed that one of the women, slightly older than the rest and no better dressed, personally served the tsar and no one else. In a long-handled cast-iron skillet she brought him a soft omelet bursting with mushrooms. As the drink enlivened Jean-Baptiste's wits, and after he saw the woman sit at table next to the tsar and kiss him on the neck, the Frenchman finally realized that this was the tsarina Catherine.

Peter gobbled up the omelet and washed it down with another pint of vodka. Jean-Baptiste then saw the tsar fix his attention on him. In keeping with his principles, the tsar shaved his face, though hardly more skillfully than his men. On his upper lip, however, he wore a thin mustache with upturned ends, so that whatever issued from the royal mouth appeared placed between whiskery quotation marks. The questioning is about to begin, thought Jean-Baptiste.

The tsar formulated a question and Saint-Août translated it.

"His Majesty would like you to tell the story of meeting Louis XIV."

Poncet was dumbfounded. How the devil could the emperor know about that? Israël Orii's letter said nothing on the subject. Who could possibly have told the tsar that he, Jean-Baptiste, had once . . .

He voiced his questions, and Saint-Août summed up their gist in Russian. The tsar laughed heartily and answered.

"The emperor asks," said Saint-Août, "what his police are for—a question you need not answer."

Jean-Baptiste bowed his head. His police! Since leaving Europe, now a very long time ago, he had forgotten all about the police. The East knew armies, denunciations, arbitrary action, and every way of speaking ill of your neighbor or doing him harm, but there existed no body dedicated to this sole purpose—a body paid to surveil, arrest, bring to judgment, and know everything about everyone: the police!

Jean-Baptiste began cautiously telling the story of his voyage to Abyssinia and the circumstances that led him to report on it at Versailles.

The emperor listened in silence but seemed to grow impatient.

"His Majesty," Saint-Août translated, "would like you to concentrate more particularly on Louis XIV. Apparently you knew him well . . ."

Jean-Baptiste assented with a smile, though it was the very thing he dreaded. His interview with Louis XIV on his return from Abyssinia had in fact been quite short. A ridiculous incident had interrupted it, and Jean-Baptiste had seen the king for barely three minutes. When his audience with Louis XIV had become known in Persia following his letter from the regent, the whole business had become embellished at the hands of rumor. Poncet was reputed to have been closeted with Louis XIV for long hours, possibly many times. He had not thought it worthwhile to set the record straight since he couldn't divulge the true facts of the story without making himself a laughingstock. These were the rumors the tsar's police must have heard. Jean-Baptiste had the sudden revelation, alas a somewhat belated one, that the crafty Israël Orii had most certainly sent on a report ahead of the travelers containing a full account of their identities and their business. It was too late for regrets. Up to his neck in the story, Jean-Baptiste had no choice but to go on for fear of alienating the emperor, whom he was hoping to enlist on his side. George, who knew the whole story, the real one, was terrified. He grew even more terrified when he heard Jean-Baptiste begin calmly:

"Sire, would you have me bore this merry company with an overlong account of the private audiences granted me by King Louis XIV—how can I hide it since Your Majesty knows everything—granted me, as I say, on a daily basis for three months?"

"Three months!" exclaimed the emperor when he received the translation.

"It's a long time, I know, but he insisted on hearing the story of my African embassy in its every detail. You ask me to speak of him, Your Majesty. Allow me to say something first of the court of France and its customs."

Jean-Baptiste launched into an interminable description of the little he had seen at Versailles, and these nothings assumed an epic stature in the telling. He had to gain time. Judging from the smell of the roasts, he guessed that they would soon be served. Toasts followed one another, and the audience, whose rumbling could be heard behind the silence, grew increasingly animated. He had to keep going until the explosion without losing face.

"His Majesty says—somewhat impatiently, I have to tell you—that he is familiar with all these settings," Saint-Août translated. "The tsar has been to Versailles. Alas, he never met Louis XIV because the king was already dead. It is about him, about his own person, that the emperor would like to hear."

A monarch's odd fancy! The man was obsessed with Louis XIV, whose glory he wanted to surpass, and was deeply mortified because the French king had not received him when he visited Europe in his youth. By the time he returned at the height of his glory, his idol had already passed away. Peter never tired of collecting reports from those who had had the good fortune to approach the Sun King and was clearly disconsolate at not having managed to do so himself. Jean-Baptiste considered the case for a moment as a doctor. Was it not time to apply the soothing balm of mourning to the wound? After extolling the king, he took the risk of going in another direction.

"Louis XIV's person?" he said pensively, surrounded by an expectant silence. "Well, if I may make a confession, Your Majesty, this great king was in my opinion . . . dreary."

The assembly murmured on hearing the translation. The more vocal uttered indignant exclamations: "Dreary!"

Peter took a great draft from his glass, tilting his head back to empty it. Then he set it down brutally, almost chipping its base, and everyone was silenced.

"He's right!" said the emperor in a virile voice.

And the tsarina, in the attitude of a camp follower, put her hands to her hips and stepped back to admire her man.

"Let me tell you something, all of you," continued Peter the Great. "The man was a great king, a very great king. The greatest? Perhaps. There have been others, certainly. But in our time? I doubt it. His palaces, marvels. His artists, geniuses. The etiquette of his court, a model. Yet this man is right: he was sad."

The roasts arrived at the table served on long pewter platters. Oof! thought Jean-Baptiste.

"An example?" the emperor continued. "His protocol: truly dreary! His levee, his going to bed, the holding of his dressing gown, his candles—can you imagine that here?"

Cries of revulsion were heard around the table.

"For my part," said the tsar, "I'd rather have you accompany me to chop down a fine old oak! That's also a protocol, if you like, and my court also has its conventions, but in mine at least you have a little fun, wouldn't you say?"

These words were followed by a new toast, which set off an explosion of laughter and joy. The meat, beautifully grilled, steamed in the plates with a garlicky exhalation. Relieved, Jean-Baptiste served George and took an abundant portion for himself. He was dying of hunger. Later in the evening, he briefly took alarm when the tsar returned to the subject of Versailles to recount his visit to Madame de Maintenon during his second trip to Paris, after Louis XIV's death. The emperor even rose to his feet to act out the scene.

"I absolutely wanted to see her," cried the emperor, in a state of excitation. "She refused! No doubt she wanted to hide her age! I insisted. I declared that her age meant nothing to me, that glory is not subject to age's indignities. Finally she agreed to receive me. I was brought to her convent. I entered. She was in bed, the curtains over the windows completely drawn and those surrounding her bed partly so. She wanted us to meet in semidarkness. What was she hiding? So that's how it was going to be! I couldn't communicate with her: there were courtiers present, but none of the scoundrels spoke Russian. She didn't either, of course, and my French is worthless, as you know. I said,

"Bonjour, Madame." What else could I do? She moaned in the depths of her dark box, which smelled of lace sprinkled with lavender. I hadn't traveled all that distance just for this. I wanted to see the wife of Louis XIV, by God! I wanted to see the person he had loved, can you understand that? But she was afraid. Of what? A moment went by, and still I couldn't see anything. Well, too bad, I went to the window and pulled the curtains back. Then I went to the bed and did the same thing with the drapes of her canopy bed. She yelped. A little yelp. Not a howl, which she would have been entitled to, but a whine, a bleat. So I stood square in front of her and looked at her. It lasted a full two minutes, maybe three. I didn't say a word, nor did she, nor did anyone else in the room. Believe me, no one had ever looked at her like that. No one has seen her as I have."

"Well?" asked the tsarina, hanging with both hands off Peter's arm, "what did you see?"

He thought for a moment, looking into the bottom of his glass where a bit of vodka still swirled, and said:

"That she made him dreary!"

He tossed down the contents of his goblet, burst into laughter, and the subject was closed for the night.

The admiral's vessel, at the heart of the great army supposedly under his command, sank gently into drunkenness. It was first tossed on a sea of shouts and bawdy songs, then rocked by musicians with strangely shaped instruments. Nostalgic voices, both from the emperor's company and from the soldiers' camps, echoed long into the clear and moonless autumn night, singing sorrowful melodies of fear and tenderness.

Before the ship foundered entirely, Jean-Baptiste managed to have a few words translated to the emperor on the subject of Juremi. Peter responded that he knew about the situation, that he had signed a pass for the Protestant which would be given to them the following day and which might be useful should they somehow find their friend. Then, pointing to a man at the far end of the table, the same man who looked like an English clergyman and had spoken to the tsar in the woods on their arrival, he said:

"For greater security, you will travel with the man you see here, Bibichev."

Jean-Baptiste's glance met Bibichev's, and though the man pretended to be addled and unsteady, Jean-Baptiste could read in his eyes that he had not been drinking.

They woke up late the following morning, their heads pounding, their clothes stained, and with no memory of how the evening had ended. Someone had put them to bed in cots under a small awning made of rugs stretched over a framework of poles. Their belongings were nearby, and Küyük, crouching quietly, watched them while chewing on a blade of grass. They washed in a great barrel that held water for the cookhouse of a Cossack regiment camped beside them.

Saint-Août came by toward noon. He said the emperor had been pleased to meet them and had given him the pass for Juremi. Unfortunately he was no longer on hand to give them an audience, having left at dawn to inspect some fortifications being built on the road to Daghestan. Saint-Août confirmed that the emperor had risen at his normal hour of five o'clock and attended mass before setting off.

The colonel brought them to an officers' mess to break their fast with skewers of grilled meat. He had made inquiries during the morning and learned that, to find the Swedish prisoners who had been deported in recent months—and those who, like Juremi, had fought with them—the best place to look was in the regions along the Caspian and the Aral seas. The first prisoners captured during this long war had been sent farther, to Tobolsk and the Far East, but the later ones had followed the direction of Russia's conquests: the empire was extending toward the Caucasus, and new colonists were being sent in that direction. For all its uncertainty, this was rather encouraging news. It gave them hope that Juremi had not strayed too deep into Siberia and that they might find him without traveling terribly far.

"According to my information," went on Saint-Août, "you should find your friend to the north of the great sea that starts not far from here and that we call the Caspian. The easiest way to get to its northern end is by boat. That will allow you to avoid the bad roads and the swampy areas around Astrakhan, where you might catch a fever."

He offered to lead them toward the nearest point on the coast, a little south of the town of Derbent, which was only thirty versts away.

"I will travel only halfway with you because I am needed here. But Bibichev will accompany you the rest of the way."

Bibichev? They no longer remembered him. With their heads pounding like trip-hammers, Jean-Baptiste and George had jumbled everything.

Yet at the moment of their departure, when they saw Bibichev's black figure approach astride a long-haired Siberian horse, his skull flat and bare
except for an island of hair clinging to his forehead, they recognized him.
They recognized him with the same displeasure one feels at finding a
rotten spot in the flesh of a tasty fruit.

19

Since arriving in Isfahan, Françoise had felt extraordinarily tired. This was no illness, no localized complaint such as medicine approves. Rather she was overtaken by a tide of weariness after the great exertions of her flight and the deprivations she had suffered in exile. The pleasantness of Isfahan, the quiet comfort of her stay with Alix and Jean-Baptiste, had overcome the defenses of her will more thoroughly than any of her previous trials.

She passed her days in the garden under a Pharaoh's fig that she liked for its dense shade. She brought along some needlework, which she left untouched across her knees while she daydreamed. Her sight had grown dimmer. Saba still kept her company and never tired of hearing her tell stories. The young redhead had also started to confide in Françoise, after a long initial period of growing used to her.

Françoise was horrified to learn how harshly the girl judged her mother. Alix was under the illusion that Saba resembled her: on the physical plane, this was patently untrue; on the mental plane, Françoise discovered, the gap was even more pronounced.

When Saba emerged from childhood in her mother's eyes, Alix had freely offered her all the instruction she herself had acquired only at the cost of enormous struggle. She took her to seamstresses in the bazaar, where she had a whole panoply of clothes made for her, and taught her their use. Saba had accompanied her everywhere she went, among Persians as well as foreigners, among the rich as well as the poor. And to equip her completely, Alix had provided her daughter with riding lessons, the real kind, so that she would know how to flee, to travel, or to fight, and also lessons in handling the rapier and the saber. Saba had willingly taken part in all of these exercises. Her skill at them had convinced her mother that the resemblance between them was henceforth complete.

Yet the young woman, who now possessed the weapons of both sexes, had no intention of putting them to the same use as Alix. Françoise was the only one who realized that the child's serious mask hid neither sadness nor timidity but a moral anger that made her condemn her parents' frivolity and the liberties they took with the truth. More than anything she hated their propensity to laugh at themselves and at everything else. Looking for happiness did not seem to her a fit purpose in life, in comparison with such true principles as the sense of duty, disciplined exertion, and the mastery of self. Where did these ideas come from? No one could say. But it is not unusual for children, when their parents raise a wall of perfect happiness before them, to reject the example for fear of being unable to reproduce it.

Almost every afternoon now Alix went out wearing her veil. These walks took the place of the gatherings and festivities she no longer had the right to enjoy in Jean-Baptiste's absence, given her supposed widowhood.

"Look!" said Saba darkly, as she sat by Françoise's side during her midday nap.

Alix was crossing the lawn, the sun in her eyes keeping her from seeing the two figures in the shade of the sycamore. She had lifted the heavy blue veil to her forehead, though she would lower it over her face when she reached the street.

"Your mother is looking younger," said Françoise, smiling, once Alix had disappeared.

"It's because of that pest who has such influence over her."

"Who's that?"

"The grand vizier's latest wife. I finally found out about it last week. My mother pretends to be delivering medicines in town but she always stops first at the house of that slyboots."

"Show a little respect to your mother's friends," said Françoise, running her hands gently through Saba's hair.

"Respect! For that Nur al-Huda! Have you seen her? She walks down the street wrapped like a mummy. Oh, you'd take her for an angel of propriety. But I've seen her without her veil when she was here, and she has the falsest face you can imagine."

Saba gave Françoise a complete portrait of the woman, in which she mixed her recollection of what she had glimpsed during their brief meeting with all the mean thoughts a virgin might harbor toward a courtesan.

The mind has an aversion to the idea of a closed sea such as the Caspian. The two words lie together uneasily. How can a sea, that infinite space with endlessly moving air, a sea that swallows everything, into which the mountains and all the continents will someday dissolve, be closed? A closed sea is a hobbled courser, a dashed hope, a conditional freedom. In short, it is a revolting idea. Fortunately, it is no more than an idea—only from looking at a map would you know that a sea is enclosed; as soon as you set the map aside to walk along the sea's shore, the idea is forgotten. The wind blows, the water ripples, you can't conceive that what is in front of you is anything but the open sea.

When the travelers came in sight of the Caspian, Bibichev, who spoke almost accentless Italian, told them to make their way down to a cove that was visible a long way off. They were to wait for him there while he hired a boat. Jean-Baptiste and George were all too happy to be rid of him and to enjoy the extraordinary landscape of the seacoast without his dark figure to dampen the effect. The late fall weather was still warm, and the impenetrable blue sky was dotted with small immobile clouds. They let the horses pick their way down the slope toward the beach along mule trails and the tracks of grazing flocks, continually branching and rejoining. A thicket of lentisk and myrtle covered the poor soil of these hillsides, gleaming with sun-pricked slivers of mica and schist under the dust of the path. Large, almost gray agaves grew on the sands at the foot of the hill. From time to time during their descent, a tall, straight pine would lift its head above the crouching vegetation and slide its cottony plume among the clouds to anchor, like a taut rope, the fleeting earth to the unmoving sky. The cove was bordered by dunes on one side and shaded on the other by mangroves. They tied up the horses under the mangrove canopy and left Küyük, who seemed uninterested in the sea, to guard them. Then George and Jean-Baptiste took off their boots and walked barefoot in the sand of the dunes along the shore. After their many long trials on land and in the mountains, the water—the living vastness of the sea, rippling with short blades of foam—suddenly gave them a feeling of deliverance. Even George no longer thought to measure the density of the air or the salinity of the water. He stood on the slightly reddish sand that caressed his feet and, with his face toward the open water and his hair flattened by the breeze, took in deep lungfuls of infinity and softness. For a moment, the pleasure made him want to open wide the window of his soul and tell Jean-Baptiste the secret that weighed him down. But despite wanting to, he could not find the strength for it and kept quiet.

The east winds, which struck them straight on, had come down from the Himalayas and dried out during their crossing of the great deserts. At the last moment, the Caspian had laden the breezes with a salty dampness, scented by its shoreline. To feel its caress was pure bliss. They sat there, on the high point of the dunes at the head of the cove, and waited, letting their thoughts go.

After a long moment, Jean-Baptiste observed to himself that he had not till now thought of Alix, or of his daughter, or of anything relating to his life in Isfahan. Of course he felt a pang at the thought of having left them behind, but their place was in his memory, not in his dreams. Traveling, he had gone back to those regions of the mind that lie, as it were, upstream from any specific love and that form, like this sky and this wind, the raw material of desire and life. He felt himself back at that distant age when everything is still possible and nothing has yet happened, an age that no doubt doesn't exist, and that one only reaches by detouring back in time.

Their daydreams had reached this stage when a sail slowly rounded the promontory that blocked the view of the gulf to the south. It was a red sail, triangular and poorly hemmed, driving a small cutter with a tiny dinghy in tow. The boat anchored in the middle of the bay, and two men jumped into the skiff to row it ashore. One of them, dressed all in black, was Bibichev. Jean-Baptiste and George went to the water's edge to meet him. The oarsman jumped from the craft as it reached the last wavelets and pulled it with great force onto the sand so that Bibichev could disembark with dignity onto dry land.

"Tell your footman to bring the baggage," he cried over the sound of the wind. "Everything is ready. We're off."

"And the horses?" asked Jean-Baptiste.

"Leave them, with their saddles and bridles. I have arranged for someone to buy the whole lot. A man is coming for them later."

They were good Tartar horses, a present from the tsar to replace the ones given them by d'Ombreval, and Jean-Baptiste felt a moment's regret at abandoning them. He had no choice, however, and resolved to do what Bibichev had asked. A half hour later they were aboard the cutter, weighing anchor.

The boat normally carried goods along the coast. No provision had been made for passengers. They had to sit on coils of ropes beside the open hold, in which a few sacks of dates rattled as the ship pitched. The crew consisted of four Russians, apparently unaware of their emperor's ukase, their long hair and beards matted with sweat and salt. A good wind from abeam drove them steadily at first. Küyük, who had made no secret of his fear of going aboard, took a seat in the bow where he clutched a bight of rope. When the boat rose on the waves and fell back into the troughs, the Mongol, whose eyes were shut, had the reassuring impression of riding horseback over the sea. George, pale during the first hours, quickly gained his sea legs and stood on the gunwales gripping the shrouds.

The crossing lasted five days. The dates, contrary to what they expected, were not the boat's freight but their own daily staple, along with some fat olives that were floating in a sticky barrel. No one complained about this diet, and they endured it silently.

On the third day at sea, they neared the coast and saw the walls and even the flag of Fort Alexander on the heights of Cape Urduk before once more making for the high seas.

Finally, on the fifth day, they hove in sight of a shoreline riddled with deserted islands and greenish shoals just below the surface of the water. When they questioned Bibichev, he told them that this was the head of the gigantic bay formed by the northern shore of the Caspian. They would land here, despite the fact that there was no town, and proceed to the province of Turgay, where Bibichev had orders to lead them.

The Russians maneuvered the boat carefully between the shoals. One of the sailors stood at the bow and threw out the lead, counting off the fathoms of water while the others maintained a watchful silence. Finally they reached a freshwater inlet at the mouth of a small river. The cutter dropped anchor. They spent a last night on board and disembarked early the next morning, the skiff depositing them a short distance upstream on a reed-covered bank.

A heated discussion arose between Bibichev and the crew. At issue, from what Jean-Baptiste could understand, was the whereabouts of a fishing village of which there was no sign. The sailors kept pointing in the direction they should go, and Bibichev was coming around to their view, though with poor grace. The travelers divided up the baggage and set off across the spongy ground, their boots sinking slightly into it.

They walked for an hour without seeing anything except the waving surface of the reeds and gorse that sometimes grew as high as their heads. White terns wheeled above them in large silent circles. The ground became hard, then soft again because of the carpet of sphagnum covering it, an indication that there were marshes nearby. At the dawn of the world the sun must have risen over a landscape like this one, before Logos had divided the elements. There was neither north nor south, nor sky, nor earth, nor extension, nor duration, but only the vacant magma of air and water mingled in this chaos of hollow stems.

Finally the curtain of vegetation seemed to part and they came out on a pond, whose waters lay still and black. It was Küyük who first pointed to the shape. There, at the water's edge, still too far away to make out in any detail, was a human figure.

They approached it silently. There was now no possible doubt: it was a seated man. He must have seen them, yet he did not move. As they drew nearer, they saw that he was holding a long fishing rod whose line dipped into the pond. Finally they were standing before him, and the man looked at them with a calm smile. He was small and ageless; his pale blond hair, almost white, stuck up from his head in a tousled crest; his eyes, which were blue, seemed entirely empty, so utterly did their pale color absorb every reflection, giving them a porcelain hue. His most surprising feature, though, was his golden yellow suit, tailored with extreme though somewhat old-fashioned elegance and decorated with silver aglets and lace sleeves, looking highly out of place.

Bibichev addressed him in Russian, but the stranger shook his head with an air of regret. George tried English, then Jean-Baptiste tried Italian and French with no more success. Bibichev then said to the stranger, pointing at his shoulder:

"Svenski?"

The Swede smiled and gave a big nod. The little group rejoiced at this discovery, though they were somewhat perplexed as to how to proceed. Then Jean-Baptiste, struck by a sudden inspiration, asked the stranger:

"Juremi?"

The other lowered his fishing rod and looked worried.

"Juremi," repeated Jean-Baptiste several times, pronouncing his friend's name in every way he could think.

Suddenly the Swede's face lit up:

"Aaaah!" he said, "Chūråmi. Tak! Tak!"

And with an intonation that sounded very familiar to Jean-Baptiste, he added with a laugh:

"Ah! Sakreblø!"

III
THE ALBERONI
PLOT

20

The orange, framed by three pointy leaves with varnished surfaces, stood out against the pastel color of the late autumn sky. The man gazed at it through a tall open window. Suddenly he turned to look at an impressive Adoration of the Shepherds on the opposite wall. They were truly the same tones: the colors of Raphael's frescoes were entirely the colors of Raphael's country, both yesterday and today, forever and ever. He looked out the window again. The colors of Italy were the colors of food, that was the source of their charm: they had a visual savor that brought together the pleasures of touch, of smell, and of taste. The orange of the orange, for instance; and the mauve-tinted pink of the sky where it met the line of trimmed yew, which was the pink of the hams from the country around Parma which his father used to send him to fetch on foot an hour away at a farm in the mountains; and that dark green, which was the green of that unforgettable parsley he had grown in the garden of his first parish.

All this filled him with pleasure, as the scene brought together his two life passions: liberating Italy and cooking fine soups.

Cardinal Alberoni sighed, closed the window, and crossed the vast room with tiny steps. He went and sat behind his always bare desk, whose red morocco surface was stamped in the center with a gold tiara surrounded by laurels.

To liberate Italy! The work was stopped for the moment; someday it would succeed; the chariot of Independence was in motion. He, for his part, had done what he could. Had it been a failure? Perhaps. But his life? Ah! no, his life was a beautiful thing, a patient and a laborious life, but also an incomparable one.

He closed his eyes for a moment. The great silence of the Vatican enveloped him. Was it really silence? He strained his ears. In the distance could be heard the tumult of the city, its shouts, the clopping of its horses and clattering of its conveyances. How pleasant the sound was! The Vatican's silence would be nothing if it did not rule over the bustle of the world. There had to be a low rumble to provide a muted reminder of the roar of the tamed monster.

He looked at Raphael's painting, those naked curves, that flesh. It was for flesh that so many people sought power. His own taste was more modest, not for the flesh in any of its forms but for what becomes flesh, what feeds it, enlivens it, instills it with motion and emotion. Beautiful meats, their succulence; the pulpy roundness of fruits and vegetables. Wine . . . And before that even, prior to it, the land, the soil of Italy, which received men's labor and bore their harvests. And then the sky, which enfolds the land in the cycle of the seasons, heats it with its celestial orb, waters it with its storms . . . Ah! The sky! . . . The sky? . . . Hmm!

The cardinal rested his forearms on a trough, a valley formed above his stomach when he sat down. Beloved gesture! How carefully he had sculpted his corpulence to make it comfortable! Never had he given in to piggishness, which is a sin, but he had cultivated his gluttony, that rare quality, with science. He had always promised himself to correct this point of scripture if he ever became pope. And who could say that some day he would not? Innocent XIII had become pope. Innocent! A good name for the pontiff, though given him for want of a better. When they had both been children, he had often enough called him *"coglione," "testadura,"* and *"cretino,"* names that would have done just as well . . . Coglione XIII! Heh! Heh! Alberoni coughed into his closed fist.

That was already a mark of destiny, the fact that he had gone to school with the pontiff. Also that this man should have become pope at the very time when his old schoolmate had been forced to leave Spain and take refuge in the Vatican. At first he had been quartered in the cellar like an outlaw, before Innocent XIII had providentially rescued him from there. A destiny, yes, truly! A life!

Cardinal Alberoni roused himself. His thoughts of the pope brought to a close the sweet bliss he allowed himself for a quarter hour at the start of every afternoon, for reasons of health.

Already a thousand projects swarmed in his head, the many letters to write, all the dreaded and beloved cares of his indefatigable life. He rang.

A secretary in a cassock with a large rectangular white collar entered and inclined his head in silence.

"Do I have visitors, Pozzi?"

"Several," said the secretary.

"The first?"

"At two o'clock."

"But it's already two-thirty! Who is it?"

"Monsieur de Maillet."

"Don't know him. What does he want? Who gave him an interview?"

The secretary raised his chin and waited before answering. This Pozzi was a man of a certain age, dried out by his decades at the Vatican like a very old and very delicate ham. His features had been arrested, like a mummy's under its wraps, in a perpetual expression of indignation, surprise, and gratitude; his interlocutors thus had the option of reading his enigmatic mask as they chose.

"Well, Pozzi," said the cardinal, "don't play at being surprised. What is it?"

"You made the decision yourself, Your Eminence, since he was recommended to you by Cardinal F."

Pozzi felt his heart beat a little faster. The go-betweens at the Vatican, like this Mazucchetti to whom Monsieur de Maillet had entrusted his business, generally worked through the secretaries. In this instance, Pozzi had inserted the meeting into Alberoni's schedule himself, at Mazucchetti's request. He took an interest in the business, and though it would no doubt be counted against him in the next world, he hoped to profit from it in this.

"Cardinal F.," said Alberoni, hesitating.

The name must have been well chosen, for he finally said:

"Fine, tell this . . . Maillet to come in."

"A docket concerning this person is on top of the visitors' pile in Your Lordship's cabinet," said Pozzi, masking his relief.

The cardinal took the docket, walked to an enormous lion's paw armchair, and sat down in it, crossing his legs under his purple moiré robes. At that moment the door opened and Pozzi ushered in the visitor.

Monsieur de Maillet took two large steps into the room, standing as straight as he could despite the pain in his hips, and suddenly stopped.

The high ceiling, the large bare desk below the monumental paintings, the chandelier . . . all the things man borrows from those giants known as governments—even Christ's government on earth!—and that they take such pleasure in enslaving themselves to . . . What memories! What regrets! A flood of emotion suddenly welled up in the former consul of Cairo, stopping him in his tracks on the brink of tears.

Alberoni, still seated in his clawed armchair, interpreted Monsieur de Maillet's immobility as respect, of which, with his rotund kindliness and short stature, he commanded little, and found himself favorably disposed.

"Enter, dear sir, and help yourself to a seat across from me."

Monsieur de Maillet recovered the use of his senses and complied. The cardinal listened to his polite expressions, signaled that his time was short, and invited his visitor to come to the point. The consul, who had gone over his speech time and again, repeated with all the fervor one puts into a last attempt: the book, its condemnation, the pope's pardon, etc. The cardinal continued to look over the docket.

"So you are the author of a work entitled *Telliamed*."

"Yes, Monsignor, I am honored—"

"And what, in a few words, is your book about?"

"Monsignor, it is a philosophical dialogue with an imaginary being named Telliamed—"

"Telliamed . . . Telliamed? A strange name, where did you unearth it?"

The consul coughed into his bony fist. Of the entire work, it was perhaps the one detail he regretted.

"That is to say," he said embarrassedly, "Demaillet, Telliamed . . ."

"Ingenious," said the cardinal, with an awful smile.

Why the devil did his colleagues oblige him to receive such utterly grotesque characters? No doubt they were aware of his admirable patience toward this tiresome lot.

"In this book," continued the prelate, rapidly consulting the folder, "you apparently assert that man arose from the sea. An odd idea, in all conscience, and a scandalous one when compared to the doctrine of our Lord Jesus Christ. Does it originate with Telliamed or with Demaillet?"

"Why . . . both, Monsignor. It is not an odd idea at all, but one that it is easy to observe in nature. Does not each species have its corresponding species in the watery realm? There are dogs of the sea, spiders of the sea, as well as those animals we call 'seals,' which are known to sailors as 'veals of the sea.'"

While the old diplomat perorated, Alberoni thought about his dinner that evening. He had invited three archbishops who were enormously important to his projects, and he counted on regaling them as usual with his cooking. Veal, he thought, an excellent idea. And he began to review recipes in his mind.

". . . And it's in the temperate regions, where the air is laden with humidity and differs little from seawater, that the marine species first came onto land. Hence the apparition of the first men on the shores of Europe's warmwater seas and—"

"Quite right," said Alberoni, making the folder snap shut, and in fact he had decided on blanquettes. "Now, Consul—"

"Alas, I am no longer—"

"I know, I know, but the title is for life, isn't it? Now, Consul, I have little time: I beg you to come, if not to the crux—for all this is of great interest—then at least to what concerns me directly. How could you sum up . . . what you want?"

"Ah! Your Eminence, I want nothing, I simply implore. I implore you to intervene with the pope to lift the condemnation of this book. It is an audacious book, perhaps, but sincere, and in no way does it contravene the holy teachings of our mother church. I am ready to do anything, Your Eminence, absolutely anything, to have my sincerity, as a man whose faith . . ."

Alberoni, in an action unrelated to this litany, rose abruptly and began to pace the room. An idea had come to him. Where did it come from? He couldn't say, perhaps from a glimpsed image, a fortuitous interplay of words, of memories: it was through these ceaseless associations that his ever active mind proceeded. No matter, as the idea was there. He turned it over in his head as though examining a fruit for wormholes. No, it looked sound. He returned and sat down.

"Consul, how long were you in the East?"

"Why . . . nineteen years, Monsignor."

Alberoni continued to reflect for a long moment.

"Let us set aside your business for the time being, we can return to it later. It doesn't seem impossible to present His Holiness with a few arguments that might allow him to review his position. *But*"—and he spoke the word very loud, holding up his hand to keep the old man from flopping about like a trout, or any other aquatic species—*"but* I would first like to solicit your advice on another matter, a confidential and highly delicate one."

"Your Eminence," sputtered Monsieur de Maillet, "my loyalty has never been found wanting . . ."

"I know. I have read your docket, and besides I have always been a good judge of character."

The consul smiled wanly.

"Here it is," the cardinal went on, springing to his feet and walking deliberately in a circle, his hands clasped behind him. "The papal nuncio who recently traveled to Persia has personally brought me strange and scandalous news. Persia is far, of course, and I care little what goes on there. But I would rather all the same that the story did not reach the pope's ears. It would do me a disservice at this critical juncture when His Holiness has been kind enough to restore his full confidence in me and name me apostolic protonotary *ad instar participandum*. Have you ever been to Persia, Monsieur de Maillet?"

"I had the opportunity to visit Hormuz and Gambrun on the coast."

"Very well! Then it may interest you to know that in this country, which I myself have never visited, someone has undertaken to defame me."

"But who, Monsignor?" exclaimed Monsieur de Maillet, showing sincere indignation.

"I don't know, and therein lies the nub. It's probably a woman. But I fear she may have associates."

"And . . . what has she done?"

"She claims to know me, Monsieur de Maillet. Me! Cardinal Alberoni!"

"Well, in point of fact, there is a possibility . . ." suggested Monsieur de Maillet in conciliatory tones.

"There is not the slightest possibility," the cardinal replied sharply, picking up a small bronze and rapping the table with its base. "You don't understand. She is not claiming to know me . . . in a general way. The woman says she has a . . . particular . . . knowledge of me. Are you following?"

Without waiting for a reply, Alberoni trotted over to a large secretary, to whose complex locking mechanism he applied several keys, one of them on a chain around his neck. He left the secretary open and returned to Maillet holding a letter in his hand.

"Consul, the document I am going to show you is highly confidential. I would like you to take a solemn vow never to disclose it to anyone, you understand, to anyone, ever."

"I so swear," said Monsieur de Maillet feelingly.

"Here, look at what they've sent me."

Monsieur de Maillet took the letter with its stained and dirty envelope, noting that its wax seal bore no arms. He read, in French:

To His very gracious, very wise, and very learned Eminence, Cardinal Alberoni, illustrious among all the peoples who follow the law of Jesus, right arm of the great lord who rules in Rome, and my dearest Jules:

My soul discovered such great happiness that all the marvels of paradise, its perfect greenswards, its beauties, which delight by night and day, are nothing in comparison with the good, the happy, and the favorable moment when my ear received, like the milk of a young she-camel tinged with the honey of most sublime bees, the blessed news of the arrival in the sainted and magnificent city of Rome, powerful as no other on earth, of Your Lordship, whose loving slave girl I am.

Persia and its very sublime, learned, and omnipotent sovereign, the adorable Shah Huseyn, star of grace, of mercy, of confidence, of clairvoyance, and of perfection, have done me the enormous favor, though I am but the humblest and most insignificant slave, of granting me the right to live in this most powerful kingdom on earth, to which the men of all nations pay sonorous and sincere homage.

O that I might soon rejoin Your resplendent and faithful Holiness in the beauty, safety, and luxury of a haven such as the blessed city of our pope. The very puissant and adorable prince, known here as the nazir, is at your disposal, my darling, who are most worthy of all sacrifices and whose image is constantly before my eyes, to make possible, *in the best possible circumstances,* my return at the side of your warm and generous heart. Quickly, quickly, answer me.

Your adored F.

"Do you not find that scandalous?" asked the cardinal, planting himself directly before the reader with his arms crossed.

"Quite," answered the consul cautiously. "The style is certainly heavy."

"What do you mean, the style!" cried Alberoni, snatching the letter from the consul's hands. "That is the very least of it! I am talking about the matter itself."

The consul sat back in his chair and assumed an air of dignity and cunning.

"It is not my position to judge the relations Your Eminence may have enjoyed with this person."

Alberoni remained momentarily speechless with fury. He was starting to regret that he had confided in this mule.

"My good Consul," he rapped out firmly, "I do not enjoy relations with this or any other person of the sort. Kindly take stock of this once and for all."

Abashed by the cardinal's tone, Monsieur de Maillet bowed respect-fully.

"They are seeking to harm me, it is that simple. Once again I am the object of a sordid cabal, perpetrated by the envious and the base, and by the enemies of Italy's freedom."

Pozzi entered the office discreetly, carrying a sheaf of folders. With impatient gestures, the cardinal ordered him out immediately and sat back down on the edge of his armchair so as to face Monsieur de Maillet direct-ly. He motioned him to lean forward.

"Someone," he whispered in the consul's ear with pedagogical patience, "is passing herself off as my mistress. Is that clear enough? This letter, the nuncio's information, and several other recent reports prove it."

Monsieur de Maillet nodded his agreement to each of these sentences without expression, as though he were listening to the rules of the game of piquet.

"To what end, these calumnies?" the cardinal continued. "Is it black-mail? Certain words in this abstruse text suggest it. They want money. Others have tried to threaten me in this way before. I am not afraid of them. But one has to get to the bottom of it. Is it the first stroke in a vast political movement?—something I might very well expect from the regent of France and his minister. Are they warning me first to alarm me and induce me to commit a blunder before spattering the venom of these supposed intimacies onto the pope himself, to discredit me and reduce me to nothing, after undoing all my work?"

The cardinal ceased leaning forward, a position for which his corpu-lence had not been sculpted, and when he continued it was from a comfortable position and in a normal voice. The rest was in any case less confidential:

"Unless . . . unless it is the coded message of one of our faithful friends, now in distress. The adverse winds of these past few years have dispersed my little band. Several of my companions have still not been heard from. I would be sorry not to reply to a friend, if perchance the author of these lines is one, a friend who was simply using this subterfuge to escape the vigilance of the Mahometans and contact me. The hypothesis is not high-ly probable, but I prefer not to neglect it."

All during this speech, Monsieur de Maillet was busy mulling over the great, the wonderful, the extraordinary news that Alberoni would in fact intervene on his behalf. He patiently waited for this confidential digres-sion to end so that he might return to his business. None of it, to tell the truth, concerned him much, and he hoped to get off with nothing more than some advice on how to deal with the Persians.

The cardinal, his peroration over, began pacing again and considered the old consul closely one last time before taking the final plunge. Of course, he thought, one could have hoped for a better agent: this one could hardly walk and was thin as a rail. Would he even last another six months? Bah! these old ships don't founder so easily. And then, Alberoni told himself, he didn't really have a choice. He was no longer, as he had once been, at the apex of a nation devoted entirely to his will, with its armies of lords at his beck and call. More particularly, and this last argument carried the day, this old diplomat, a discreet man from an excellent family, who was familiar with the ways of the East, would cost him nothing—he simply wanted an indulgence, which is to say the coinage of heaven, a commodity the cardinal saw no reason not to spend freely.

"Monsieur de Maillet," he said, "we are going to engage in a solemn covenant, being the men of honor that we are. For my part, I will have the condemnation that weighs on your innocent work lifted, however great the difficulty—and I know it to be considerable."

"Ah!" moaned the consul.

"But do you, as a gentleman and plenipotentiary of the king of France, give me your assurance in return . . . to set off as soon as possible for Persia to shed some light on this compromising business?"

The consul received the proposition as though a mace had landed on his feet: he jumped backward.

"Set off for Persia! Me!"

The cardinal, in a show of good nature, kept his eyes lowered and his arms hanging at his sides like a penitent. He left the old man to debate the bargain he had set before him, to moan, to blanch, to mumble, and finally, under the spell of the enormous hope of pardon planted in him by the cardinal, to capitulate and accept. Then Cardinal Alberoni rose and, with a generosity that he never managed to conceal, paid the consul in advance and in full with a warm embrace.

21

Magnus Koefoed was one of those men whom life favors with successive titles, which they adopt easily one after another. He had first been a knight, then a baron at the death of his father; afterward King Charles XII, whose favorite he was, had made him a general; since becoming a prisoner, the pastor in him had taken the upper hand, and no one called him anything but "Reverend."

To him and the two thousand other Swedes captured at the same time, the Russians had given no other jailer than the kindly thickets, the wild ponds, and the motionless sky of the Turgay steppes. On his arrival at this far confine of the earth a year before, Reverend Magnus had immediately taken charge of his little flock and courageously gone to work.

When Jean-Baptiste and his companions were brought to him by the man they had met on the edge of the pond, the reverend, who spoke French very well, rejoiced at their coming and looked forward to showing his visitors the work he and his countrymen had accomplished in a few short months—but these fanatics were interested in only one thing: if he knew where Juremi was living.

"As chance would have it," said Reverend Magnus, annoyed but maintaining his equanimity, "the first man you encountered was Lars, who served as an artilleryman in your friend's regiment. We have with us several other soldiers he commanded, but Juremi himself, alas, is not in our community."

Jean-Baptiste was unable to hide his intense disappointment. Since the exchange at the pond, he had been convinced that fate had led them straight to their goal and that their troubles were over.

"Don't worry," said the reverend, "we will soon know where he is and I'll have you taken there. All our little camps—we prefer to call them villages—are linked by a postal system that allows us to contact them easily. You'll see, it's not the least of the improvements we have brought to this country."

Jean-Baptiste urged him to dispatch a message immediately. Hardly accustomed to such haste, the reverend nonetheless agreed to write a letter then and there calling on all the other heads of communities to write back to him with information on where Juremi was living. He then handed it to a young man who served as his secretary with instructions to copy it and send it out as soon as possible throughout the Turgay and the Ural Area.

"There is nothing you can do at this point but to settle down here and wait," the Swede concluded amiably, glad that he could now turn the discussion to more important matters, which is to say his village.

He arranged for them to live in a little wooden house at the settlement's center next to the church. Jean-Baptiste, George, and Bibichev each claimed one of the rooms and insisted on going to bed immediately. Küyük, for his part, spurned both of the two remaining rooms and settled to sleep outside on the wide wooden porch surrounding the hut.

The following morning the reverend came to them bringing a copious breakfast of dried fish, berry tea, and barley cakes. He was visibly delighted that the heavens, to which he had often directed his secret prayers, had dropped these unexpected visitors in his lap, the first to whom he had had the chance to exhibit his flock's hard work. As soon as the meal was over, he took them on a tour of the camp.

The unhappy Swedish exiles displayed a state of mind that combined despair and enterprise, like those sailors voluntarily marooned by the early navigators on distant and deserted islands with the promise that their ship would return soon. They were alone in the midst of virgin nature.

Most of the prisoners were too old to forget their culture and abandon their native customs but young enough still to want to reproduce them. Unfortunately, their country had managed to cultivate—before going down to defeat—the most refined and brilliant civilization in Europe. What the reverend wanted to show them with such touching pride were the shards of this great jewel, scattered in the midst of the steppes.

The village was situated on a stretch of well-cleared land whose raked soil was marked off into alleys and squares. Small houses dotted the area in an orderly way, their shingled gables opening onto the street, their walls daubed with dried mud of different colors. Despite their soiled appearance, these surfaces created lively tonal contrasts. Every type of skill was needed in this wasteland, and there was no dearth of them in the village. Yet because of the extreme rarity of metal, the majority of artisans were unable to put their talents to full use.

While technology remained at a primitive state, the arts were flourishing. The visitors admired an entire display of portraits inspired by Velázquez, which had been painted with linseed oil and required several weeks in the sun to dry for lack of turpentine, an ancient technique also used by van Eyck. Musicians were widely represented among the captives, whose main concern was to procure instruments. The travelers visited a dark workshop where an aged artisan, a former drum major in the royal armies, had hand-built a small barrel organ. Its pipes were made of bamboo, neatly aligned and bound together with willow strips. The mechanism was activated by turning a large wooden drum set with thousands of small nails. The contraption made a sound like a cart rolling over paving stones, but by listening intently one could just make out the moving strains of a Lully cavatina.

"'The Triumph of Love,'" announced the reverend proudly.

As luck would have it, one of the company was a luthier. He had supplied the community with violins, which he built with considerable skill. Regrettably, he had neither glue nor varnish, and his instruments, with their pegs and nails, looked like coffins for newborns. The cords, made of stretched sinew, gave an odd, hoarse, plaintive sound. Yet three musicians, summoned for the purpose, executed a number of chamber pieces on these instruments that were lovely enough to draw tears.

The reverend's greatest interest was in dance, and he saved its demonstration for last, after he had conducted them everywhere, from the dairy to the stables, and from the bakery to the brewery. Everyone was converging on the large low room used for assemblies, councils, and celebrations. The reverend had asked the women to convene there so that he might present them to the visitors.

As the Russians had deported only men, the prisoner communities normally contained members only of the male sex. No doubt the prisoners could, in this realm as in others, have come to each other's assistance and thereby experienced relief, perhaps even pleasure. But the human propensity to hand down one's work to posterity had won out: they had coupled with native women.

Most of the Tartars living in the area called themselves Kalmuks. These Buddhist Mongols had come from the far reaches of Asia during the previous century, shoving aside everyone in their path. Curiously, contact with the peoples of Russia had had the effect of making them entirely peaceful. The Kalmuks became sedentary and gathered into villages, where they fished, practiced a little farming, and mixed easily with the foreigners. They had welcomed the Swedish deportees with open arms and were now even related to them, having allowed the Swedes to take their women in marriage, though still consorting with them discreetly.

Nothing was so surprising as the juxtaposition of these two races. The Swedes were smooth, white as turnips (or at most reddened by the summer sun), and had pale eyes and long noses. When they considered their bronze-skinned wives with their square faces, flat noses, and almost total absence of teeth, it was more with astonishment than with intimacy. Human history has witnessed stranger unions even than this, thought Jean-Baptiste, and nothing kept them from being happy. Yet he remained uneasy, though unable to explain it to himself.

The first dances started. They were slow minuets and gigues, which the reverend himself directed by brandishing a long ceremonial cane.

The men, whom Jean-Baptiste had seen walking about the village in their coarse cotton clothes, had put on military dress. The uniforms varied in color and cut according to the regiment. In its hour of glory, Sweden had had the means to equip its armies sumptuously. Unfortunately the Swedish defeat had not been kind to the uniforms, which became torn in battle and threadbare in exile. The dancers wore tatters whose elegant cut and exquisite fabrics only emphasized the hideousness of their innumerable patches, which stood out like sores on a well-formed limb. The Kalmuk women had been even more sadly tricked out. The village tailors, with what they could find in the way of sacking and animal hides, had confected court dresses for these gallant ladies which were of the most complex and recent style, with puffed-out hoops and skirts made of materials it is best not to know. They had even gone to the extreme—and cruel—length of covering the women's heads with wigs of tow, very ingeniously made, but which put the finishing touches on the outrage.

Jean-Baptiste could now explain his own uneasiness, a fact that didn't lessen the strength of his feeling: these Swedes hadn't married Kalmuk women, they had simply used the raw material, which they regarded with disappointment and resignation, to try to manufacture Swedish wives, with the same care and the same means that allowed them to take their crates for violins and their creaky carts for carriages.

"Isn't it a lovely picture?" whispered the reverend into Jean-Baptiste's ear, pointing admiringly at the dancers.

He had left the task of conducting the last galop to another musician.

"What grace! What feeling!" he continued, practically in tears. "Can you imagine them at Versailles, or at Charlottenburg?"

"Yes, exactly . . ." said Jean-Baptiste vaguely, unable to hide his discomfort entirely.

This trying spectacle lasted another hour, and they were obliged to witness it several more times during their stay. Contrary to what they initially thought, it was not a gala given in honor of their arrival but a simple entertainment such as the villagers enjoyed every day.

Jean-Baptiste was actually the only one to be disagreeably affected by the spectacle. Küyük took great pleasure in these balls, as did all the other Tartars. Ignorant of the original these rituals were intended to copy, they saw nothing in them but an amusing way to have the women take a turn with their arms bare. George for his part was filled with admiration for the work the Swedes had accomplished. Visiting various workshops in the village on his own, he was constantly discovering new examples of ingenuity and reporting them to Jean-Baptiste. He claimed that Reason had been carried in triumph onto the tabula rasa of the steppes and was almost ready to say that these men had found happiness.

Every day messengers came and went through the archipelago of the camps. The reverend questioned them on their arrival. None, unfortunately, had any knowledge of Juremi's whereabouts. Finally, after three long weeks, the news they had been waiting for arrived. Magnus Koefoed announced with dismay that they could at last resume their journey.

The distance to the place where Juremi had been found was not particularly great, though with the winter's cold settling in, they might have to travel for two weeks with heavily laden horses to reach it. His village was on the fringes of the Aral Sea, directly to the east. They should only be careful not to provoke the nomad hordes, if ever they happened onto them. Aside from the Kalmuks, who had become sedentary, there were Kirghiz nomads moving through the area. They lived in hordes and roamed freely in the area between the prisoners' villages, sometimes attacking them to great effect. The travelers were not to stray from a designated path where, at long intervals, they would find other deportee camps.

On the eve of their departure, the reverend seized on some pretext to take Jean-Baptiste aside and speak to him alone. For a moment, in the deserted space between two wooden buildings, the pastor dropped his exquisite politeness to reveal his more political side.

"Forgive me," he said in a whisper. "I lumped you all together at first, and that explains why I welcomed you as formally and coldly as I did."

"Lumped us all together . . . ?"

"Yes, with that man in black, the Russian."

"Bibichev?"

"That must be the one. You put me in a tight spot asking 'Why don't you run away? Why don't you build weapons to use against the Russians?' etc. with that man standing right there. Did you think I could answer in front of him?"

"Why . . ."

"No matter. But since we are alone for a moment, let me simply say that we don't leave because the area is surrounded by agents of that stripe. If we attempted it, and this is the truth, they would call in the Cossacks immediately. By the way, where did you get this . . . Bibichev?"

"The tsar assigned him to us as a guide and dragoman."

"The tsar! I understand. Well, I don't know what you plan to do once you find your friend, but you had best beware of that Russian, believe me, and get rid of him if you can. It's never a good idea to sleep so close to an officer of the Okhrana."

22

Winter is the most beautiful of seasons in Isfahan. The sky has the purity and depth of a sapphire, polished by the soft, deft winds that sand the face and fingers of all who venture outdoors. Everything looks sharp and clear, both the near and the far, and in the pale rays of the sun colors—even those of fabrics and flesh—take on the cold brilliance of metals and gems.

It was barely two o'clock in the afternoon when Alix arrived out of breath in Nur al-Huda's room. She expected to find her ready for their walk, since they had agreed three days before to meet at that hour. But the young woman was without her jewels or makeup, and wearing a housedress of beige cotton with a simple woolen shawl over her shoulders.

"I thought I was late," said Alix in surprise, "and you haven't even started getting dressed?"

"It's no use hurrying," said Nur al-Huda in lugubrious tones, "I am penned up here on orders from that monster."

"What monster is that?"

"What a question! My dear husband, of course."

"Forgive me, Nur, but I have never known your dear husband, as you say, to have managed to forbid you anything."

"Well, he has now!" said the young woman, rising. "True enough, when it concerns only me, he can't generally impose his whims, but I'm powerless against collective measures. Today and for a full week the entire harem, eunuchs included, is confined within these walls."

"A week! How extraordinary!"

"Oh, he didn't dream up the idea himself, you can be sure. There's been a big hue and cry that will soon engulf the whole city. It's just that we, who have the privilege of sitting in the first tier, are the first to experience its disagreeable effects."

"But what's it all about?" asked Alix, who understood less and less.

"What's it all about! Lord knows I love you, Alix, but you ask very silly questions. About the disaster, that's what."

"The disaster?"

"The disaster brewing to the east. The Afghans have surrounded Kirman. The king has decided, somewhat belatedly, to send a large army against them, whose defeat would leave the country with no further defenses."

"All this is common knowledge," said Alix, somewhat provoked.

"Yes, but what is not widely known is that the battle will be decided this week. The priests and the astrologers are working full bore to see who can predict the greatest catastrophe, those who listen to God or those who read the stars, and who can conceive the severest penances. The king has therefore decided to impose public purifications: streetwalkers and dancers are to be thrown into prison, wine is to be forbidden more strictly than usual, and women of virtue are to stay in their harems for good measure. As the streetwalkers will all take shelter with their protectors and the wine barrels have very little to fear from this king, innocent women will in the end bear the brunt of these harsh measures. And as my dear husband learned of this before everyone else, he seized the opportunity to show his zeal and put us in seclusion starting today."

"Well, that's unfortunate," said Alix, starting to remove her large veil. "Let's hope it all serves some useful purpose, and in the meantime let's drink a nice cup of hot tea . . ."

"No, no," said Nur al-Huda, rushing toward her friend. "Keep your veil on. You are a foreigner and can go out. You will carry on as if I were with you."

Then in a low voice:

"And you will bring word of this latest development, along with your medicines, to the usual place."

The suggestion surprised Alix, who had grown used to her role as accomplice but had never thought to penetrate any further into the secret of her friend's meetings at the royal palace. And though their conversations were filled with playfulness and laughter, she had never dared question her friend on this subject. Nur al-Huda, who talked readily about everything and spoke of herself frankly when she wanted, had never said much about her lover.

Alix had learned his name not long before but had never spoken it. When the guard opened the palace gate in response to her knock, Alix asked with some confusion to see Reza Alibegh. She followed the soldier along a cold gallery, lit by simple windowless openings set so high on the wall that they showed nothing but sky. This entrance must have led to the rear of the barracks, allowing the officers to come and go without being seen at the main gate. The guard led Alix across two courts and up a stair-case. She had a moment's fright when he invited her to precede him down the corridor. She was supposed to have been here often and to know the way . . . She pretended to sneeze, and this slight delay kept the guard in the lead. Finally she entered a square, high-ceilinged room whose modest area was all but filled by four banquettes along the walls and a round brassware table. Reza stood waiting for her. In this narrow space, he seemed curiously smaller than he had appeared on horseback, but his head was more impressive than one might have expected from his body. Two enormous eyes the color of green water shone from his face, with eye-brows forming a precise and elegant curve above them as though cal-ligraphed in India ink.

He took the medicines she held stupidly in their package and set them on the table; with the same gesture he carried her hands to his lips to cover them with kisses. It was only at this moment, belatedly, that Alix realized with a pang of self-reproach that she was hidden under a heavy veil, and that this man had taken her for another. She removed her veil with alacrity, and Reza backed away in surprise.

In this narrow chamber, however, it was impossible to back away far or put much distance between oneself and another. His astonishment sub-sided, and he invited her to sit down and explain. She did so, taking care to hold herself as modestly as possible, though she wasn't used to keeping her eyes lowered.

"May I . . . speak?" she asked, glancing toward the door.

"As in the middle of the desert," he answered.

His voice was agreeable, not unduly deep for a Persian, and made the long vowels of his language sing.

Without giving her own name, Alix explained that she had come on behalf of Nur al-Huda and repeated all that her friend had instructed her to say.

"A week's absence," he summed up pensively.

For a moment he stayed deeply silent, his eyes unseeing. Alix was not surprised to find him saddened. After all, she brought bad news. But his expression suggested a deeper and more lasting sadness than could be explained by the present adversity.

"Are you a foreigner?" he said finally, examining Alix.

"Yes."

"Just as she is . . ."

"But not from the same country," she cut in sharply. "No, I am only
. . . her friend."

Really, she would have preferred to leave at that point, as it was
painful to witness the man's agony and be unable to relieve it.

"Did she tell you our story?" he asked after a long silence.

"No," answered Alix, and her clear and unwavering eyes told him
that she was not lying.

He waited a long moment. No sound filtered through the window of
opaque red and yellow glass. Alix ransacked her brain for a phrase that
would prepare her exit from this room and cover her flight.

"She should have," said Reza. "As long as you know our secret, you
may as well know the whole of it. I am going to tell you why we see each
other this way."

"Sir," said Alix, "I would rather—"

"I take responsibility," he interrupted, "for asking you to listen. You
are committing no indiscretion, you are simply doing a favor to a man
who stands in great need of one and who begs you to relieve him of a
secret that he cannot confide to anyone else."

Behind the evident courtesy of these words, Alix sensed a tone of
authority that did not suffer contradiction. As she was dying of curiosity
in any case, Alix capitulated with good grace.

"My family," he started, "comes from Asterabad, south of the Caspian.
It is at the far reaches of the Persian Empire, constantly attacked by raiders
and turbulent neighbors. My father was a governor of this province, as
was his father before him. Shah Abbas the Great appointed him to this
post immediately on conquering the area. I am the second son, and my
elder brother will follow in the footsteps of our forefathers if, that is, our
land remains free. Children in our country, as you may know, are less constrained by caste than in yours. They know who they are, of course. But
the son of a shoemaker can play with the son of a governor without causing any eyebrows to raise. There was a small band of us, all about eight
years old, who used to go off fishing in the spring along the great rivers
that pass the foot of our town on their way to the Caspian. We would come
in late, and sometimes not for days on end. The houses were so big that it
wasn't always noticed immediately. In the course of our explorations we
discovered a band of Circassians living in a meager, gorse-ridden field—
they claimed to be nomads but never seemed to leave this quiet spot. We
often went there to fish, not because the fishing was better there but to
hear the sound of their tambourines and their singing. Nur al-Huda was

the link between these Gypsies and us. When she wasn't dancing with them, she would come and join us in our huts. She was an unprepossessing little girl with curly hair, which was her one beautiful feature. She spoke Farsi poorly and was not yet known by her present name. We called her Ozan, which means "red." I've never known why, because she didn't have red hair. Maybe because she was as quick and darting as a fire? or that she singed the hearts of those around her like a flame?"

Alix didn't move, for fear of breaking the thread of these confidences.

"We were always fighting amongst ourselves and I was a rough-and-tumble little leader. I already wanted to become a soldier, and at night walking back to town, we would talk about battles and armies. Everyone would say why they wanted to fight: for their country, or their family, or to conquer kingdoms, or acquire riches, or glory, and I would invent something, but I always knew that what I would fight for was Ozan. Childhood memories are always a little silly. You shouldn't judge too severely on that basis. And this is a memory that has only come back to me recently.

"The Bohemians left before the third winter," he continued. "Ozan never warned us. They were gone without a trace. Snow fell that January and painted over the past in white. I forgot. I grew up."

Holding the package of medicines between the tips of his long fingers, he had turned it over and over before finally opening it. Now he played with the small packets of powder.

"I saw her again four years ago in Tehran. It was she who recognized me, probably because someone told her my name. She was a dancer. You know how powerful these women are in our country and how odious their reputation is. She came to see me, citing some memories we had in common. She called herself Nur al-Huda. As these courtesans customarily go unveiled, her beauty shone on me full force, and was all the more troubling for being mixed in my memory with the child I had been drawn to long ago. I fell in love with her, more deeply than I had ever been in love before. I was delirious. Crazy. I thought of nothing but of being with her, although it hurt me to see her and hurt me to be away from her. Anyway, I won't describe all this to you, as you've surely been in love . . ."

Alix lowered her eyes, flustered.

"Forgive me," he said, suddenly noticing her dark veil. "Have you recently been widowed?"

"Yes," she answered, instantly regretting that she had lied with so little hesitation.

He remained silent for a respectful moment, then continued:

"I'll finish, because the story is very simple. Two years before, my father had married me to the daughter of the director of the mint, who is a considerable figure in our part of the world. I cannot repudiate my wife. And neither my family nor hers would accept a second marriage to a dancer."

"I believe," said Alix cautiously, "that Persian law allows a number of accommodations in these cases . . ."

"Ah! You say that only because you know very little about Ozan, your Nur. She has never wanted anything of the kind. She is brutally jealous and rejects any notion of a shared marriage. The subject soon became the source of violent, almost daily quarrels, and caused a horrible misunderstanding. I came to believe that she was more interested in my wealth and title than in myself. And she kept accusing me of not considering her my social equal. That's how she conceived the plan of marrying the despicable Hutfi Ali Khan. In our country, a disparity in age between husband and wife mitigates any disparity in station, and for all that he was prime minister, he could marry her without a scandal. She thus proved that she could attain to fortune without me, and that she deserved to become a great lady as much as anyone else."

Poor Reza finished his story on the verge of tears. It's unfair, thought Alix, but sadness is infinitely more affecting when it's attached to beauty. She felt sincerely sorry for the man.

"And now?" she said.

"Well, each time she has managed to come here, thanks to your help—for I take you to be the accomplice she has spoken of—she has heard me say that I love her and has responded in the same words, to which I can't object. But she says that she will follow me anywhere on condition that I give up all my attachments."

At these words he raised his large, grief-swollen eyes toward Alix, before going on with difficulty:

"The king has put me in command of his personal guard. My country is under threat, and I may be called on to fight at any moment. Ozan asks me to forget all this, to say nothing of my family and responsibilities. But where would we go? If I were to do it, I would be pursued with such hatred and thirst for vengeance, the king's to start with, that we would have to go to the far ends of the earth to escape. Oh! why won't she understand? Madam, I beg you, tell her to respect my suffering and not ask for the impossible."

An hour had passed. The time normally allotted for these meetings was coming to a close, and the young man clearly had duties to perform, as he formulated his last few words hurriedly.

"She won't visit for another week? That's terrible news—though I'd like to think it could be a relief. At least in the coming week, she won't be lighting fires that our hand-holding can't put out—for she never consents to any fuller display of our feelings. But though I say that, I know in fact that it will be painful and that waiting will be an agony."

Having spoken these words, Reza seemed for a moment to contemplate an inner image, then he turned his eyes toward Alix. His gaze was so intense, so eager, so hungry from the deprivations of unhappiness, that she was moved.

"Thank you for listening to me," he said, taking her hand and looking steadily at her.

"You have done me much good," he added.

And though she sensed he might have been willing to prolong the moment, he bowed and withdrew. He hadn't asked her name. She found his tact in this instance irreproachable, while at the same time tasting a slightly bitter tang of regret.

During the evening that Alix spent at home immediately afterward, the image of this noble and unhappy young man stayed with her. She felt no trace of reproach toward Nur al-Huda: she understood her. Yet she couldn't help blaming her just a little. Far into the night, she came across a sentence that summed it all up and made her laugh: "Whenever a woman encounters a man who is both handsome and unhappy, she inevitably thinks, At least I would have loved him better." The next moment, she fell deeply into a dream.

23

Monsieur de Maillet sighed deeply as the money changer placed the last gold coin on the last pile of his last reserve of money. Through two large windows giving onto the Sacchetti Palace and the reddish waters of the Tiber, a pale sun shone down on the three little stacks of coins lined up on the dark leather of the desk. The money came from the sale of his last property, a plot of land that had once been his wife's. A neighboring farmer had bought it, moaning and groaning, at half price. Then the couriers, notaries, and bankers had taken their regal share. What remained were the thousand écus that had so resonated in the poor old man's mind these past weeks, the same thousand écus that were now stacked in miserable piles of worn coins before him.

The consul stuffed his savings into a little cloth pouch with a long drawstring and tied it around his neck. This way he could feel the gold against his heart, which they would have to stab to take his treasure away.

He walked down the two flights of marble stairs holding tightly to the banister. Before going into the street, he called over a boy who was playing in the courtyard with a cat. Promising him a copper, the consul asked him to look for any suspicious characters who might be lurking in the street. The boy brought back a reassuring report, and he went out.

In point of fact, the consul was in an extremely precarious position, and the sight of the gold had done nothing to quiet his fears. In the heat of his benevolence, Cardinal Alberoni, O sainted man—Monsieur de Maillet never said the cardinal's name without signing himself and blessing the man's charity—had overlooked one small detail: the former diplomat whose spiritual interests he would be protecting had, materially speaking, not a penny with which to undertake the voyage to Persia.

Monsieur de Maillet had momentarily thought of drawing the prelate's attention to this point before leaving him. But right until he stood outside the cardinal's office, the great man had discussed lofty topics, large-scale projects, one might almost say matters of state. The consul, lost in admiration, would have committed a breach of taste by introducing the specter of his poverty into so distinguished a conclave.

The streets were fairly empty, the Romans mostly staying home at noon on a winter's day. The consul looked over his shoulder several times, turned back on his tracks, changed sidewalks suddenly: no one was following him.

It was all very clear, he had turned the problem over in his mind enough to know. The possibilities came down to two: either he paid Mazucchetti the thousand écus he had promised him for interceding with the cardinal—in which case he would never go to Persia and would lose his last chance of salvation in this world and the next; or he kept the money for himself, set off down the road, and fled—running the risk of being murdered by the crook Mazucchetti.

Who could have imagined that a man of his eminence would one day be reduced to so sordid a pass? Monsieur de Maillet sighed. Only the prospect of committing a sin distressed him, as his decision was already made. He was determined to keep the thousand écus and do the cardinal's bidding whatever the consequences. After all, this Mazucchetti had been sucking his blood for several months without producing any results and had eaten his fill of the consul's fortune: he had been paid. The consul's only mistake had been to promise him more, which was why today he found himself countenancing a lie; but fortunately there was confession to absolve him.

Since the interview with the cardinal, Mazucchetti had been coming by every day to claim his due. Every day the consul led him to hope that the moneys would arrive the following day, while enduring ever more violent threats. When faced with force, to what else does one turn but cunning? Monsieur de Maillet had hatched a plan that he believed to be extremely clever: every morning he went punctually to his money changer's and returned empty-handed. That way, the day he came into his treasure would seem a day like any other. He himself knew not, as the Gospel says, either the day or the hour. He kept his clothes ready in a bag; when the time came, he would only have to grab them and take discreetly to the open road. The only problem was the hirsute Paolo in his cubby. To keep him from seeing the bag, the consul would have to leave at night when the landlord went to lap up his stinking soup in the kitchen at the back of the hotel.

The great day was at hand. Excited at feeling the thousand écus over his heart, though less so than he had expected when rehearsing his part beforehand, the consul proceeded with his plan. He made long detours through back alleys in the direction of Trajan's Column and the Coliseum, as was his custom. His rheumatism made these walks somewhat painful, and he was not a person to draw relief from the sight of beautiful monuments. Besides, his eyesight was dim, and he could hardly see them. Fortunately this was Rome, and in walking over the toppled stones at Caesar's Forum or Octavia's Gate, he was penetrated by the city's moral sternness. The great stoic consolation of the Latin tradition cast an armor of bronze around him. The example of Marcus Aurelius helped him bear the thought of Mazucchetti.

He then went to sit in a café near the Montecitorio Palace, where he watched the chess players. He was careful not to order more than usual, so that no one in the disreputable den—if any informants were about—could report his newfound prosperity to his persecutor.

Around five o'clock, he hobbled back to the Laughing Bull. To the west, nightfall had thrown a purple stole over the Vatican's shoulders. The hotel entrance was deserted except for Paolo slumped at his desk. The consul nodded amiably at his landlord as he did every day. But what happened? Did he seem in too great a hurry? or too relaxed? or too confident? Or was it simply that such brutes could smell money? In any case, Paolo's glance was a little too bright. Without a word having been said, the consul understood as he mounted the stairs that the jig was up.

He walked to the fourth floor, saw no one in the hallway, and closed the door behind him, shooting home the bolt, which suddenly looked frail. What should he do? Paolo was not rotten enough to run and denounce him. He would wait until Mazucchetti came, then tell him everything. How much time did that give him? Very little, probably. The consul sat on his bed, his old heart beating so hard that the gold coins vibrated on his chest. And he had always been a man of action! Ah! Saints above! To be in such a fix! Overcome at the thought of being under attack with no hope of rescue, he gave in to utter panic. He tugged on his bed, pushed it, puffing like an ox, and butted the iron bedstead against the door. Anything rather than to see that wretch again! In one corner was a small empty dresser: he tipped it onto the mattress to give the thing more weight. There were still a flimsy table and a chair by the window; he wedged these against the foot of the bed—the pile of furniture was now buttressed against the wall facing the door and made a reasonable obstacle. The old man sat down, panting, on a corner of the mattress and would almost have felt a sense of calm if at that very moment he had not heard rapid steps in

the stairway, then in the hall. It was he, right there behind the door!
Beating on it with his cane.

"Am I disturbing you?" bawled Mazucchetti.

The handle turned and the lock offered an eloquent but ephemeral
resistance.

All is lost! thought the consul darkly. The Lord is my witness that I
tried everything. O God, if your mercy is as great as I believe, you will
receive me among the just!

He rose and glided like a sleepwalker toward the window.

Mazucchetti had gotten past the lock, and the door opened a crack
before butting against the stacked furniture.

"Resistance is useless, Maillet! No one is going to come to your help
here," shouted the assassin, and a knife gleamed through the opening of
the door. "Come on, open up! All right, I'll break the door down."

He took a few steps backward for a run at the door. During the pause,
the consul opened the window and straddled the sill. The Roman winter
night, clear and cold, with a tremor of chimes and sighing breezes, offered
his nearsighted eyes a last vision of blueness and purity.

"Justice" he cried, clasping the bundle in which his dear and innocent
Telliamed nestled.

And he jumped.

Fyodor Nicolaievich Bibichev would have liked to become a priest. At
seventeen, however, finding himself an orphan and alone, he had taken up
with a pauper girl who had given him eight children. The service of heav-
en in the Orthodox religion requires long years of study and does not feed
a family well: he entered the police instead. So as not to go against his
vocation, he had been assigned to keep watch over the clergy. He assidu-
ously attended service in a number of churches, where he tidied, cleaned,
and sometimes even helped celebrate the holy office.

Probably from his observations of himself, Bibichev was profoundly
convinced of man's imperfection. His deference to rank was equaled
only by his harshness toward individuals. Here, according to him, was
the true function of the police: to defend institutions against the men
charged with embodying them; to save the mechanism by keeping the
gear wheels under surveillance so as to quickly change any that proved
defective.

Thanks to his philosophy, he had no qualms about making denunciations. He served two vocations at once, giving praise both to God and to the tsar, purifying both the church and the state of their human failings.

His zeal led to his rapid promotion. He was sufficiently versed in theology to become an Orthodox priest. But to answer the needs of the moment, he was instead given a false diplomatic title and sent to spy on the Vatican. He returned two years later. Since then the Okhrana had assigned him to special missions of a diplomatic or religious character. He was dispatched to the tsar's entourage on the Caspian to learn the thinking of the clergy in those parts. It would never do, when the Russian army entered Persia, for troubles to erupt at its rear.

A few weeks earlier, a dispatch from Isfahan had alerted the Russian agencies to a conspiracy involving the famous Alberoni. Bibichev knew from his travels how dangerous the man was, and he had happened to be in the tsar's entourage when the individuals signaled in the dispatch tried to make contact with the court. It was due to this unfortunate coincidence that he had been assigned to watch over these persons.

He had hoped to return to Moscow to spend Christmas with his numerous family, but he was stuck here on a complex and dangerous matter of state, one whose mystery was far from resolved.

Bibichev saw no end to the failings of those who had the gall to claim that they served God, or country, or the general good. Yet he was always ready to attribute great powers to men whenever they turned to the service of evil. Hence he had immediately recognized these suspicious characters as having awesome powers, almost to the point of genius.

The first of these powers was for dissembling. Despite his long acquaintance with ecclesiastic circles, Bibichev could truly say that he had never met such singular personages: that handsome devil of an apothecary, always in a good mood, smiling like a donkey, elegant in nothing but a handful of rags, who had the brass to claim that he could cure people with his tinctures . . . And then the boy, his son. His son! As though a giraffe could point to a beaver and say in all seriousness: "my son." And to cap it all, that Mongol—a man so mysterious and formidable that Bibichev had not even managed to find out his true religion.

By all the tsars! Even in defeat, Alberoni showed that his talents were undiminished: to dig up such specimens as these to enact his plans, that was the hand of a master!

And then there was the plan itself. What audacity! Choosing Persia was the first stroke of genius. To come back from the direction least expected of him, that took some imagining. And now the conspirators were confounding all predictions by heading toward Central Asia when the obvious step would have been going toward Europe.

Bibichev had been taken totally unawares by this new turn. He had no experience of the desert, and even less of the desert in the cold season. Who would have ever thought that a Vatican specialist would be heading east across the steppes? Yet that's what it had come to, and the contents of his court baggage were not up to the task. His boots were soaked and the right one split along the side. His black suit, sticky inside from sweat, was plastered on the outside from the muddy rains, and the whole was starting to freeze as a unit. He had finally been obliged to accept help from the tailor to whom the Reverend Koefoed had kindly introduced him.

The skillful Swede had fashioned a pair of breeches of gray squirrel on the same simple, comfortable model as the trousers worn by the Gauls during their triumphant advance on Alesia. On top of this, and despite his initial refusal, Bibichev was forced to wear the innovation that the tailor was most proud of: a short quilted sheepskin coat decorated on the outside with otter tails. At rest, the thing looked like a normal fur, but as soon as Bibichev made the slightest movement, the appendages flopped and fluttered, giving the policeman the frightening aspect of a centipede.

He spent the two first stages of their journey tearing the tails off discreetly one by one and throwing them into ditches. Soon he had none left except on his back. He now looked like a porcupine, but this was less disturbing to him.

Every evening, Bibichev wrote out a short memorandum on the actions of the suspects. The Okhrana had intermediaries across all of Russia's territory. Even the camps of the Swedish deportees had been infiltrated by Okhrana agents, whom Bibichev knew by the signs he had learned at the most secret police schools. He gave them his dispatches, which they rapidly sent on their way.

Thanks to this zealous agent's regular reports, Moscow was able to follow—with some perplexity—his slow progress over the steppes.

After leaving Reverend Koefoed's village, the little band of riders had met with two heavy snowstorms, then been slowed by an uneven terrain from which all tracks had been erased. Despite every effort to break down the suspects' guard through what the manuals called "the camaraderie of travel," Bibichev had never been able to catch them out. The one of the company who seemed weakest, Poncet's pretended son, had held endless conversations with the agent in which he discoursed on and on with disarming naiveté about his faith in progress and the sciences. But he had never once pronounced Alberoni's name or referred to him even indirectly. This showed truly admirable strength!

Finally, just before the Catholic Christmas, they reached the camp where the man whom the foreigners claimed to be looking for was detained.

The following dispatch took almost three weeks to reach Moscow:

This afternoon reached pioneer village of G. Deposited our luggage as usual in guest room near the church. A Swedish reverend informed us that the suspect was five hundred meters outside the village. We found him behind a frozen dune, on a trampled area that serves as a playfield. He was teaching a group of eight young Swedes to fence (indoctrination? recruitment?).

He is a tall man, corpulent, his hair and beard curly and gray, his eyes black. His face is deeply wrinkled. His energy is unabated. When we first saw him, he was fencing in the air alone, shouting in several languages (Italian, most certainly; Arabic, probably; and French, which seems to be his native language). The Swedes were smiling (but we know that this people always wear that expression, even in prison).

Suspect Ponc—took his so-called son by the hand, and at first they simply looked at this scene from a distance (precaution? signal? uncertainty as to identification?). Then he called out to suspect Jur— in a loud voice. The latter did not hear him. Ponc—repeated his call. Your agent was then witness to the following scene. First, suspect Jur—heard the call and fell silent. He had unmistakably recognized the voice. After a long moment he went into a violent tantrum. He broke his sword over his knee and threw the pieces away with great force. He started jumping up and down, tearing off his clothes, and shaking his fist at the sky. The wind carried off some of his words. He was saying: "I didn't want it" (repeated several times); "I asked you not to send them" (to an invisible interlocutor in the sky above); "All this is my fault" and also "I'm just an old codger." The suspect spent all his strength in this outburst. He finally fell to his knees in the snow. Tears were running down his face.

These gestures convinced your agent that there is grave dissension among the members of the group. But the faction represented by Poncet seems to have won the day. The latter suspect advanced. He knelt in front of Jur—. They fell into each other's arms and cried, clasped closely together, each with his head on the other's shoulder. Everyone watching this scene cried, including the Swedes.

The most startling thing was that everyone came back to the village laughing loudly. Suspect Jur—seemed highly interested in getting to know Ponc—'s so-called son, whom he had apparently never met before (different cells? sham? replacement of personnel?). As I write this report, they are all in the performance hall. As in every village, we will have to sit through a ballet put on by the Swedes and their Kalmuk mates. The suspects have resigned themselves to it with good grace tonight. They have already drunk a bottle of aquavit presented to them by the reverend. I imagine things will come to a head in the next few days. Your agent is listening to conversations more carefully than ever. He will keep you apprised of any developments.

Signed: B.

P.S. Kindly transmit to my wife and our children their father's Christmas greeting. He is fine.

24

"*Kiss me,* Lorenzo!"

That night, Marcellina looked more beautiful than ever. For two whole days she had had her hair—the thick tresses of a brown-eyed blond—combed and braided. Her complexly woven coiffure gave her the geometric and sensuous purity of the Roman beauties of the Renaissance.

They were now standing near the damasked drapes that framed the windows. In the distance the Vatican raised its broken outline against the dark of earth and sky. The room's mirrors, interrupted by the dark piers framing them, echoed the clear melody of the silver chandeliers.

"Are you really leaving?" whispered Marcellina as her soft lips parted from those of her lover.

"Really," he said.

"Tomorrow?"

"Tomorrow."

She held his eyes in her dark gaze, then gently placed her hand on the collar of his blue outfit. It was impossible to imagine greater refinement, or greater elegance, than this young man possessed. True, he might not be handsome exactly, but he was infinitely charming.

"Imagine falling in love with a soldier!" she said, laughing.

"The idea!"

They both laughed, all the more readily in that each knew the other to be unfaithful yet loved the other still. A summer of festivities had brought them together. Rome had afforded them the highest pleasures. Marcellina, the daughter of a family of rich bankers, found herself alone in the world when, the previous year, her parents and all her brothers died in an epidemic. She had kept this palace for herself. Nothing so disposes one to make joyful use of a house as to have received it through a tragedy. The gaiety of this Roman summer had given Marcellina the sense that winter would never plague her again. Yet Lorenzo was going to leave.

"Our last night . . . " she said in a voice of sweet regret, on the point of leading her lover off by the hand.

Suddenly, a thud shook the room and the crystal pendants of the large chandelier tinkled. The two froze and silently strained their ears: nothing.

"What an astonishing city!" said Lorenzo dreamily. "Here it is December, and yet there are still people crazy enough to be setting off fireworks."

He pulled Marcellina toward him. They intertwined and stood there, breast to breast, rocking gently to a melody that only they could hear.

Suddenly Lorenzo felt his mistress stifle a cry and slump in his arms. Distressed, the young man supported the unconscious woman, looking around him desperately.

It was at this point that a man's voice—hoarse, powerful, and lugubrious—resounded at his back.

"Justice!" it cried.

The young soldier turned, still holding his tender burden, filled with a terror more acute than he would have felt under fire.

A figure stood framed in the dark doorway. The stranger held a package tightly in his arms. The torch in the foyer lit him from behind, ringing his head with a halo of spiky hair.

The apparition lasted no more than a second. The man repeated, though more softly: "Justice!"

Then the ghost advanced a few limping steps into the room. Under the light of the candles he resolved into a tattered old man who went and sat down at the table where the remains of a delicate meal still gleamed.

Lorenzo regained his self-possession and set Marcellina gently down on the other chair. She was recovering consciousness, and the young man, in deference to his charming audience, straightened his collar. In martial tones he asked the rumpled old man what he was doing in this house.

"I am the French consul," said Monsieur de Maillet, waving placatingly at his hosts. "That is, I was. But none of this is of any great importance. I ask for justice, that's all."

"Sir," said Marcellina, who had recovered from her fright and was angry at this beggar for interrupting her happiness. "Will you kindly tell me how you entered my house?"

"Would that I knew it myself!" said Monsieur de Maillet, shrugging his shoulders.

He gave a great sigh of weariness.

"I wanted to die, madam. Is there anyone in this city who is capable of respecting an old man's pain?"

The old man was so pitiful, really, that Marcellina grew calm.

"At least tell us the way you came," she said gently. "Where did you start from, first?"

"From that accursed hotel with the ridiculous name, 'The Laughing Bull.' "

"It's a hideous rooming house on Bear Street, behind us," said Marcellina, looking toward her lover.

"I was trying to escape from a thug who was intent on robbing me," went on Monsieur de Maillet as though speaking to himself.

At these words, he probed his shirtfront in the region of his heart and seemed relieved.

"A thug! Yes! I preferred to die. Ah! you are young. Life smiles on you. God grant that you never find yourself in a similar situation: jumping out the window to rescue one's honor, at the cost of one's life."

"You jumped out the window?" cried Marcellina.

"Exactly!"

"And you didn't die?"

"Believe me, madam, I regret it keenly," said the consul with dignity. "I did my best. How was I to know that there was a terrace below the window of my room?"

"Did you never look out your window?" asked Marcellina in surprise.

"Yes, madam, but always toward the sky!" answered the consul, joining his hands together.

He paused, then went on:

"At any rate, this is how things stand: there was a terrace in the path of my fall, two stories down . . ."

"Two stories!" exclaimed Lorenzo.

". . . And a servant girl, or at least I suppose it was one, had scattered laundry, wicker hampers, and other items of the sort to keep me from accomplishing my purpose."

"You fell on hampers?" asked Marcellina, and the two youths exploded, at those words, into laughter.

Monsieur de Maillet shrugged.

"And from the terrace . . . to here?" asked the young girl, repressing her hilarity with difficulty.

"I tried to trick death, madam, that is the truth and the cause of my punishment. Instead of stepping over the terrace and having done with it,

I was afraid. Yes, I admit it. I had struck the small of my back against those hampers and found it very painful. I had set out to die, you understand, not to get knocked about."

"And then?"

"And then I saw a gable on the next house over, with the roof sloping away on either side just like in my own country."

"That is my house!" said Marcellina. "It was built by my grandfather, who admired the Fuggers and traveled to Flanders . . ."

"I grabbed a ladder that was lying on the terrace, and without letting go of my precious *Telliamed* . . ."

The two youths looked puzzled. Monsieur de Maillet tapped his package.

"A book, madam, but no matter. Without letting go of my luggage, as I said, I climbed up to the roof ridge and crawled along it astraddle to the middle. Then I chose a side, the left—in the direction of the setting sun and our very Holy Father."

"The cold frame!" cried Marcellina. "You know, Lorenzo, the cold frame that broke during the last hailstorm . . . I forgot to replace it and now water comes into the attic room. Poor man!" she said to Monsieur de Maillet, "you did just what the rain does. You slid down the roof and fell . . . into my attic."

Highly amused by this story, the two young people offered the unhappy old man something to eat and drink. The fatigues of the day, the emotional tension, and also perhaps the wine made the Frenchman doze off, and they laid him out gently on a banquette.

Then, resuming the gesture that had been interrupted when this meteor landed in their midst, Marcellina dragged her lover into the bedroom. Lorenzo found the interlude so funny that he half suspected his mischievous mistress of having organized it on purpose. She denied it laughingly. But whether the design was hers or belonged to divine providence, the presence of a man, albeit an elderly one, in the adjoining room gave added impetus and spice to their lovemaking.

They rose at eleven o'clock the next morning, prodded by a strong sun that forced its way above and below the drawn bedroom curtains. The consul stood waiting for them, his hair combed and his clothes brushed, before the windows of the drawing room.

"So, dear guest," said Marcellina, laughing, looking even more resplendent by day than she had by night, "do you still want to jump out the window?"

"No, madam," answered the consul gravely, "but I am going to set off for Persia."

The two young people thought him completely mad but only liked him the better for it. It was thus that at two in the afternoon, under a pale sky etched with long white clouds, a comfortable cabriolet left Rome in the direction of Naples. Its passengers were a young man, his body half out the window, blowing kisses to his rapidly receding mistress, and an elderly man, who stayed prudently in the shadows—as befits the dignity of a cardinal's emissary.

"Sacrebleu! but it's good to speak one's mother tongue," exclaimed Juremi.

He was walking, flanked by Jean-Baptiste and George, their heads aching from the long night of emptying bottles and discussing their lives. The village was already far behind them. A white sun shone low on the horizon in a sky made vitreous by the wind.

"Boil my boots if there aren't days when a word comes into my head and I find myself saying to it: 'What are you, anyway? A Turkish verb? an Arab city? some bit of French?' Sometimes it's a piece of the flotsam that drifts by here like old boards around a port: Mongol? or Russian? or Chinese? or who knows what? People manage by cobbling all of it together the way the Swedes do with their old furs. And speaking of furs, Jean-Baptiste, is that cur whose snout I don't much care for going to follow us around like this all the time?"

Bibichev jogged along ten yards behind them, his back still riddled with his black otter's tails. In the cold, they had stiffened and stuck out horizontally like so many daggers planted in him from behind by a band of cowards. He bobbed along trying to catch up with the conversing friends, whose words he could no longer hear.

"I'm afraid so. He's a spy in the service of the tsar," said Jean-Baptiste.

"A spy?" cried Juremi, who kept the pace up as protection against the straggler. "And what is he spying on?"

"I don't know. Us . . . you!"

"Lately he has asked me a lot of questions about religion," said George.

"So that's it!" said Juremi. "They're suspicious of Protestants here too. There isn't a place on earth, even in the depths of this forsaken backwater, where they'll let us live our lives in peace!"

"That's possible, but why should he be particularly interested in you?" asked Jean-Baptiste, puzzled. "The Swedes are Protestants too, whereas George and I, whom he's been following up till now, are not."

"Yes, it's odd," said the old giant, scratching his stiff beard, which was hung with small bright icicles. "But if there's one thing I've learned about the Russians it's that there's no point in trying to understand what they're doing. They landed in these steppes directly off the moon. The tsar can order them to cut their hair, shave off their beards, and scrape every last hair from their bodies, but he'll never turn them into people like us."

Bibichev had finally caught up with them: they felt the steam he puffed warming the backs of their necks.

"A beautiful country, truly," said Juremi loudly, "and one that I will miss. Do you know, my friends, that I found something absolutely extraordinary here? The desert. Yes, a desert that looks nothing like those sand-filled ovens of Africa, which you can cross so quickly on a camel. No, here it's a desert with vegetation, an endless moor."

"Damn me if you haven't become a poet," said Jean-Baptiste.

"Maybe I have! In any case, I went walking every day in those solitary wastes. Every day without exception. People will tell you that it's danger-ous, isn't that so, Mr. . . . —by the way, what is your name?"

"Bibichev," muttered the spy, toward whom Juremi had turned.

"Well, it's false, Mr. Bibichev, entirely false. It's a good idea to observe certain precautions, that's true. But the nomads you meet are for the most part friendly. Bands of raiders roam these parts from time to time, but if you take care to avoid them, you have nothing to fear from the others. They are even quite hospitable and would gladly give you everything they own. Ah! nomads! these are people who really speak to my heart. Nothing is solidified about them the way it is with us sedentary people. Even their gods aren't frozen in place. They don't shut them up in churches but let them run with the wind and the clouds and the snow. It's no coincidence that from time to time this cauldron boils over and spews a hallucinatory horde to the far ends of the earth—the Genghis Khans, the Tamerlanes, the Baburs, and the Huns have all come from here . . . By the way, where is our Mongol?"

"Küyük?" said Jean-Baptiste, laughing. "I have the impression he found a soul mate in your village."

"Good for him, then."

While they were talking, they had covered a good deal of ground. The camp was no longer in sight, hidden by a fold of the landscape. The cold desert sparkled all around them, extending flat to the horizon, which seemed farther away than anywhere else in the world.

"Look," said Juremi, who had spread his arms wide and was revolving in a circle, "you're at the center of the world, in the workshop where gods are born, where man fashions them himself for his own use . . ."

An enormous cloud, tapering into a claw, was tracing a mysterious rune onto the first page of the book of heaven.

Embracing the whole horizon, Juremi finally stumbled on Bibichev. At the sight of this creature, who, from the back at any rate, had not completely detached himself from the animal realm, Juremi returned to earth.

They resumed their march in silence. A little farther, gaining height at the crest of a slow undulation on the steppe, they saw a surprising irregularity in the distance.

"Do you know what that mountain is?" Juremi asked his two companions.

They had no idea.

"A tomb," he told them. "A gigantic earth tomb, as big as a hill in our part of the world. The ancient inhabitants of the steppe built it to bury their king or some other great figure. All around it are standing stones, somewhat like our menhirs. The natives call these mountains *kurgans* and think they contain their ancestors, who are of course sacred."

Shading their eyes, Jean-Baptiste and George examined the strange earthen monument that rose above the green line of the horizon.

"How did they ever build such things?" asked George.

"'How'!" Juremi repeated in severe tones. "Now there's a question for this age of prigs. At your age, my boy, I would have asked 'Why?' The rest means nothing."

"All the same," said the young man, upset, "the technical ability—"

"What technical ability? Do you think the Scythians had no skill with their hands? Look."

The Protestant pulled a bright object from his pocket, which he lifted toward the sky between his thumb and forefinger. It was a gold jewel in the shape of a buckle, extraordinary in its purity, whose spare and elegant curves represented a stylized animal folded in on itself.

"Gold!" cried George.

"Yes, gold. The purest gold. And worked with more skill than our best jewelers have. Yet there is something there that has nothing to do with technique. It's beautiful, do you see? It's inspired. It has in it a morsel of that immaterial substance, human genius, which allows a man to create things greater than himself."

Juremi made the jewel shine for a few moments, then put it back in his pocket.

"The tombs are full of them," he added. "Unfortunately, wretches come to loot them every spring. Most are poor Russian peasants. Whole bands of them go there with picks and shovels, they dig any old place and stuff whatever they find in their haversacks. Then they run back to their villages and melt everything down into ingots over big bonfires that they light in their forests. The nomads are extremely cruel with them if they ever catch them. They're convinced that the desecrations of the grave robbers disturb the spirits of the steppe and set off disasters. The looters captured by them are never seen again."

"So these barrows are now empty?" asked Jean-Baptiste thoughtfully, eyeing the distant kurgan.

"Not entirely," said Juremi. "The peasants are poorly equipped. They only scratch the surface. But the great funerary chambers are at the center of the tumulus and often stay intact. They are apparently pure marvels."

"But who's to know," George objected, "since no one can get into them?"

They had started walking back toward the village, as the sun was almost touching the horizon. Bibichev had gone off to answer the call of nature. It took him several minutes to make up the lost ground.

"I've met a Scotsman," said Juremi softly in the spy's absence, "an old campaigner like myself, who was taken prisoner in Poland almost ten years ago. He was brought to a camp farther north but escaped and now lives entirely like a primitive. I came to know him on my walks. It's the same thing everywhere: a man has some disease that tracks him to his lair, even when the whole world has lost him from view. I took care of him, and he was grateful. Now he tells me his secrets."

Jean-Baptiste and George turned and looked out over the steppe. It was hard to believe that anyone could survive in those solitary wastes.

"He's the one man who knows those burial mounds like the back of his hand," went on Juremi. "Of course, he traffics, but he doesn't loot the mounds. In any case, he knows what he's doing. When he finds an intact grave, he removes the most remarkable jewels without disturbing anything. Then he closes the opening through which he entered and carefully removes any trace of his passage."

"And what does he do with these treasures?" asked George.

"He passes them along to a network that includes the Swedes and ends, apparently, in Holland, where the great collectors are."

"He must be extraordinarily rich, out there in his cabin," said Jean-Baptiste.

"I think he sells the jewels for a tenth of the value of their weight in gold."

"Why does he do that?" asked George somewhat hesitantly, as he was now afraid of the giant's reactions.

"Because he likes his life, that's all. And then he's convinced that in sending the jewels away he's actually saving them. Maybe he's just crazy. In any case, if you hadn't arrived I was planning to accompany him next week on one of his explorations. Apparently he has discovered a new royal tomb, an extremely beautiful one, and still has several rooms to visit."

"Well?" cried George, "let's go!"

"Yes," said Jean-Baptiste, "why not?"

"Well, of all the . . . " said the Protestant, shaking his head. "I thought you were in a hurry to get back to Isfahan. I wouldn't want—"

"How long will it take?" asked Jean-Baptiste.

"Less than a week, maybe, if I let him know tonight."

"Count us in!" said Jean-Baptiste, and the three slapped each other's hands noisily to seal the bargain.

Bibichev caught up with them in the middle of this joyful outburst. He looked at them crossly, furious at having missed something of possible importance.

On the way back, he arranged to walk in the rear with George, saying he needed a steadying hand as his game leg was acting up. He plied George with skillful questions, and the young man, full of enthusiasm, discoursed freely on kurgans, gold, and a certain Scotsman. Without revealing the plan in full, he left the able spy in little doubt as to its main elements.

It took Bibichev more than an hour to compose his dispatch that night. It ended as follows:

Suspects have made contact with a Protestant in the service of Sweden and a possible Stuartist Scot. Removal of a treasure belonging to the soil of our motherland planned. Plot is taking shape. Its goal is finally clear: to procure funds. Suspects avoid mentioning it, but the hand of Alb— is perfectly visible in this contrivance

25

Certain men, born on the margins of the human community, are never entirely convinced that they belong to it. Such was Malcolm Halquist. Providence had tossed him into the world one angry day on the island of Foula. This tiny canoe of land, escaped from the Shetland Archipelago, tries in vain to counter the always adverse currents and rejoin the flagship of the British Isles.

Halquist's life as a mercenary with one or another fleet of war had been nothing but a long series of falsehoods. He had returned to truth when the Russians captured him. His Siberian exile had restored him to his place: on the fringes of the human race, alone in the middle of a sinister ocean of land.

Juremi went to visit him in his lair to see if he would allow the two others to follow them into the tombs. The Protestant guaranteed their loyalty and gave a glowing description of Jean-Baptiste and George. Halquist listened without moving an eyelash, like a stalking predator. After a long period of immobility, the Scot rose and unhooked a flintlock from the log wall of his cabin. In silence he began greasing its hammer.

"All right," he said finally. "But I'll carry the only gun. And if anyone should take a fancy to touch the gold . . ."

He pressed the trigger and the flint hit the striker sharply. Luckily there was neither primer nor load, but the message was clear.

"We leave tomorrow night, before dawn," he concluded.

Once back in the camp, the three had to prepare the way for their upcoming absence. Jean-Baptiste explained to Küyük as best he could that he and his friends were taking a small trip into the steppes and would be unable to bring him. It would be useless, even dangerous, to alert anyone to their brief disappearance. The shaman looked at Jean-Baptiste with a strange expression, showing his concern, along with what was probably disapproval.

The Mongol had changed a great deal since their arrival. This was perhaps due to the influence of his Kalmuk companion, with whom he found joyous solace—yet without unduly riling the Swede she was married to. Juremi looked at this ménage à trois with misty eyes and pointed out that Protestants might not give freely, but they knew how to share. Küyük's fame as a shaman brought him more and more clients. He kept open house in the morning after chapel, where he attended service as dutifully as everyone else. None of the Tartars who consulted him seemed to find any incompatibility between worshiping Jesus Christ and appealing to the spirits of the steppe. Despite his easy circumstances, Küyük would have left everything to follow his friends if he had thought they ran any great risk without him. But he preferred to go on quietly about his affairs, business and otherwise.

Küyük knew that Jean-Baptiste was going to be with Halquist, who distrusted Mongols. He didn't insist on coming with them and was reassured to know that his friends would be in the company of a man who knew the steppes like a native. The Mongol wished his companions good luck. That night, though, he took his leave of them with a little more solemnity than usual, as if, among the hypotheses he entertained, the thought of never seeing them again was not the weakest.

Bibichev was extremely easy to convince. He swallowed a fairly crude fabrication about hunting martens without putting up much resistance. Jean-Baptiste pretended to have rented a sled in a neighboring village, one that, to his great regret, carried only three people . . .

The Russian had seen enough of the apothecary, his son, and the Protestant to know that they lacked any interest in hunting, or any use for martens if perchance they should catch one. It took a great store of indulgence not to laugh at so stupid and clumsy a lie. He was kind enough, however, to appear convinced. He even extended his courtesy so far as to invent a story of his own, which was almost as ridiculous, saying that he had a high fever and would stay in bed.

Night came. The three exiles slept a short, dream-filled sleep and rose quietly at two o'clock in the morning. They made their preparations in silence before walking out into the cold night. The date had been well chosen: the moon, as they proceeded in Indian file into the frozen desert, was high and nearly full; its pale, bluish light seemed to penetrate the ice, making its surface translucent, almost phosphorescent. They advanced at a quick pace. In less than an hour they were at the Scotsman's cabin. They saw it only when they were almost on top of it, as it was set on a rock plinth and covered with a flat roof made of tree trunks hidden under the snow.

The hermit did not vouchsafe them the comforts of his lair: he was waiting for them at the door. When Juremi introduced him to Jean-Baptiste and George, they had the impression of meeting one of the mummies they were going to visit underground. The Scotsman's flesh had been frozen and thawed so many times that it had assumed the parchment-like consistency of those animals from the distant past recovered intact from bogs. It seemed that nothing could affect him anymore. Despite the biting cold, his emaciated forearms and scrawny neck were bare, without causing him the least discomfort. A large copper ring hung from his left ear. The hole through which it passed, right in the middle of his earlobe, was easily wide enough to accept his little finger. His face, which had the typical impassivity of the Scots, was further rigidified by the cold: only at rare intervals would he sometimes blink.

For all that he seemed frozen, the Caledonian was extremely agile: he galloped like a reindeer and the others had a hard time following him. After a two-hour run that left them exhausted and sweat-soaked under their furs, they reached the foot of the colossal tumulus where the Scythian tombs were buried. Around the kurgan stood huge blocks of rock, upright and pointed. These stones seemed tiny from a distance in comparison with the bulk of the artificial hill, yet when they walked below the mound, those same stones towered above them. These lugubrious monuments clearly elicited Halquist's approval. Without quite smiling, the Scot showed a marked animation as they drew near. He even insisted on making Juremi and his companions follow his example: he placed both palms flat on the rough and crystalline surface of the cold rock, then breathed in deeply, as though inhaling a telluric force hidden in the stones. In fact, these lithic rows were altogether similar to those left by the Celts in Europe. Through the intercession of these cromlechs, the strayed druids no doubt recovered their ancestors' trace.

Once the four men crossed an imaginary circle traced by the line of upright stones, they had the disturbing sense that they had entered a sacred place. Its spell was wholly spiritual. If the kurgan had been a natural hill, they would have considered it a modest, even a small, hill. But they knew that men had carted this earthen mountain here, thousands of men. It was certainly admirable that they had raised it so high, but it was to a greater degree pathetic that despite their desperate efforts to leave a mark on this vast expanse, they had finally managed only to imitate a simple ripple of nature by erecting this modest arch, this risible bulge, this wart on the giant skin of the world.

The constant back-and-forth in their perceptions, the impression at one moment of great size and at the next of smallness, instilled in them a deep uneasiness. Earlier, on the approach to the kurgan, they had convinced themselves that the mound was modest in dimensions. Now they were no longer lofty observers, measuring things against the backdrop of the universe, but tiny figures clinging to the hill's steep slope, crushed by the majesty of this earthen monument, which had been created by living men in ancient times to bury their dead kings.

From a distance the surface of the hill appeared smooth. When they stepped onto the kurgan, they realized that it was actually very uneven, strewn with rocks large and small. Their feet occasionally sank into ruts, depressions, and crevices. They had to be careful not to fall into any of the many galleries dug by the looters. The openings of some were dangerously hidden by high grasses, by tufts of broom or holly. Halquist, who walked in the lead and knew every inch of the terrain, pointed out the pitfalls to them.

Halfway up, they reached a gallery that, while indistinguishable from the others, was apparently their destination. The Scot set down the jute sack he carried on his shoulder and removed from it a brass candle-lamp, a flint and tinder, and a pick made of hardwood from Siberia. He entered partway into the tunnel, struck the flint, and lit the lamp. The other three explorers, without a glance at the magnificent panorama of the moonlit steppe, stared fixedly at the dark opening that their guide was inviting them to enter. George, who was not normally fearful, started to tremble all over, his teeth chattering noisily. His body was rigid, and his eyes were opened wide. It was clear that he was prey to one of those irrational but stormy terrors that uproot all the mind's constructs, a holy terror. Jean-Baptiste thought the boy was going to scream. He was disturbed at seeing him so terrified and anxious to avoid an incident with the Scotsman. At the same time, he was secretly pleased that George had started to sense presences lurking behind things.

The heavy eyelid of the sky was opening on a new day. Cold swirling winds arose with the purple dawn and whistled over the kurgan's slopes.

The Scot came back out of his hole to see what was keeping his companions. He swore, in English, and the familiar language had the effect of bringing George back to earth. They were all able, one after the other, to enter the chute. George followed behind Halquist, and Juremi brought up the rear.

The shaft was less frightening on the inside than it had seemed from the outside. The narrow tunnel through gray and friable earth was supported at intervals by wooden struts. As they sank into the depths, the air grew pleasantly warm. The gallery forked repeatedly into a network of galleries.

"The Scythians lived in antiquity, at the time of Herodotus or earlier," Juremi observed in a loud voice, clearly finding reassurance in playing the role of guide. "According to Halquist, these people moved from Greece to China. They rode horseback on the steppes. They were free men."

The Scot signaled them to stop. They must already have reached far toward the center of the mound. There was nothing remarkable about the spot. It was a portion of the shaft like any other. Halquist started to stamp his heel on the ground in different places. Suddenly there was a hollow sound. The Scot knelt and swept away the dirt with his fingers. A flat stone appeared. With his wooden pick, he levered up one corner, raised the stone, and set it back down on the adjoining ground. Through the breach thus created came the clear echo of their every whisper, reverberating off unseen walls in the dark below. Jean-Baptiste and Juremi looked at George, anxious about his reaction, but in surmounting the great panic that had assailed him at the entrance to the kurgan, George seemed to have gone through the looking glass. He had learned all at once how to navigate the obverse side of the world unafraid, and he was the first to lean over the dark square, his eyes burning with curiosity, to the point where the Scot had to restrain him firmly. Halquist even made George step back and, in consolation for treating him harshly, gave him the lamp. Then, without an instant's hesitation, Halquist threaded his long fur-wrapped mummy's body through the cavern's opening and slid in. A moment later, only his hands were visible gripping either side of the orifice. They could hear his feet striking out in search of a foothold. As soon as he found one, he let go of his hands and disappeared into the dark. A moment passed, full of anxiety for the three novices. Then Halquist's voice came up to them, echoing as though in a chapel, to ask for the lamp. George handed it down to him and, after the Scot took it from his outstretched hand, rejoined him without hesitation. Jean-Baptiste and Juremi followed.

When they were reassembled, Halquist shone the light around them. What had echoed like a chapel was in fact a vast straight hallway with perfectly dressed stone walls crowned by a vault, also faced with stone, in the shape of an upside-down staircase. The stone block they had removed was at the top of the vault, where the two facing flights of stairs that made the roof came together. The slightly sweet and dust-laden atmosphere they had been breathing since entering the dirt tunnels was gone, but what replaced it was not the humid, stony smell of a church crypt that they had expected. It seemed rather a domestic scent, though cold and confined, made of mixed humors, table leavings, clothes impregnated with the exhalations of the body, a scent that is both common to all human habitations and peculiar to each. There was no doubt about it: they were in someone's house.

Halquist set off and the others followed him along the hallway, whose perfectly clean floor echoed under their feet. At a T junction, the Scot took the right fork, lifting his lamp. His three comrades cried out. Ahead of them, an arm's length away, were a dozen horses, rigid in death. Their hides were almost intact, stretched over the bones, and kept the animals arrested in the attitudes they had held when they were slaughtered. The nearest, supported by the mass of horses immolated before it, was almost standing, and its enormous head, pierced by a pickax blow to the forehead, towered over the intruders and glared at them with an expression of terror, anger, and eternal reproach. Halquist approached the first horse as familiarly as if it were alive and, as though to pat it, rested his bony hand on its fleshless neck. To those who affix a boundary to man's life, this striking group offered a troubling denial, like a sign of intelligence exchanged between accomplices on either shore of death.

Without giving his companions time to recover, the Scot abandoned this ghostly stable and set off down the other fork of the hall. This branch was longer. Part of the ceiling had caved in and they were obliged to climb over broken blocks strewing the ground. Along the flat stone walls, at ground level, openings had summarily been made by removing one or two blocks.

"He visited all the rooms in the last few weeks," explained Juremi knowingly.

The spot was lugubrious enough that they tried not to think what a lone man might feel there. At the end of the hallway they saw Halquist prepare for another search. He started with a minute exploration of the wall, rapping the stones with the handle of his pick and running his fingers over the joints between the stones, doubtless in an effort to find even a slight discrepancy to indicate the presence of a funerary chamber. Finally, he restricted his examination to a single area and traced a rectangle on the wall with the sharp edge of a pebble. He then calmly removed his fur tunic, revealing an undergarment that had more holes in it than cotton. Taking up his pick, he scratched at the joint between two stones.

Lacking tools, and perhaps courage as well, the three visitors convinced themselves that there was nothing for them to do. They looked at Halquist with a mixture of admiration and horror, careful to turn their backs on the mares that still eyed them viciously from the depths of the hallway. The workmanship of the tomb was excellent and it took some time to pry the first stone loose. Afterward everything went much quicker. Soon an opening similar to the others had been created. Halquist straightened up, put his pick aside, dusted off his hands, and slipped his fur jacket back on. Was he afraid of the cold inside the sepulcher? or was he concerned to appear correctly dressed before these witnesses from the beyond? At any rate he seemed to be taking his precautions before crossing the sacred threshold. He drew a rye cake from his sack and bit into it. As no one else in the group was hungry, he ate alone, drank three swallows from his waterskin, and only then decided to enter the funerary chamber that he had just awakened from its three-thousand-year sleep. He crept into the black gully on all fours, but was at first unable to progress beyond his waist. One last obstacle stood in his way. At his request, Juremi passed him a dagger he had brought in his sack. They heard him scratching and striking at a wooden panel, which gave with a sudden crack. Halquist disappeared into the hole, then called for the lamp and told his acolytes they might follow him. They joined him one after another, each new arrival stopping speechless with astonishment on rising to his feet.

The room in which they were standing was rectangular, small, cluttered, and barely able to contain all four of them. Their heads touched the ceiling, forcing Juremi to keep his knees bent. The boards paneling the walls and floor gave the room a dull hue and exuded a scent of freshly sawn softwood. The lugubrious Scotsman had set the lamp down on a wooden shelf. Spreading his arms as though he were their host who had just led them into the dining room, he said:

"Voilà, Messieurs."

His features, without actually moving, registered a jubilant expression. But his eyes shone with intense excitement.

"It's the royal chamber," whispered Juremi, "the one he's been looking for."

In the millennial silence, the giant man's voice, even hushed, sounded like the trumpets on Judgment Day.

The solemn announcement let Jean-Baptiste and George know the full extent of the discovery, as the impression of chaos on entering the room was so strong that they were afraid they had arrived too late and grave robbers had already ransacked it from top to bottom.

Several dozen amphorae, emptied of their contents by the passage of time, stood leaning against each other. Beside two great copper cauldrons an entire battery of plates, vases, and ceremonial vials was stacked. As they soon came to understand, the amassed objects only seemed helter-skelter because of the narrow space of the room, which was in fact very rigorously organized and recovered its meaning when one connected the objects to their purpose, which was to accompany the defunct on his eternal voyage.

And that's what was missing from this sanctuary: the deceased. This well-furnished house was certainly meant to be used by its master. But where was he resting? In the supernatural atmosphere, the visitors had the fleeting suspicion that the dead king might have fled to another abode (and why not?) or reached some subtle paradise of the just.

Halquist brought them back to the real world by making the heavy lid of a wooden sarcophagus creak.

"Would you give me a hand, Juremi?"

The Protestant grabbed the other end, and the Scot was able with his help to fold back the large panel. The king appeared, or rather his adornments. The corpse was literally covered with gold and bronze from head to foot. He wore a helmet, greaves, and a breastplate. His weapons were laid along his right side. Around his neck was a wide torque of incised gold. His face was the only part of his body visible. Time had not decomposed it, only dried and tanned it, following the same process whose early steps Halquist had undergone. His eyelids opened on empty sockets.

This encounter made them horribly uncomfortable. Not that the remains were horrible to see—the king could even be said to have a certain grace. Their unease came from the presence of death, revealed by the mummified flesh, which rendered useless, even absurd and revolting, all the attentions surrounding the defunct. This plate, this chariot, these foods: why? And especially, for whom? The human belief that had caused these objects to be out there had been cruelly misplaced. Nowhere in the world was the imposture of faith more plain. Yet this spiritual edifice was all that was left of the Scyths. They did not have eternal life, yet they entered into contact with the eternal life of humanity—witness the meeting in the here and now of a king dead for millennia and four very living men.

This solitary king in his tomb would not have expressed his humanity so strongly had he not been surrounded by objects and art celebrating the life, joys, and struggles of those over whom he had reigned. All the poignant emotion of the place lay in this obvious fact: that the whole kurgan was a hymn to strength, to royalty, and to the gods. Yet it was neither that strength nor that royalty, nor those gods who allowed these men to survive through the centuries, but the greatness of their dreams, the beauty of their imagination, and the power of their art.

As the visitors reflected along these lines, they began to feel more at ease. After all, the place was made for dead men who were much like the living. Juremi fingered the amphorae, picking up the olive pits that lined their bottoms, and found a comb, which he sank into his curly beard. Jean-Baptiste and George admired the design of the jewels, and the figures in relief on the platters. It wasn't a profanation, rather a fraternal communion across the divide of the centuries.

Meanwhile, Halquist had inventoried the pieces that interested him. He asked George to get the sack left in the hallway. With a jolt the three friends remembered the awful truth: they had not entered the tomb for peaceful ends. They had come to rob the grave, even if their approach was expert and Halquist took care that no one followed in his tracks to finish destroying the sanctuaries.

The Scot, unbothered by such scruples, approached the sarcophagus and started the meticulous work of stripping the dead man. He planned to attack the torque first. His two desiccated hands slid around either side of the royal neck to reach the clasp at the rear. He had almost managed it when George called to them from the hallway outside where he had gone to fetch the sack.

"Come," he cried, "come quick."

Halquist let go of the jewel. They passed through the crawlway one after another. In the hall, George gestured at them to keep still.

"Shouts!" said Juremi.

They ran to the opening through which they had lowered themselves. Echoing through the earthen tunnels came repeated calls.

"A man's voice," said Jean-Baptiste.

George, who had hoisted himself to the hole in the floor of the shaft above, cocked his head and shouted:

"Bibichev!"

26

The battle of Kirman took place on the last day of the weeklong period of penance and purification that the Persians had set for themselves.

It was once more apparent on this occasion that war is devoid of morality. The Afghans, presented with the base but seductive prospect of rape and pillage, fought with passion. The Persians, recently deprived by their priests' zeal of the good wines and free women they might have hoped to receive in reward for a victory, showed much ill will. The battle was long and confused: the Afghans, full of audacity, displayed their courage in the open; the Persians, full of caution, hid their discouragement behind walls. The city fell after three days.

Mounted couriers left in the evening for Isfahan to bring the king word of the battle. Each message that arrived at court was already five days old, which was the time it took to reach the capital even at a fast gallop and with fresh relays of horses. How could one confidently eat food that was so far from being fresh? Despite the victorious proclamations of the palace, the greatest pessimism reigned among the people. The streets of the capital remained deserted and lugubrious. All the men were either away fighting or afraid they would be sent if they showed their faces. The women were confined to their harems. Alix was one of the few people, in her treble capacity as a foreigner, a widow, and an apothecary's wife with medicines to deliver, who could move freely about the city at this period.

She visited Nur al-Huda twice and was terrified to see her friend so heedless and full of gaiety. In fact the prime minister's harem had never been the theater of such prolonged merrymaking. The poor man's three other wives, though they might at an earlier era have been mutually jealous, were now elderly, and their only rivalry was in promoting the luxuriance of their mustaches, an adornment welcomed among the Persians as a sign of maturity and experience. They treated the young Circassian as their daughter and smiled indulgently at her whims. Such unanimity deprived their husband of the slightest chance of policing the interior of his gynaeceum. It was so well protected from his sanctions, so quick to learn of his slightest inclination to visit, in a word, so safe and so secret, that Nur al-Huda had the idea of inviting several of her dancer friends, whom the strict new laws were threatening. Five women of all ages, disguised as servants, snatched up their tambourines at nightfall and created scenes of the most joyful animation in the little rooms with their drawn curtains. When she was not dancing herself, Nur al-Huda lay stretched out on cushions and smoked a little narghile stuffed with cinnamon and flour, which made her head spin agreeably.

She laughingly introduced her protégées to Alix. One of them was a relative of the patriarch Nerses who told the false widow of the old man's confusion at Jean-Baptiste's sudden death. He had counted on the apothecary to rescue him by interceding with Alberoni and had been saved only by the outbreak of the Afghan war, which had first diverted the community's attention, then allowed him to be pardoned.

Alix thus learned how Nur al-Huda had found out that Jean-Baptiste wanted to leave Persia. Wanting to get to the bottom of the mystery, she asked:

"But who was it who told you that Jean-Baptiste . . . intended to die?

"My dear husband," Nur al-Huda laughingly confessed, "reported Jean-Baptiste's conversation with the king in front of me. I knew that he wanted to leave and was being prevented. I told you: I was interested in seeing my benefactor again. I wanted to know what he would do in this critical situation. All I had to do was to post one of our little beggars day and night in front of each of your doors."

The admission no longer had any importance, and Nur al-Huda proffered it negligently sucking on the amber mouthpiece of her water pipe. Alix couldn't help thinking that it showed excessive solicitude on the young woman's part toward a doctor who had taken care of her during childhood. For a moment she wondered whether she shouldn't see this interest as masking less admissible feelings. The idea displeased her. Yet she was also aware of an infinitesimal nub of satisfaction, as though by finding the beginnings of a cause for jealousy she might dissipate the slight shame she felt at having listened so indulgently to Reza's confidences.

In talking with her friend, Alix took care to avoid showing any of the emotions she had felt during her meeting with the officer. She nonetheless acquitted herself scrupulously of her mission by giving an exact account of her interview with the unhappy captain of the royal guard. Nur al-Huda listened with no expression either of satisfaction or of displeasure.

"Why did he tell you all that?" she asked at the end.

"I think . . . he's very unhappy," offered Alix. "He is passionately in love with you. Yet the situation he's in—"

"What situation?" muttered Nur al-Huda with great impatience. "He still hasn't made his choice, that's all."

"But isn't the choice you're asking him to make too harsh?"

Nur al-Huda shrugged for all answer. Then, to change the subject, she rose abruptly to her feet and launched the dancers into a new round of games.

Alix got nothing more from her. Nur al-Huda did not ask her to return to the royal palace during that week of seclusion. When she happened to pass the little gate through which she had visited the officer, Alix found herself thinking long and sorrowfully about this man who suffered while the woman he loved lived among pleasures and festivities. Once Alix even crossed the square where the changing of the guard took place and saw Reza from a distance, fortunately by chance.

As soon as the news of Kirman's fall became known, Isfahan resumed its normal aspect: men and women once more went about their business through the streets. Yet from the rhythm of their steps, the tone of their voices, and the frightened darting of their glances, it was clear that the crowd had only returned to the outward form of its old habits: a deep panic had taken hold of it. The only news that, while not exactly good, was somewhat reassuring was that a great portion of the army had taken flight. Rather than fight to the end and leave the empire defenseless, the Persian soldiers had preferred to desert en masse and withdraw by stages toward the capital. After the fall of Kirman this cowardice began to look like cunning, almost boldness. The deserters were practically applauded on their return to the city.

Although his troops had been spared, the king was all the same in a difficult position. The Afghans would regroup their forces in Kirman, and there was nothing to stop them afterward until they reached Isfahan. If they thought it worth the taking, the Afghans might pause along the way to capture Yazd. They could also bypass it without tactical loss. So it was to be expected that within a few weeks the Afghans would appear in the area of the Chahar Bagh.

How could the Persians resist them? What could still save them? Defeat makes an army vulnerable, not so much by reducing its effective force as by giving the lie to its claims of divine protection. The Persians had performed severe penance in the past weeks to punish their corruption and please God. Kirman had fallen nonetheless. Men of little faith concluded that the whole business was useless; they saw themselves as alone with nothing to expect from heaven. The more faithful read the defeat as God's verdict and considered themselves damned beyond repentance. Only the Magians and the Shi'i clerics would not give up. They searched for ways to recover control and for reasons to intensify the program of expiation. Strange phenomena in the heavens came providentially to their aid, justifying the call for new decrees, first of all, then the great and unexpected sanction, whose originator was never determined.

It all started three days after the defeat at Kirman, the news of which had still not reached the capital. Early in the morning, a gray veil of cloud covered the sky, and the sun failed to burn it off. Ordinarily, Isfahan experiences either a pure blue sky or bursts of storm. The steady curtain of vapor drawn between man and the heavenly body venerated so long in these highlands caused some surprise. That evening as it plunged toward the horizon, the sun set the whole west ablaze. It was one of those days a person is eager to see the last of, full of indecipherable but probably bad omens. The next day, however, the veil of vapor was still there. It had kept the ground warm during the night and the brisk cold of winter was replaced by a humid and unseasonable warmth. At dusk, the sun was immolated more bloodily even than the previous evening, as though thousands of sheep slaughtered for the Feast of Eyd had splattered the sky with their severed carotids. The news of the defeat arrived the following morning under the same shroud of vapor, and the message of the heavens was finally understood. There was a feeling almost of gratitude toward the sky, which had the decorum not to post a jubilant sun at a moment of such grief. The whole city climbed to the roofs and terraces at nightfall to watch the horizon honor the blood of the dead.

When the phenomenon continued for another two days, there was some confusion as to its proper interpretation. In the first place, the residents of the capital came to realize as descriptions trickled in that the battle had been anything but bloody: the Persian army had had the good sense to decamp. This hardly seemed to call for such a gaudy festival from the skies. And when the dates were calculated, it became clear that the veil had not appeared on the day of the defeat but well after. This tardiness clashed with the idea men generally have, and Persians in particular, as to the rigorous and punctual providence of the stars. Why the delay? The holy men and astrologers met and conferred. The nature of their discussions was never known. One can only conjecture that they were rightly concerned with taking care of the future—their own of course—by inventing new causes for alarm, requiring their costly but indispensable intercession.

The sun had been gone five days when the magus Yahya Beg came before the king to inform him of the conclusions that he and his colleagues had reached.

"Sire," he announced, "the situation is extremely grave. If these phenomena persist until tomorrow dawn, we must expect to see earthquakes such as those that destroyed Tabriz last month."

Poor Shah Huseyn had fasted conscientiously right up to the battle of Kirman. He had barely recovered, after two days of libations, from this cruel and useless privation, and his greatest fear was that he might have to undertake a new round. Thus he was relieved to learn of Yahya Beg's diagnosis.

"We believe that unless the sky returns to normal by tomorrow morning, it will be necessary to . . . evacuate the city."

"Evacuate it!" cried the king in surprise. "What do you mean?"

"Drive all the population outside the walls, which God may cast down on our heads at any moment. And advise all the sinners to take the sky as their shelter and to wait until God has purified the city Himself. Our efforts thus far have, alas, not purged it entirely."

The following morning, the warm atmosphere had grown moist under its lid. The cloud cover, smooth and gray like a vault of dressed stone, extended to the horizon in all four directions. Not the slightest breath stirred the air, and even the birds were not flying. At midday, a decree from the royal palace was shouted from the rooftops and echoed to the farthest corners of the city, commanding everyone, old and young, male and female, foreign and Persian, to pack up the barest necessities and prepare to leave for the countryside.

This time Nur al-Huda, secluded in the harem and absorbed in her diversions, was unable to warn Alix of the danger. The news reached the apothecary's house with the same abruptness as everywhere else. Things had to be done in haste, and decisions on serious matters taken instantly—should money and jewels be left at home, hidden, at the risk of being found by looters, or was it more sensible to take them along, despite the possible violence and confusion? Saba, calm as usual—almost calmer for the adversity—persuaded her mother to divide their valuables into two portions and bring one. In siding with her daughter's opinion, a small capitulation, Alix signaled that she was abdicating the leadership role in favor of her daughter. Françoise at first refused to go: she didn't have the strength for it and was likely to slow down the whole group. Saba had the idea of modifying a stretcher used by the gardeners to carry dirt and stones. Two men supported the shafts at either end, while Saba settled Françoise on the slightly hollow square of cloth nailed in the center of the crude litter, to which she added a small cushion and a wooden backrest.

Alix meanwhile ran from room to room with mounting anxiety. In losing her house, which she had so little expected, she suddenly became aware of how alone and exposed she was. When she entered the laboratory, she thought suddenly of Jean-Baptiste, but only to blame him for abandoning her. She restrained herself from crying and went on filling a large leather sack at random with superfluous items while neglecting the essentials. She didn't even take the precaution of packing a firearm, so foreign to her present thinking was the notion of fighting. It was Saba who, this time, recommended to her mother and Françoise that they wear a veil, while keeping their faces uncovered: best to look as little as possible like foreigners at a time when the people might be tempted to appease the heavens' wrath by finding scapegoats.

In less than two hours everything was ready. Saba and Alix walked on either side of Françoise's litter. Behind came the small band of servants, who, for reasons having to do with Jean-Baptiste's departure, were limited to four, plus the two porters. The old gatekeeper closed the gate behind the procession and remained alone in the house, in accordance with the orders of the king, who had authorized two guards to stay behind in palaces, only one in the houses of the rich, and none among the commoners.

No animals were to accompany the evacuees, to avoid the congestion of mule and camel trains carrying household furniture. The crowd of pedestrians was so dense, so given to shouts and tears, so nervous and quarrelsome, that it took several hours of treading in place to reach the gates of the city. The flood of people in veils and turbans formed an even and regular sea of whitecaps, broken only by the bundles floating here and there at head level. At rare intervals, a horseman of the guard would fend a way for himself through the viscid waters, striking out on either side with the flat of his sword as though rowing.

One of the horsemen, whom Alix and her group encountered somewhat before arriving within sight of the city walls, was a giant with a shaved head, who had lost his turban in the fray. He brandished a great long dagger over the heads of the crowd, threatening to strike down anyone who stood in his path. From time to time he would bring his sword down hard on a door or a post and use the anchor thus provided to haul himself forward. Coming level with Françoise, the madman sank his blade into one of the uprights of her litter. In pulling himself forward, he threw the porters off-balance; Françoise, unable to catch herself, fell heavily to the ground. The ensuing melee was short and brutal. As the crowd drew near the gates of the city, the current grew more impetuous; it was practically impossible to stop. Saba and Alix were instantly separated from the rest of the group and believed that Françoise must have perished. Luckily the giant who had caused the whole incident, continuing his flight, slowed the crush behind the litter somewhat and unwittingly allowed the porters to raise Françoise and dump her in the improvised seat, where she lay curled up and moaning. It was not until they had passed through the tall gates and could walk freely in the countryside that the little band was able to regroup. Saba made a resting place for Françoise on a garden bank, gave her something to drink, and asked her if she had sustained any injuries from her fall. The brave woman assured the others that she was fine, but her changed face, her pinched and bluish lips, gave a clear indication that she was in pain. Gently parting the woman's veil, Saba discovered that she was supporting her right arm with her other hand, as a person does who has just broken a bone. Saba ran her fingers over Françoise's shoulder and found a place so painful that the patient cried out at the slightest touch—for all that she was hardened to pain and making an enormous effort to let nothing show.

"How horrible!" said Alix at the sight of her friend's pain. "We've forgotten to bring our medicines."

Saba went without a word and rummaged through the bundles the servants had set down on the bank. She had had the foresight to bring a vial of willow water, which she now gave Françoise to drink.

While the crowd rested in the gardens, the sunset began its parade of blood. Muezzins, perched on stone walls or on the roofs of huts, gave their piercing call, sending the soothing vapor of their incantations skyward and causing to be spread over the reddened earth around them the balm of thousands of the faithful prostrating themselves to the greater glory of the one true God.

The prayer over, the crowd resumed its tramping as far as the eye could see. It was then that Alix and her companions saw the royal litter, carried by twelve slaves and covered in a betel-dyed Indian cloth, pass out through the gate through which they themselves had just emerged. The procession passed slowly by, to the regular step of the porters. A detachment of mounted guards opened a path in front. Behind came the sovereign's litter and another half dozen carrying his wives and concubines. Closing the rear of this silent march was a second company of soldiers, on foot this time, in formation around an impassive rider. Alix recognized the horseman as Reza, whose eyes scanned the surrounding scene for the slightest sign of disturbance or danger. Their glances crossed, and he indicated with a slight smile that he had recognized her.

27

A curtain of bare hills formed a horseshoe around Isfahan to the northwest, a half hour from the city. The inhabitants, either on their own initiative or under the guidance of some unknown person, directed their steps toward these heights and installed their makeshift camps on the slopes. The weather stayed hot during the day and kept its warmth through the night—providentially, given the difficulty of finding even a stick of firewood in those steep ravines. It wasn't until the second night that wood arrived in carts from the irrigated gardens below, where the hedges and even the fruit trees had been ordered chopped down by government.

Dawn arrived on the eighth day with the sun still trapped behind its veil of clouds. Its milky light seemed to come from all the sky, and it was hard to find a spot more blindingly bright than the rest where the sun might be hiding. For their camp Saba had chosen a square patch of ground at the slope's midpoint. It was not entirely comfortable because the ground was irregular and strewn with sharp stones, but it was convenient for bordering the road used by the carriages to bring water, wood, and fruit. The high ground also offered a wide panorama of Isfahan in general and of their house in particular, whose roof could be seen among the naked branches of the garden.

The days passed quickly in attending to the thousand needs that the sedentary suddenly discover when forced by circumstances to assume the life of the nomad. Françoise's arm caused her pain, though Alix and Saba had bound it to her side by tearing a shirt into strips and wrapping them around her. Toward four o'clock their meager campfire finally finished cooking the pot of vegetables and stale bread they had brought with them. They shared this, their only meal of the day, with their servants. At five o'clock, in heavy silence, the same vermilion dusk re-created across the sky its mysterious and unsettling sacrifice. The Persians had by now grown to regard this singular celestial tragedy as normal. Saba, Alix, and

Françoise, on the other hand, who had not been unduly struck by this curiosity of nature at first, found it that night to hold unprecedented terror. Isfahan lay at their feet deserted, without one light or fire, painfully enduring the heat of the sky that turned the minarets pink, inflamed the ocher walls of the city, and made the green-tiled domes of its mosques crackle with light. What new page of the Sacred Book was this people exiled on the threshold of its city writing? Its prophets had called for a terrifying encounter with punishment. But from what direction would the blow fall? From the sky, which for the time being held its fire but might not much longer? From the earth, long irritated by man's sinful prurience and whose imminent vengeance the holy men were predicting? Or from man himself, for no one had heard since the defeat at Kirman whether the Afghans were not already on the way to bring the Persian Empire to its knees?

Night fell at last, a black night. It was an odd effect to hear the city silent and the countryside full of voices. Those who had been able to light fires now snuffed them out to save wood. The camps were sinister without their souls, and the fleeing populace wanted only to flee further into a deep sleep. There was the brief sound of bedding being spread, hides unfolded, and children calmed by soothing words, then a great silence spread over the hillside. Françoise and Saba, the one wearied beyond endurance by her pain, the other not free of all the frailty of childhood, fell deeply and immediately asleep.

Alix, who had set a few embers aside in putting out the fire, watched dreamily as the green sticks slowly reddened and consumed themselves in smoke. She couldn't think of Jean-Baptiste without feeling singularly resentful toward him; she blamed him for leaving her and beyond that for stamping her life with departure and exile. Perhaps he had even deprived her entirely of her youth . . . The feeling was so unfair and at the same time so strong that she chased it from her mind. Other images came to her from the most distant past, aureoled in the wonder of things that are buried and protected from time: her childhood in the boarding schools of France, her arrival in Cairo and the life she had lived with her parents there. She had never regretted even for a moment leaving her gilded cage, yet she now looked back on it tenderly. Her mother, so sweet and so subjugated, poor woman! Alix had never written her for fear that she would show the letters to her husband and that their hiding place in Isfahan would be discovered. And her father, her poor consul of a father! Was he alive or dead? With the passage of time, the man's ridiculousness seemed no more than an amusing foible, behind which his shyness and a great goodness were no doubt hidden.

She was lost in the maze of this subterranean memory when she noticed figures coming and going along the path left open for wagon traffic. She was soon able to see that they wore white soldier's uniforms. Some held resin torches, unfurling their strands of dark flame into the still night air. They went from group to group holding the light over the sleepers as though looking for someone. With fright she saw one of the guards approach her and she lacked the presence of mind even to veil her face. The soldier saw her and ran to the path calling the others. A cluster formed, from which a man emerged who was hidden by the light of the torch. Only at the last moment when he stood near her and bowed respectfully did she recognize Reza. Françoise and Saba slept peacefully. Alix rose to her feet and at her visitor's invitation followed him to the hollow road. He ordered his men to return to camp. Alix and he sat side by side on the steepest portion of the bank, and Reza planted his torch somewhat off to the side in the sandy dust.

"I noticed earlier that you were accompanied by an injured woman," said the Persian in a low voice.

When he had passed them with the royal litter, Saba had been putting the last touches on the bandage around Françoise's arm.

"Thank you," said Alix, touched by this mark of attention and experiencing a strong pleasure at the man's protection of her. "She is a relative who lives with me in Isfahan and who took a bad fall in the crush."

"Would you like us to have her carried to our doctors? The one assigned to the royal guard is not bad. He has set up a small station on the other side of this hill, near the tents of the king and his court."

"No," said Alix hurriedly, "it's not necessary. We have medicine. Everything is fine, thank you."

On no account did she want Françoise thrust before the nazir and the whole superstitious court, where the arrival of the cardinal's putative concubine at this critical juncture might give rise to some disastrous scheme, and Françoise would undoubtedly be the one to suffer from it.

"At least let me arrange to have supplies brought to you tomorrow morning so that you can have a good fire and three meals a day."

Reza's solicitude was so sincere, so natural, and so touching that Alix accepted without reserve and thanked him with visible emotion.

Having disposed of this subject, they abandoned the solid ground of conversation to rise, thanks to long silences, toward the more vaporous and inexpressible region of their thoughts.

"Have you . . . seen Nur?" asked Alix timidly.

Reza kept his eyes on the ground, as he had done at the palace, and ran the ends of his long fingers over the fine pebbles on its surface.

"No," he admitted.

He paused, then went on, raising his eyes:

"Anyway, I believe that I am healing. Do you know, this week was not painful for me. Not like before at any rate."

"I'm happy for you," said Alix feelingly. "And what have you done to finally achieve this serenity?"

"I simply followed your advice."

"My advice! I gave you advice?"

She remembered that she hadn't been able to say anything after hearing his story. She had left him muttering a few civil phrases of encouragement and thanks.

"I don't know whether you gave it to me," he said, "but I heard it anyway."

So saying, the officer held his eyes on Alix. Darkness hid his pupils; all she could see was the pure line of his eyebrows, from which she could not detach her gaze.

"And what advice," she asked unsteadily, "might I have suggested to you?"

"The very simplest: that I was not to suffer and . . . "

"And?"

"That I should love another."

The torch held the scene in its red light smelling of camphor and resin. The least gesture, breaking the charm, would have sent them flying from each other, whereas this scented and vermilion distance brought them together as if entwined. Thousands of recumbent shadows around them, steeped in blue sleep, seemed already to have fallen victim to the foretold scourge. They alone had survived and carried in them on behalf of humanity all that was left on earth of lust and pleasure.

The gods may have created the innocent just to keep the unwary from falling into serious danger. This, at any rate, is what a simple, open-faced fellow accomplished who approached Reza for permission to light a stick at his torch. The man's child had a fever and he wanted to rekindle his campfire.

This intrusion returned the talkers to an awareness of themselves, the place, and the hour. After a few embarrassed exchanges—they now had the feeling that the whole world was listening to them—they parted until the following day, bowing awkwardly.

The following day, again veiled in clouds, was dismal and unending. Soldiers came bringing wood and victuals for Françoise, but Reza did not appear. Alix was almost relieved, as the pleasure she had first felt at seeing Reza had become increasingly tinged with anxiety during the day. What was she doing? The apocalyptic atmosphere of the sunsets and nights had turned everything topsy-turvy and made the exiles feel that they had already passed over into some limbo where time did not exist. But daylight came to dispel these illusions and restore hunger, thirst, worry, children's crying, and the straining of heavy convoys climbing the hillside under the lash of the whip. Alix wondered with some trepidation where Nur al-Huda could be. Then she forgot it all. The sun had still not set entirely when, after two sleepless nights, she fell sound asleep.

Late the following morning, after ten days in its shroud, the sun reappeared as pure as ever, full in the middle of an indigo sky. The city took on color again, and the air its hint of biting cold. Sunset gaily flapped a few pink aprons across the evening sky and gave way to the familiar Iranian night, riddled with stars and lit by a paring of moon. The holy men held a conclave that lasted until dawn, making learned calculations of the orbits and constellations. Finally, they announced to the king that their prayers had taken effect: the earth, relieved of the burden of this repentant population, had decided to suspend its punishment. At noon, the haggard residents, smudged with dirt and ashes, passed word of the royal decree from camp to camp: everyone could go back to the city.

Bibichev was no coward. To go out into the frozen night at three o'clock in the morning with no light and to follow at a cautious distance (which is to say out of sight) after a little band that was moving swiftly over the snow in single file is neither easy nor without risk. But an agent such as himself was not going to give up so near the goal. The great achievements of his trade lay along the ridgeline where the two slopes of theory and practice meet; each supports the other, but a person venturing only on one side or the other would surely slip into the abyss. The theory in this business was clear: he had powerfully represented to his superiors the plot of this conspiracy. Now he needed to obtain concrete proof. Might the fruit only be harvested at three o'clock in the morning on the frozen steppe? Then so be it.

Several times he came within a hair of being discovered by those he was tracking: once when they met up with that devil of a Scotsman who popped up out of God knows where, and again when Bibichev had had to fight down the urge to sneeze and had finally won. When they drew near the kurgan, things grew easier: he had simply stood behind an upright stone and made a note of the shaft into which the suspects disappeared, then he had climbed up afterward at his leisure. It was too dangerous to climb down into the shaft after them: he knew that these molehills were full of branching tunnels, and anyway he had no lamp. He crouched down near the entrance to the tunnel and decided to wait. The weather was bitter cold, but the furs sewn by those damned Swedes kept him warm. The otter tails, he had to admit, brought him added comfort in this frost; in fact, he missed them on his stomach, where he had ripped them off, and in order not to lose heat he curled up, leaving only his back, bristling with black fur, in contact with the cold night. This position was his downfall.

As the sun rose over the white vastness of the steppe, a band of Kirghiz slowly made its way past the kurgan, bows drawn, their steel-tipped arrows nocked, their eyes peeled. These nomads belonged to a small tribe that, unlike the Kalmuks, was greatly to be feared, as they knew nothing but hunting and brutal pillaging.

Reaching the circle of upright stones, one face of which the dawn was turning blue, the nomads regrouped, then set off individually, radiating outward from each other star-fashion with the barrow at their backs. At midday, the hunters would follow their own back trails to reconvene at the starting point. Only one of the hunters was sent in the opposite direction to hunt for any game that might be hiding on the kurgan itself. That day they chose a boy named Iakash, who was about fifteen years old and was taking part in only his second adult hunt.

Iakash was familiar with all the ways of the steppe tribes. He knew how to move without making a sound, in leaps, and how to melt into the general stillness by making long stands by a rock. He knew how to recognize the saiga, which is an antelope of the steppes, from afar, and also the fox, the wolf, and even the large black lark of the desert.

But an animal such as the one he saw halfway up the kurgan, huddled in the entrance to its den, was something he had never seen before. The most fantastic stories of the ancients came back to him as he approached it. In order to come at the animal from downwind, he had gone around the top of the mound, from where he could see only its rounded back of black fur. For lack of anything to give the scale, he had no idea of its size: it could be one of those large tarantulas that spin their webs between rocks, or a huge bear that they didn't have in this region but that his father had once seen near the Caspian coast. The animal didn't move. Iakash drew his bow to the breaking point as he walked forward. He was now less than two strides from it. Despite his youth, the boy knew that you should never aim at the back of an unknown animal. Many species have carapaces that can turn the best arrow, and once alerted by the ineffective shot, they will charge the disarmed hunter. In contrast there are few instances in nature when a blow to the head or stomach is not likely to be fatal. Despite his fear, the boy had to signal his presence by making a noise, so that the startled animal would stand up and expose himself. Iakash shouted a Kazakh oath. The black shape unfolded. For a crucial instant the boy held still.

Bibichev made no gesture either, not even raising his hands. It was this impassivity that saved his life, as the hunter, before making any conscious decision, mirrored his prey's movement and froze too, in the interval realizing what he had captured. He had hoped for an aurochs; it was a government official.

The discovery seemed to reassure him somewhat. He took three steps backward, loosening the strain on his bow while keeping his arrow pointed at the man, and decided to call his friends by uttering an agreed signal.

Bibichev was soon surrounded by a dozen cautious savages who examined him in silence. After a muttered conversation, they approached the hole, and one of them stuck his head in the shaft to listen.

They knew that Bibichev was not alone and took him for the lookout for a band of grave robbers. The nomad tribes hate nothing so much as the desecrators of tombs. Though they may show the greatest contempt for life, their own and those of others, they have great respect for the dead buried in these tombs, to whom they erroneously claim a relation.

Still covered by the bows of Iakash and two other hunters, Bibichev was pushed roughly toward the tunnel's mouth, where the nomads, using unmistakable gestures, ordered him to call his companions. This he did at first with an expressionless voice. A well-directed kick to his breeches made him repeat his call with more feeling. He chose the words that carried best, and soon the repeated sound of his cry echoed through the invisible tunnels:

"Help, Juremi! Help me, Poncet! Come quick!"

IV
CAPTURES AND DISASTERS

28

In the sixth century before Christ, on a warm night in the month of August, Nineveh, the formidable capital of the Assyrian Empire, was taken. The orders of the conquering Medes were clear: no looting or rape, but no survivors either. The city's three hundred thousand inhabitants were murdered in the many days of carnage that followed. The site was destroyed as brutally as the population. No house was spared. Even Assurbanipal's cedar library collapsed in flames onto its thousands of clay tablets.

Few dead cities retain so strong a hold over the souls of the living. From Mosul, on the opposite bank of the Tigris, one can survey the skeleton of Nineveh's walls, on which nobody in three thousand years has ventured to set one stone on another. Arriving at this most famous site, Monsieur de Maillet's first care was to have himself driven to the ancient capital, where he might meditate while walking over heaps of stones overgrown with thistle and pellitory. The consul found much in the desolate sight to encourage him. The passage of the Medes here indicated that Persia was not far away, as the Medes were the Persians' ancestors: he was drawing close to his goal. And the advance of the desert, clearly visible on this mound of dust and tears and in the new city built at a lower elevation on the far side of the meager river, confirmed that the earth was slowly drying, as it had started to do long before historical times—this was the genial and harmless conviction at the root of his *Telliamed*.

Monsieur de Maillet breathed easier. Everything had worked out for him since leaving Rome. Boldness had definitely succeeded. He had crossed Italy and boarded a tartan in Manfredonia that had taken him all the way to Greece. Then, after traveling on a variety of caïques, all of them fast and new, and making several stops on attractive islands, he had reached Jounieh, in Lebanon.

The caravanserais in this region were comfortable and safe. He reached Aleppo, then Mosul, without difficulty. The winter was not a harsh one. The consul was in fine health, and the idea that he was advancing toward his deliverance helped him endure every fatigue.

At every stage Monsieur de Maillet stayed the night either with local inhabitants or at an inn and carefully avoided any contact with the Frankish consuls. His mission was a secret one and of no concern to official diplomats, in whose company he now felt uneasy, ashamed at having lost caste. In Mosul, the French legation was fortunately at some distance from the city, on a hill, as though the diplomats were not entirely convinced that Nineveh had been destroyed for good and had thought it best to choose a site halfway between the two cities.

On making inquiries, Monsieur de Maillet learned that he might choose from among several caravanserais for his stay in the town, all of excellent repute. One was pointed out to him as being a European-style inn with a small number or rooms; its cooking, though strange, was famous. The consul was struck by the name of this establishment: it was a French name that the Turks understood poorly but that they had learned to repeat like an exotic sentence. It was called "A l'Ami du Négus."

Monsieur de Maillet had himself taken there. The building was in a corner of the Turkish city above the bazaars. One ascended to the ground floor via a short flight of steps adorned with succulent plants to find that the opposite side of the building was really quite high. Its four windows provided a vast panoramic view of the river and of the ocher line of Nineveh's walls in the distance. The maid who showed the new guest to his quarters on the floor above was blond and quite elderly, though her hair was braided like a little girl's and hung down gaily on either side of her head. The room she showed him was modest but clean, with a red tile floor, a wooden bed, and a dresser on which sat a ewer and an earthenware basin decorated with blue borders in the style of Rouen. All this was charming and the price reasonable. The consul appeared highly satisfied with the accommodations, though slightly worried about some raucous shouting he had heard coming up the stairs. The clamor redoubled while he was examining the room, and the maid, learning that he would take it, appeared primarily intent on answering the vehement calls. She excused herself with a curtsy that made her braids dance and disappeared full speed down the corridor. The consul had not even had the opportunity to ask for an explanation of the hotel's unusual name.

Day was rapidly fading. Monsieur de Maillet allowed himself a little rest on the bed, watching the ruins turn pink on the horizon. Then he realized that he was hungry, that the room had no candle, and that it would be best to inquire about these necessities before darkness fell.

He went out into the hallway, which was now dark, descended the stairs, and found the room below occupied by a half dozen silent diners seated on stools around low tables. Each helped himself from a common bowl in which food for two or three persons had been arranged. Monsieur de Maillet had the privilege of being served a bowl for himself alone, and he took care to roll up his lace cuffs before he plunged his fingers into it. His Turkish guides had spoken the truth: the cuisine was strange. On a large crêpe covering the bottom of the basin were stacks of the most mysterious and unexpected foods. Some were recognizable: a vol-au-vent, an almond trout, a mango sorbet. Others, while very uneven, still gave proof of familiar ingredients: a ball of rice pilau with raisins, a spinach purée, a crumbled pile of dry cheese. But other of these mouthfuls provided no clue as to their origins, other than that they were too fiery a red in color to be judged harmless. All the cuisines of the East had combined to inspire these mixes, according to criteria that had less to do with taste than with the nostalgic reminiscences of the cook.

In bringing out these dishes and beverages, two serving maids assisted the woman who had shown Monsieur de Maillet his room. These poor women dressed and wore their hair in the same juvenile style as the first, though they were more than old enough to be grandmothers. They tried, by their game efforts at small talk, to make bearable the sight of their ruined breasts, pushed up by their lace-trimmed bodices, which cast a more melancholy pall over the unhappy diners even than the ruins of Nineveh.

Monsieur de Maillet honored the cooking with what he could salvage of his appetite. He found this way station very satisfactory, though he continued to feel some apprehension. Twice during dinner came the same booming shouts from the top of the stairs that he had heard in his room. His neighbors, for the most part quiet foreign merchants, many of them Greek, seemed unbothered by the noise and continued eating without raising their heads. He modeled his behavior on theirs, but his quiet anonymity was not to last. Hardly had he finished his meal and drunk a last glass of tea than the serving woman with the braids came up to him and spoke in his ear:

"Sir," she said in French, "the ambassador is waiting for you upstairs."

The ambassador! Monsieur de Maillet was greatly alarmed. He readjusted his cuffs, dusted his clothes. Could he appear without his peruke?

He was growing increasingly anxious when another thought struck him: What was an ambassador doing in a place like this? And anyway what country was this diplomat from? It was useless to pursue these questions with the poor serving woman, whose entire store of French had just been expended in a single sentence. Monsieur de Maillet rose to his feet and, plucking up his dignity, bravely followed the wench upstairs.

On the landing, across from the hallway leading to the rooms, a low door hidden behind a hanging led to another wing of the building. Entering it, Monsieur de Maillet saw that it had once been a pergola terrace. The beams had been covered over, on the ceiling and along the walls, with oddments of boards and the gaps covered with rough sacking, bellied out by the wind. The effect was part house and part encampment, the mixture being as bizarre as the cooking in the establishment. From the scaffolding of this nave hung an odd jumble of African-seeming objects: hippopotamus-hide shields, a pair of crossed lances, a dusty tiger fur. Occupying the center of the room was a monumental piece of furniture, heaped with soiled carpets and worn cotton shawls. It resembled at one and the same time a bed, a throne, and a catafalque; two or three people could have stretched out on it side by side, but the man who lay there was large enough to occupy the entire bed. The giant caftan covering his form, big enough to wrap two horses in, made it impossible to distinguish the outlines of his monstrous body, but stretching out from under the caftan toward the door were two legs, bare from the knee down, that exactly resembled elephant trunks: same striking size, same thick and wrinkled skin, same blackish color tinged with violet. The feet were covered with two woolen caps. When Monsieur de Maillet was able to detach his horrified gaze from this sight, he directed his eyes to the other end of this unusual platform. His poor eyesight detected the presence, at the summit of this massive shape, of a head, also laden with fat, and featuring an impressive pair of lips, which, against all expectation, were human and even smiling amiably.

"Have a seat, please," said the same rasping voice he had heard giving orders that afternoon in accented French. "I like to meet my new guests."

Monsieur de Maillet placed a cautious buttock on the edge of a wooden chair.

"How did you find my cooking?" the man asked, his voice making the suspended leather shields vibrate.

"Why . . . excellent!"

"Wonderful! Here is a man of taste. Do you know that I will not countenance any insults on the subject. The reason is very simple: the recipes were given me by a great king, yes, the greatest king of all, who reigns on earth by the will of God and executes God's orders."

"And who is this monarch?" asked Monsieur de Maillet, who judged it prudent to show an enthusiastic curiosity.

"Ah! Ah!" the man bellowed. "Is it possible that anyone who comes here does not yet know it? The negus of Abyssinia, of course, the king of kings, whose ambassador I am, and whose friend I am also, as the name of this establishment indicates."

At these words, Monsieur de Maillet leaned forward in his chair to get a better look at this person, whom the poor oil lamps lit insufficiently for his tired eyes. He could tell only that the reclining man was surrounded by clay plates full of almonds, pistachios, and dried fruits. These victuals occupied all the free space around him on the bed. He delved into them with his pudgy fingers as he spoke and stuffed great handfuls of peanuts into his mouth at every breath, swallowing them whole.

"And you, dear sir," this strange host pursued, chewing all the while, "I know that you are a Frank, from a nation familiar to me. Might I know your name? And don't hold it against me if we are already acquainted, as I have lost my eyesight almost entirely."

"My name is Maillet."

"Maillet? Maillet? I knew a scoundrel years ago in Cairo with a name something like that, though with a 'de' in front of it. He sent me through hell, the very place I hope he finds himself these days."

The consul rose to his feet. Now he understood: Murad! The Armenian cook brought back from Abyssinia by the impostor Poncet. The man who had actually had the gall to want to go all the way to Versailles, but whom he had fortunately stopped in passage. The glutton had gone back to Abyssinia again with a gaggle of Jesuits, and Monsieur de Maillet had hoped that he would stay there. But no, these adventurers have neither hearth nor home, and now he found him again along his path.

"I say that," said Murad in a quieter voice, "but in fact I forgave him long ago. The hours that I spent back then in Abyssinia and Cairo are so dear to me . . . And there is no one that I can share them with anymore."

Poor Murad was genuinely moved and liberally seasoned his bowls of dried fruit with tears.

"Am I to conclude," Monsieur de Maillet articulated with all the vigor he had once employed in dealing with this miscreant, "that you are the same Murad who lived for a time in Cairo fifteen years ago?"

"Is it possible?" cried the Armenian, simultaneously making a hideous effort that resulted in projecting the mass of his guts forward so that he might truly sit up. "Maillet! Monsieur de Maillet! Yes, I recognize your voice. Ah! Excellency, how happy this makes me! What an honor this is!"

Then, with a shout that practically knocked over the old diplomat, he clapped his hands:

"Here, girls! Drink for Monsieur de Maillet! Quickly, Cathy, Leandra! Come! Wine, right now, and the best in the house—none of your disgusting syrups."

This accomplished, Murad fell back on his couch burbling with pleasure. The consul hardly knew how to react. The night was pitch dark, making flight imprudent, perhaps impossible. Furthermore, though this meeting was unpleasant, it did not promise to be dangerous. And he had no time to deliberate. The worn dolls had all three materialized and were busily filling two glasses. Murad, in his excitement stuffing raisins into his mouth by the fistful, made a noisy toast, and a delicious Bordeaux trickled soothingly down Monsieur de Maillet's constricted throat.

"Did I have any idea that you would one day come to see me in all my prosperity?" cried Murad, still astonished. "In this house, which I bought with my own hard-earned silver, through my own labor! Isn't it magnificent? And these lovelies, what do you think of them?"

He had passed an arm around the backsides of two of the poor servants, who quaked under their lace aprons and laughed, showing all the teeth they no longer had.

The consul armed himself with great patience to wait out these effusions. Finally they were alone and Murad, starting in on the second bottle of wine, grew calm enough for them to hold a genuine conversation.

"So, dear Monsieur de Maillet," he said, mouthing the other's name with pleasure, "I suppose that you are stopping here on your way to Egypt."

"No," answered the former diplomat somewhat embarrassedly, "I no longer live in Cairo."

"You are no longer consul there?"

"Neither there nor anywhere," said Monsieur de Maillet gruffly. "I left the diplomatic corps, that's all."

"And . . . what are you doing here?" asked Murad without a trace of malice.

"I'm traveling," said the consul in definitive tones.

The Armenian inhaled a great quantity of chopped nuts, thought for a moment, then winked a whole half of his face, to the point where even Monsieur de Maillet noticed this gesture of complicity.

"Secret mission! Eh! All right, you won't tell. And you're right. But just between us diplomats . . ."

The consul shut his eyes momentarily. For man to have emerged from the sea was a fine idea of God's. But why had he pulled onto dry land this despicable sperm whale?

"Might I at least know where you are going?" pressed Murad.

"To Persia," the consul admitted, knowing that he could not hide his destination for long.

"To Persia! With all that's going on there!"

Murad had been unable to pull himself upright, and he waved his hands about with his head tilted back.

"Do you know that the Armenians captured Erevan last year? that the Russians have just advanced on the Caspian, led by the tsar in person? and that the Afghans are at the gates of Isfahan?"

"I know," said the consul impassively.

"He knows! I must have misheard. Believe me, dear Consul, this is not something to be ignored. This time, the end is near. Persia's day is done. I see many people go by, I ask questions, I listen. Sensible foreigners are leaving the country now as fast as they can. And here you are, planning to walk straight into the lion's mouth!"

"How many days' travel are we from Isfahan, with a good team of horses?"

"Isfahan! But how many times do I have to tell you that the city is on the point of being besieged! At this very moment, the Afghans may have already reached its walls."

The conversation went on in this vein for a considerable time, but there was nothing for it. The consul was determined, though he never explained why, to walk into the Persian trap. With a heavy heart, Murad finally agreed to help him with his tragic plan. He offered the consul the use of a carriage he had formerly built for himself. Made to measure, it now lay unused in the inn's stable. He attached one condition: that the vehicle not enter the town of Isfahan but return with its coachman after dropping the consul off at the city's gates.

As the night wore on, a sort of trust gradually developed between the two men. Monsieur de Maillet concluded that poor Murad was harmless, even well meaning. He decided to ask him for help in a matter that had been troubling him since his departure from Rome. On one point

Monsieur de Maillet had spoken the truth: he was not afraid to go to Isfahan, even if he were to meet his death there. But he did not want all traces of his mission to vanish with him, along with the cardinal's commitment. He had conceived the outline of a secret memorandum in which he would expose the entire business, from the concubine's dubious blackmail to his petition to the pope concerning his book. But where could he find a safe place to deposit this document?

"I am grateful for your many kindnesses, my dear Murad," said the consul after long thought. "Might I ask you for yet another favor?"

"Please. Anything, any service at all."

"Very well. Could you put a strongbox at my disposal, leaving the key in my hands?"

"A casket? Choose one from under the bed. There are two of different sizes."

Monsieur de Maillet took the smaller of the two coffers and hoisted it onto the bed, setting it down between two troughs that had almost been emptied of their pistachios. Murad rummaged under his tunic and brought out two small keys.

"Put any papers you find there into the other casket, the bigger of the two. And keep this one, it's yours."

"I thank you very kindly," said Monsieur de Maillet, overcome at finding a solution to his difficulties. "Tomorrow morning I will return it to you closed, while keeping the key myself. If anything should happen to me, if I sense that the danger is as great as you describe, I will make sure to send you the key, and I will then count on you to make these documents known and to ensure that they arrive at their destination, which you will find written on them.

Murad promised to do all this. The surprise and excitement of their reunion had tired him. The consul allowed him to doze off, taking the opportunity to return to his room and put his plan into action immediately.

A half hour later, no doubt sent by her master the ambassador, Leandra came to rub the end of her braid softly against the consul's door, moaning unequivocally. Intent on his writing, the consul barely heard her and didn't open.

29

It is best to be abducted by rich captors, as any hostage will tell you. The little band of Kirghiz raiders that captured Bibichev and his henchmen as they exited the kurgan were not. Their aoul was a gathering of small round tents such as all the nomads of the steppe build, but over the wooden poles joined into a stack were only meager pieces of camel felt, yellowish gray and extremely thin, that let in icy drafts and even a bit of rain. There was no rug on the ground, only some repulsive flea-ridden furs that were constantly shedding their hairs. The most wretched of these huts, or kibitkas, was used for storing the saddles and the milking equipment that went unused during the winter. It was there that the four prisoners were brought, their feet still hobbled, their hands tied behind their backs, and a rope attaching one to the other. There was no point in guarding them closely in the midst of this frozen wilderness: the nomads all left them alone to go and celebrate the capture in their elder's tent.

"The Scotsman was clever, wasn't he?" said Jean-Baptiste to dispel the heavy silence in their shelter. "We should have followed him."

"What do you mean, follow him!" cried Juremi, who had been simmering with anger since the morning. "When someone calls to me for help, I go."

He cast sullen glances in the direction of Bibichev, who maintained a dignified and abstracted air. In point of fact, they had all three been scooped up without the slightest resistance as they rushed wholeheartedly to the help of the policeman. Halquist had had the sense to stay behind, and he fled when he heard Juremi shout that he had been captured. Although the Kirghiz had lit a grass fire in the mouth of the tunnel to smoke him out, the Scot never reappeared. He knew the passages through the molehill so perfectly that he had probably gone out the other side, unless he had settled down there for a week.

"I hope," said Juremi wickedly, "that right around now he's having a meal of Scythian horse."

The wind gusted over the snowy crust of the steppe and slipped through the felt tent, boldly tickling the prisoners' spines. This time it was a more serious business than when they had been captured in the Caucasus. And Küyük was no longer there to save them with his trances. How could one summon the spirits of the desert without knowing their language?

At times, when the wind swirled in their direction, they caught bursts of laughter, or snatches of song coming from the tent where their new masters were celebrating.

"Ah! Ah!" cried out George all of a sudden, though he had never been known to lose his patience before, "the center of the world, that's a good one! The workshop of the gods, hah! A great idea to go and visit that tomb. Now we're really in for it."

And he went on muttering into his furs.

"Is your offspring addressing me?" asked Juremi, turning toward Jean-Baptiste.

When he received no answer, the giant spoke to the young man directly.

"I have gone out among the tribes a hundred times, do you hear? And I have never once encountered hostility. If this clown hadn't provoked them by dressing like a polecat . . ."

Bibichev pretended to hear nothing.

"That's enough!" George exploded, his handsome face, still blackened from the dust of the tunnel, a frightening sight. "Ever since we set off, we've been constantly disguising ourselves. We've listened to the superstitions of the Armenians, the tricks of a supposed shaman, and soon we'll be asked to believe that we're in the hands of a peaceful and good-humored people . . ."

"All right," said the Protestant, waiting for the rest with a severe expression, "what do you propose?"

"Oh! to let my throat be slit quietly, don't worry. But at least, at least, admit that I might be right: these lands will only become hospitable when superstition has been eradicated and the light of reason has replaced it. I don't mind dying, but I want to be able to point out the cause. All right, well, I am dying a victim of fanaticism and barbarity."

"The light of reason! Why you brat! Listen to him—"

"Come, come," said Jean-Baptiste, who wanted to step between them and felt stymied at not being able to pull his hands free. To compensate he raised his voice. "We're in a bad enough way as it is without ripping into each other."

Possibly he had shouted too loudly; the singing in the neighboring tent stopped, and the silence also had the effect of cooling the captives' temper. A few minutes went by, then the felt door of the kibitka was brutally swept aside and three Kirghiz entered. Warmed by the celebration, they had taken off their furs and wore variegated tunics of different fabrics crudely stitched together. Their wide faces with their high and prominent cheekbones were flushed with the joyful spirits of the festive ceremony, and their skin, made leathery by the wind, had the bright reflections of glazed pottery. Although they all looked quite similar and wore the same multicolored khalat, two of the nomads turned out to be men and the third a girl. She smiled as she looked at the prisoners one after the other; they saw with dread that her teeth had been carefully dyed black. Her arms hung by her sides, and in her right hand she held an object they only discovered at the moment she brandished it in front of her. It was one of those heavy steel scissors in the shape of a compass, with sharp, pointed blades for shearing sheep.

The two men laughed and egged her on as she examined each of the hostages in turn. Finally she walked up to George, and the two Kirghiz clapped noisily. Jean-Baptiste was terrified. He had done everything he could to draw the attention of this fate to himself, foreseeing that no good would come of it. When he saw her focus on George, he couldn't help crying out. But the young woman was not to be distracted. She knelt in front of George, grabbed his head, and placed it forcibly on her lap. Everyone held their breath. The square, plump hands of the savage girl plunged into the English boy's blond hair and lifted meshes of it, which she stared at pensively. At last, she raised the shears high and sliced a large hank off at the roots. She was on her feet a moment later, running away with shouts of laughter, followed by the two raucous men.

"What the devil was that about?" asked Jean-Baptiste when calm returned to the kibitka.

George, his hair still rumpled, had been so scared that he couldn't say a word.

"One of those dangerous superstitions that our young friend proposes to eradicate," said Juremi, still vexed.

"What do you mean? Tell us," prompted Jean-Baptiste anxiously.

"They believe that the hair of foreigners has special properties, especially blond hair, that's all," Juremi explained irritatedly. "Mine are gray, and no one wants them—though I have on occasion bestowed a hair or two upon the poor, who had no Englishman to scalp."

216 THE SIEGE OF ISFAHAN

"This is reassuring. It means they haven't marked George for some sacrifice or torture they are planning."

"No, alas," said Juremi, "though he certainly deserves it. What's most likely is that a woman in one of the tents of this aoul is expected to give birth soon. The young lady so recently among us will suspend the lock of hair right in front of the parturient, and the delivery will thereby be hastened, for these primitive souls believe that their attraction to these endive-colored hairs is shared by the infant."

George shrugged. Though he forced himself not to smile, he was decidedly relieved.

"Not only is there nothing to fear," went on Juremi, whom the incident had put in sparkling form, "but it all seems a very good omen."

"How the devil do you mean?" asked Jean-Baptiste.

"Did you notice how the girl looked at George? How carefully she laid his head between her firm young bison's thighs? Take my word for it, the girl has lost her heart."

Jean-Baptiste found this talk highly inappropriate and was afraid that it might spark a new quarrel with George. But they were all tied together, for better or for worse, and couldn't get away from Juremi's rantings.

"You don't believe me?" the Protestant went on. "I'm serious. Let's take a cold look at things, as if we had a choice. We're sunk. That's the truth of it. Our coming across these renegades was a pure stroke of bad luck. Do you know what they will do to us? They are going to drag us to Bukhara or Khiva and sell us as slaves. The Turkomans will take pleasure in buying us, and we'll spend the rest of our lives, which will fortunately be very short, wearing shackles and absorbing blows."

Bibichev, exhausted by his icy early-morning chase, had dozed off in his fur.

"Unless, unless," said Juremi with a hungry look, "we use our reason, our intelligence, our lights as it were."

"Leave off, I beg you," said Jean-Baptiste.

"I'm serious!" the Protestant interrupted.

Then he went on in a low voice:

"Tomorrow and the next days, when they form up a caravan, we'll see this girl again. This band of beggars can't be very numerous. George has only to smile at her! To cultivate the dominion he has gained over her through his charms!"

"That's enough, Juremi," cried George. He moved as far away from his companions as he could, given the tight rope, and turned his back on them.

"I'm serious, I tell you. You don't want to hear about superstitions? Fine. I understand. But this has to do with the human heart and its most universal laws. Plus, the young women of these tribes are capable of absolutely anything. You see them flee on horseback and gallop for days, pursued by their father's horsemen, to reach the man they love."

He continued on the subject for a long time, but the others no longer listened. George was sulking, and Jean-Baptiste, at the mention of these abductions, thought of Alix in Cairo, of moments of warmth and love that brought tears to his eyes and happy images to mind.

Everything happened just as Juremi had predicted. A woman gave birth on the day after their capture. The Kirghiz allowed the young mother two days of rest, then dismantled their huts. The nomad band consisted of eight men, twelve women, and ten or so children. To carry the wooden poles of the kibitkas, the pieces of felt that covered them, and the wooden chests in which they kept their household utensils, the raiders had only six large camels, short-legged animals with humps grown soft from lack of forage. The men rode small steppe-bred horses, usually with a woman in croup and two or three children in front on the horse's neck. Taking turns, one of the party would follow on foot, cracking a big whip at the flock of long-haired black sheep that trailed confusedly after the convoy. The prisoners, still hobbled, were tied one to another, and the first in line, generally Juremi, was attached by a cord around his neck to the saddle of the camp elder, the band's leader.

Despite the harsh measures, there were also signs of attention, even sympathy. The Kirghiz felt concern for their hostages, whom they hoped to sell dearly. They fed them with care, sacrificing a sheep every week and serving them the best pieces, grilled to perfection.

Each day the steppe presented the travelers with the same landscape, always moving past yet always standing still, unrecognizable yet sempiternally familiar. For weeks at a time they trudged through frozen dunes, gray grasses, and, while they were turning the south end of the Aral Sea, thickets of saksaoul, a shrub with a stunted trunk, its wood so hard it couldn't be carved, so brittle it couldn't be used for anything except charcoal.

They marched for endless days over stretches of salt flats that wore out their boots in a week. The nomads sewed new ones for them with great solicitude. At night when they lay down in these salt marshes, horrible itchy rashes would break out on their faces and hands, and their captors experienced the same irritations.

These common hardships, the death along the way of two children, and the eternal silence of the desert in the end created a bond between the men and women traveling together—on whichever end of the rope they were. The daily routine almost took on the color of friendship.

Yet conflicting dreams were harbored on either side, and the captives continued to watch for the slightest opportunity to escape.

There was none. Without help, or equipment, or food, or horses, it was a fantasy to imagine that one could live in these wastes. As the weeks wore on, it became clear that the only reasonable plan was the wild one proposed by Juremi at the outset.

The young Kirghiz girl who had shorn George's mop was the only marriageable woman in the band, a fact signaled by her long and free-flowing hair. Kutulun, as she was called, or "Lucky One," came every night with three other women to bring the prisoners supper. Not to risk untying their hands, the prisoners were spoon-fed by these helpers. Kutulun would only put food into George's mouth and watched him chew with fond eyes.

One day Kutulun would be married, but for the moment she was free, and her father, one of the old chief's brothers, saw no harm in her looking after the human cattle that they planned to sell. No one imagined that the young woman could have other desires than those consonant with her fate as a future mother. What's more, the Kirghiz elders were certain of being obeyed as the punishment for disobedience was harsh.

Juremi saw a little further into the souls of women, or in any case he read there something different. He convinced his companions that this young woman was capable of a grand passion that would make her break her chains and, more pertinently, theirs. But George would still hear none of it.

"Is it because her teeth are black?" asked the Protestant, trying to discover what was making this impossible child resist. "And what of that? Will death have white teeth, do you think?"

He generally made these comments during mealtimes, between mouthfuls offered by the hideous hag assigned to slop him.

"Just compare her to the three others," Juremi would insist. "Gently, madam, if you please, with that mush!"

George for his part was only sorry that he had not confessed his secret to Jean-Baptiste when the two were alone. They would leave him alone if they only knew . . . But now, how could he bare any part of his soul before the terrible Juremi, who turned everything into a joke?

The season advanced and, making steady progress, they reached more southerly latitudes. The snow disappeared, and the steppe from one day to the next assumed the brighter colors of spring pasturage. Tufts of wild sage and arrowroot relieved the monotony of the prairies. The air was tinged with the smell of garlic and wild onion. Large flights of storks blackened the sky over the salt marshes left by the Aral Sea in its southern wake. They finally reached the valley of the Amu Darya, which was cool and green, full of flocks and shepherds. The moment for action had arrived.

30

With the return of gentle weather, humidity, and good pasturage, the flock of sheep accompanying the Kirghiz band rapidly regained its strength. Each night the clear sounds of milking could once more be heard. Milk flowed from ewes, mares, and she-camels into leather buckets to enrich their owners' cooking and was fermented into cheeses and potent drinks.

At every camp, the whole aoul would become impregnated with the smell of whey and carry it along from stage to stage. The kibitkas, heated by the sun, exhaled terrifying smells of matted felt, sweat, and rendered fats, augmented by the sweetish aroma of dairy produce and fermenting milk. Most of the nomads now slept outside. During the beautiful nights, the world seemed to have capsized, with the earth a dark and deserted covering, while the sky flared with a thousand fires.

On Juremi's orders, the prisoners opted to continue sleeping in the shelter of their hut. The nomads took too good care of their hostages to refuse them this satisfaction. At nightfall, the little procession of hobbled men took a last breath of pure air and, their gorges rising, slid into the fetid entrails of their kibitka.

Juremi's whole plan depended on this nighttime camouflage. He had watched the passion in young Kutulun's heart mature and judged that they were approaching the decisive moment. The lummox George could easily have hastened its arrival if he weren't so stupid. The night the Protestant had been waiting for finally arrived. The prisoners had been asleep for about two hours when the felt flap at the tent entrance opened for a moment on the black, moonless night. The form that glided in was easily identified, or at least imagined, as Kutulun.

The captives, their hands and feet still tied, were also roped together less than a yard apart. Whatever discretion they might have liked to show toward what was to follow, their bonds kept them from moving away. Groping in the dark unerringly, Kutulun found George, whose hair she grabbed lovingly. With his hands tied behind his back, he was relieved of having to return her gestures with the same ardor. In fact he was far from any intention of the kind. Juremi had talked to him at length during the past days about what, according to him, would happen, and the boy had prepared himself for it without losing all hope that he would be let off. And now the moment was upon him.

The young girl let her khalat slip to the ground and crept naked under George's furs with him, adding to the symphony of animal smells a few new and rather sharp notes, in the oboe register.

"I am going to scream," said the young man.

The caressing sounds of the French language, to a woman used to the harshness of the steppes, unleashed on her part a purring sound replete with lust and perhaps already satisfaction.

"Consider," Juremi had said each time he spoke of the scene to come, "that if you shout out, it will spell death for her as well as for us."

It took all the young Englishman's revulsion toward committing multiple murder to keep him from denouncing the assault being made on his person. This moral conflict elicited groans from him, in which his mistress thought she heard the tenderest adjectives of the Tartar idiom.

The other prisoners, and Bibichev in particular, who did not belong to the family, brought credit on themselves by their perfect discretion, though the action lasted a great while and was, at certain moments, slightly indiscreet. The young Englishman was able to accept his defeat like a gentleman and even gave the impression finally of entering into the spirit of the act.

In the morning when they took their places around the little fire where the nomads cooked the morning meal, Juremi was beaming and George kept his eyes to the ground. Young Kutulun came and went about the camp with a morose air, and no one could have guessed that this was the same shadow that had left the kibitka at first light.

"I've calculated that we still have about ten days to go before reaching Khiva," said Juremi. "We don't know for certain that they will sell us there. They could be on their way to Bukhara. But my impression is that they'll decide to go to the nearer city. So you're going to have to act fast, George."

The young man, resigned to passive submission, did not yet seem ready to move on to voluntary action.

"We'll help you," said Juremi by way of encouragement. "First you have to make this glutton understand that she'll get more from it by untying your hands. Believe me, women have no trouble picturing this sort of thing. Follow this regimen for two nights, then talk to her about horses and make signs that you want to ride to the horizon with her. Now, I've done some research on this subject. For three days I've been listening to their conversations, and I'm starting to collect a nice little vocabulary. For example, the desert that's near here is called *Kara-Kum,* which means 'black sands.' Horses, from what I can tell, are called *kulan,* and you can also talk to her about the *kamcha,* which is that big whip the riders carry."

Jean-Baptiste felt torn. He knew how disagreeable the whole situation was to his son. And if he wasn't entirely sorry to see George get a first installment on real life, he was afraid it might lead to an act of despair or revolt. He had to concede Juremi's foresight, though. And in their critical situation, there hardly seemed another solution.

"But how can we possibly flee?" Jean-Baptiste asked the Protestant. "Are you forgetting that there are four of us?"

"Three," said Juremi sharply, sneering at Bibichev. "So we only need three horses. She just has to get one for George, one for herself, and a third for their baggage. That's the lot. After she has freed his hands, he borrows her knife and cuts our ropes by way of farewell. She won't object. Then they leave the kibitka and walk toward the horses. We follow them. At the last moment we grab her, gag her, and leave her tied up somewhere ten minutes from the aoul. We're free."

"Do you want the poor girl to die?" cried George.

"I knew it!" said the Protestant. "Yesterday, milord wouldn't have her; she had black teeth, or she looked like a Breton armoire, or who knows what it was? Today he is in love with her and no one can touch a hair of his lady's head."

"In love with her!" the young man repeated, looking up at the sky.

"George is right," Jean-Baptiste intervened. "The poor girl doesn't deserve to be betrayed like that. Why not bring her with us?"

"All right, as you like. Their horse will have to carry two of them. I warn you that if they follow us . . ."

"That's a risk we'll have to take," said Jean-Baptiste after studying George's shuttered face for a moment.

Even under those conditions, it wasn't certain that the young man would agree to take part in such a plot.

Yet that night brought their plans a step forward. Without having to be told, Kutulun cut the rope around George's hands and replaced it on leaving with a hemp handcuff that was easier to tie and untie. The following night she showed great tact in staying away altogether, which gave everyone the chance for a good night's rest. The following evening, Juremi renewed his exhortations: the moment had come for George to speak. Regrettably, the night passed in wordless rustlings of fur, to the usual tempest of animal fleece and ripe cheese.

All day, George brooded and refused to utter a word. When their nocturnal visitor appeared, Juremi took it on himself to intervene, staking everything on the outcome. The girl had hardly slid into George's bed when the Protestant started whispering insistently:

"*Kara-Kum,* young lady. *Kulan! Kulan!* and wham, wham, *kamcha,* giddy-up, *kamcha!*"

The nomads are not offended at promiscuity. The crowding of their families into tents accustoms them from childhood to discreet observation of the frolicking that maintains the species. The young girl was not unaware that her lover's three companions lay nearby attached to them by ropes. Yet she froze on actually hearing Juremi speak to her. Did she feel indignation at finding this old man, whose malicious glance she knew, talking in her ear of hot sands, wild horses, and the whip? In any case she dealt him a resounding slap in the face and disappeared.

The night was a gloomy one. The captives, now believing that George's sacrifice had been for nothing, uttered not a word.

The following days, the caravan advanced by long stages at a distance from the river, among rounded sand dunes devoid even of shrubs. To make a fire, the Kirghiz searched the ground for tiny plants with yellow flowers, whose woody roots reached the size of a man's arm under the sand. Suddenly the nomads seemed in great haste. They plodded on interminably, unloaded a minimum of utensils at night, and no longer pitched any tents, which put an end to Kutulun's little game. What's more, she was now the object of everyone's attention. On the caravan's third night in this desert landscape, the women shaved the head of the supposed virgin completely; far from being a punishment, the operation was performed with laughter and festive preparations. The next day, they angled southward and came nearer to the river. At midday they reached a large aoul surrounded by abundant herds, to which a strong band of Tartars welcomed them with whoops and ululations. The khalats of these graceful hosts were tailored from colored samite and embroidered with gold thread. The captives recognized a man among them whom they had met with a group of horsemen not far from the Aral Sea. He had stayed with the little band for three days, during which he had held long councils with their elder.

Only now did they understand the subject of these talks: a marriage had been agreed to, and Kutulun was to be one of the parties.

Everything in the large aoul had been prepared for a wedding. A beefy young man of yellow complexion, his eyes so epicanthic they seemed to remain continuously closed, had been designated to marry George's lover. From the admiring way their hosts came to examine them, the prisoners understood that it was only thanks to a discount against their future sale that the elder of the band had been able to wrangle such a rich prize for his niece. Two poor wretches, who were servants to the prospective groom's rich tribe, were assigned to guard them day and night, lance in hand and suspicion in their eyes.

For three days the unfortunate hostages, still securely tied, had to endure the sight of endless festivities, in which their only share was dripping hunks of lamb held out to them to peck at. The bride, her head adorned in the large white veil that covers the shaven head, the nape of the neck, and the chin of married women, had not a glance to spare for the young man she had until recently been assaulting.

Juremi hadn't come to terms with his slap in the face, nor with the shipwreck of his plans. He showered the young bride with vengeful and indignant mutterings. This affair proved, according to him, that a savagess was in no way inferior to a so-called civilized woman, at least when it came to perversity.

He hadn't conceived the full extent of it, however. When the time came for the two bands to part, the smaller tearfully said goodbye to the young woman forsaking her first family to stay with her husband. They wished her good luck. Endless blessings were made in the name of Allah, for the nomads claim allegiance to Islam though they perform none of the prayers of this religion and seem unaware of the existence, never mind the direction, of Mecca. The horsemen were already in the saddle, the camels loaded, and the prisoners in marching order when the dreadful Kutulun uttered a loud cry. They watched as she ran into a kibitka and back out again only to swoop down on George. Brandishing her sheep shears, she cut off a last lock of his hair to the emotional cheers of both tribal groups, then returned to nestle against her husband, the talisman pressed to her stomach in pledge of her future fertility.

"That way," said Juremi darkly when they were once more on the road, "if the little minx gives birth to a blond child, the credit will go to your hair, George, and not to the husband's horns."

In two days they reached Khiva, under the rule of a fiercely autocratic khan. No infidel entered the town except as a captive, or left it except as a slave. Their first glimpse of Khiva was partly obscured by a curtain of trees. The road into the city led between high orchard walls, above which they could see the foliage of alders and willows. Finally they reached the city's outer rampart, a formidable wall consisting of bricks along the lower portion and clay along the top, so tall that even the highest painted minarets and tile-covered domes could hardly be seen. They entered through a massive door with iron bolts to find themselves in a large sandy open area, beyond which was a second wall, lower than the first, with the town behind it. The space served as a market on one side, while on the other, scattered randomly, were a multitude of Mahometan graves. The rich streets of the city were lined with shops offering goods of every sort. By contrast, their own poor procession appeared mangy. The prisoners lowered their eyes and showed their shame at the furry rags they wore, which were too warm for the climate and dirty from the hardships of the journey. Their jailers, on the other hand, held their heads high, proud to parade their considerable booty before the whole town.

Either because they were unfamiliar with the bazaars or because they wanted to extend the pleasure of this parade, the Kirghiz made numerous detours before arriving at their destination. The sun was already setting below the walls of the city when they arrived at the stalls where slaves were bought and sold.

31

In Isfahan nothing had been touched during the brief exodus of the city's residents to the surrounding hills. There was no looting to deplore, nor the slightest theft. Yet the city was no longer the same. Life did not resume its usual course. People made the same gestures, found the same smells and street sounds there, but having seen themselves from the outside, having contemplated the finitude, the fragility, and the derisory character, perhaps, of their lives, the city's residents felt a change in their souls, to the point where they were strangers to themselves.

Alix felt these changes more than anyone. She found everything as it had been, yet she recognized nothing. Besides, what was there to hang on to? What she had shared with Jean-Baptiste was dislocated by his absence. What she had been occupied with since his departure seemed childish and dull.

Françoise, in pain from her broken arm, remained in bed and suffered in silence. The servants had resumed their posts but showed by a discreet change in their attitude that they recognized Saba as the only one capable of making important decisions, and therefore the only one who could legitimately give orders about small decisions. The rosebushes needed tending, as did the medicinal plants, having suffered much neglect from Alix in the past months. Saba gave all her time to them and spent the better part of her days in this garden, which was neither quite her house nor quite the outside world.

For about a week after her return, Alix avoided thinking about Nur al-Huda and especially Reza, so strong was her feeling that she had ventured down a dangerous path with him. Showing a child's naiveté, she convinced herself that by chasing these memories from her mind she could erase their existence.

She had succeeded so well during that week that, on seeing the eunuch Ahmad's pointed hat above the garden wall, she felt a stab of emotion. At the same instant, the bell rang and Nur al-Huda, her chaperon in the lead, bustled into the garden.

She kissed Alix as soon as she had taken off her veil and dragged her friend into the house as though she were at home.

"Brr," said the young Circassian, "let's go inside, it's still winter, and I don't know how you can stand to have your arms bare."

The two sat down at a small octagonal table inlaid with mother-of-pearl. Nur al-Huda's blue taffeta dress was closed up to the base of her neck, and on this bodice swelled by her breasts shone a double row of sapphires and diamonds.

"What a horrible week it's been!" she said forcefully. "First, during all of that ridiculous excursion I was deprived of my companions—as you can imagine they stayed hidden in the harem. And as if that weren't sad enough, I've now been back a whole week and you haven't visited me once. What have I done? Tell me? Do you not like me anymore?"

Her thin face registered such sincerity, and her voice was so clearly pained, that Alix felt terribly ashamed and wanted to ask her friend's forgiveness.

"Don't go imagining anything of the kind," she said with difficulty. "I've had so little time, believe me. With Françoise being ill, and all the things we had to do when we got back. And then I've been afraid of going out . . ."

"I know all that," said Nur al-Huda, taking her hands, "and that's why I came myself. Come, I'm not angry with you . . ."

To maintain her composure, Alix called out for tea and cakes.

"Besides," her visitor went on, "it's not the moment to complain or quarrel. The worst is yet to come. It's now a certainty: we can expect the Afghans at the gates of the city from one day to the next."

Although they had all known it for weeks and had seen proof of it in the fall of Kirman, the residents of Isfahan could not bring themselves to imagine thirty thousand brutish Afghan shepherds camped in front of their refined capital. Among the feelings elicited by the invasion, indignation held a greater place than terror.

On this veranda, laved in the gray sunlight filtering through the yews, the imminence of the invasion was even harder to accept than elsewhere.

"Will they mount an attack or settle in for a siege?" asked Alix.

"No one knows, and my dear husband less than anyone. The army itself has received no orders. Officially, they are making preparations, but in reality they are just waiting. If the Afghans attack, our army will defend itself, but it may not happen right away. A true siege is apparently impossible at this time of year because the city can't be fully encircled: it's protected by the river, whose bridges we control."

"How fortunate!"

"Yes and no. My dear husband, whom I approve of for once, is for negotiating with these raiders and offering them a sum that will make them go quietly home. Alas, his opinion is in the minority. A faction now gaining ground with the king is urging him to use the rest of the army to mount a powerful strike. It's possible that even the guard . . ."

Alix winced. Nur al-Huda had stopped for a moment and showed great emotion, to the point where for the first time her friend saw tears glaze her eyes.

"Reza no longer wants to meet with me," she said in a broken voice.

"But how . . . how can you know?" asked Alix, flustered.

"Through the usual channel, the woman who helped arrange the meetings we had thanks to you. She's the wife of one of his junior officers, who has been passing messages to Reza and sending me back the replies."

A pause.

"When there is one."

Alix was deeply moved by her friend's suffering. So as not to give in to a confession that would have relieved no one but herself, she tried to think of objections that would also exculpate her.

"Maybe he hasn't been able to see you because of all that's happening."

"Nothing prevents him. The woman has seen him. He himself said as calmly as you please that he had nothing to say to me."

"I don't understand, Nur," said Alix a little too quickly. "You always seemed so indifferent. And when I came to you with his message . . ."

"What can I say," said the girl, raising her head. "Yes, I could afford to seem indifferent since he wasn't. What message did you bring me except that he was suffering. Therefore I knew he loved me, so why should I have shown any alarm?"

"But," argued Alix, pained at this admission, "what about the things he told me, the passion he's expressed for you and that you've rejected, your marriage . . ."

"Alix, please. Don't oblige me to lose all honor before you . . ."

"What do you mean?"

"Don't oblige me to tell you the whole story, which would reveal me in all my weakness, and which would contradict his version on every point. His passion! Just the word makes my blood boil. Because I know what passion is. I know that it has no limits, that you accept damnation for it. Since childhood, do you understand, I have been consumed by this poisonous flower. Since childhood I have not been able to conceive of living without him, or of sharing him, or of being despised and treated as a mistress—loved, perhaps, yes, but surreptitiously, within the bounds of family propriety. I disappeared in order to escape this torture. But by ill fortune I met him again, and ever since I have sunk further and further. My marriage! Do you think I would have gone and married here, under his nose, and to a person like my husband, if I had really wanted to escape him and hadn't wanted instead to call out to him, make him understand how much I despise all that he sets such store by. I only ever had one thing in mind: him! And he never made the smallest step toward choosing me, preferring me to everything and everyone. Even now he's going to risk his life to defend that crazy king. Is that what you call a grand passion?"

Nur al-Huda finished her sentence with a sob and hid her face in her hands. Alix rose so as not to watch her cry and came to stand behind her. When the young girl had composed herself again and wiped away her tears, Alix sat down again.

"Forgive me," said Nur al-Huda. "None of my friends can understand it. They are women who have endured too much misfortune, perhaps, to feel sorry for themselves as I do."

And have I not endured enough? thought Alix. She had never before felt so guilty at not having been unhappy in love. Perhaps that was all that she had been looking for.

"In any case," continued Nur al-Huda, straightening up and in a new tone of voice at once energetic and nasty, "I'll know what caused it. He didn't change as he did for no reason. Whenever he has put distance between us before, he has always left a door open. There must be another woman who turned him away from me for him to shut me off like this. But who? I don't know, but I'll find out, believe me, and my vengeance . . ."

She didn't finish. Alix had dropped her cup of boiling tea onto her knees. The rest of the visit passed in taking care of her slight but extensive burn and in going to sit with Françoise to entertain her.

The Kashan caravanserai had only just recovered from the turmoil caused by the discovery of a woman disguised as a male traveler. The merchant Ali, who hadn't been seen again since that time, was often mentioned at night in the conversations held in the cool of the great courtyard. But the rumors of war had gradually taken precedence, and now that the

Afghans were within sight of the capital, the main attraction at the inn was the procession of foreign carriages fleeing Persia at top speed. Since the start of the tragic events, they were invariably heading in the one direction, away from Isfahan and toward the Turkish border. This detail in itself was enough to make the arrival of a carriage traveling in the opposite direction noteworthy.

This vehicle, rustic in construction and dilapidated in appearance, was remarkable for its enormous leaf springs, which a skillful blacksmith had doubled, even tripled, so as to cushion a considerable weight over the worst bumps. But instead of the mastodon or the numerous party that one might have expected to emerge from such a coach, in the doorway appeared a little wizened man, who jumped to the ground with a display of bad humor.

"Finally!" cried Monsieur de Maillet, setting his foot on the steps of the caravanserai.

He shouted to the coachman to bring in his luggage immediately. It consisted only of a simple bundle, but one he considered it beneath his dignity to carry.

Entering the establishment, the consul was disappointed at eliciting no more than a mildly contemptuous curiosity, and in any case nothing like helpfulness. He was given, grudgingly and at a very high price, a small room on the upper floor. After casting a quick glance around the room, he went back downstairs among the merchants to catch up on the latest news. But conversations broke off as he approached, and he ended up by himself, his arms folded, near one of the fountains decorating the corners of the courtyard. It was there that the coachman came to join him.

"You look worried, Beugrat," said the consul acidly.

"Worried, me?" answered the coachman, looking around as though the comment might apply to someone else.

The driver was a gigantic Swiss whose head bristled with red hair. He had landed in Murad's service after his meager career as a mercenary ended with an inglorious broken knee, sustained during a bout of drunkenness.

He now put all his honor into asserting his origins as a native of the Swiss canton of Vaud, and he constantly lampooned his neighbors and enemies from the canton of Valais for their stupidity and filth. His favorite joke, in fact his only one, which he repeated constantly, was contained in the following two sentences: "Why is the air so pure in the Valais? Because its inhabitants never open their windows."

Finally grasping that the consul was indeed addressing him, Beugrat made great forward strides in self-awareness.

"Yes, sir," he said, "you're right: I am worried."

Then, pursuing his introspection further, he went on with difficulty: "Or rather I'm not. Well, not anymore. In fact, not at all."

"Explain, Beugrat," said the consul impatiently.

"Well then, my master, the Ethiopian ambassador—"

"Call him 'Murad,' as it's just the two of us."

"Well, my master particularly told me to take good care of his coach. I've gathered some information. The road from here on out is terrible, and there's the threat of war. That's it in a nutshell: I'm not going any farther."

This scrupulous coachman knew only one thing in life, how to look after Murad's carriage, and nothing could sway him from his decision. Monsieur de Maillet came to realize this. Neither threats nor magnificent promises of money, nor entreaties worked. The only concession he could wring from Beugrat was to wait for him at least two weeks in Kashan. Monsieur de Maillet thought to accomplish his business long before that, and if he was detained any longer, it would be, as he commonly put it, "for that encounter each man must prepare himself for, though knowing neither the day nor the hour."

In fact, the coachman's capriciousness was almost a good thing: the coach, standing out as it did, would make his entry into the threatened city difficult. Monsieur de Maillet was convinced that a simple mule would better serve his ends. While he was bargaining over the price of his mount, a fine equipage dashed noisily into the caravanserai. On inquiry, it turned out to be a detachment of the royal constabulary of France. These soldiers had guarded the precincts of their embassy to the very end, and were finally obeying the order to draw back.

The provosts in white and blue uniforms took the best table in the vaulted hall where meals were served, and called for wine with boorish cries. Monsieur de Maillet let the squadron slake its thirst, then on a hunch approached the man on the end of the bench who seemed to be their leader. The officer's regulation wig, flattened like a beret, sat askew on his enormous square head, which seemed on the verge of exploding. The red wine that the fellow took in at the mouth seemed not to bother detouring through his intestines before lighting up his face from the inside and radiating across his bulging eyes. A plant watered in this fashion cannot grow in the wrong direction, and to sum up Monsieur de Maillet's thoughts, "the brave fellow inspired confidence."

The former diplomat asked permission, in the name of their shared fatherland, to join the soldiers at table. He toasted their health but remained, despite his every effort, a discordant note in their midst, like a daisy in a field of poppies.

Fortunately, these brave and simple lads rose from table almost immediately and went to lie down. Only the officer stayed on: being older, he needed a double dose.

"So," said Monsieur de Maillet admiringly, "you are leaving Persia, poor country! And who is left to protect the French ambassador?"

"The ambassador! It's been ages since he left, and all the other diplomats with him. It makes no difference if the pigs in the constabulary face the fusillade."

"You left the embassy empty! Are you not afraid of looters?"

"We're afraid, all right, but mostly of what they'll do to us. If they loot the embassy, we'll build another just as good, or then again maybe we won't. But that's not our business. First they'll have to wait for all these hotheads to agree amongst themselves, which will take years."

Until now the soldier had answered carelessly, paying little attention to this sentimental elderly gentleman. But once he had finished the second carafe, he looked at him more closely:

"How is it possible that you don't know all this? There isn't a Frank in Isfahan who doesn't."

"It's just that . . . I'm not from Isfahan," said Monsieur de Maillet, "I am going there."

"You are going! Lunatic! Do you want to lose your life?"

The consul was satisfied. Since he had started acting for the salvation of his soul and for his reintegration into the body of the church, he felt capable of anything. There was no means that was not justified by this noble end. The plan taking shape in his head required a great lie: he proffered it without the slightest contrition.

For almost a quarter of an hour he described his situation to the officer in poignant terms. Not only did he invent a name for himself and hide his former position, but he pretended to have suffered a considerable number of horrible misfortunes to himself, his children, his brothers and sisters, and even his favorite hound in the pack. To escape this hellish cycle of misfortune, the bishop of his parish had personally recommended a pilgrimage to Isfahan, where Saint Thomas had preached the gospel of Christ. For the intercession to be effective, he had to find himself in the very crypt where the apostle had preached on the morning of the spring equinox, which was in two weeks.

This tale was so long and told with such talent, emotion, and suffering that the soldier had to help himself to two further carafes so as not to burst into tears himself, or just burst, plain and simple. At the end he seized the consul's arm:

"I understand. Better yet, I approve."

Then, looking cautiously around, he added:

"And if you'll allow me, I'd like to help you. You're going to Isfahan? Very well. But where will you stay? The caravanserais in that town are places where you will get your throat cut, now more than ever, especially a foreigner."

Monsieur de Maillet blinked and allowed his eyes to tear up from snuff.

"That damned embassy residence is empty," went on the constable. "We left it in the hands of a Persian who is honest only because he's too lazy to thieve. As soon as the first squibs go off he'll wake up and be at the forefront of the pillaging. Go there!"

"What do you mean?" asked Monsieur de Maillet, pretending great surprise.

"Go there, I'm telling you. Tell Hasan, that's his name, that I sent you—Chauveau, can you remember that? And here, take the key to the legation, go on, take it, we weren't so foolish as to leave it with him. At least for the time you're living within those walls, you'll protect them, and they'll protect you. Well, a little, because I don't think the Afghans know a great deal about diplomatic protocol. In any case, you'll see. And good luck to you."

So saying, the policeman abandoned the realm of earthly thoughts. He finished his tumbler, then crossed the courtyard, his eyes glassy, his walk firm though a little wide to the sides, and went to lie down beside his men.

32

In the silence of the spring morning, all of Isfahan's residents stood quietly on the roof terraces of their houses, and all of the army gathered on the southern embankment to look beyond the sparkling river at the black mass that had come to a standstill on the plain. The Afghans were there! The barbarians! Death! Mothers clasped their children to them, husbands their wives, and the elderly shook their heads. Everyone suddenly felt there was too much blue in the sky, too many silks draping these bodies, too much delicious glaze on the enameled wall tiles and magnolia leaves. Isfahan, which was all beauty, tenderness, sensuality, and refinement, like a young woman in love, like a happy girl, had simply forgotten about death, which was now here, black and immobile on the plain.

The Afghans were coming no nearer. Being at a considerable distance, nothing about them could be made out. Were they building a camp? No smoke of a campfire rose into the air. Had they even dismounted from their horses? Was it only an advance party, waiting for the bulk of the troops?

Mounted Persian scouts made large circles that brought them momentarily close to the invaders and returned to bring news to the city. Four ominous buzzards imitated these circles in the sky, and as though this hour of tragedy were also the birds' hour, turtledoves seized on the silence in the gardens to fill them with their crooning imprecations.

At the royal palace, the place with the widest view was a watchtower next to the kitchens. It was on this terrace that Huseyn, king of Persia, protected under a red canopy held up by four slaves, gazed at the black seeds of disaster far off across the plain, which no doubt contained the germ of his own downfall. Courtiers and high officials formed a circle to one side, each, for once, vying not to be in the front row of the little crowd. Wielding a savage politesse, they attempted to conceal themselves behind someone else. In contrast to apoplectics, who breathe more easily when they are bled, the sovereign found his ill humors relieved by seeing others bleed. The fear on this morning was that he might feel the pressing need to see a few heads cut off.

In truth, Huseyn was beyond such diversions. Wine, his only succor, had taken full control of him, in the form of a dazed, almost indifferent calm. He stared fixedly at the horizon, and no one could have said what he might possibly see there.

Yet the court's terror and the gravity of the moment had not swept aside the many plots and rivalries dividing the royal entourage. Imminent catastrophe is a call to those whose ambition has till then been constrained by overly peaceful times. If peace favors reasonable men with settled ways of thought and delicate habits, tragedy and chaos free the initiative of those great beasts of the supernatural who have kept their huge prophet's or hero's body squeezed within the narrow coffer of ordinary life and now seize the moment to deploy it far above other men.

Such a man was Yahya Beg, magus and astrologer, king's favorite as well, but one who had suffered at having to share his dominion over the monarch with many others, and above all with the mullahs, the whole Shi'i court clique. Persian superstition, which is ubiquitous, borrows its forms from Islam but comes from much farther afield, from those primitive ages when the cult of Mithra reigned and there was human sacrifice. The Magians, who were the guardians of these ancient divinatory traditions, had only grudgingly shared their power with Muslim officials and continued to contest Muslim influence. A great tragedy could be the perfect opportunity for settling these scores.

While the circle of courtiers backed away, quaking with fear, Yahya Beg strode forward on the terrace and dared to stand alone before the king.

"Your Majesty," he said in a loud voice, "I must announce some important news to you."

Huseyn turned toward the astrologer, his black eyes barely visible behind eyelids swollen to the size of small sausages.

"What do you want?" he groaned.

"To speak to you, Sire, but what I have to say is not for indiscreet ears and concerns only your sovereign self."

The holy man's tone was so firm and laced with so unmistakable a threat that, despite the effort the gesture cost him, the king raised both arms and dismissed the entire court. Only the four slaves holding the canopy were left. Yahya Beg insisted that they leave as well, and Huseyn, who had been shivering a bit in the shade, gladly accepted the chance to warm himself in the lovely morning sun.

"Speak," he said.

"Sire, what I have to tell you is of the utmost gravity. I hesitated for a long time, believe me, and I am proceeding only after having read and reread the clear proof of what I have to say in the stars themselves."

In the distance, on the plain, two columns of blue smoke rose toward the sky near the Afghans. Had they pitched camp?

"Now," said Yahya Beg, and his tall thin figure stood out against the distant line of Iran's snowy plateaux, "I'll speak frankly: have the Prophet Muhammad and his son-in-law Ali protected us against our enemies?"

He made the silence last, and the ruler answered with embarrassment.

"Not enough, I agree," he murmured. "We have, no doubt, sinned greatly . . ."

"No, Sire. Your ancestor Shah Abbas had the same habits as ourselves, particularly as concerns the pleasures of the table and the body. Yet he conquered. The clerics asked us to perform acts of penitence, and we did. They were of no use."

"Are you implying that God . . . ?" Huseyn said worriedly.

"Exists, Sire, I do not contest it. There is no God but God, the point is agreed. But . . ."

"To say 'but' is already to disown God."

"No, Your Majesty. I said 'but' not in relation to God, whose strength is infinite and whose power is without limit. It applies only to those who pretend to interpret God."

"The mullahs!"

"Your Majesty, here is my belief. This country is not just a country like any other to God. He summoned a great prophet here . . ."

"Zoroaster."

"The very one, who showed us the way for many centuries. He revealed to us the sacred name of Ahuramazda and instructed us about the diabolical plans of Ahriman, god of evil. For centuries the great kings of Persia have drawn their strength from this god of sun and fire, who lights, warms, and renders invincible."

With his black hair hanging to his shoulders and his staring eyes, Yahya Beg had a terrifying majesty.

"Are we not being punished for forgetting this god who elected us in the first place? Are we not guilty of having made His image disappear behind the very true but very general God of the Muslims? In fact the one has covered over the other. Has He replaced Him? Is He not simply the form in which Ahuramazda chose to appear to us and manifest His presence in the world? Allah is the name behind which God hides for all the peoples of the earth. Ahuramazda is the name by which He reveals Himself to the one people He has chosen among all others. Is this not what He wanted to tell us by spreading that immense fire over our heads during the hour of defeat?"

Then, pivoting somewhat to the side, Yahya Beg swept the air with his right arm and pointed at the menacing shadow of the Afghans on the plain.

"Their God is the same as the God of our mullahs. Why should they be conquerors?"

He allowed Huseyn the time to ask himself the question, during a long pause.

"Because, Your Majesty," he continued, "we are not using our true strength. It is time to tear the veil and show that we are believers in the one God of this country. It is time, in order to avert these misfortunes, to call on the eternal God who has formed an alliance with this country, the millennial God of our ancestors, Ahuramazda."

"But," murmured Huseyn under his spell, "what does He want us to do?"

"To worship Him in the correct manner, Your Majesty, and to consent to the sacrifices He may ask of us."

"Sacrifices? What sacrifices?"

"I don't know, Sire. We will know it by tonight if you choose."

"A dreadful choice, in truth, between abjuration and defeat," said Huseyn, biting one of his hands.

"No, Your Majesty, victory and reconciliation with the very sources of your dynasty are within your grasp."

Huseyn, deeply uneasy, fidgeted on his throne and whimpered. The four buzzards chose this moment to make their circles over the castle. Did he read this as a sign?

"And where will we perform this ceremony?"

"Ideally," answered Yahya Beg sternly, mastering his triumph, "we would hold it in Persepolis, at the altars of your ancestors. At present it is out of the question. But in the suburb of Abbas Abad there is an ancient temple that may do."

"And . . . when?"

"Time presses. We will start this very night, at four o'clock, in time for dawn."

Hasan liked only one thing: having his beard trimmed. He never felt as well as when he reclined in the barber's chair, his neck caressed by a warm towel, surrounded by perfume flasks and mirrors . . . He decidedly had but one regret: that his hairs did not grow any faster so that he might resort to these delights more often. According to popular wisdom, one's beard grows faster during periods of sleep, which gave him a reason to prolong his siestas until five o'clock in the afternoon. He had arranged a rug and some cushions in the shelter of the wooden gallery formerly used by the gendarmes: from there you could see the entrance gate, the first garden, and the steps to the French embassy with its five French windows. Hasan at first thought that he was dreaming when he awoke to find the middle door ajar. He cautiously approached the door, pushed it open, and entered. It was the first time he had gone inside the legation since the Franks' departure. All the large pieces of furniture were in their accustomed places, a beautiful sight to see, the curved chests of drawers, the long tables, the large armchairs covered in silk plush. The diplomats had carried off only the small things in their chests: the silver, the candlesticks, and the portable paintings. The rooms were at once sumptuously furnished in the European style and stripped of all the details that show a room to be lived in.

The evening sun bounced from room to room, striking gold reflections off the moldings and blue iridescence from the crystal of the chandeliers. Out of caution, Hasan walked softly and silently. He saw no one in the entry or the drawing room, poked his head into the kitchens, which were empty. Finally he walked toward the ambassador's office, which opened directly onto the garden. From lingering scruple, slipcovers of unbleached cloth had been placed on the furniture in this room. The embassy's majordomo had been resigned to the idea that the embassy would be looted, but he could not stand the thought of the furniture collecting dust. Hasan had to scan the room a moment before making out, in the midst of these white ghosts, the figure of a small, dignified, and withered old man, who had stiffly taken his place behind the large Boulle desk.

Hasan had obtained his post thanks to his serviceable French, learned as a child from playing with the children of a French merchant. Yet when Monsieur de Maillet told him rather curtly to enter and sit down, the Persian asked him to repeat the statement three times, so sure was he that he did not understand the language of ghosts.

"Brigadier Chauveau told me you were an honest man," the consul went on without allowing the poor man to recover from his astonishment. "My compliments! Nothing has been moved. You have guarded the embassy well."

"But . . . who are you?"

"Monsieur de Maillet, French consul."

Speaking these words, his hands flat on the leather of the desktop, sensing the portrait of Louis XIV above him—for there hadn't yet been time, in the tumult of the Regency, to replace it—Monsieur de Maillet felt his lip tremble a bit but was able to contain the emotion that overcame him.

"Have you a courier?" he asked, turning to the calmer realm of practicalities.

"A what, Your Excellency?"

"A messenger, someone who can travel about the city carrying messages."

"My sister's eldest son, if you please."

"Perfect. I'll need him today. Tell me, do you know which of the personages at court is called the nazir?"

"The nazir? Of course, Excellency. He is the great chamberlain of the king's house."

"Well, I would like to convey a message to him this very evening. Does he read French?"

"I don't believe so, Excellency, but I can translate it for him, unless it's secret."

Monsieur de Maillet, rummaging in a nearly empty drawer, had found a pen, some ink, and a small piece of paper. He wrote the following lines:

> Milord,
> If you would be so kind as to come at the earliest possible moment to the French embassy. It concerns the Alberoni affair.
> Signed: B. de M.

He folded the sheet and, not finding an envelope in any of the drawers, entrusted it to the porter as it was.

"Tell your nephew to replace you in the garden and carry this message yourself to the nazir immediately."

Hasan ran out into the street with the letter, a bit sorry that he had not profited from the brief respite of the last two days when he could have stolen something from the embassy. Yet at bottom he was rather pleased that life had resumed its normal course.

An hour later, the nazir's carriage was entering the open double gates of the French legation, and the heavy official nimbly climbed the entrance steps.

On receiving the consul's note, the nazir abandoned all his other business instantly. The coming of the Afghans had brought an atmosphere of rout into the city, and each person was concerned to gather his belongings, prepare hiding places for them, and organize his possible flight. In the panic, all debts were being called in. The nazir was busy day and night trying to recover those still due him and avoid paying those being clamored for. The balance sheet was disastrous at the moment. Then all of a sudden Alberoni reappeared, offering the prospect of help from abroad. At a time like this, it spelled fortune, freedom, life itself, perhaps. He would have to see to these negotiations immediately.

The nazir was at first surprised to see the man chosen by the powerful cardinal to represent his interests. The worn and patched suit the old man wore, for instance, yellowed from many washings yet soiled at the sleeves and collar—was it due to the war, or was it rather an extraordinary ruse? At any rate it in no way affected the man's high valuation of his own dignity. And what was hidden by the white veils mysteriously covering the furniture in this office? The nazir seated himself on a small sofa whose slipcover came down to the ground. He immediately had the disagreeable sensation that a man might have slid under the trailing skirt. He renewed his caution.

"I will be perfectly direct," said the consul after a brief exchange of greetings. "Cardinal Alberoni wishes to know the truth as soon as possible about . . . the letter he received from Persia, sent by a woman who claims to know him and who mentions you specifically."

The nazir pulled on one of his mustaches and released the long gray spring after it reached its full extension. It immediately coiled back up under his nose. Hasan interpreted, and the nazir merely nodded to show that he had understood.

"The cardinal's orders," the consul went on, "which I am blindly following, are categorical: I must meet this woman."

Meet her, thought the nazir, his mind racing. He'll have to. But not at Poncet's house, as this emissary mustn't know where she is hiding. Otherwise he'll take her and she'll get away from me. Keeping control of this business is the key.

He had Hasan translate a florid reply, in which it came out that he was dazzled by the glory of Alberoni, that the consul had no more devoted slave on earth than he, and that he would arrange for the consul to perceive His Holiness's very considerable concubine the following morning.

Perceive her! thought Monsieur de Maillet. You're a sly one. You want to keep me from talking to her and exposing her imposture.

"At least," he protested, "allow me a word with her, that I may reassure her as to the cardinal's concern for her."

"Ah! Excellency," cried the nazir, "that would be to kill her. No, no, believe me. First the two of us will come to an agreement here and fix the conditions for her departure, then I will prepare her for it with all necessary gentleness."

During the long silence that followed, the nazir pulled out a snuffbox and buried his mustaches in it.

"Tell him to be careful of the slipcovers!" cried Monsieur de Maillet on seeing the grains of black powder spilling.

The nazir decidedly found the place strange and this man unusually agitated.

"It is regrettable," said the consul finally, "but if I cannot speak to her, it is useless for me to see her. I'm afraid my mission has come to an end."

It took almost an hour of maneuvering for the two foxes to reach an agreement. A rendezvous was made for the next morning at the nazir's house. The interview would take place through the Persian himself, with two interpreters, so that the consul could not give the woman any message directly without the chamberlain knowing it.

Once the business was settled and his visitor was gone, Monsieur de Maillet dismissed Hasan and remained alone in the office as the violet shadows of the evening lengthened. He opened the door onto the garden and went out for a moment into the cool air. It was just what he had used to do in Cairo after a day's work. The same cries, the same barking of dogs, rose from the city. The sensual pleasure of power was all contained in this bitter solitude. A slight evening breeze made him shiver, and he went back inside. The chairs held their arms up under their veils and stood out against the growing darkness. All the torches had disappeared. Feeling his way with his hands among the ghosts, the consul went to the door, down the hallway, up the big staircase, and finally reached the floor above. In the first room he felt the mattress of a large bed, which had been stripped of its sheets. He stretched out on it fully dressed, and the big gentle hand of nostalgia immediately carried him off to sleep.

33

If you should feel the urge one day to found a great religion, it is incumbent on you to speak, teach, live, perform exemplary acts, but on no account to write anything. Not one of the great founders—Jesus, Muhammad, or Buddha—wrote anything in his own hand. No doubt this is what has preserved the vital and original force of their message. Afterward, generations of toiling priests had the time to solidify this burbling source into the ice of their writings and commentaries. Zoroaster did not have this misfortune or this luck. His teaching was not codified, and the most extravagant magic practices have claimed descent from him with no one able to disprove it.

At the time Yahya Beg was trying to restore the Zoroastrian religion to official status, it had grown so neglected that any innovation was permissible. The temple of Abbas Abad was a plain stone altar at the center of an open space that was also used as a trysting place and a garbage dump. In preparation for the ceremony, the astrologer sent a small group of his slaves to clean the precincts and to lay palm branches along the perimeter. The main thing was to keep away the usual idlers and loiterers. It was announced that the first person who approached the area or even looked at it from a distance would be sentenced to death. By midnight the bundles of firewood had been carted in and the logs stacked behind a low wall. Yahya Beg, wearing a red simar, set off a bit later in his own sumptuous carriage to fetch the king. By the time the monarch was readied and brought to the site—alone, a crucial condition—it was four-thirty in the morning. An enormous bonfire had been lit by the astrologer's numerous henchmen. Large embers of pine, crackling with pungent resin, burned below the flames so that only a great red light showed. Yahya Beg settled the king on a rug near the inferno and facing the altar. Within moments, the unfortunate Huseyn was dripping with sweat. But the swirling spectacle set in motion around him by the holy man dissuaded the king from moving. The clapping of many hands to a slow beat, the insistent chanting of deep voices, and the staccato rhythm of the tabors, their drum-heads stretched tight, combined with the heat and the red glow of the embers to make the scene mesmeric. A flask containing holy liquor was then given to the king, who pleasantly discovered that another fire was being kindled deep in his innards.

After an hour of these trances, the sun rose. The king was positioned with respect to the altar so that the red disk just kissed the surface of the large flat stone. He had the illusion of seeing the sun emerge blood-covered from a sarcophagus.

"Look, O Huseyn," murmured Yahya Beg, "son of the Sun. Look at it."

The king wanted to blink, but the holy man forced him with all his might to open his eyes wide.

"Light banishes evil," cried the magus. "Ahriman is drawing back. He is growing weak. He is running away. Look, Huseyn."

The sun had risen completely from its tomb. It dominated the altar and mixed its light with the heat of the embers burning by the king's feet.

"Now," cried the holy man, "the God will tell us what will satisfy Him. Ahuramazda, what do You want?"

The king, his eyes still staring at the sun, was completely blinded, dripping with sweat, and rather limp. It was in this state of trance that he heard expressed the desires of the celestial orb that ruled the world. A rasping voice rose from behind the altar, the voice of an accomplice of Yahya Beg, who had been carefully chosen to speak for the divine being: during childhood the membranes of his throat had suffered a festering infection that obstructed his larynx and made the noises he uttered sound barely human.

"I want three bowls of good red cinnabar," bawled the supernatural voice, "to burn day and night in the palace of My son Huseyn."

"Three bowls of red cinnabar!" Yahia Beg took up, yelling into the ear of the dazed sovereign.

"I want Hutfi Ali Khan to be whipped in public until his hide is a welter of red wounds."

"The grand vizier, whipped to the raw," cried Yahya Beg.

"I want one hundred twenty-carat rubies to adorn the robes of the priests of Persepolis."

"One hundred rubies of twenty carats!" repeated Yahya Beg.

The sun now shone full force, but the king, his eyes still staring in the sun's direction, seemed not to feel its scorching heat.

"Is that all?" cried Yahya Beg.

"It is not! I want the entire royal guard of My son Huseyn to mount an attack in full red uniform tomorrow."

"Attack of the royal guard tomorrow."

"My personal guard . . ." murmured Huseyn, now in an entirely different world.

"And is that all?" asked Yahya Beg, who expected no further requests.

"No! I will be satisfied only if a red virgin is immolated in this spot within three moons."

"A red virgin?" cried Yahya Beg, turning to look at the altar himself.

The most likely explanation is that his acolyte had grown carried away in the heat of the moment. They had agreed that the Sun would ask for the punishment of the prime minister and the destruction of the royal guard—being the two rivals Yahya Beg feared most. And now the man who spoke from the shadows in the name of the Sun had had an inspiration and added demands of his own. Zoroaster's teachings, insofar as they were known, disapproved of this sort of sacrifice and had moderated the crude practices of Mazdaism in this regard. In his zeal, the idiot had allowed the ancient instincts of Iran to speak through him and had invented this absurd business of a red virgin. But how was one to get around it now?

"A red virgin," repeated Huseyn, showing that he had unfortunately heard.

"Yes, Your Majesty, within three moons," Yahya Beg confirmed, furious, but obliged to bend to the Sun's wishes. "I believe that is now all," he said in a loud voice, to put a stop to the fantasies of his accomplice.

"That's all?" said the king, putting his hands to his eyes. "That's all! Wonder of wonders!"

And suddenly he collapsed from his trance, disjointed as a puppet, into the arms of his victorious astrologer.

In the chaos that visited Isfahan after the arrival of the Afghans, the least occurrence took on an ominous cast. The summons to Françoise to appear before the nazir threw the whole household into turmoil. They were afraid that some action would be taken against the poor woman, though she had not yet recovered from the injury to her arm.

The Persian authorities, humiliated by their defeat, were making the most extravagant decisions. Were people not saying that the king was now completely under the influence of his magus, to the point where they now missed the harshest and most fanatic mullahs? What ignominious acts might the nazir not stoop to when it was known that he would do anything to retain his place and his privileges?

It was in a state of extreme alarm that Françoise climbed into the carriage sent for her by the high chamberlain. Alix and Saba said goodbye to her as though she were leaving on a long voyage, though she was barely going across the Chahar Bagh. The poor woman was a sad sight. Tired, her features drawn, she still wore a small wooden board strapped to her arm as a splint. It was difficult to undress her, and for several days she had been wearing the same simple dress of brown wool, which showed unpleasant signs of neglect.

Helping her from the carriage, the nazir wore a look of distress as he noted the extent of the damage.

How, he thought, am I ever to get the bids going on so sorry an article?

With smirks of courtesy, he showed his visitor in. They did not enter the palace proper but directed their steps toward the small circular pavilion where Poncet had once waited for his client. Of openwork design and somewhat dark despite being open on all sides, this garden folly was surrounded by a moat floating with water lilies. This was crossed by a little wooden bridge, arched in the middle in the Chinese style. The nazir graciously preceded Françoise, installed her on a chaise longue inside the shelter, and disappeared.

Hardly had she taken her seat than Françoise jumped. Someone was behind her crying. She turned around and saw at the other end of the little pavilion a creature so horribly deformed that she did not at first distinguish it from the vine branches climbing the columns. She suddenly felt in the best of health, compared to a person whom life had crumpled so mercilessly. The man was bent over in a wheeled chair and sobbing.

"My God!" whispered Françoise, standing right next to him. "Poor, dear sir. Why are you so sad?"

She reproached herself for asking the question—as if anyone in such a physical state could retain the least glimmer of happiness.

"It's my cat," said Leonardo with a sniff.

"Your cat! But where is he? Have you lost him?"

"He's dead," bawled the poor invalid, opening wide his pink hippopotamus mouth.

"What a shame . . . And when did this happen?"

"A week ago."

"Well then," said Françoise cautiously, "it's time to let go of his memory a little—"

"Let go of his memory!" Leonardo interrupted, looking at her as if she were a viper. "Madam, I'll have you know that Piano lies at this very moment in a wooden chest on my worktable, and that nothing in the world will persuade me to close it."

Françoise backed away in horror.

"Madam, he was the gentlest, the most exquisite animal . . ."

As he spoke, Leonardo grabbed Françoise's good hand and squeezed it in his. The very hands, she thought disgustedly, that had only recently been rifling an inert carcass.

"And might one know," said Françoise, discreetly withdrawing her hand, "what has driven you to leave your dear departed and come to the cool of this arbor?"

"The nazir! Who else would show such cruelty, madam? Today he needs two interpreters, and I have the misfortune of being one of them.

He was on the point of going back to sobbing when they noticed a movement in the garden. The nazir practically ran across the little bridge, making it shake. He seized Leonardo's wheelchair and pushed it forward to block the bridge entrance to the pavilion. Françoise sat back down in the chaise longue, and the nazir, having reviewed the situation, took up a position on the bridge, at its raised middle. Two men appeared on the other side of the moat, a Persian with an impeccably trimmed beard and an elderly Frank, who shaded his eyes with his hands and squinted toward the pavilion.

The Persian was shouting words to the nazir in their language.

"What are they saying?" Françoise asked Leonardo, who hid them from her view.

"I am only allowed to translate what the nazir says to you," said Leonardo with dignity.

What was this pantomime all about? Françoise couldn't understand it at all. Finally the nazir turned back and uttered a short sentence.

"Greetings are being conveyed to you from the far bank," said Leonardo, brushing away his tears.

"But who from, for mercy's sake?"

"And you are asked whether you are in good health."

"Yes, yes, I am in good health, but couldn't you tell me . . ."

Leonardo sent back the translation, which was repeated toward the garden, where the bearded Persian translated it again. A reply came back in the other direction.

"Would you like to return to Europe?"

"Come, sir, won't you kindly tell me—"

Impatient with this absurd interrogatory, Françoise elbowed Leonardo aside and stood in the doorway of the pavilion.

"Good Lord! The consul!"

She drew back quickly into the shade, yet she had stayed frozen in astonishment a moment too long, and Isfahan's pure spring light had drawn her features so sharply that even Monsieur de Maillet was able to see them. He too stepped back, then asked a question in a low voice, which was translated to the nazir, and which Leonardo finally delivered to her.

"Are you not called Françoise?"

The nazir knew her name. He had simply judged it more politic to let her answer the question herself.

"Yes," she said, closing her eyes.

No sooner had this admission been transmitted than a violent agitation shook the garden. The old man began to shout and she could hear an outburst of voices.

"A washerwoman!" he yelled. "My servant from Cairo . . . The plot has been uncovered . . . Ah! Ah! Impostor!"

At a signal from the nazir, the guards stationed behind trees on every side came forward to lead the old man hurriedly to the house. His interpreter was likewise hustled off, even more unceremoniously.

When everything was calm again, the nazir returned and presented his apologies, without explaining the incident.

"An old madman," he said. "He wanted to see you, and I was quite certain that he planned to make a scandal. Don't worry, madam. Return home, but kindly don't hold this regrettable incident against me."

Françoise said nothing, thanked her hosts, and climbed with great dignity into the carriage, which took her home.

A little earlier, barely ten minutes after Françoise had set off for the nazir's, a stranger rang at the garden door. It was a Persian soldier, wearing a felt coat over his uniform, but unmistakably a member of the royal guard from the white trousers visible at his shins.

Alix joined him on the lawn, as he refused to come any farther. He

handed her a letter, bowed, then disappeared into the street. After looking
around her, Alix opened the letter and read:

Madam,
The king has just ordered the guard to mount an attack tomorrow in full red uniform. We will perhaps enjoy victory. I will work
toward it with all my might. But though I may play a part in bringing it about, I will not live to see it, as I will ride in the front line
where the battle will not spare me.

The certainty of dying has its privileges, the greatest being that
one may speak sincerely. You cured me of one love by making me
discover another. Were I to have gone on living, a single thought
would have troubled me: when and how to tell you of my feelings.
Dying, I have the great good fortune that I may leave this simple
statement behind. Thanks to you, I have seen happiness, I have
smiled at it, I know that it exists, and I will die without regret.

R.

Alix crumpled the letter as though to make it disappear. She wanted
to throw it far away, to run after the soldier and give it back to him, so that
none of this might have happened.

But she had no time to delve further into her feelings, as at that
moment the cook and the coachman entered the garden and hurried
toward her.

"Where is Miss Saba?" they asked together.

"I don't know. In her room, I suppose . . . What has happened?"

"I've just come back from the market," said the cook.

"And I've just come from the mosque," added the coachman.

"Calm down, and tell me what it is."

The cook spoke first:

"The king's criers have been announcing everywhere that they are
looking for a red virgin, and they have ordered anyone who might know
of one to deliver her to the king."

"A red virgin!" cried Alix with an expression of horror.

"Oh! madam, we will never turn her in. But she mustn't go out into
the street."

"Yes," added the groom, "luckily last week when the sky was in
flames, you all took the precaution of wearing veils."

"But who are you talking about?" asked Alix.

"Of the young mistress your daughter, so pure and with her red hair."

Saba, thought Alix. A red virgin.

She would never have described her daughter that way, yet she could see how it applied. And it was under that designation that she was in danger.

"No one knows her," said Alix. "She never goes out."

"We must be very careful, madam," the coachman insisted, "someone might denounce her . . ."

"Denounce her!" cried Alix, dumbfounded.

Suddenly it all came back to her: the letter she had just received, Nur al-Huda's suspicions. She uttered a moan of terror. Denunciation . . . She ran to the kitchen and threw the note into the fire after tearing it into small pieces. Come, she said to herself, there's no cause for alarm; she will never know. Thus reassured, she went back into the house to look for her daughter.

Meanwhile, the soldier who had brought the letter finally reached the guards' gate at the royal palace. He knew what was going to happen the next day and was in no hurry to leave the city, its narrow streets, and its fresh smells. Before returning to his quarters, and as a goodbye gesture to life, he searched his pockets and found three copper coins. He handed them with a smile to the ragged beggar girl who had been following him through the streets.

"Here, you can sing for me tomorrow, little gypsy."

34

At winter's end, in Khiva, the stalls of the slave dealers were not very well stocked. The great raids didn't generally occur until later in the season when peasants and hunters were more likely to stray beyond their usual range. Demand was not very strong either. The merchant who bought the four men practically drew tears from the Kirghiz, complaining of the sacrifice he was making as he counted out his money. In private, however, he was quite satisfied that he had made a good bargain.

Despite their long journey, the four new slaves were in strapping shape. The gentle spring in the oasis had restored the color to their cheeks. Fed for long weeks on sheep from the steppes and raw milk, they carried no excess fat and their bodies were hardened to outdoor exercise.

They parted from their Kirghiz captors with sincere regret, so close had they grown to these companions in hardship. Though slaves, they would be staying on in a prosperous city filled with people like themselves, while the poor Kirghiz were returning to their formidable deserts. They wished them good luck.

From the start, the slave trader took good care of his newly purchased stock. He first made the four take off their rags, which smelled so strongly of fur and milk curds that they would have driven away even the most determined buyer. He next took them to the hammam, still tied to one another, where they soaped themselves happily in the warm waters gushing from the earth. That night the trader allowed them to wrap themselves in cotton tunics. He conveyed to them that the next day they would be offered for sale in scantier attire, made of a piece of white cotton twisted three times around the waist and crotch. That way their qualities and flaws could be readily admired, their physical ones at least.

The stall where they were exhibited might hold some twenty slaves, but when they arrived it was empty except for a small man, very thin, stooped, his ribs prominent, whom it hurt to look at. He was a Montenegrin, ordinarily a robust race, but the rule had its exception in him, for this Nicholas, as he was called, had never been any stouter or stronger. According to him, he had even put on a bit of weight in captivity. He refused to say how he had landed in this slave market, possibly a sign that he was an informer. On the other hand, he was free with his advice on how to carry oneself.

"If you want to sell nicely, you have to stand straight, here, like this, look."

He swelled out his scrawny chest and beat with his bony fists on the wishbone that was prominent just below the skin.

"But why should we try to get ourselves sold?" asked Jean-Baptiste. "Is there anything enviable about being a slave?"

"Enviable, maybe not. But in any case preferable, believe me, to being a slave without a master. At least out there you walk around, you're active. People in this country are not too hard on their servants. I've seen many pass through here and they all say the same thing. Anyway, you've heard it yourselves: in the East, everyone claims to be everyone else's slave, and there is no more honorable title than to be slave to a king. Watch out, stand straight, someone's coming."

Three or four buyers wandered by dispiritedly, stopping in front of the store for a few moments.

"If you want my opinion, they're worried you'll turn out to be too expensive. Look at those muscles, those teeth, that hair. Who ever thought of being built like you? I can't wait until you're gone. As things stand, I soon won't be any use at all."

"Not be any use?" asked Juremi in surprise.

"Come, you're all being very nice, but don't pretend you haven't noticed: I'm unsalable. I was almost set free, I'm so useless. But a merchant had the idea, not such a bad one either, to buy me for nothing and use me as a foil. Next to me, the feeblest slave looks well endowed. Why do you think I always stand next to this fellow?"

He pointed at Bibichev. With his knobby knees and long, hairless trunk, hollow in front as though it had been punched in, the policeman did in fact made a jarring sight next to the insolent good health of the other three.

George, who had listened to the conversation in silence, intervened:

"The thing is, we don't want to be separated."

"Well, there isn't much you can do about that," said the Montenegrin, shaking his head. "It's in the hands of fate. Though your interests and those of the merchant selling you coincide on this point. He'll surely do what he can to see you go off in a batch."

"In a batch!' repeated Juremi darkly.

He was revisited by nostalgic thoughts of flight, images of kibitkas in the snow. He remembered Kutulun and the opportunities that dunce George had missed. He sighed.

The following days passed at the same slow pace. Boredom, in fact, did set in. For lack of interested buyers, a week went by. This at least afforded them the chance to return to the hammam.

"Out of curiosity, I've asked about your price," said Nicholas one morning. "It's very reasonable. But I still believe that clients are turning away because they are afraid you're worth a fortune. I think I'll take back the recommendation I made to you earlier. Don't stand too straight, it makes you look insolent and martial. They might worry about a rebellion. Even slouch a little. They'll think you're more affordable."

Except for Bibichev, who could only stand straight, the three others slouched as much as they could, until they seemed almost slovenly.

"This is not an improvement," said Nicholas in perplexity after two more fruitless days. "But don't get discouraged. Now that spring is here we'll start to see the farmers coming in. They have less experience, and if we can just get one whose eyesight is a little dim . . ."

It was as though the old rogue had a sixth sense. Not two days had passed before they saw that rare pearl come and stand before them. A desiccated old man in a long woolen cloak whose trousers narrowed at the ankles, he held a thick wooden staff across his shoulders, over which he draped his hands as though crucified. His flat felt hat, jammed down on his head, looked like a bellows.

"Look," whispered Nicholas, "an Afghan."

The old man continued to stand and look at them. This was annoying because for the last two days a breeze had been coming down off the mountains, giving them goose bumps and turning their hands blue. They worked hard at not looking quite so chilled.

"Don't try too hard; he can't see a thing," observed Nicholas.

In point of fact, the peasant's wizened eyelids opened on pupils clouded by cataracts. He wasn't blind, as he walked without feeling his way, but he must not have been able to make out many details. A long moment passed, then he gave a high crooning shepherd's call. The merchant appeared at the door to the teahouse where he spent his days and came to his client's aid. The Turkomans and the Afghans, while neighbors, speak very different languages, but the old man must have been from a border region as he spoke Turkish quite fluently, and the bargaining took place in that language.

"How many do you need?" asked the shopkeeper.

"Two."

"In that case, don't hesitate, take the two best."

He grabbed Nicholas the Montenegrin and Bibichev and pushed them in front of the Afghan, who, leaning his cane against the side of the shop, approached the two slaves to feel them with his bony hands, which were expert at palping sheep. He looked at them one after the other, turning his head down and away to align them with the only opening through which light could reach the back of his diseased eyes. He immediately and angrily rejected poor Nicholas.

"What did I tell you?" crowed the Montenegrin. "Even the blind . . ."

Having examined Bibichev, the Afghan turned back to the merchant.

"This one might do, but don't you have anything else for comparison?"

"Ah! I see that the aga is a connoisseur. Tell me what you think of this one."

He pushed Juremi toward the front of the stall. The old Afghan ran his hand over the Protestant's gigantic torso, crisscrossed as it was with horrible scars. But these old wounds impressed the farmer less than the size of Juremi's chest and the hardness of his muscles.

"A real giant!" he exclaimed. "Yes, yes, this one suits me perfectly. But don't you have any others to go along with him?"

"The two I have left, I'm afraid, go as a pair," said the merchant briskly. "If you take both of them with the giant, we can come to an agreement. But I don't want to separate them as I wouldn't get half price for either alone."

So saying, he brought up Jean-Baptiste and George. The Afghan was clearly satisfied with his examination of them. He then started to reflect.

"The fact of it is, I am not exactly buying for myself," he explained. "In my valley we've lost many men. The winter was bitter cold this year and full of miasmas. I've been asked to fill an order. I could take three of them, but the price . . ."

A long discussion started. Fortunately the morning was far along, and the sun, beating on the palm roof, had warmed the shop until the men on display found their billowing trousers sufficient, even comfortable, cover. The idea that they would all three leave pleased Jean-Baptiste, George, and Juremi enormously. The only one whose face was somber to the point of despair was Bibichev.

Throughout the whole adventure, the spy had not given up hope of finding a connecting thread, a clue, in short the framework that, though carefully hidden, necessarily underlay this plot somehow. Had the Kirghiz raiders happened on them by accident? Certainly not. In fact, the other three captives had made friends with the nomads very quickly. One might wonder whether the three hadn't simply been waiting for the raiders at the bottom of their hole. Was this not the conduit they had chosen for exporting the gold they took from the kurgan? What easier method of putting it on the market?

All this was extraordinarily skillful, thought the policeman, but the suspects had made one mistake: relying on his naiveté. Each night since they had begun their journey toward Khiva, Bibichev had been composing a dispatch to Moscow in his head and learning it by heart. As soon as he could put his hands on pen and paper, he would transcribe it all. In the meantime, he had to find his way out of this latest trap. These formidable conspirators had simply, in their good-natured and hypocritical way, found a means to get rid of him.

The dealer and his Afghan client were on the point of concluding their bargain, making final adjustments so that the one's money would exactly fit the other's price. The Russian at this point noticed that the Afghan was often turning his cloudy eyes toward him.

The shopkeeper had set Bibichev aside from the three others, whose sale was almost final. Yet there could be no doubt about it: the Afghan was staring at him, Bibichev. Perhaps he wanted to include him with the others to round out the price. In any case, the Russian started to hope. He assumed a flattering position, swelled out his narrow chest as much as he could, contracted the stringy muscles of his arms like a gymnast, flexed his legs, and smiled to show his teeth. The others were touched to see this zealous policeman work so hard to find a buyer.

The old Afghan approached to watch these exercises, and Bibichev redoubled his heroic poses and athletic gestures.

"No," said the Afghan finally, shaking his head, "that one is too restless. He'll eat too much."

He pulled out his purse to pay for the three others.

Having come so near salvation, Bibichev now assumed an expression of despondency. He appealed to the humanity of his companions, though he hardly credited them with having any.

"Have pity on me," he said. "I have eight children. What will happen to me alone here?"

It was the Montenegrin who providentially came to his rescue. He had no desire to be supplanted by this Russian as a foil. After his long residency in Khiva, Nicholas spoke the Turkoman dialect well enough to call out to the shopkeeper and whisper a few words to him that the Afghan could not understand.

"You are getting an excellent price, even a somewhat inflated one," murmured Nicholas. "Ask him for two tomans more and throw in the Russian. You won't get any more for him alone."

The trader, while saying nothing, rapidly fell in with this sage advice, and all the more so as the sight of the Afghan's gold had given him a fierce desire to conclude the bargain and take possession of the money. By noon the deal had been struck. Jean-Baptiste, George, Juremi, and Bibichev, once more fully dressed, were joyfully following their Afghan buyer through the streets of Khiva.

He led them to another part of the bazaar, to a blacksmith who fitted them with chains fastened to their ankles by two riveted steel rings. The chains were long enough for the slaves to take big strides, but too heavy for them to run with, and so noisy that they couldn't move without making a clinking sound. This arrangement made it possible to keep them prisoner without having to tie their hands or rope them together. As soon as they had their new irons, the three had the sensation once more of having been born free.

They accompanied their new master to the caravanserai where he had left his pair of donkeys. The next day at dawn they set off once more along the Amu Darya. To the south, the river ran through a fertile valley planted with tamarinds and aloe trees. Fat flocks wallowed around wells and drank from the clear water raised to the surface in leather buckets by laughing, half-naked boys working wooden hoists.

But the river narrowed as they traveled toward its source and began to look more like a mountain stream. The nights, at first cool, started to become truly cold, swept by glacial gusts that tumbled down from the mountaintops. Soon they branched off directly south toward Herat across a range of desolate plateaux.

All the joy they had felt in Khiva was gone. They were once more in a travel rhythm that they knew all too well; it had been a source of enthusiasm to them at one time, before becoming a source of misery. They had lost all freedom and hope. Their souls captive, they found that even watching the men and activities of great cities or small villages no longer diverted them. What was left them was pure despair, as rough and cold as the rocks planted in place of vegetation on the lunar landscape of the mountains.

It was while pitching camp late one afternoon that Jean-Baptiste was suddenly visited by an atrocious vision. Before him appeared Saba, his beloved daughter, as real as life with her fiery hair, black eyes, and child's softness. She was in great danger, she was screaming. He stopped, looked at the stony desert where the wind advanced over the ground with a piping noise. He wanted to hold out his hands to touch his daughter, take her in his arms, protect her.

I am going mad, he thought.

Unknown to him, at that very moment in Isfahan Yahya Beg's henchmen were beating down his door and, with the confidence of well-informed men, proceeding to Saba's bedroom, where they seized the screaming young girl. Yet Jean-Baptiste could hear her. As he could hear, without knowing their source, the sobs and curses heaped by Alix on his empty grave as she knelt among her roses until long past nightfall. Was it she who called to him, or was it the wind off the Himalayas carrying the mutterings of the Tibetans, whose shrines it had overflown? And the consoling words that reached him afterward, as smooth and round as pebbles on a beach, and whose meaning he could not grasp, how was he to know that it was Françoise who spoke them as she stroked the hair of her despairing friend. Alix cursed herself, blamed herself for everything, cried out Jean-Baptiste's name. But her soul, still too much a stranger to the East, could not conceive that the deepest griefs can mix with the elements and travel across the earth to be heard in its far reaches.

Jean-Baptiste, for his part, was starting to believe in such mysteries. He could not shake the notion that the apparition was more than a dream and might actually have occurred somewhere.

In truth, during the long marches, the empty nights, their dreams had become their companions. They related their dreams to each other in the morning, sometimes continuing on until the evening halt. Juremi thought of Françoise, relived happy moments with her, and imagined great journeys on which he would take her. Jean-Baptiste, since the brutal apparition, constantly saw Alix and Saba and, between the past and the present, never left their company. Even George abandoned himself to his thoughts.

But as they concerned his famous secret, he refused to speak of them and kept his chimeras to himself.

They did not bother much with knowing where they were, or whether Herat was still far, or even if that city was their destination. They walked the way a person lives: without imagining resting points, or a purpose, or even an end. Perhaps they might have convinced themselves that they were already dead had not Jean-Baptiste remembered one night a proverb told to him long ago by an Abyssinian: "If the beggar saw no butter in his dreams, he would die of hunger."

V
THE LAST HAPPINESS
OF ISFAHAN

35

Nothing would have happened had Mir Vais not been made to suffer so much fifteen years before.

The Afghans of Kandahar had been Persian subjects since Shah Abbas's conquests in the preceding century. Although Sunni Muslims, the Afghan feudal tribes adapted calmly to the suzerainty of their distant rulers. In fact they governed themselves, and the true power resided in the hands of the kalantar, or first magistrate of the city. But kings like to reassure themselves of their might, and all the more so when they have little. The Persian sovereign one day had the idea of sending a strong man to govern Kandahar, a Georgian convert to Islam who showed all the anxious and awkward zeal of a new believer. Mir Vais, the peaceable kalantar of Kandahar, bore the brunt of this appointment, finding himself arrested by the Georgian and taken to Isfahan for imprisonment. Few decisions have had such nefarious consequences.

Rulers always profit from being seen at a distance. As soon as he reached the capital, Mir Vais took stock of the decadence of the Persian court, which until then he had respected. He saw that it was weak, corrupt, and indecisive. Not only did he note its vices, but he immediately demonstrated his skill at using them to accomplish his ends. He exerted his charm, obtained his freedom, paid court to the king, and made such a show of his great virtues that he was able to cast total opprobrium on the man who had been so blind to them as to have made him prisoner. Mir Vais returned to Kandahar his head high: the king had restored him to his former position.

The Georgian governor, wanting to show that he had capitulated and was eager to seal an alliance with his former enemy, thought it would be politic to ask Mir Vais for his daughter's hand in marriage. The Afghan accepted and sent his child to him with surprising good grace. He even went so far as to organize a great feast, to which he invited all the chiefs of the tribe over which he ruled. For three days and three nights, the rugged

Afghan warriors drifted down from the mountains to take part in the wedding. An enormous tent was erected in the center of town to welcome this solemn multitude, and the Persian soldiers of the garrison mingled trustingly with them. In the midst of the festivities, the governor rose to consummate his marriage. He saw the whole thing in a flash of insight, but too late. The girl whom he held by the hand was no more than a trollop sent by the Afghan in place of his real daughter. She fled immediately. The Georgian was unable even to move before Mir Vais's dagger had slit his throat. At this signal, all the Persians in the tent and in the entire city were murdered. The war had started.

After throwing off Isfahan's dominion and declaring Kandahar a kingdom in its own right, Mir Vais had taken every opportunity to humiliate Persia. His hatred was founded neither on a desire for conquest nor on the vision of an empire builder, nor on religious proselytism, nor on a sacred mission conveyed to him from on high. The only issue at stake was honor, and his only motive to avenge the wrong that had been done him. So great was Mir Vais's contempt for all concerned that he considered the offense inexpiable.

Mir Vais accumulated victories over the Persians until sickness unexpectedly laid him low. After the accidental death of this great rebel, his brother succeeded him and made the mistake of showing more moderation in the exercise of his vengeance. His reign lasted three years, the time it took Mahmud, the eldest son of Mir Vais, to reach the age of eighteen and bring adult judgment to bear on his uncle. He carried out the sentence by slitting his uncle's throat with his own hands—such henceforth appeared to be the founding ceremony of every reign worthy of the name in this manly dynasty.

Acclaimed for his resoluteness, Mahmud had been governing Kandahar for three years when the weakness of the Persians more than his own strength finally led him to the plains before Isfahan. The long march toward the heart of his ancestral enemy had first made him proud, but he was now starting to be highly embarrassed by this gift of Providence.

What was he to do once he reached the walls of this fortified city? Among his thirty thousand men, Mahmud could count on barely a third who were true and loyal warriors from his own tribe. The others were auxiliaries picked up along the way, either bought, rented, or lending their support in return for the eventual chance to pillage. The entire mass was exhausted and scorched by the desert sun; their horses were emaciated and covered in sores; there wasn't a tent among a hundred men. It took all the cowardice of the Persians not to tear these ragged beggars to shreds. But in the minds of the rugged Afghan mountain men, this was a given: the degeneration of the Persians exceeded all limits. Had the Persians not sent another of their grotesque embassies only a week before to plead for mercy? A courtier in a richly colored and brocaded robe, mounted on a superb horse ajingle with bells, surrounded by a guard of well-armed and well-fed soldiers, had come to prostrate himself before Mahmud, who was black with dirt and wearing the same stinking cloak he had worn on setting out from Kandahar. This messenger from the king of Persia offered the Afghans fifteen thousand tomans if they would spare the city.

Were the Persians really surprised that Mahmud slit the throats of this hideous herald and all his little retinue himself? It was just the sort of proposal to renew his respect for his father's foresight and rekindle his desire to avenge him. He decided on a siege.

But not withdrawing was one thing, and taking the accursed capital was another. The six hundred thousand poltroons inside it counted for nothing! The crux of the situation was the protecting walls. They girded the city, and Mahmud had no cannon capable of breaching them. The best he had were small culverins, called zumburuk, strapped to the flanks of camels. They shot one-pound balls that had just the force to tear a man's head off, but bounced off a rampart like pebbles.

The Afghans also didn't have the means to starve the city out, unless they could cross the river that transected it. In the spring, the river is wide, fast-flowing, and too deep to ford.

Mahmud had the entire countryside sacked on the near side of the river, but there were gardens on the far side where the purple flowers of the lilac could be seen in bloom and the trees were bent under the weight of ripe cherries.

For the first time since becoming king, Mahmud felt irresolute, a state of mind that suited him poorly. Short, bony, the hollows of his cheeks filled with patches of chestnut beard, Mahmud, at once intrepid and anxious, was constantly in motion. He paced to and fro, met with his counselors while walking, his hands clasped behind his back, and ate standing. If ever he was forced to hold still for a second due to danger or surprise, his black eyes continued to rove to right and left like sheepdogs herding a flock. His prodigious activity, day and night—he hardly slept three hours, and was constantly restless even then—allowed him to perform every function himself. He gave orders and supervised their execution, visited every unit of his army, and interrogated prisoners, travelers, and traitors himself, for there was a constant stream of them leaving the city and offering him their services. None of these renegades had to date brought him very interesting information. Mahmud sometimes reproached himself for his scruples. If the Afghans, instead of conducting long and patient interrogations of these cowards, would simply slit their throats, they would gain much precious time.

After two weeks of hesitating, the Afghan decided that he could take satisfaction in having come this far: his victory entitled him to return home with his head high. Persia had been penetrated right to the heart, humiliated beyond the original affront, and half of her territory had been damaged by pillaging. The Turks and the Russians to the north were busy completing the task. Isfahan could be spared. This huge head, which the sick body no longer had the means to feed, would surely rot on its own.

Mahmud had decided to order the withdrawal on the following day when, one after another, three different fugitives brought the same news. King Huseyn, under the influence of his astrologer (his astrologer!), had eliminated the grand vizier, the very man who had sent emissaries to buy clemency from the Afghans. The royal guard was on a footing of war. And the general commanding the guard had been given authority over the entire army and was preparing a sortie in force.

The royal guard! The elite corps of the Persian Empire! There, finally, was an enemy worthy of Mahmud. Until now he had only ever had to do with ordinary troops, who were distressingly weak. The business was now becoming serious and risky. The Afghan knew the poor state of his own forces: would they resist the assault? Would it not be better, since nothing had yet been made public, to give the signal for withdrawal right away before he was forced to retreat? Mahmud, in reality, was deliberating with himself only so as to justify his perpetual excitement, which had doubled in intensity. For his soul of a mountain warrior commanded him to run toward this formidable enemy, with no thought of turning back, so as to bathe his honor forever either in blood or in victory.

The very next day, he arrayed his army in battle order. There were three corps, one in the middle, which he would command himself, and a cavalry unit on either wing. His meager mobile artillery, that is, the fifty camels carrying a culverin on each flank with a basket of stone balls on their backs and two attendants sitting on their humps, would wait in the rear. This reinforcing fire would come to the aid of whichever part of the army was subjected to the fiercest assault.

Two days passed before the Persians were ready. Finally, on the third morning, in the darkness just before dawn, the besieged troops let themselves out through the bronze gates of Julfa, which closed immediately behind them. The sun rose on an imposing sight. The royal guard, dressed all in red, curved swords upraised, formed a first line of impassive cavalrymen. Behind and to the sides, on horseback and on foot, came all that remained of the Persian army after the fall of Kirman, a fraction that still formed a great multitude, about twice the size of the Afghan forces. Mortar pieces were installed in fixed positions along the ramparts. They had never yet been fired, the Persians not having wanted to initiate hostilities while there was still hope for negotiations. Aside from the fixed battery, there was the field artillery, which had exited through the gates at the same time as the soldiers and immediately taken positions in two corps on the right and left extremities of the Persian army.

Mahmud, across from them, was elated. He shuttled back and forth from one meager army corps to another. His shouts were met by savage, angry yells. For all its raggedness, and probably because it lacked for almost everything, this ill-nourished, barefoot, shivering army was pricked by the unbearable and all-important goad of hatred and raged at its destitution, in contrast with the state of the brightly colored enemy, who were weighed down with all the luxurious trappings of prosperity. Every one of the Afghan horsemen and auxiliary troops from distant India felt a personal need to punish these soft men, who had become effeminate from a life of too much ease and happiness. The have-nots felt both a great contempt for riches and the violent desire to appropriate them. They hoped to acquire them cheaply: the sacrifice of their own lives meant nothing to them, since they put them at risk routinely for no reason, at no profit, and without fear.

Mahmud had only to make the slightest signal and his orders were executed at a fast gallop. The Afghans' horses pawed the ground and fidgeted in place. Their mounts were worn, but every soldier had one; there was almost no infantry to impede the restless mobility of the cavalry corps.

The Persian ranks were more static and indecisive. The slow movement of the many foot soldiers, the hauling of the heavy artillery pieces, and perhaps also a certain subtle dissension in the command slowed the progress of this massive army. More than three hours passed before it had spread its two wings against the cork-colored ramparts, like a butterfly pinned to a naturalist's mat. Mahmud feared the Persian artillery, but he was quickly reassured. The mortars on the ramparts were firing over

them, and by the time their aim was adjusted, the battle would be joined
and they could no longer be used. As to the field artillery, the proper elevation of the guns was determined by firing a shot or two, and the
Afghans simply had to move to make the gunners do their calculations all
over again. In short, artillery was ill adapted to the battle at hand. The day
would be decided by the horsemen.

The attack of the royal guard at noon indicated that things were coming to a head. The Persians had decided to break the right wing of the
besieging army, and it was this wing that bore the brunt of the assault. The
red horsemen of the royal guard were armed solidly and protected by
good armor, as were their horses. The valor of this elite corps in no way
fell short of its reputation. The Afghans, with their lances and short
swords, had great difficulty resisting the pressure of the attack. While
none retreated, they fell by the dozens under the blows raining violently
on them. Within minutes, the guard had butchered the Afghans' right
wing. The Persian horses trampled corpses underfoot, and the bright red
uniforms, soaked with blood, lost their satiny sheen and turned a dilute
purple, horrible to see. Absorbed in their murderous task, the Persians
thought only of victory, which was visibly approaching as they reached the
last ranks of the Afghan army. The fact of Mahmud's absence from the
field of battle caused them no alarm.

The Afghan ruler, confronting this disaster, boiled with impatience and
the desire to strike. He nonetheless made an extraordinary effort to restrain
himself and rein in the central corps of his army, which champed at the bit
to join the fray. It took all the terror that Mahmud inspired to keep his soldiers from crossing the invisible line of his command and rescuing their
murdered brothers. All wondered what their sovereign was waiting for.

Reassured by the success of the royal guard, the bulk of the Persian
army decided to fly to the rescue of a victory that appeared all but complete.
They left the foot of the ramparts and advanced in turn on the enemy's
right wing. The first combatants of the royal guard had practically annihi-
lated it. But the Afghans, before dying, had fought so well that the Persian
guard lost about half of its own men. The commanding general fell in the
first engagement. As a consequence, Reza, who led the sovereign's personal detachment, assumed command of the attackers. Now, beyond the last
remaining line of Afghan horsemen, at the far edge of this forest of men,
Reza could see the open country, the untamed land of his ancestors. His
final adversary was a large Baluch, wearing the embroidered cap of his
native region. The poor man was probably more adept at looting and pil-

laging. Despite his fatigue, the Persian cut him down with two energetic strokes. It was as the lummox fell noisily to earth that Reza froze before an apparition. Was it due to the violence of battle? to the hunger and thirst that tortured him? to the sword stroke that was making blood seep from his shoulder? The young officer, erect on his horse at the far end of the field of corpses on which the bulk of the Persian army was now exhibiting its courage by stabbing the wounded and sabering the dead, experienced a moment of dismay and terror at the sight of the open desert ahead of him. There, no more than a few paces away, some fifty sphinxes were drawn up, their gray knees resting on the dusty floor of the plain. Their dark eyes were directed at the human carnage and at him, Reza, the victor, reproving him with the millennial patience and wisdom of their animal nature— Mahmud's mobile artillery, arrayed to cut down the attackers!

What have I done with my life? thought Reza, instinctively lowering his eyes to his vermilion hand.

He shouted:

"Ozan!"

Fifty camels loosed their fire at that moment. The culverins on their flanks shot one hundred granite balls at the astonished guard, who thought they had won the battle, wreaking dreadful carnage. No officer was spared. Reza, transpierced at stomach height, fell dead with staring eyes. This was the moment Mahmud chose to finally launch his center and left wing against the Persian flank and rear. Just as they thought victory was theirs, the Persians saw themselves caught in a net, cut off from all retreat toward the ramparts, in disarray, and deprived of their elite corps of guardsmen.

The massacre lasted two hours and was atrocious. Not a single fleeing soldier was spared his life. Three quarters of the army perished. Mahmud consented to take prisoners only with the approach of night, less from mercy than from weariness at the thought of finishing them off. The Afghans' victory was total. Their only failure was in not capturing the field pieces, as the Persians had taken the precaution of bringing them back into the city during the fray. This detail was extremely vexing to Mahmud. Isfahan had been purged of its defenders, but hardly captured. The troops devoted themselves noisily to praising God and His Prophet, then to sharing out the vast booty stripped from the corpses of the dead. But the victorious king was somber: he still faced the same irritating problem. How was he to take control of this disarmed capital, whose enormous riches were now within reach, when those accursed ramparts still protected it?

36

Alix remained prostrate for three days after the arrest of her daughter. It staggered her to the point where she could no longer act, or think, or even rise from bed and feed herself. Whenever she regained consciousness for a moment, she experienced such sharp, such painful, and such inexpiable remorse that she withdrew wailing and once more took refuge in her dreams. Françoise kept vigil over her despite her own great weariness. Three times in the night she would call the cook and another servant to change Alix's sheets, which were soaked with fever.

In her carapace of dream, Alix nonetheless felt a peace she had all but forgotten. She was in Cairo, preparing to rejoin Jean-Baptiste. She met him on his return from Abyssinia, touched his body, kissed his lips. All that she had left of him were those first moments of passion, of parting, and of reuniting. Nothing had changed them: neither their life in Isfahan, steeped in the mediocrity of dailiness, nor the unbelievable fickleness that had led them to separate, he to chase after the memory of a friendship, and she to taste a freedom she had never lacked. After three days and three nights of tormented peace dreaming of a golden age, Alix slowly came back to herself. She rose, dressed, gave orders around the house, and reproached herself only that she had not yet tried everything she could to free Saba.

She picked up the thread of these terrible days. First she learned the extraordinary news of her father's return. Françoise had absolutely recognized Monsieur de Maillet. What was he doing here? Alix felt a strong desire to see him. She nonetheless feared that the formidable old man might have harnessed his pompous naiveté to another of his disastrous causes. Had he not been in the nazir's company? Had he not cried out that Françoise was his washerwoman? It seemed as though he might be taking belated revenge against Françoise by denouncing her to the Persians, who had welcomed her on false premises. Even if Alix managed to see him— which was not at all certain—it might be to find herself still unpardoned and the target of her father's vengeance. Best to leave the whole business lie for the moment. The urgent issue was Saba. Where had she been taken? The cook had heard servants' gossip that the red virgin was in a wing of the harem in the royal palace. She would be kept there unharmed until the day of the sacrifice, which the magis had announced for the third moon, in fifty days. This immolation, ordered by the sun god and ruler of the world, would occur no matter what, even if the city had been spared. Then it would be an act of thanksgiving.

No visitors were allowed to see the prisoner. Yahya Beg's henchmen guarded the first door of the harem themselves night and day. Alix made calls on numerous well-placed Persians, some with excellent connections in court. They all told her how great was their sorrow for her, yet for all the sincerity of their regret they could do nothing. Alix would have done anything to save her daughter, including humbling herself before Nur al-Huda, who she was certain was responsible for her daughter's denunciation. Everything had changed so much in a very short time. The army had been destroyed and Reza killed while Alix lay prostrate and cut off from the world. This was one of the first items of news she heard on waking up. It had no effect on her. She had put shame behind her now. Serious things had occurred to reduce this childish and stillborn passion to insignificance. What a gulf separated it from the things that really mattered to her! Besides, Reza had warned her of his fate in his last message. The official news of his demise added nothing to this knowledge, unless it was the slight ease that Alix felt on knowing that a page had been turned. She wondered whether Nur al-Huda would feel a similar detachment. Would Nur be able to forgive, and help? There was nothing to be lost in finding out. Alix decided to search for her.

But the prime minister, her "dear husband," as the Circassian always called him, was in disgrace. Despite his venerable age, he had been given fifty lashes in public. Next he was thrown in prison. His palace was closed to visitors and kept under guard by the henchmen of the nazir. The building, once a gift from the king to his grand vizier, had officially reverted to the king. The servants and eunuchs in the minister's household had been sent away. What had become of his wives? Alix was told that they had all returned to their families. Nur al-Huda, who had no relatives in Persia, had disappeared without a trace.

One last card was left to play: a pardon from the king. Alix sent him twenty moving entreaties and even offered to take her daughter's place under the executioner's blade. She received no answer. In despair, she

went so far as to slip into the palace past the guards. She was arrested at
the second court and, in deference to her widowhood, led back into the
street with no more punishment than a severe reprimand.

Françoise tried every night to console her. But though Alix had
recently found absolution for her acts of folly from the quiet older woman,
that time was now past. Françoise was an aged, spent, and weary woman.
Experience is simply the mask we give our optimism when we seek to
share it with a younger person, but Françoise's mask had slipped from her
now elderly features.

In reality, Alix was alone: alone to think up a solution, alone to decide,
and alone to act. For two long days she walked in the rose garden, moved
by the regrowth of her beloved flowers. On the last night she sat on the
stone bench, took a heavy, half-open tea rose in her hands, and breathed in
its smell deeply. It was an improbable scent, yet one that held off all the
corruption of the world, as certain persons may, whatever their era, by
their beauty, their purity, their inner peace, which is stronger than the vast
movement of death, though it will destroy them. She felt suddenly that
her doubt had disappeared. Life was opening its doors again at the simple
sound of those magic words: "I want" and "I will."

Nerses, the Armenian patriarch, was not a mean man, and he did not
blame Jean-Baptiste for dying. It would be more accurate to say that he
was even grateful to him for it. The Alberoni business had failed, of
course, but the unexpected death of the apothecary had marked as with a
crash of cymbals the destiny of the unfortunate patriarch. Everything had
started to stir after that and changed in rhythm and color. Today, after
having known opprobrium and flight, Nerses had returned to glory. The
war freed the Armenians of their debt to the Turks and erased the past
errors of their clumsy patriarch. The defeats Persia suffered at the hands
of the Afghans had made the community close ranks, and the divine pro-
tections offered in return for cash by a helpful and understanding church
had again climbed in value. Since Mahmud and his soldiery started camp-
ing under the walls of the town, and more particularly under the walls of
the Armenian suburb of Julfa, the patriarch had once again become the
symbol of salvation, the gilded standard that the merchants waved desperately to attract God's attention and pray for mercy.

Nerses received Alix in the presbytery, to which he had returned in
state. Situated at the high point of Julfa, in a bosket of black cypress, the

presbytery was adjacent to a large chapel and consisted of four stone buildings arranged in a square. In the middle of the little central garden, two
paved alleys drew a cross dividing plantings of gourds from others of
watermelon.

"There will be two of you, you say?"

"Yes, Monsignor," answered Alix.

"Well, it seems to me that it's perfectly feasible . . . shall we say . . .
tomorrow night. Does that suit you?"

"As soon as possible."

"Tomorrow is the earliest possible," the patriarch confirmed.

"All right, then."

The old man clapped his hands. Two lightly clad serving girls, very
young and pretty, came to pour tea for the patriarch and his visitor.
Prosperity had not, on its return, entirely done away with avarice: the
kitchen had standing orders not to send out cakes at every turn and to be
sparing with sugar. Nerses tasted the boiling tea to check that it was good
and bitter, and being as economical in his movements as in everything else,
he finished off his cup at the same time.

"Beware, madam!" he continued, stimulated by the crackling of his
innards around the boiling liquid he had just tossed down, "I hope that the
person accompanying you is agile. This is no pleasure jaunt. Even yourself—"

"I'll manage, believe me," Alix interrupted. "I have always taken part
in physical exercise: fencing, riding, hunting. I hardly think this business
will be any more difficult. As to the person accompanying me, Monsignor,
have no fear: he is a workingman, a gardener and a former soldier."

"Very well, if you say so," said the patriarch, whom this subject did
not enthrall. "In any case, I've warned you. What happens is your own
responsibility."

"The price you mentioned, Monsignor, does it pay for both of our passages or is it the price per person?"

"Per person. For which you can be entirely thankful to me, I may as
well say. Those who perform this work take an enormous risk. Usually it
costs twice as much."

Alix smiled to show that she forgave him this lie. She removed the sum
in question from a leather sack. It disappeared inside the patriarch's tunic.

"You were naturally aware of the affairs of your late husband Jean-
Baptiste Poncet?" he asked to change the subject.

"Most of them."

"Alberoni?"

"Yes," Alix admitted with some impatience.

It now seemed to her that this first practical joke of Jean-Baptiste's was at the bottom of all the mishaps that had happened since: she didn't like to remember it.

"Well, it turns out that your husband was right," whispered the patriarch, leaning toward her and lowering his voice. "That devil of a cardinal, as I've discovered, is truly attached to his mistress, just as Poncet said. By the way, is the courtesan still staying with you?"

"Yes," said Alix, with some acerbity, "but, Monsignor, she is not a courtesan. Besides, the poor woman is very ill."

"She is staying with you," the patriarch repeated in perplexity, "and yet you know nothing?"

"But what is there to know?"

Nerses, his eyes sparkling, answered triumphantly, for nothing so delighted him as scandalous gossip, especially when he had the opportunity to pass it on to the last person not to have heard, yet who was the one most personally concerned by it:

"Why that Cardinal Alberoni has sent someone all the way here, to Isfahan, an emissary to inquire after his concubine."

This, then, was what the old man had learned, and the thing that was bringing a bit of heat to his face—when the boiling water had not provoked even a shudder. This horrible patriarch decidedly knew everything, and Monsieur de Maillet's visit had not escaped him. Alix took no pleasure in the business, but she couldn't resist trying to find out a little more about Alberoni's emissary. It amused her that she was just the slightest bit ahead of the Armenian on one point, for he seemed not to know that Monsieur de Maillet was her father.

"Do you know what has become of this emissary? He hasn't come to my house," she said ingenuously.

"The nazir has arrested him, or so I hear, and shut him up in his palace for unknown reasons. Presumably he is planning to make use of this hostage at some point, especially if the city falls and he has to flee."

"Is the emissary . . . well treated?"

"Very well, by all reports. The nazir visits him every day with his horrible interpreter Lorenzo to make him sign papers. The man refuses and they leave him alone. What do you think? Isn't this all very strange?"

Alberoni! thought Alix. So that's what had brought her poor father all this way. Would nothing ever stop the infernal progress of this lie?

"In any case," added Nerses, "I want to get to the bottom of this story. I'm going to send a messenger to the nazir's hostage tomorrow. We have secret contacts in that house, and my man will be able to talk to him."

"What will you say to him?"

"Why, that the cardinal's concubine is safe and sound, that Poncet has welcomed her into his house, that he was my friend and had promised to have Alberoni intercede in our favor."

"What good will it do?" asked Alix, who watched in horror as these stories became entwined.

The patriarch, in a state of high excitement, seized her hand.

"What will happen to this city, madam, is something no one knows. And what will happen to us poor Christians is even more uncertain. Imagine for a moment that we manage to help this emissary escape—just as you are going to escape tomorrow, though in a different direction, naturally. Now suppose that with our help he should return to Rome. In your opinion, toward whom will he show his gratitude? To the nazir? or to your humble servant?"

Alix didn't want to contradict the old man, for under the chain of errors and misunderstandings there remained a breath of hope. Help her father to escape? Why not. She herself could do nothing for him, but at least she could protect other agents of fate who might possibly lend him a helping hand.

"Your plan is excellent, Monsignor, but may I make a confession and offer you a tiny suggestion?"

"Please."

"I didn't tell you the whole truth at the beginning of this conversation, not realizing that you were so well informed."

The patriarch smiled craftily.

"I knew of this man's existence," Alix went on. "He has met the person he came to see."

"Ah! really, the concubine?"

"If you like. But out of precaution, and so as not to give in to the nazir's extortion—the nazir has set a price on this man's freedom, a passport for Rome . . ."

"A passport for whom?"

"Why, for himself, of course."

"Swine!"

"So as not to give in to the nazir's extortion, this emissary pretends not to have recognized the person he saw. He is claiming that she is not the cardinal's concubine."

"I understand," said Nerses, winking.

"As to my late husband, this man pretends for the same reason to wish him nothing but harm."

"God rest his soul!" said Nerses automatically.

"So," said Alix, "while it appears to me highly politic on your part to rescue this very influential personage and help him recover his freedom, you should do so without asking for too many explanations, without talking of concubines or Poncet, or anything else. Tell him simply that you are acting on behalf of . . . the brotherhood of Christians, for example."

"Your suggestion is well advised," murmured the patriarch, who now had a deeper insight into the intrigue and understood the need for the greatest discretion. "I'll follow it scrupulously."

He clasped Alix's forearm warmly, then rose to take his leave of her. It was time for the main service in the nearby chapel, and the shrill sound of a small bell was already ringing in the still night air. As she took leave of the ancient Armenian, Alix hesitated. She held the old man's fleshless hand in hers and added:

"Monsignor, I almost forgot an important detail. There is one thing that can most assuredly win you the confidence of the cardinal's emissary."

"And what might that be, madam?"

"This man is the father of an only daughter, who is living in the East at this very moment. Life has separated them. Time has passed, and she is a woman now, but he has had no news of her. This woman is someone I have known well. If I were not leaving tomorrow, I would go to her father myself and say: Your daughter is happy and in good health, and she loves you.'"

"Very well," said the patriarch, held in the spell of Alix's soft, warm hand. "I will tell him that."

"She loves him," repeated Alix. "And you might add that she hopes he has forgiven her."

While she walked back down Julfa's hill, along the dusty path, the churchbell rang to the rhythm of her steps. So great was the city's upheaval in these tragic days that no one turned to look at the pretty woman in tears.

In Isfahan that year, the Afghan horde and spring arrived together. The first was camped in front of the town, the second had captured it entirely. The Chahar Bagh had grown as dense as a forest. The great

Oriental plane trees cast a thick shadow on the avenue and dyed black its narrow canal, dotted with water lilies. The sycamore figs and cedars, which had kept watch through the winter, now faced the onslaught of a crop of young elms and willows, their fresh leaves snickering in the spring breezes. Slender threads of light angled through the undergrowth to stretch this canopy of leaves around the pickets of the large black trunks. In the beds around the alleys, in the middle of the clearings kept open around the fountains, the gardeners continued to tend flowering beds of poppies and cineraria, tulips, lilies, and white carnations. Roses were bursting out everywhere, this year of disasters having proved particularly favorable to them. They were early, abundant, and more scented than ever. The city was covered in roses, far beyond the center and the Chahar Bagh. The lowliest wall in the most impoverished alleyway proudly supported with its stones the heavy heads of these beauties.

Françoise's room, which opened onto the flower garden, was filled with these sensory consolations. Alix came in to kiss her gravely at the end of the morning. Every arrangement had been made so that the remaining servants would provide the poor woman, whose arm was still fragile and whose health was failing, with everything she might need. Françoise was afraid neither of being alone nor of dying, but only of not seeing her friend again. More than anything, she wanted to let Alix accomplish her business with no dragging remorse. She maintained as gay a demeanor as she could muster, kept their farewells short, thanked Alix, and, by way of wishing her luck, gave her the blessing that is the particular prerogative of older women: a kiss delivered with eyes closed on the top of the forehead.

Alix carried a canvas bag slung over her shoulder, large enough to hold what she needed but small enough not to be taken for luggage. The entrance to the arched bridge crossing the Zayande Rud was strictly guarded by a civil militia, recruited in haste after the massacre of the army. The shops on the bridge were closed, and lookouts perched on the roofs kept watch over the roiling water that sparkled in the sunlight below. The Afghans were so terrifying that people expected them everywhere, even in the fast-flowing waters of the river, on which they might float into town.

From a distance, Alix scanned the entrance to the bridge and was relieved to see the man she was looking for: Dostom, leaning on the parapet in the midst of the crowd, gazing down at the water. She walked by him without a word and continued on to the sentry post at the start of the bridge. Fortunately, the militia were not stopping anyone and allowed her to pass, scrutinizing her mercilessly. At the far end of the bridge, she glanced back to see that Dostom had started across the bridge himself, walking at a leisurely pace. She angled off toward the maze of Julfa's streets. The shopkeepers' stalls, still laden with goods, were crowded with idlers and merchants. She turned right twice, then left, and arrived at a small sloping square paved in stone. Alleyways with stone arches led off from each of its four corners. It was here that Dostom joined her.

"Is everything all right?" she asked.

"Everything," said the young man with a slight smile.

A boy who had been eyeing them approached and gave Nerses' password. The two countered correctly. The boy set off through the streets, motioning them to follow. After a long walk, probably intended to disorient them, they reached a small whitewashed house with a narrow blue door onto the street. The child knocked. A servant ushered them into a small courtyard where laundry soaked in clay bowls. They waited there almost an hour. Finally an Armenian appeared wearing baggy woolen trousers and a quilted vest. Without introducing himself, he said:

"The changing of the guard on the outer wall is at five o'clock. We'll hear them file past this door and that will be our signal to act."

The man spoke of the guard in contemptuous tones. In common with other Armenians, he was offended that the Persians had denied his people the right to defend Julfa themselves. The community derived its name from a town in the Caucasus conquered by Shah Abbas, who had deported its inhabitants to his new capital, Isfahan. Many Armenians died during the exodus, but they had since accepted their fate and, in building a new Julfa on the outskirts of Isfahan and devoting themselves single-mindedly to trade, they had shown themselves loyal to the Persian king. Confronted with the Afghan menace, they were prepared to do battle in good faith to safeguard the king and his capital. As Christians, however, they were not deemed trustworthy. They had been made to give up their weapons, and a Persian guard had taken up position on the ramparts of Julfa. Now that the army had been destroyed, the guard consisted of a hodgepodge of green recruits and scallywags. The Armenians felt entitled to deceive them whenever they could.

At five o'clock, they heard a disorderly cavalcade of footsteps pass the door, accompanied by sounds of jostling and swearing. The Persian soldiers had left their post. Alix and Dostom followed the Armenian into the street and mounted a steep staircase to the crenellated battlement. In a moment their guide had knotted the rope around a stone projection and tossed the free end to the foot of the wall. The daylight was still strong, though the sun was low and the shadows were lengthening. In the distance across the devastated countryside sprawled the Afghan camp, blue smoke rising from its cook fires. Frighteningly far off at the bottom of the wall, the ground was rocky. The man made Dostom climb down first. He advised him once more to stay hidden at the base of the rampart until nightfall. The relieving sentries, busy settling in for the night, rarely looked over the walls when they arrived. They didn't bother fugitives anyway, and when darkness came the two could safely leave the shelter of the wall and walk openly away.

Dostom lowered himself over the edge and disappeared. The rope was knotted every three or four feet to make the climbing easier. Once the rope was slack again, the Armenian offered it to Alix. She took hold of it without hesitation and climbed into the crenel. A warm wind carried a last breath of roses and warm stones up to her. She launched herself into the air and started down.

37

After his victory over the Persian army, Mahmud enjoyed a brief respite, as victory celebrations and the division of spoils kept his restless troops occupied. Yet as he still could not bring himself to mount an assault on the city walls, the Afghan once again sensed a nervous agitation around him. To gain a bit more time he sent his mercenaries against a small fortress only two miles from Isfahan. Known as Ferrahabad, the fort housed beautiful gardens and a palace belonging to the Persian king. The terrified garrison surrendered without a fight, conveniently allowing the attackers to cut their throats one by one, at their leisure, in the cool shade of the lofty umbrella pines in the park. The Afghan army took possession of the barracks, while Mahmud was able to lie on silk cushions in an actual palace for the first time in his life. He felt truly a king. Following the same course of action he had condemned his enemies for taking, the path that had in fact led to their downfall, he abandoned himself to luxury. There was less anger in him now, as he leaned on his windowsill in the evening watching Isfahan turn pink. The swallows circled, cheeping, over the park; no mountain raised its craggy wastes into view; there was nothing to be seen but the quiet undulation of the high plateau. The hated word "peace" might very nearly have sounded sweet to Mahmud's ears.

An incident occurred, however, to give him a grip on himself. Defectors had grown rarer lately. No doubt the townsmen had heard what happened to those who relied on the enemy's indulgence. Yet two more defectors had been caught that night. They were waiting in one of the palace antechambers for Mahmud to order them brought in. At noon, Alix and Dostom appeared before the king.

The large hall where Mahmud granted audiences had originally been a terrace, but a cedar roof with lacquer arabesques had been added onto it, darkening the space, which was lit only by a glass wall on the far end facing the park. Mahmud was having lunch—that is, a great steaming bowl of meat and vegetables sat on a table by the window with a silver ewer beside it. The fear-inspiring ruler came and went before the landscape, grabbing a mouthful on the fly, or sometimes a swig of water, pacing all the while. He did not immediately pay attention to the prisoners, who only saw him against the light. Yet when he did see them, he stopped dumbstruck. Alix, having removed her shawl, was dressed in a tight-fitting hunting outfit, which, despite its sturdy cloth and masculine cut, only revealed the gentle particulars of her form all the more. Her loose blond hair fell to her shoulders. She thought at first that the king's astonishment was directed at her and trained her pale gaze levelly at him by way of defense. But Mahmud crossed the length of the room with great strides, not paying the least attention to her, to stand full before Dostom. He paused, looked at the young man intensely, and, when he was sure of having recognized him, clasped him in a brotherly embrace and burst into laughter.

After this warm greeting, he ordered them both untied and led them to a terrace where they sat down. Alix, who couldn't follow their conversation in Afghan, had no trouble guessing what the two were discussing so loudly.

In Isfahan she had been one of the few to know Dostom's story, or rather to remember it, and it was this that had led her to choose him for a companion in flight. The young man's father had been an Afghan, a companion of Mir Vais, who had followed the kalantar into captivity and stayed faithful to him. His wife and children had joined him in Isfahan. When Mir Vais returned to Afghanistan in state, he had accompanied him back to Kandahar. His eldest son, Dostom, however, stayed on in Persia. Was this prompted by caution, in case Mir Vais met with a poor welcome in Afghanistan? Or had Mir Vais already begun to weave his web around the Persian king? In any case, Dostom lived in Isfahan, and his origins were gradually forgotten. He took a wife locally and raised his children in a modest quarter of town. He was known as an honest, if untalented, trader who was often away on business and returned from his trips hardly the richer. Jean-Baptiste had come to know him from treating his eldest child. Dostom had taken a Persian name, he dressed as a Persian, lived as a Persian, and no one remembered his ancestry. During his long conversations with Jean-Baptiste, the talk often drifted to plants that grew in the mountains. Dostom exhibited a remarkable knowledge of the subject. He knew species that did not grow in the climate of Persia. When his son recovered, he showed his gratitude to the doctor, who had never asked him for a toman in payment, by offering to bring back a few of the rare plants they had discussed and that Jean-Baptiste needed to make his preparations. Swearing him to secrecy, Dostom revealed the reason for his long absences. Trade was only an excuse; in fact he went back and forth to Kandahar bringing news of Persia with him. His information had been extremely useful to Mahmud in his military campaign. Since Isfahan had come under siege, Dostom had stayed in the city, since there was no way to reenter if he left it. He was waiting for the final assault so that he could help the attackers from inside. Yet when Alix asked him to take her to Mahmud, Dostom didn't hesitate. She had not told the spy of her relation to the red virgin, saying only that she had a terrible secret she urgently needed to reveal to the Afghan king.

When the two men finished their excited greetings, Dostom presented Alix to Mahmud, offering to translate for them.

"So, madam," said the king, "you are the widow of a Frankish doctor?"

He was not accustomed to speaking in this way to women. In the mountains he received no women at all except captives, for whom he reserved a different welcome. Petrified of making a faux pas, he froze, looking like a lumberman who has just felled a tree on his own head.

"Yes, Your Majesty," said Alix, herself intimidated.

She had been pondering this interview for a long time. How could she best persuade this warrior to attack Isfahan and to do so with all speed? The sensible course was to wait until summer when the river was low and easily forded, so that the town could be surrounded on all sides and effectively starved out. But by then Saba would be dead. What could she say to make him try to capture the capital immediately? And what advice could she give so that he would succeed? The city could not possibly be betrayed from within. Even Dostom, who had been considering it for weeks, training all his faculties on the problem, had concluded that it was hopeless. The Armenians were willing enough to pocket a few coins to throw madmen over their walls, but when it came to delivering their city to the enemy, not one of these Christians would consent to it, no matter how badly they had been treated by the Persians. Since the siege began, the city residents had been on a war footing. While there had still been an army, the civilians had placed their safety in its hands. Now they were attending to their own safety with a zeal and a vigilance no one could hope to outwit.

Alix was reduced to hoping that Mahmud himself, as a well-informed leader, would discover some crack in the city's defenses or a way to bring in artillery. But how long would it take to bring mortar pieces this far? There was one last solution, which Alix invoked in secret: that the king's desire to conquer the capital was strong enough for him to agree to sacrifice half his army to do it. If they advanced with ladders, the first five waves would be decimated, or the first ten, but the eleventh would claim victory.

She couldn't trigger a massacre on this scale by appealing for her daughter to be rescued.

"Your Majesty," she said, determined to risk everything, "all my deceased husband's duties toward the king of Persia—"

"His duties! I understand he was an apothecary. Did he treat the royal dog?"

"He avoided doing so for a long time, believe me, as the king is extremely unjust and my husband did not like him at all, but he was finally forced to. You know the position foreigners are in . . . As I was saying, my husband's duties all fell to me after his decease."

"Are you a doctor as well?"

"Let's say I know how to prepare the medications, so I have continued to bring them to the royal palace."

Mahmud stretched out full length on the carpet, a thing he rarely did, while his guests remained seated. It was not unpleasant, in fact he was surprised he had not discovered how comfortable it was long ago. That a beautiful foreign woman sat facing him who had only recently conducted a similarly elegant conversation with Huseyn of Persia gave him a pleasure he would have believed highly improbable only a month before.

"It was there, Your Majesty," Alix continued, somewhat reassured by the sovereign's welcome, "that I caught wind of the operation they are planning. Dostom, to whom I revealed it, thought the matter serious enough for us to come tell you about it."

"An operation!" cried Mahmud, turning toward the spy.

"Go ahead, Dostom," said Alix, relieved to have her weak lie delivered by another, "you can explain it better in your own language, and it will save the king time."

She looked calmly at the swallows while the young Afghan repeated the fabrication she had told him when they arrived in Ferrahabad. The palace of the Persian ruler, he told the king, had considerable treasure hidden in it, the fabulous booty amassed by Shah Abbas in the course of his conquests. These wonders, contained in fourteen sealed chests, were hidden in a place that the foreign woman had learned entirely by chance.

With the nazir's help, Huseyn planned to move this great wealth out within a month and put it in a safe place, beyond the Afghans' reach. Then he would abandon the capital.

Alix thought the story so simple and stupid that she would have been ashamed to tell it herself. Her lack of imagination dismayed her. She could create long romances in her head featuring the people she loved or who had harmed her, but she was hopeless at imagining the beautiful abstract constructions that Jean-Baptiste conjured up so well.

Her one chance was that the rugged Afghan, whose mind was not without its subtleties, liked clear and straightforward ideas. This was one. She had convinced Dostom of its truth, despite his long acquaintance with Persian culture. And she inflamed Mahmud's imagination, to the point where he could no longer keep still.

It wasn't that the Afghan king was in transports about this ridiculous business of treasure. Of course, it would be good to capture such rich booty. But what most infuriated him was to learn that the Persian jackal was still trying to deceive him. Honor was his driving motive, and Alix, in thinking to excite his greed, had unknowingly set this secret cord vibrating.

"One month, you say?" the king asked.

That would bring them to the third moon, counting from the time of Yahya Beg's prophecy. Alix nodded.

"That's not much time," said Mahmud, pacing up and down.

A final doubt came to him suddenly. He stopped in front of Alix.

"And what is your interest, madam, in informing me of this?"

She had foreseen the question.

"I hope, Sire, to obtain your gratitude."

"In what way?"

"When you have captured the city, as I'm certain you will, and so quickly as to confound your worst enemies . . . I would like to ask you for the lives of three people."

"Their lives? And what for?"

"To save them . . . or put them to death, as I please."

Mahmud recognized this as a woman's folly, authentic in every detail. He no longer doubted her sincerity. Without even asking the names of the three persons, whom he almost certainly did not know, he accepted.

"Leave me now," he said. "Make yourselves comfortable in the camp."

To Dostom, he added in Afghan:

"What shall we do with this foreign woman?"

"Your Majesty, she is a courageous woman," the young man answered. "She'll take part in the battle herself if need be."

Mahmud took such keen pleasure in his new civility as a parvenu king that he felt full of gratitude toward this elegant woman who had just inaugurated the new manners of his court. Yet it was a little early to impose the new customs publicly. A remnant of caution suggested to Mahmud a provisional solution.

"In that case, have men's clothes issued to her, a uniform such as we all wear, and let her stay in the palace. We will treat her . . . as an officer. Translate these words to her."

Alix thanked him and withdrew with Dostom. She couldn't help questioning the spy immediately: what decision did he think the king would make with regard to attacking the city?

"When he accompanied you to the door," said the Afghan, "the king was speaking to himself, did you notice? He was heaping curses on Huseyn, but he also said: 'Oh! if only they get here in time . . .' I have no idea who he could mean."

Afghanistan is a desert in a rage.

Gray and unvarying with its scaly surface of pebbles, it has the harshness, the denudement, and the aridity of the desert. But instead of lying flat like the steppe, or rolling gently, the Afghan desert rears up and coils on itself violently. It is all rifts, sheer drops, and sharp ridges. The higher one climbs, the more forcefully does this anger from the depths lift and agitate the landscape. Nothing calms it. One never finds the high, peaceful summits, foursquare on their environing slopes, that give the Alps or the Caucasus Mountains their serenity. At most the mountains show their horrible teeth, broken by gusts of wind, their jagged passes where frozen squalls howl despairingly and plunge into the wet gullies, as black as the insides of a gargoyle.

The four slaves followed their master silently along the narrow paths of this hostile environment. The altitude, which made their heads light, the sharp cold of the shadowed slopes where their hands turned blue, the desiccation of the south-facing slopes under the white light of the spring sun—everything contributed to their estrangement from the world, and even from their own bodies. They daydreamed, not saying three words to each other all day. And they spoke even less to their owner. Since leaving Khiva, the slaves had heard unpleasant conversations about themselves in every village where they had stopped. The old Afghan trusted neither his own eyesight nor the Khivan trader who had sold him these dubious specimens, and at every stop he asked for reassurance about his choice. But there is a common form of meanness, owing as much to stupidity as to jealousy, that inclines men to denigrate what another has bought and they don't have the means to buy themselves, if ever a doubt is raised or an opinion imprudently sought.

These advisers had in the end convinced the old Afghan that his slaves were poor recruits, that they had flaws, some hidden, others clearly apparent, like Juremi's scars and Bibichev's camel knees, and that he had paid too much for them.

The slanders had the practical effect, first, of delighting the people who spread them, and second, of making the slaves' conditions harsher. The old man now cut back on the rations he fed twice a day to his human flock, which consisted of some rice, a few vegetables, and boiled beans. He also started venting his ill humor on the captives, treating them roughly and forbidding them to speak to each other. Jean-Baptiste was convinced that what frightened the old Afghan most was the thought of arriving home with them. He had spent his community's money and was going to be reproached for it. The detours through the mountains were probably intended to delay the settling of accounts. The old man might even be looking for a way to sell them at a bargain and thus recover his money, at least in part. Better for him to return to his village empty-handed, saying he had found nothing worth buying in Khiva, than to bring back damaged goods, which he would never hear the end of.

Spring had come to the Afghan mountains, but it remained orbiting in the heavens with its palette of colors, finding nothing on the ground to paint: no bush to turn green, no flower to hang petals on, no animal with winter furs to brighten. One morning, though, after the travelers climbed a long rocky trail, they reached a high, scooped-out valley set in a cirque of jagged peaks that offered them a less sinister, even a thoroughly pleasant, sight. At the bottom of this combe lay a lake. In all their travels in the area they had seen nothing like it. The lake was of astonishing beauty for its freshness and purity. Its waters, when one approached close enough to touch them, were as black as obsidian. But their darkness made the lake a perfect mirror, so that from a distance it reflected the sky and took on its pale azure hue. It had the appearance of a great floating well set among rocks. At the end of the lake, where it was fed by a narrow torrent flowing hidden under pebbles, fringes of dark green algae and yellow splashes of water lilies defined the contours of the great circle of liquid pastel.

By their groans and a great show of stubborn ill will, the slaves finally managed to make the old Afghan pitch camp near this watering place. They built a fire of the dried cow dung Juremi carried on his back. Jean-Baptiste brought out the cauldron he was in charge of, and George poured in the dried vegetables and the rice. Bibichev, for his part, was responsible for drawing water—an easy task here—and stirring the pottage with a long spoon. The policeman, who like the others daydreamed a great deal, imagined that he was holding a large quill in his hand and tracing on the broth's ephemeral surface the immortal dispatches he continued to compose in his mind.

After their meager meal, the four of them sat on the ground with their master, cross-legged, silently contemplating the lake. Suddenly, a great noise drew their attention to the far end of the valley where the path rose to a high pass. An enormous block of stone had come tumbling down the slope, breaking into three pieces when it reached the bottom of the gorge. A caravan must have been coming through the saddle in their direction, and its travelers must have been extraordinarily clumsy, or else very heavily laden, to topple such a huge mass. Before another minute had passed, a second rock, bigger than the first, rolled down the incline. Four more boulders fell, each unleashing a set of explosions that reverberated around the cirque. The caravan was now coming into view. The four slaves stood and squinted at it.

"Is it horses making all that rumpus?" asked the old Afghan, who couldn't see them yet.

"No," answered Jean-Baptiste. "Not horses or mules."

"Camels?"

"No, but wait, it looks . . . yes. Aren't I right, Juremi? Those are elephants!"

As the party worked its way down the looping trail below the pass, they could be seen more and more clearly. There were eight animals in single file, swaying along the narrow path and brushing against the large stones bordering it. Two men herded this impressive troop, one running in front and the other in back, shouting and waving their arms to make the train move. Finally the caravan appeared on the edge of the lake and reached the spot where Jean-Baptiste and his companions had pitched their little camp. The animals' tread made the ground ring, and even the lake quivered. The leader of the herd, a thin, agitated Afghan, all arms and legs, stopped the animals by waving his hands wildly in front of them, then leading them gently to the edge of the lake. Eight trunks lined up and plunged their tips in the water. From the sucking sounds that echoed through the valley, it seemed that the entire lake might soon be swallowed up by the pachyderms.

The herder, all the while keeping an eye on his mastodons, approached their camp and greeted his fellow countryman. The slaves watched the two perform their salamalecs, unable to follow the conversation in Afghan. From the difference in their outfits, it was clear that the new arrival belonged to a different tribe than their old master. Afghanistan is a feudal mosaic without much cohesion. Each region has its own costume and character. The elephant driver was a Pashtun, most likely from the south, near Kandahar. But the very depths of Afghan culture contain an admixture of Persian and even Hellenistic influences, as Alexander the Great crossed the country on his way to Sogdiana, and the amber blond hair of the Pashtun was perhaps a distant heritage from the Macedonian leader and his warriors.

The old Afghan, after a few minutes, motioned his slaves to help the other member of the elephant convoy feed the animals. Large wicker trunks were tied to the beasts' flanks, some of them full of fodder. The little man they were to help had climbed onto one of these and was pitching bales of dried hay and straw down with a wooden fork. He hopped to the ground and showed them how to distribute the rations among the animals. They saw that, like themselves, he wore a chain around his ankles. He spoke neither Persian nor Arabic, nor Turkish, nor French, nor Italian, nor English, so that it seemed all communication with him would be impossible. When Bibichev tried Russian, however, the other replied: he was a Bulgar.

The two Afghans had meanwhile walked some distance off and were talking animatedly. The new arrival glanced often toward the group of Franks. The Bulgar, with Bibichev interpreting, offered the glimmer of an explanation.

The tall blond Afghan, whose name was Amanullah, had left Kandahar two weeks before with two countrymen and five slaves. They had ridden with all speed to Samarkand, where they had bought these elephants. They were now returning just as quickly, but directing their steps toward Persia. In the last few days, though, a mysterious fever, probably contracted in the fetid plains of Uzbekistan, had carried off the two other Afghans and four of the slaves. The only ones to have survived were the strongest, Amanullah, and the frailest, which was to say himself. This was far from enough manpower to keep such a large herd of pachyderms in line. They could no longer ride them one to an animal and had been forced to attach them to each other by the leg. If one of the elephants ever lost his footing, the entire line would be dragged over the precipice.

"Does your master have any gold?" asked Jean-Baptiste.

"He still has a great deal," said the Bulgar, "because he brought enough to buy fifteen elephants but despite all his efforts could only find these eight in Samarkand."

"Then all will go well."

The conversation between the two Afghans was taking an animated and decisive turn. Before long they were gaily slapping each other's hands. They retired behind a rock to complete their transaction, then came back, both radiant, toward the elephants. The old man was visibly delighted.

"Hey, all of you!" he shouted at his little band, "I have big news for you. You no longer belong to me. From now on you will obey the great lord that you see here and whose name is Amanullah."

The four Franks bowed respectfully.

Amanullah was not one to linger over a ceremony. As soon as the beasts had been fed and watered he had them untied, except for two that remained shackled together. The slaves and he climbed onto the animals' necks and took up the goad used to steer them.

Amanullah said a brief goodbye to the old Afghan and, not bothering whether his new recruits could manage their unusual mounts, set off down the slope. Only when night had fallen completely did he give the signal to halt. After their long ride, the new mahouts were stiff and sore. They were all the same delighted to have proven themselves in this trial by elephant. They slept like stumps. Only on the following day, when they were loading the animals for another stage to the west, did they think to ask the Bulgar why they were making such haste.

"He says," Bibichev translated, with the ironic expression of someone informing his interlocutor of a well-known fact, "that they are expecting our reinforcement. To capture Isfahan."

38

Amanullah, a devil of a tall, fair-haired Afghan, was driving his pack of elephants toward Isfahan at breakneck speed. Almost standing on the animal, he belabored its trunk with blows of his elephant goad to drive it on as quickly as possible. The elephants, as it happened, needed no urging. They gathered their mass into a shambling, powerful gallop with all the more pleasure and the less effort as they were now descending from the heights of Afghanistan toward the lower lands of Persia.

Still wearing their leg shackles, Jean-Baptiste and his companions rode their elephants sidesaddle, gripping the long strap around the animals' necks with all their might. Rounding a bend, a load came loose on one of the elephants, and the two wicker chests dashed against the rocks. The novice mahouts thought a thousand times that they would be thrown from their mounts, or go hurtling with them over a precipice. Amanullah never stopped. They saw his heavy blond mane floating in the air ahead of them and heard the howl of his war cries and mountain ditties.

He was neither mad nor cruel, as they had at first feared. He was simply an Afghan warrior. Never having seen one, the poor Frankish slaves had not imagined such men existed: absolutely devoted to honor and to battle, indifferent to death, and intimate with the sacred exaltation engendered by danger and solitude, and maintained by every decoction of the poppy. Other than the hellish pace he made them keep up, Amanullah treated his company quite well. He showed not the slightest contempt for these infidels and shared the little there was to eat with them fairly. He regarded them less as slaves than as soldiers, and they were all partners in this rude brotherhood. To help them overcome their pain and weariness and function on the small amount of food and sleep they received, he gladly shared with his companions the miraculous resins that he smoked. With the exception of Bibichev, who declined contemptuously, all the mahouts leaped onto their mounts in the morning, the Afghan in the lead and the Franks close behind, after having inhaled deeply of these God-given essences; it gave them the feeling of riding not elephants but eagles, and they took off unafraid.

The eight beasts, charging at top speed, made the ground tremble long before they came in sight. The villagers in the foothills of Afghanistan took the dull rumbling of the earth for the first tremors of an earthquake and rushed out of their houses, dragging their most valuable belongings out with them. Amanullah's yelling band would descend on them during their panic, never passing a village without seeing the inhabitants standing outside haggard, mattresses on their heads and cribs in their arms, looking on terrified at this unlikely vision of unfettered beasts and shackled men.

Amanullah always made camp in deserted places, probably because he was not on his own tribe's lands and he wanted to avoid having to give explanations. They stopped only at the very end of the day, moving the flat stones of the scrubland aside to lie down and sleep. The animals, loosed in the cork oak and oleander bushes, spent the night trampling down the plants. A sliver of moon lit the feast of scented foliage, eaten to the joyous sound of crackling branches and heavy bumping. One night they saw a long procession of laden camels pass in the distance: it was the spring caravan on its way to Kandahar and the India of the Great Moghul. They avoided making the least sign that might draw attention to them. Amanullah kept his distance not only from his enemies—many in this caravan must have been his own tribesmen, from whom he could expect only help—but also from anything that might slow the party down, if even slightly, so crucial to his mission was haste.

When the descent was over they started off across the great salt desert. Without hesitating, Amanullah took the shortest route directly west, through a region where the salt crust had for centuries decimated all life, except for the black vultures who found nothing there to feed on but each other.

The Afghan knew even the smallest wells. Most were brackish or tainted with alum. Luckily it was not yet too hot in these first days of spring, and the animals traveled so fast they did not stay long in this hell.

The change in climate, the mountains dropping behind them, and the slower progress of the elephants on the loose ground brought Jean-Baptiste, Juremi, and George down from their initial carefree state. They returned to very practical concerns and, so as to consider them more fully, refused the Afghan's consolatory drugs. As his supply was dipping low, he didn't insist that they partake.

The mahouts, balanced on their monsters' withers, had rejoiced at first to be returning to Isfahan. But they were sorry now to be bringing the Afghan army decisive reinforcements for its assault on the city and looked for some way to delay or even forestall entirely this disaster.

The little Bulgar was very talkative. He had told the story of his life to Bibichev in detail and insisted that the Russian translate it for the other three. But to his discomfiture, neither Jean-Baptiste nor his companions paid the least attention to the vagaries of his existence, governed as it was by an unlucky star. They had simply had enough of the extraordinary, the picturesque, and, a fortiori, the tragic. Their only thought was to return home. The questions they asked the Bulgar all pertained to the siege of Isfahan and the plans of the Afghan army. The poor man knew very little except that the city could not be encircled because of the high waters of the river. He had also heard Amanullah talk of the massacre of the Persian army, and there his knowledge came to an end.

"I've got it!" cried Jean-Baptiste one night when they were stretched sleeplessly on the rock-strewn salt crust.

He shook Juremi beside him. The Protestant groaned.

"The goat crossing!" said Jean-Baptiste.

He looked toward Amanullah. The Afghan was asleep, his eyes open to the stars. George rose on one elbow:

"The goat crossing?"

"Yes," said Jean-Baptiste, "it's about a mile from Julfa, upriver on the Zayande Rud. When the water level drops in the summer, it's the first place that can be forded on horseback. A few days later, the shepherds drive their goats across it."

"So?" grumbled Juremi, who hadn't lost hope of finding sleep.

"So at the moment it can't be forded either by horse or by goats, but possibly—"

"By elephants!" cried George.

"That is what we are now doing," said Jean-Baptiste. "We are bringing Mahmud a way to get his troops across the river."

"With eight animals?" Juremi objected disgustedly.

"Each elephant can carry ten men: that's eighty per trip. Ten trips a day, eight hundred men. In three days you would have enough troops across to encircle the town, pillage the convoys bringing supplies, and destroy the countryside immediately outside the ramparts. Have you been listening to the Bulgar? The Persians have no army. The poor townsmen will have to watch this disaster from behind the walls and do nothing about it."

"We have to find a way to keep that from happening," said George, who had sat up, feeling a keen anxiety.

The great shadows of the elephants were scattered widely in the desert around them as the animals foraged for small succulent acacias whose flat foliage extended low over the ground.

"If we drive the elephants there ourselves, we can then turn them against the Afghans—" George started.

"Don't count on it," interrupted Juremi. "The Bulgar has talked about it to Bibichev: as soon as we get to Isfahan, Afghan soldiers will climb aboard and we'll be lucky if they let us run along behind the brutes and give them forage at night."

There was an embarrassed silence among the three after this outburst. It was clear that only one option was available if they wanted to deprive the Afghans of their reinforcement. Out on the great lake of salt, which sparkled like diamonds in the moonlight, the large animals lumbered peaceably, amiably. They were superbly oblivious to the petty quarrels of men; yet men had just condemned them to death.

During the following days, Jean-Baptiste hardly dared to look at his companions, and he felt a similar discomfort on their part. Courageous and willing, the pachyderms walked tirelessly on despite the growing heat and the irritation of the salt crystals to their feet. They were sturdy Asian elephants, with short ears held flat against their necks, prominent foreheads, and long tusks sawed off to a third of their length for fighting. Between them and the little men who had been hanging on to their necks for so many days, a genuine familiarity had grown up. George in particular had developed a camaraderie with his elephant: they played like children, even arm-wrestling, one with the end of his trunk, the other with his fist, sailor-style. Probably because the animal was particularly greedy, George had baptized him Garou, from the French name for a leafy mountain shrub. Garou came docilely at the sound of his name when he was off masticating among the others.

What method could they use to destroy the poor animals? There was not a prayer that the beasts would run away from their butchers: they had grown so accustomed to their keepers that they never even needed to be tied at night. Every other solution called for some hideous act, the mere thought of which disgusted them.

From the place that Amanullah had bought his Frankish slaves, it had taken barely three weeks at their hellish pace to cross the salt desert and reach the foothills of the plateaux on which Isfahan was situated. The climb made the elephants swing their heads from side to side, breathing heavily. They were happy at night to find thickets of hawthorn and serviceberry. The sloping meadows with their covering of mountain flowers provided the travelers cooler and more refreshing halts. Given the effort of climbing, even Amanullah agreed to rest the animals two or three times a day; otherwise they would stop on their own, half choking, a frightening pink froth collecting on their lips.

During one of these halts, on a beautiful sunny day, Juremi called to his companions excitedly. He pointed toward a stony slope along the edge of a wood where tall purple flowers grew, covered with berries.

"Do you see what I see?" asked the Protestant.

"Deadly nightshade!" said George.

"Which your father and I, when we were in Italy, learned to call *belladonna*. Wealthy Venetian ladies use a tincture of it dissolved in collyrium to dilate their pupils and create the deep black eyes that lovers adore."

They looked at each other, smiling: the same thought had crossed all their minds and given them hope. Belladonna blurs a person's vision and makes him very sick. But used in the right dosage it is not fatal and leaves no trace. They glanced over at the elephants. How much would it take to incapacitate them and prevent them from carrying out the task they were destined for, but without killing them? They had a brief discussion, and George walked away to make his calculations.

"Half a pound per head," he announced on returning.

"Two kilos in all, then," said Jean-Baptiste.

Amanullah was below them, behind a hedge. He had started on his prayers. The Bulgar was chewing a grass stem and reciting more of his life story to Bibichev, who was dozing.

"Let's go," said Juremi.

He took off the cotton vest he wore over his shirt, spread it on the ground, and started to throw handfuls of belladonna berries into it. The two others followed suit. They stripped off a large quantity, which Juremi weighed in his hand.

"Barely two pounds," he said, frowning.

They went back to frantically picking. It was painstaking work, which absorbed them entirely. Suddenly Amanullah's voice made them jump. The Afghan was standing three feet from Juremi's vest, studying them.

They straightened up, panicked, dropping the berries from their hands. The blond warrior repeated the same sentence. The guttural sounds of the Afghan language always made him seem angry, this time more than ever. They had to wait for the Bulgar to come translate and for Bibichev to translate his translation.

"The Afghan wants to know if you can smoke it," said Bibichev finally.

There was visible relief in the faces of the three herbalists.

"Tell him yes," said Juremi quickly. "It's truly fantastic. I'm surprised he doesn't know about it. It will take us a few days to dry our harvest, crush the berries, and make a preparation that I think he'll find very satisfactory . . ."

The Afghan let them pick a good two kilos, almost three, while a fond and greedy look played in his eyes.

The next two days they crossed a deserted countryside. Jean-Baptiste had often traveled in the area around Isfahan, but it was unrecognizable now. The gardens lay untended, the fruit trees had been hacked off at the ground, the wells poisoned, the huts burned. The soil of these regions is very fertile but entirely without water. By irrigating it carefully, the most beautiful flowers and the most delicious fruits can be grown there, but let this program be interrupted and everything perishes, with hawthorn and goat grass invading the abandoned land. Ever since the Afghans had passed, sowing terror in their wake, these vile thorns were the only crop remaining along this shore of the river. Thanks to Amanullah's elephants, the Afghan force was now planning to extend this desolation to the opposite bank. Before such cruelty, Jean-Baptiste thought of Alix, of Saba, of Françoise, of the horror they faced, and he felt himself capable of anything. The sack of berries more than ever represented their only hope.

On the second day, at one o'clock in the afternoon, Isfahan came into view. The three Franks let their tears run at the sight. Above the ramparts, which shone with majesty in the sunshine of the high plateau, the Mongol minarets, the tiled domes, the tall alignment of poplars in the Chahar Bagh sent signals of friendship and understanding. Their loves were there. All beauty and refinement, all joy and pleasure were also there. By rotten luck, however, they were on the wrong side of the walls, and their arrival spelled the city's downfall.

They intended to execute their plan immediately. Unfortunately, everything happened on this first day more quickly than they expected. Mahmud, king of Kandahar, came out to meet them with a detachment of horsemen on learning of their approach. The large encampments of the Afghan army were visible in the distance, black on the horizon, but the elephant herd was not led in that direction. Amanullah, who had entered into discussion with Mahmud, gave his slaves no explanation. All they knew was that the king's retinue showed extraordinary impatience. Without allowing the animals or their drivers a moment's rest, Amanullah lolloped north behind the king, his blond mane flying. Before long they reached the riverbank at some distance above the city. Jean-Baptiste had been right. Hoofprints in the dried mud showed that they had come to the goat crossing. The river, swollen by heavy rains, was more impassable than ever. But as they had foreseen, the Afghans were preparing to make the elephants cross there. For them it was a question of putting into effect a plan they had been hatching for weeks.

Just as the Bulgar had said, the Frankish slaves were asked to dismount, and their places were taken by actual soldiers. Jean-Baptiste and the three others, on foot, took up a position on the bank among clusters of bamboo—a ringside seat from which to watch the action. The Afghans took the precaution of sending over only one elephant at first. It was the one belonging to Amanullah, who had proudly retained his position of mahout. He prodded his mount, which advanced heavily down the embankment as far as the water. Amanullah turned around, saluted the king, and, urging on his elephant, stepped into the water at the supposed ford. The animal advanced cautiously. Within a few moments, it was in the water halfway up its body and sinking heavily at each step. The king was pale. Jean-Baptiste felt a stirring of hope.

The elephant driver seemed to hesitate for a moment. If the river bottom continued at the same slope, the pachyderm would be swallowed by the current long before reaching the middle. Courageously, Amanullah directed the animal to continue forward. Another step and the slate-colored water rose even higher on the elephant's flanks. No one on the bank spoke. The only sound was the swishing of the water and Amanullah's shouts as he urged his mount on.

After a long hesitation, the pachyderm, perhaps guided by a mysterious instinct awakened in him by danger, decided not to follow the exhortations of his mahout. He started pawing at the bed of the river to the right and left, his trunk upraised. Suddenly, the animal pivoted to the side a bit and seemed to come up against something solid. He took another step in that direction, and his body rose more than a meter out of the water. He had found the narrow, solid strip of the ford. The elephant then turned back toward the center of the river and reached it in a few strides without sinking any deeper. Arriving at midstream, Amanullah let out a yell of victory, rose in his seat shaking his elephant stick, and looked with a radiant expression toward his sovereign. A joyous clamor greeted this victory from the bank. The Frankish slaves, of course, took no part in it.

But it had been ordained that nothing was to happen simply on that crucial afternoon. So far there had been no sign of anyone besides the Afghans. Now the Persians entered the scene. We have mentioned that they watched the river day and night and feared an attack on the city from this quarter. In their imaginations they had foreseen the boldest plans, even those that might enlist the help of supernatural agencies; they had not, however, considered elephants. Fortunately, in expectation of what would happen a few weeks later when the goat crossing became passable, the Persians had prepared an ingenious device, which they now set off earlier than they had planned to, seeing the elephants approach. The ford, being in an exposed area, could not be defended from the bank. A bit farther upstream, though, the river ran through groves of elm trees, planted, appropriately enough, by Shah Abbas. These were sturdy, hundred-year-old trees, yet the Persians, feeling justified in using any means at hand to spare their capital, had cut them down. No sooner did Amanullah begin his bold crossing than watchers on the Persian side gave the signal to loose five or six of these giant trunks, lined up along the bank and held with ropes. The logs were cast adrift with three strokes of an ax, and the current swept them downriver straight at the elephant. The poor brute avoided the first one, which passed just ahead of him. Two others struck him on the side; the elephant lost its balance and keeled over, like a tall ship flattened by a storm. Amanullah passed directly from his moment of triumph into the cold water. They saw him float a few moments before sinking down into the muddy flood. The elephant, unable to regain its footing, floated off like a giant gray buoy. A little later the Persians guarding the Chahar Bagh bridge were surprised to see it pass under one of the arches. The beast became stuck there, and the frantic crowd pelted it with spears and projectiles before realizing that the poor animal had drowned. It sank during the night and no more was ever seen of it.

This reversal filled Mahmud and all the other Afghans with bitterness and anger. The other elephants and the slaves who were responsible for looking after them were installed in a camp not far from the river, at some distance from the rest of the army so as not to arouse too much curiosity.

All further attempts to cross the river were for the moment suspended. This setback had to be kept from dampening the besiegers' morale and making them mutter more about their leader's indecision. To restore his authority, Mahmud ordered a great parade for the following day, so as to properly mark the arrival of the mastodons and pay homage to the courageous Amanullah, who had brought them so far, so fast, and for so little.

39

It was not a prison. The nazir had emphasized this point repeatedly. The small pavilion was simply at a distance from the others that made up the palace of the high chamberlain. True, the space around it was enclosed by walls, but these had been tastefully obscured by trimmed arbors. The inevitable fountain plashed in the center of the square lawn fronting the little building. This charming spot, enveloped by the scent of clematis, had been built for a favorite mistress. This made the nazir sigh each night as he turned the key to the great blue door on his way to visit Monsieur de Maillet. Times had certainly changed. Now that everything teetered on the brink, he found himself shutting an anorexic old man in a place where nature would more readily have celebrated youth and its appetites. One simply had to accept it.

It might have been simpler and more sensible to have done away with this person straight off—death would in any case visit him before long. Nothing could induce the man to silence—he claimed to have left instructions outside town that would keep his disappearance from going unnoticed—and as he declared himself determined to broadcast the truth at any cost, the nazir could have brought the curtain down once and for all on this bothersome consul. In the chaotic atmosphere of Isfahan, no one would give much thought to the fate of a half-crazed old foreigner.

Yet, humanitarian considerations aside, the nazir considered it more adroit to hold on to his hostage. An emissary of this kind was a simple and useful asset. The information he had provided clearly showed that he was Alberoni's envoy. While the prelate might not have cared to pay anything for his presumed concubine, he would assuredly give something when the time came for this undoubted messenger. If the city fell, if flight was necessary, the nazir had determined his course of action: he would take Monsieur de Maillet with him and set off for Rome.

In the meantime, he continued to visit his prisoner in an attempt to make him weaken. Nothing was having any effect. The old man stubbornly continued to claim that this supposed cardinal's concubine had in fact been his servant in Cairo, that she had fled the city with an adventurer, that she had given innumerable proofs of her evil, lying nature . . . in short, that the whole thing was an imposture. The nazir tired of it finally and started visiting only twice a week.

Monsieur de Maillet passed his time in the garden beside the fountain reading and rereading his beloved *Telliamed,* savoring its beauty ever more fully. For him it was not a book of philosophy but the story of his life. He remembered the very first day, the day he had experienced his great, his first, intuition: he was walking that morning in the streets of Cairo and had left the city without noticing it. It was already hot. After passing a small shipyard where half-naked carpenters were building feluccas, he had reached a tiny cliff on the edge of the river. He sat down there and saw seashells. Seashells! So far from the sea! It had all unfolded from this vision.

The consul closed the book and took a deep breath. What happiness! Thought! Pure ideation! The very movements of the mind! Yet a certain bitterness rose up in the midst of the sweetness, spoiling the taste. What was it? He had already experienced it several times without managing to explain it to himself. He considered. A mourning dove cooed in a yew tree in a corner of the wall. What a bizarre call, really! It sounded like a stubborn question. The bird repeated it. When it did so a third time the consul rose in his chair. He had understood. "What were you doing that day in the streets of Cairo?" the dove was asking him. It was true. At the time he had hardly been in the habit of going about on foot. Probably it was even . . . the first time.

The first time! Why? But because *she* had just left. The answer came to Monsieur de Maillet of itself, and the fact suddenly pierced him with sharp grief. Yes, Alix had just left, or rather, he had just learned the truth: that she had fled with the apothecary, that they had killed a janissary and the guards from the consulate, that he had been betrayed, dishonored, by his own daughter. And he had walked straight before him through the streets of Cairo.

His theory! His seashells!

The old man gave an abrupt sob, more of a hiccup really, that shook him to his entrails. "Alix!" He clasped his beloved *Telliamed* in his arms.

"Can it be that this little book, what am I saying, this great book, has until now spared me this grief . . ."

The leather-bound tome fell from his trembling hands into the grass. He picked it up and collected himself:

"Come, one has to fight off abandonment!"

It was all due to the inactivity forced on him by his unfair detention. He rose and began walking with his hands behind his back. He had hardly made two circuits of the garden before a servant appeared and bowed to him respectfully. The consul approached but failed to recognize his usual chambermaid.

"My name is Gregory, Your Excellency," said the man softly. "I am your new servant."

"You mean my 'new guard,' surely," snickered Monsieur de Maillet.

"No, Excellency, I did say 'servant.'"

Then, in a lower voice:

"I count on your indulgence not to denounce me to the nazir."

"Denounce you! Whatever for?"

"Why, for what I am about to tell Your Excellency."

The consul examined this servant. He was young but, being stout and bald, looked older. Men who are round all seem to have reached a far shore of wisdom, where time unwinds at the pace of their pleasures, rather than at the pace of life. Something in this frank delectation touches on eternity. This Gregory, with his long shirt distended by his stomach, had the figure of a monk and the sly smile to go with it.

"And what would you like to tell me?" the consul asked, the other having clearly cast him in the role of midwife to the conversation.

"That I am Armenian, Excellency."

"All the better for you. Some of your race are perfectly honest. Don't worry, it won't be from me that the nazir learns you are Christian."

"He knows it, Excellency. There are several of us in his service."

"Well then, everything is for the best," said the consul tartly. "Is there nothing else you would like to confess to me that the whole world knows already?"

"No, Excellency, but there is something that no one knows but me and, shortly, you."

This devil of an Armenian would have exhausted the patience of a stone effigy.

"Would you just say what you have to say!" exploded the consul.

"Shh! Excellency, someone could hear us."

"When you're ready," murmured the consul, resigned.

"Well, Excellency, our patriarch Nerses is a saintly man. It distresses him that an injustice should be committed against a Christian, namely yourself. Alas! we are all too used to such mistreatment, especially from the person responsible for your suffering."

"Kindly thank your patriarch for these thoughts," said Monsieur de Maillet, genuinely moved.

"They are not only thoughts," Gregory persisted enigmatically. "There could also be actions, if Your Excellency should wish it."

"Actions? What actions?"

"Might Your Excellency perhaps wish . . . to return to Rome?"

"Do I wish to return to Rome!" said the consul with a jump. "Well, I certainly plan to, my friend. It is my firmest intention to do so."

"In that case, we might arrange . . . an exodus."

The consul stared hard at this strange servant. He leaned toward him and repeated:

"An exodus?"

"Yes," Gregory confirmed in a whisper. "I mean, of course, an escape."

Monsieur de Maillet, reacting to this word, started to his feet.

"Never!" he cried.

"But—"

"Do not insist, Gregory. I said 'Never.' I want justice, do you understand? And I will obtain it. My mission requires me to unmask a certain impostor, whose game I have discovered and am on the point of wrecking once and for all. I've asked for an audience with the king of Persia. The nazir is a bandit, yes. But he was all the same obliged to take my requests into consideration. I have remitted three letters to him for his ruler. I'm waiting for my audience."

The servant, after a moment of astonishment, resumed his thin smile.

"Do you seriously believe the nazir intends to deliver your requests?"

"Of course! His honor demands it, my friend, have you forgotten his honor?"

"His honor . . . of course . . ." the Armenian replied with the patience of a merchant who sees his client choose an expensive garment but one that is much too small. "It is possible, however, that the nazir will have a different idea of it than Your Excellency."

The consul was irritated by the man's quiet confidence and had the unpleasant feeling of being naive in comparison.

"Don't insist," he countered with asperity. "I shall stay here until my mission is accomplished."

Having thought for a moment, he added:

"The one thing you might do that could be useful . . ."

"I am entirely at your disposal," said Gregory, noting the old man's hesitation.

". . . would be to get this key to a person who is waiting for me at this very moment at the caravanserai in Kashan."

Grasping the key at his neck that opened the chest he had left with Murad, the consul thought: Well, from one Armenian to another . . . And it may have been this thought that decided him.

Gregory took the key and listened to the diplomat's instructions.

"I would be happy to perform this service for Your Excellency," he said. "I hope to prove worthy of the trust, and perhaps Your Excellency will let Cardinal Alberoni know how much the Armenian Christians of this country count on his support."

"I solemnly promise to inform him of your devotion," said the consul in a voice of authority. "If possible, you will submit a brief on the problems faced by your church, and if I have the good fortune to see the cardinal again . . ."

Gregory kneeled and kissed Monsieur de Maillet's hand, which the latter permitted. He was accustomed never, in the Orient, to resist even the most singular act of obsequiousness.

The servant rose and started away, then came back.

"I forgot," he added. "The patriarch asked me to give Your Excellency news of your daughter. She is well, apparently, she is happy, and—if you will forgive my indiscretion—she hopes you have forgiven her."

At six o'clock, with the chill of nightfall upon him, Monsieur de Maillet still stood unmoving in the garden, overcome by the emotions stirred in him by this news.

According to Juremi, who knew a thing or two about it, the Afghan mahouts now in charge of the elephants were clumsy and unskillful handlers. Reenacting once again the marriage of incompetence and vanity, they treated the slaves who fed and cared for the animals with harsh contempt. Fortunately, these soldiers were so sure of their great importance that they spent the better part of their time in the barracks in Ferrahabad, near King Mahmud and his court. Jean-Baptiste and his companions were on their own for the greater part of the day. They could come and go as they liked, since their noisy leg chains would keep them from attempting an escape. Discussing Amanullah's watery end among themselves, they agreed that this first setback would probably be followed by other attempts—and they shouldn't give up their project of incapacitating the animals. On the very morning after the unfortunate accident, they once more discreetly undertook to prepare their potion. They spread the fresh berries in a large basin, which they left out in the sun. Juremi mixed them lovingly by the handful as he watched them dry.

"I'm wondering," he said with a nasty smile, "whether those scrimshanking mahouts don't also deserve a share of these."

Jean-Baptiste, for his part, had gone off looking for a concave rock to use as a mortar, and George was carving a pestle out of holly. Bibichev watched these preparations discreetly, pretending little interest in them. In fact, his attitude had changed enormously. At this point he could hardly keep himself from admiring the suspects deeply. To have completed such a journey, made contact with so many intermediaries and agents, each more extraordinarily disguised than the last, only to end up bang alongside the Afghan army at the very moment the town was being assaulted, it was all too much. He waited serenely for the next development, like a man confidently on his way to a performance by an artist who has never let him down.

Landing in the midst of a heterogeneous army, Bibichev was able to gather useful information from the Slav mercenaries and slaves who served in it. Thus he learned that the Persian Empire, aside from having its capital threatened by the Afghans, was being carved up by its other neighbors. The Uzbeks had taken Khorasan; the Turks had advanced into Azerbaijan; and as to the sainted armies of Peter the Great—tears started to his eyes at the thought of them—they had led a successful campaign into Baku, then followed the Caspian shoreline and taken control of the sea's perimeter. For the moment the Russians seemed content to go no farther. Bibichev calculated that he was therefore quite close to his own lines, and that once the river had been crossed, he could easily find a way to transmit a dispatch to Moscow.

The captives' midday meal consisted only of some grayish rice and a few pieces of a highly unusual animal made entirely of bones and without the slightest trace of flesh. Not long after, they saw the mahouts return.

These proud soldiers wore the same felt tunic that the other Afghans wore, but they had shined their belts and combed their beards. Their flat caps were artfully cocked and carefully hid their hair, which was less disorderly than usual. In a word, they had made themselves ready for the great parade. Two of them carried a square trunk by the handles, which they set down near the elephants. It contained fabrics that had been carelessly heaped together, but that the soldiers unfolded with admiring eyes. These were unmistakably prizes gathered after the massacre of the

Persian army. The mahouts first removed seven richly colored blankets of Kashmiri samite, fringed all around with gold. From the size of them, they must have served to cover the prize warhorses of the Persian officers. The slaves were given the task of spreading these fabrics over the elephants' backs like saddle blankets. The animals wore these appurtenances elegantly. Using a complicated arrangement of straps made from horse harnesses, they next made the elephants a sort of helmet that was anchored to the tusks and under the throat. This allowed bells to be hung from their heads and a large pennant of green silk from their foreheads. Both mahouts and slaves were very happy with the results. The remainder proved more painful. At the bottom of the trunk, in a wrinkled ball, was the regalia intended for the Franks, as it was customary for parading elephants to be followed on foot by their grooms.

Juremi exclaimed that he would never fit into such a tunic. The garments were narrow, sleeveless sheaths that fell to the ankle without widening. It took two men to slide this covering over Juremi's bulky and uneven form. Bibichev and the Bulgar slipped them on without difficulty or distaste. George and Jean-Baptiste were the last to don them, and the example of the others was hardly encouraging. Soon all five were enveloped in their white muslin sheaths, an outfit more appropriate to a procession of virgins on their way to first communion. Bibichev's bald and lugubrious head and Juremi's rumpled gray thatch were both highly incongruous crowning these white surplices. The mahouts, without irony, declared themselves satisfied with their helpers' looks. The captives complained, but to no avail. The Afghans' only concession was to slit the seams of the tunics to the knee so that the slaves could run alongside the elephants. The final outrage was still to come. Reaching into the bowels of the trunk, one of the mahouts pulled out five pairs of those colored Indian slippers that have bells hanging from their raised, pointed tips. Part of the booty taken from a caravan, these items had found no taker—for good reason! As they were adjusted with a lace, the Franks couldn't even claim the excuse that they were too big.

After prayer, which must have been the signal to gather for the parade, the mahouts mounted the elephants and headed toward Ferrahabad. Beside each animal trotted its keeper, to the clanking of his chains and the tinkling of his bells.

The palace of Ferrahabad had been developing in two different directions since Mahmud had settled there. In material terms, it was declining precipitously. The occupiers had vented their destructive rage on the buildings, even those that quartered them. The doors and windows, not to mention the furniture and hangings, in fact everything, had been torn down, scattered, resold, dispersed, or burned. Even the park, where the horses had been allowed to graze, was starting to look like the steppes. A plan to build a raft, though soon abandoned, had called for felling the umbrella pines that shaded the park. The char marks of great campfires blackened the ancient paved terraces. But in diplomatic terms, Ferrahabad had taken on an importance inversely proportional to its decline. Mahmud's camp had become a court, even a sort of capital. Emissaries from the Grand Signor of the Turks had arrived to pay homage to the future victor. The Uzbeks and the Afghan tribe that ruled Herat had also sent messengers. Even the East India Company had thought it prudent to offer its services by naming a highly cultured Dutch resident to attend the king of Kandahar, who might soon be king of Persia.

Mahmud received these homages in the hall where he had first encountered Alix and Dostom, which remained the only one in the palace not to be reduced to rubble.

There is a general delusion about what cutthroats feel. Some undoubtedly find pleasure in killing. But most, and Mahmud was among their number, go about the business without enthusiasm. They look upon it as their duty—but let the obligation be lifted and you will see these same cutthroats converted to the gentlest humanity. The young king of Kandahar was perhaps not yet quite at that stage. He continued to nurse the bitterest hatred toward the Persians, a feeling revived every morning by the sight of the intact city. One sensed, however, that after he surmounted this obstacle, he would become a peaceable, perhaps even a good-natured, king. A worrisome gap was already developing between himself and his brutal and sanguinary army. To mitigate it, Mahmud wore two faces. As commander of the army, he remained a pitiless warrior. As king, he made daily efforts to learn the ways of the world. Regrettably, there were few in his entourage who could help him in this. It was thus that Dostom, who had long lived in Persia, and Alix, a well-traveled foreign woman, seemed to him such valuable advisers. He solicited their opinion constantly on questions of protocol, and when drafting diplomatic messages. Dressed as an Afghan, Alix was treated as an officer and even as a man by the king. Mahmud had enough lawful wives, slave girls, and female captives to staunch any feelings of desire—fellings that, as it happened, he did not experience in the presence of this foreign woman with the troubling glance. He almost felt a small boy again in her presence, and she did in fact have to teach him the ABC's of kingly behavior.

The parade, though conceived after Amanullah's failure, was meant to celebrate the strength of the Afghan forces. The king had summoned all the foreign emissaries to join him for the occasion. They were given seats on one of the ramparts of the Ferrahabad fortress. Alix and Dostom were posted immediately behind the king so that he might discreetly ask them for advice should any question arise.

The first troops appeared below the walls at three o'clock in the afternoon. They walked parallel to them, hardly more than a few paces away, and saluted as they passed in front of the king. The bulk of the army consisted of horsemen, to whom the very idea of presenting themselves in orderly rows had never occurred: they arrived in packs, yelling, raising clouds of dust, bumping and jostling each other, and making their horses whinny. The animals reared, foaming at the mouth, their eyes starting from their heads at the sound of the weapons and the blows of hooves. Bits stolen from the vanquished army stood out here and there amidst the general impoverishment—the new leather of a saddle, a brocaded caftan, an incised lance—floating on the tide of rags and grimacing features. Alix was horrified at this violent and uncouth mass of humanity, hardly daring to imagine how much damage it would wreak on delicate Isfahan should the city ever fall into its hands. Yet fate had ordained that she would pin her hopes on just such an apocalypse and even wish for it to happen soon. Five days remained before the term set by Yahya Beg.

Finally, when the horsemen had all swept by, a last contingent came trampling over the mingled dust and manure, filling the air with a majestic rumble: the elephants, their mahouts, and their grooms.

40

The tunic was bunching up under his armpits. Despite Jean-Baptiste's efforts from above, and George's and even Bibichev's from below, the muslin sheath was stuck. From under this cotton casing came the sound of Juremi's swearing and abuse.

"Pull, sacrebleu! Go on and pull, you blockheads!"

The team's joint efforts were rewarded by a great cracking noise. Split in two, the tunic fell limply to the ground, freeing the Protestant, flushed with rage, standing in his underwear, his scars all showing, shod in a pair of belled ballerina slippers.

A young Afghan looked on, smiling. Jean-Baptiste turned around, saw the man, and rushed toward him.

"Dostom! Dear Dostom!"

They embraced warmly. Jean-Baptiste introduced George and Juremi, who was trying to get dressed again. Bibichev bowed politely, absorbed in recording the name in his mental files for his dispatch: "D-O-S-T-O-M."

"You looked wonderful, really," the young man joked, still with his hand on Jean-Baptiste's shoulder, "running beside your elephants, a gold tassel in one hand, the other saluting the king."

Poncet shrugged.

"This explains it," he said unsmilingly as he displayed the shackles around his ankles.

"I noticed, and that's why I wasn't sure I'd recognized you at first. Oh, Jean-Baptiste, what a wrenching it gave me when I convinced myself that it was really you. Luckily, I realized fairly quickly. I put my hand on her arm, and that's how she kept from crying out when she saw you."

"She? Who do you mean?" asked Jean-Baptiste, hardly daring to imagine the answer.

"Why, Alix, dear friend! Alix herself, who is there beside King Mahmud. I can understand how astonished you might feel at the news.

She was equally flummoxed to learn that you were a slave and looking after elephants."

This was too much. Jean-Baptiste, worn by the fatigues of his journey, with all its hopes and difficulties, felt swallowed by despondency. He fell sobbing into George's arms. Everyone was moved, and if the mahouts had not been afraid of the Afghan Dostom, whom they had often seen in the king's entourage, they would have scattered this sentimental gathering with their shouts. But nothing put an end to this affecting scene; on the contrary, Juremi, George, and even Dostom joined their tears with those of Jean-Baptiste. Bibichev, for his part, didn't know what to admire more, the ingeniousness of his suspects' plans or the apparent sincerity of their acting.

The first to be afflicted, Jean-Baptiste was also the first to regain control of his emotions.

"Let's go to Alix!" he cried. "Quick, Dostom, take me to her."

"Alas! Things are not so simple," said the Afghan, wiping away the last of his tears.

"What!" growled Juremi. "She's here, and so are we, and yet we can't see her . . . Is this Mahmud keeping her prisoner?"

"Ah!" sighed Dostom, "it will take much time to tell you the whole story in detail. She is free, and the king has given her his protection . . ."

Jean-Baptiste frowned.

"Without requiring anything of her, so you are not to worry."

"Well then, let's go," said George, also growing impatient and looking at the Afghan with a residue of distrust.

"To put it in a nutshell for you," said Dostom quickly, "Alix is known here as a widow. We mountaineers are simple folk: the dead are dead, as far as we are concerned, and they stay that way. We don't have the same facility as the peoples of India for believing that the living return eternally in the cycle of life. Mahmud thinks you are dead and buried, Jean-Baptiste, have I made that clear? He wouldn't understand at all if you suddenly reappeared, particularly as you look today . . ."

"But . . . that's terrible!" said Jean-Baptiste.

Then drawing himself up, he said with all his might:

"I want to see her, do you understand! I want to see her! I will die for good and all if I don't . . ."

"Calm down," said Dostom, holding both his hands out, "it can be done. I am here to work out certain details with you so as to avoid an incident. Alix will arrive in a few moments."

"Here?" he asked, looking at the rags he had put back on after the parade. "Now? Isn't there some other place, and at a time that's more . . ."

"Listen carefully," said Dostom, gesturing to the three Franks to step aside with him, "there can be no question of your true identity at this point. The Poncet who was an apothecary in Isfahan is dead, do you understand?"

"Ah!"

"No, wait. You are Frankish slaves, captive soldiers, it doesn't matter where you come from. The beautiful foreign woman sees you. She takes a fancy to one of your number, and something tells me that she may choose you, Jean-Baptiste. Oh, and that will be your name: the coincidence will remind her of her dead husband, which will play in your favor."

"And then?" asked Jean-Baptiste despondently.

"Then you'll see each other again. She will seek you out, and I'll do what I can to encourage the affair. The king, who values this foreign woman at his court, will have no reason to forbid her a fling . . ."

"A fling!"

Jean-Baptiste was dumbfounded. In the weeks he had been imagining his reunion with Alix, he had envisaged every possibility: saving her from the flames of a sacked city, finding her in exile, a captive, or hiding in a cave—every possibility except that he should woo her in the disguise of an elephant keeper, his feet ignominiously chained.

He had no time to deliberate as a group of horsemen was already approaching the elephants' camp.

"Here she comes," said Dostom. "With her are two officers of the court. Be extremely careful."

The slaves busied themselves without further ado around the feeding racks, pitching forkfuls of hay for the animals.

Alix, wearing the same felt uniform as the two officers, had to maintain an attitude of authority and decisiveness. Yet she felt herself tremble inside with all her poor being. On seeing Jean-Baptiste, George, and Juremi from the ramparts, she had at first thought she was going mad. Opposing gusts within her heart had fanned her hopes: the desire to confess everything to the king, then her resignation toward Dostom's plan, and now, in the last few moments, her shame. Had she not cursed Jean-Baptiste for having abandoned her, when he was traveling to the ends of the earth to bring his friend and his son back safely, enduring the hardships of slavery? Had she not even betrayed him, in thought if not in action, by allowing and nurturing a culpable attachment to that hapless

Persian officer? In truth none of this weighed very heavily on her in comparison with her one overwhelming desire, which was to throw herself into the arms of the man she loved. In addition, she was afraid that she might burst into tears and be unable to bear the sight of her loved ones in their unhappy circumstances. This fear made her keep her eyes lowered. She put such passion into looking at the pachyderms and so little into looking at the slaves that Dostom started to think the whole plan was ruined.

"Would you like to ride one of the animals, madam?" he asked to get the business going.

Alix agreed, and Dostom elected to bring her to the elephant being fed by Jean-Baptiste. The mahouts kept at a respectful distance from this foreign woman. Dostom called out peremptorily to Jean-Baptiste, motioning him to help the rider onto the mastodon. With a little tap on the animal's shoulder, Jean-Baptiste made it lower its trunk to serve as a mounting block. Alix took hold of the tusk in one hand, Jean-Baptiste's arm in the other, and hoisted herself onto the rough-textured spiral held out to her by the animal. The elephant lifted her gently to his neck, which she bestrode. The foreign woman remained there a moment, apparently delighted, then asked to get down. Unfortunately, just as she was putting her foot on the tip of the beast's trunk, she lost her footing and slid into Jean-Baptiste's arms.

This fortuitous incident was just what Dostom had been hoping for, as he could not think how to bring two such awkward lovers together, their twenty years of conjugal life not having prepared them for such an exercise.

No sooner was she in Jean-Baptiste's arms, no sooner did she smell his body and his breath, see his hair, eyes, and mouth so close, than Alix felt an inner turmoil that nearly propelled her from an extreme of shame and caution to a dangerous excess of tenderness and self-abandon. Jean-Baptiste was no less shaken by the total and vivid assault on all his senses.

They both, however, had enough restraint to let nothing appear in their faces but pleasure—perceptible, certainly, but within bounds. Their expressions were unmistakable enough for everyone present to be touched by the charming encounter. Such a sudden mutual interest confirmed the powerful attraction that the sexes exercise on each other independent of social circumstance, for the greater happiness of all.

Dostom arranged for a message to reach Jean Baptiste that very night telling him that an identical visit was planned for the next day. The slave readied himself for it by taking a bath in the river: he rubbed himself with cakes of ash and tallow, washed his hair, and had his beard trimmed by Juremi. When the Afghan officers arrived in camp, smiling complicitly toward Alix, Jean-Baptiste saw that she had taken as great pains over herself, though without being able to change out of her unfortunate uniform. They exchanged long looks that filled them with desire. Alix took a little walk on the elephant's back, while Jean-Baptiste held the animal from the side by its leather collar. They could have exchanged a few words when they were at a distance from the others, but neither even thought of it, so forcefully did their entwined glances talk of secret things that no words could translate.

This pleasurable encounter was unfortunately followed by another separation, and they wondered whether they would ever see each other again. They waited for these moments with the agony of two adolescents who have just noticed each other for the first time. Their daily routine as man and wife in Isfahan had dissipated all feelings of uncertainty and surprise between them and buried the feelings of awakening love that they now rediscovered intact, thanks to a proceeding they would have been hard put to recommend to anyone else.

The third visit, though, showed the limits of this mute and public exchange. It seemed very short and very conventional. The equivocal smiles of the onlookers, to which they had at first paid no attention, now struck them disagreeably. The thousand things they had to tell each other came almost to their lips before they remembered there was no proper way to put such words into the mouths of an elephant keeper and a female officer of the Afghan army. Life doesn't prepare one for every role, and the only way they found to play this one was wordlessly.

This padlock on their lips was more intolerable than all the chains a slave wears. Something had to happen.

Dostom did what he could for them, first by starting a rumor, then by speaking directly to Mahmud. On the morning of the fourth day, Alix was summoned to the king.

She went to him in a state of wild uncertainty, similar to the anxious feelings of an artless girl in love.

"My compliments, madam," said Mahmud, greeting Alix with a gracious bow he had learned from her. "I am told that your widowhood is behind you. Spring has returned to your heart."

"Your Majesty, it's just that—"

"No confessions, no avowals! I know everything and I support you entirely. It may please you to learn that I myself am waiting for some twenty women captured by my soldiers in Kirman, who are expected to arrive here for my use any day now. By God! We are soldiers!"

"Yes," said Alix, standing very straight in her uniform and grasping the pommel of the sword hanging at her side. All the same, she thought, twenty!

"So, let's get to the point," went on Mahmud Shah. "This Frank is to your liking? Very well, he is yours."

"Oh! Your Majesty! Thank you. I am extremely grateful for the favor. Then, you are going to free this man?"

"Who said anything about freeing him? No, believe me, it's not in your interest. As soon as these people are freed they have only one idea in their heads: to disappear and betray you. Take him as he is. Nothing could be simpler: I will assign him to you this very day. You can do whatever you like with him."

For a moment, Alix entertained the idea of pleading on behalf of George and Juremi as well. But though three is a very small number next to twenty, she feared that this display of appetite might make her appear somewhat too free, a circumstance the king might think to profit from. She bowed, thanking him at length, and withdrew.

Since her arrival, she had been quartered in a wing of the palace near Mahmud's apartments, which for this very reason had not yet been too thoroughly devastated. Her room was a former cook's cubby; her only piece of furniture was a narrow wooden bed that could be raised against the wall. The ground was paved in stone, the walls were plaster-coated and echoing. At her request, Dostom had a second mattress brought to her and some blankets. She spent the afternoon preparing this wretched sleeping place, horrified at its lack of comfort.

At five o'clock, two soldiers appeared, leading Jean-Baptiste between them. She ordered them to leave him. The sound of his chains resounded horribly off the walls when he entered. He busied himself with the lock to make sure the door was closed. This diversion over, they remained a moment facing each other, stupid and at a loss, frozen with fear at making the first gesture. Then she threw herself against him, entwined with him, gave him her mouth, made him fall on the soft nest she had prepared. For a while they took precautions to keep the prisoner's chain from shaking too much and ringing out like church bells. But it is impossible to say whether, though at first irritated by this restraint, the lovers did not eventually take a secret pleasure in it. Soon they allowed this voluptuous angelus to have full throat, and it was heard in the palace long into the night.

The patriarch Nerses stood on his terrace looking off into the distance in the direction of Ferrahabad. Since the elephant had drowned, the Afghans seemed indecisive. One saw them parading, first for themselves and now right under the Persians' nose. Every day they came near the city walls to perform incomprehensible cavalry and elephant maneuvers, probably to instill fear among the defenders and make them capitulate. This was hardly the spirit reigning among Huseyn's entourage, however. The king more than ever had confidence in the stars. It was known that a spectacular act of thanksgiving would be performed on the morrow, the day of the full moon. The word "sacrifice" had been officially broadcast. Some who were in the know spoke of the red virgin. Paganism was returning. Nerses had no cause to praise the Mahometans, but he still preferred dealing with them than with the Magians. He sighed.

The old attendant who served as his sexton announced Gregory, who arrived on the terrace dripping with sweat.

"So," asked the patriarch, "did you deliver the key?"

"Just in time, Monsignor. The road to Kashan is very crowded, what with all the people fleeing Isfahan. I arrived just as he was leaving."

"What does he look like?"

"He is a Frank unlike any I have ever seen, and I had a great deal of trouble understanding his language. His name is Beugrat. When I found him, he was on the point of leaving the caravanserai."

"On foot?"

"No. He drives a carriage such as there is not another example in all the world. You could, let's see . . ."

The deacon looked in the distance toward the Afghans. The troop of elephants was perfectly visible in the front ranks.

". . . seat one of those beasts in it!"

"Are you joking?"

"No, Monsignor. It is a carriage, but of monstrous proportions. I looked inside, and there is only one seat, but a gigantic one."

"Quite," said the patriarch, dispelling the topic with a wave of his hand. "What did he tell you?"

"He took the key that the nazir's prisoner gave me. All he said was that it was high time, as he was going back to Baghdad."

"Baghdad, really? These people truly have outposts everywhere. Did he say anything about the cardinal?"

"No. But I asked him to convey the cardinal your greetings."

"And what did he say?"

Gregory's customary smile disappeared and he blushed a bit.

"You will think, Monsignor, that I am joking . . ."

"Say it anyway."

"I may have understood him wrong, though I did make him repeat it."

"Well?"

"He asked me if the air inside a manservant is pure."

The patriarch stiffened in indignation.

"Air? In a manservant? Fawgh! No, these Catholics are decidedly impossible to come to terms with. What did you say?"

"Nothing. So he laughed and told me to open the windows. Upon which he whipped up his horse, and the monstrous stagecoach set off jolting down the road."

"Taking the key?"

"Yes, Monsignor."

But the patriarch did not have the opportunity to listen to the deacon's answer, so singular a turn did the proceedings at the foot of the ramparts take.

41

The moment he woke up—and after obtaining permission from the woman he now served—Jean-Baptiste ran to the elephant camp. But lovers, no matter how hard they try, can never rise as early as soldiers: when he finally rejoined his former companions, they had been up and about for more than two hours. Juremi had taken advantage of the confusion in this irresolute army to finish confecting the belladonna potion, and George was stirring it slowly in a great earthenware pot. To test its potency, the boy had dabbed a drop on each eyelid: his pupils were maximally dilated, and his vision blurred.

Jean-Baptiste ordered them to leave off preparing the potion and to follow him immediately. Bibichev was as usual prowling in the vicinity. Jean-Baptiste led them out of his earshot. Where to start? There were so many things to tell, which Alix had revealed to him during the lulls in their lovemaking. He told them everything all at once: how Françoise was in Isfahan, ill, how Alix had fled from the city and her reasons for it, chief among them being Saba's horrifying capture and the threat that hung over her.

"When is she to be executed?" asked George, beside himself, his large collyrium-darkened eyes giving him a frightening expression.

"Tomorrow, the day of the full moon," said Jean-Baptiste darkly.

For a moment they were silent. Not only were all their plans overturned, not only must they make sure that none of the elephants took the potion, but all the energy, imagination, intelligence, and guile of the three of them—not to mention their strength, which was derisory and enchained—should be put to use in the forthcoming hours to achieve exactly what they had been trying to avoid: the city had to be captured, and as quickly as possible.

The mass of Afghans around them all of a sudden struck them as disorganized, incoherent, lacking in boldness and purpose. But what to do, good God! Juremi started pacing up and down. Passing near the cauldron of belladonna, he dashed the contents into the sand with an angry shove of his foot. George, still on his knees, devastated, his eyes staring into space, kept repeating:

"Saba! Tomorrow, on the day of the full moon! Tomorrow!"

Jean-Baptiste bit his knuckles.

Suddenly they became aware that the Afghan mahouts were calling them and had been for some time. One of them came to shake them roughly from their stupor. Maneuvers were planned again for that day, absurd maneuvers intended as a show of muscle that the army was in fact incapable of using. The elephants played a prominent role in this representation of terror. They were made to approach the city walls, their mahouts riding them and their grooms following. Their ears were then tapped to make them trumpet horribly—the Afghans hoped this noise would undermine the enemy's morale. Fortunately the mahouts were too far from the walls to hear the shouts of laughter among the Persians each time the elephants' ears were thus tweaked.

That morning the whole business was reenacted. It happened just as the Armenian patriarch was talking with Gregory on the terrace. Everything started off as usual, but nothing turned out as expected.

On the point of ordering their slaves to make the mastodons trumpet, the mahouts found themselves caught in a volley of musketry. With the Persian army gone, the attackers had convinced themselves that they need no longer fear any such retaliation. Things had apparently changed and the people of Isfahan were arming themselves, or else this was something prepared by Yahya Beg and his overexcited Magians to justify the blood they were going to spill the following day. At any rate, two mahouts fell dead to the ground: the one accompanying the Bulgar, who took to his heels immediately, and the one whom George served. The Afghan landed almost on the boy's feet. George took a moment to make up his mind. Jean-Baptiste shouted at him to take cover. He saw the young Englishman turn his head in all directions, but the effects of the belladonna had not yet worn off—he could see nothing but blurred shapes. The rest took only a moment. Already holding his elephant's girth, George quickly vaulted onto the animal's back. Garou knew the boy and was used to obeying him. When George urged him on, he began to run, freeing up all the power of his musculature. Following a long curve to the right, Garou headed straight for the city walls. The Afghans, from whom the elephant was drawing away, were dumbstruck, unable to mobilize an attempt against their own animal. The defenders and all the residents of the city who, like the patriarch, were watching the scene from their roofs remained mute with astonishment at the solitary charge of the pachyderm. His mahout, hair streaming in the wind, shouted in English, a language that the beast, bounding straight before him, seemed to understand. Placing his hand on the animal's forehead, George made him lower his head and retract his trunk. They were now galloping full tilt, and there was no longer any doubt about it: the elephant, on orders from a boy, was charging the walls of an entire city.

A great silence fell over the desert and the town. The only sound was the heavy tremor of the animal against the ground. Whatever impression of power his running gave, Garou took an interminable minute to cover the long distance to the walls. The emotion of the spectators in both camps was extreme. Finally the pachyderm reached the stone embankment from which the walls rose. He was seen hunching his shoulders even more, lowering his great, bulging forehead until it formed a vertical line, a living, mobile wall launched against another, inanimate wall, which did not at all seem majestic but rather frozen with the fear that things sometimes exude at the moment their reputation for beauty, for everlastingness, or for strength is about to fall. The shock was phenomenal. Walls trembled, and people who had not been watching thought there had been an explosion. A cloud of plaster dust surrounded the animal and fell to the ground in a rain of pebbles with a sound like machine-gun fire. The sentries and the crowd along the battlements had instinctively closed their eyes. When they opened them again and leaned over, they saw Garou seated on his backside with his little eyes trained toward the sky, which he presumably did not see entirely in its proper place. George, half sprawled over the animal's flank, had not let go of the neck strap. He also took a moment to come to his senses. But before the defenders had time to think of throwing anything down on him, the boy had mounted the elephant again, made him stand, pivot around, and take off for the desert as fast as he had come.

Jean-Baptiste and Juremi were at last able to breathe again. On the ramparts there were shouts about a madman, a sick animal . . . The Afghans, for their part, were silent. Like all those on the plain, they had seen the fresh crack ten cubits high that split the wall from top to bottom. Jean-Baptiste knew Julfa's fortifications well and had often heard the patriarch complain of them. They would stand up to the fire of a culverin, of course, but they had been raised much too high for their width. The Persians claimed that it was the fault of the Armenian masons who had stolen the cobbles instead of using them for construction. And after the heavy rains of the past few weeks, the bottom of these walls of brick, mud plaster, and straw had absorbed much water and become friable. The end result was that a single blow had created this large crack. Did George know it? His blurry vision had made him bold enough for this first assault, but would it allow him to measure its results? He was still galloping toward the Afghan camp. Juremi was swearing a blue streak, enough to damn him for all eternity. Suddenly, Garou's course shifted, he started to bend around, then completed a full turn. The Protestant let out a great cry of joy and lifted his arms in the air: Garou was renewing the charge.

This time the Afghans were no longer thinking of restraining the intrepid mahout and his mount. Messengers had set off in haste to bring the news to Mahmud, who was now arriving at a gallop from Ferrahabad. All the Afghan horsemen were in the saddle waiting for the shock.

The Persians disappeared from the ramparts at a run. Garou, directed more by instinct this time than by George, and proving himself a methodical artilleryman in his own right, came charging at exactly the same spot as before. A section of wall collapsed on either side of the crack, approximately the width of the elephant's forehead. A roar of triumph went up from the Afghan camp and the cavalry moved toward the breach. Garou, who recovered more quickly this time, busied himself at George's urging to enlarge the hole by battering the bricks with his tusks and trunk. When the opening was big enough, the elephant backed away and quietly rejoined the others. Mahmud and his horsemen, riding at the galop, leaped over what remained of the wall and disappeared into the city howling.

Here and there small disks of light green algae hid the blue and gold tiling of the pool. It had been built without a raised edge, and the shimmering surface of the water, flush with the floor, occupied the space of several squares of marble, so that one almost believed the stone to be liquid and was tempted to test the water's solidity. Saba, her knees drawn up under her chin, spent hours sitting next to this limpid square, one hand trailing in the cool water. Two goldfish that lived in this puddled rain had grown so familiar with the white skin of her hand that they now came to rub up against it like cats. The court, located somewhere inside the maze of the royal palace, was surrounded by a windowless gallery with a lower course of tile. Above the tile, at head level, the walls were decorated with plaster arabesques that confused the eye. An enormous door of carved wood, which Saba had never seen except closed, presumably led out to other courtyards. For sleeping, she had a little room covered by a low, dark stone vault. She stretched out on rugs at night, her head on a velvet cushion, and listened to the slightest noises. She could hear even the rustling of the east wind in the poplars of the adjacent gardens, despite the high walls around her. Twice a day, a bolt was shot back, echoing in the patio like a cannon shot. A servant girl's slippers swished across the floor, and she set a tray down by the prisoner's door with a crash like crockery breaking, though it was only two cups and a carafe clinking together.

Two months of this horrifying solitude had shattered the young girl. She had first been filled with shame. The red virgin! That was what they had labeled her. All the world of feelings, fears, hopes, memories, and attributes within her, all that made her a human being quivering with weakness and determination, had all been summed up in the obscene signpost symbolically hung on her door: the red virgin. She had been singled out by her color like an animal, a thing. And as to being called a virgin, it exposed the most intimate part of her body to the world at large, as though remaining a virgin or ceasing to be one were not first and foremost a freedom that concerned her alone. With time, she had overcome her initial modesty and been willing to take pride in the title she had been given. Virgin, yes. Pure, innocent, intact, insolent, passionate—she was all of these things. Virgin, then. And red. Was there another color she would have wanted to exude, as wool from her skin, as an ornament, as gleaming armor? The red virgin. So be it. They had asked for it.

The great shame was that all these qualities made her fit for battle, whereas she was going to offer her neck to the sacrificial knife like a lamb.

The spring sun warmed first one side of the court, then the other. She moved with it, feeling well only when irradiated by its gentle heat; within its veil colors softened, blurred, and harmonized with her daydreams. Her solitude brought back her childhood, which surprised her, as no one could have been more lovingly looked after in her early years. In large Eastern households, there is always someone to take care of little children, caress them, cradle them, tell them interminable stories. Saba had grown up hearing fabulous tales, of diamonds growing on trees in lost valleys where the ground is paved with gold, where beautiful lovers are kept captive by spells. It took her a long time to escape from this gentle prison of legends herself and to realize that she had been shut up in it by her parents. She was six or seven and had started to tire of the company of servants and nursemaids. She suddenly realized that Alix, this beautiful princess whom she saw so little and who was constantly organizing a parade of visitors and entertainments worthy of the Thousand and One Nights, was her mother, and that she might have liked to confide in her. Alix's affection for her child was deep and sincere—she had just not taken the trouble to express it. She saw her daughter surrounded by servants, chasing butterflies in a garden filled with birds and flowers. It simply never occurred to her that Saba might need something more. Alix would have been very surprised to hear that her daughter, whom she embraced every day, felt as abandoned as she herself had when her parents had sent her to boarding school in France.

It was from this time that Saba's fierce solitude dated. She had remained aloof from dreams as well as from life, and her only consolation was to see, to understand, and to judge. With her red hair and sapphire eyes, she took to thinking that she was a sort of jinn that had emerged from the forests of dream to contemplate objectively the lives and morals of humans. Her parents became the prime subjects of her observation. She learned in detail of their past life, of their commitment to treating the sick without regard for their material wealth. But all the reasons she had to love and admire them only increased the bitterness of being unable to express those feelings.

Trained to love, Saba discovered that hatred gave her more freedom. She hated all the important people who came to their house and whom she saw in their fine clothes. She was repulsed by parties, by spending, by the whole life of pleasure, lies, and artifice that deprived her of the simple happiness of having parents.

Now, against the smooth screen of her jail, these moments played back to her. The idea that she would soon be dying made her see all this not against the yardstick of eternity, which the young believe to be their allotted time on earth, but as human and ephemeral gestures, awkward but worthy of compassion. She had believed her parents to be futilely seeking pleasure, whereas they were trying instead to live their happiness. This simple idea made Saba smile and soon called up her tears. Alix and Jean-Baptiste had long ago banished the vast sorrows that made their love impossible. They had chosen to leave everything behind and be free. The perpetual bustle of parties had had only one purpose: to justify their agonizing choice and show each other that there was no reason to regret a fate that had brought them so much joy. Deep inside, she thought, they were afraid. If unhappiness or plain boredom ever proved their choice mistaken, they would have no one and nothing to blame for having forced their decision. Everything had to be beautiful, easy, funny, luxurious, alive. Their child, in this setting, was an added ornament of happiness and mustn't become a hindrance. Little by little they had reassured each other, but their daughter's outrage had not in turn decreased. It had taken this seclusion and the expectation of imminent death for her to dispel these reproaches and simply love them, sure of their feelings and consumed by the desire to see and embrace them.

And George? Where was he? What was he doing? She recalled him as he had been when he first came to live with her family; she felt as strongly as ever the enormous pleasure of having a companion enter her life. In George, life had given her an extraordinary present: someone whom she could simply love, a brother, and what's more an older brother, to whom she could freely open up the lake of her accumulated tenderness, the overflowing reservoir of her unused love. Had George confessed to Jean-Baptiste, during the course of their travels, the pure and joyful games they had played in the garden in Isfahan, the great bowls of fresh milk they had drunk at night returning from their long jaunts through the Chahar Bagh, their walks along the riverbank and onto the islands that rise in summer from the low waters, and the fishing expeditions, the afternoons when they slipped away, their first caresses? Had he confessed the secret they had sworn one April evening never to reveal until the right day came, when they were old enough? A secret! She smiled. The promise to love each other always, never to love each other less, nor ever to love another. A child's secret, and the only one she had ever shared. It was this infinitesimal part of her life, tiny, unknown, and unfulfilled, that, as she came to die, gave her the greatest happiness.

One morning Saba, still seated in the patio of her jail, heard the far-off sound of cannon fire carried on the wind, sharp and brief. She did not know Reza, nor did she learn of his death or of the destruction of the Persian army on that afternoon. Everything turned calm again. The days passed. She had known, even before she was chosen for the ominous role herself, that the red virgin was to be immolated on the third moon. Each night she watched this orb appear above the court, where the porphyry still shone with the sunlight trapped within its crystals.

And so the end would come tomorrow. Alone, she had already been deprived of the dramatis personae of her life, now she would be separated from the scenery as well. The play was ending after the first act.

Toward the end of her morning of reflection, she felt almost irritated at being bothered by shouts, coming from a considerable distance to the south. Most likely it was some further trouble among the Armenians, maybe a quarrel between merchants. Then there was silence and a dull percussion, not cannon this time, repeated twice, like a gigantic shock.

"Oh! if only they would stop bothering the red virgin," she groaned, "since she is preparing to die."

But the noise did not diminish. On the contrary, it seemed to grow more diverse, still far away to the south, but also growing closer. Saba listened for the slightest sounds. Her hearing, after her long solitary confinement, was so quick to catch even the slightest whispers that she almost cried out when she heard the bolt on the door brutally pulled back. It wasn't mealtime. She rose and bounded lightly into the violet shadow of the gallery, behind a pillar.

A woman entered and ran to the little room. Saba caught only a glimpse of her, but enough to know that it was not the serving girl. Finding no one in the bedroom, the intruder came back to the patio and emerged into the light. She carried a bloody dagger in her hand. Saba cried out: it was Nur al-Huda!

"Come, Saba!" said the Circassian, blinded by the sunlight all around her and unable to see the prisoner.

The girl hesitated for a moment. She had never imagined that her death would be like this. She had prepared herself for a pyre, incantations, a ritual. But it was to be simply an act of vengeance. There would be only the silence, the sunlight, a blade.

"Don't be afraid!" said Nur al-Huda without raising her voice. "And please, don't dawdle."

Saba walked two paces toward the light. The red virgin! No one would be able to say that she had shirked her fate.

Her face was so grave and so proud that this time it was Nur al-Huda who stifled a cry. But she quickly regained her composure, approached the young girl, took her gently by the hand, and pulled her in her wake.

"Can you tell me . . . ?" asked Saba, hesitating to follow her.

"Later. For the moment, let's get out of here."

Saba could hear the sincerity and controlled fear behind these words. She followed Nur al-Huda.

As they were emerging from the court, Nur unfolded a long blue veil she was carrying and covered Saba's face and upper body with it, then she opened the door to the outside. A corpse lay on the threshold in a pool of blood. Saba recognized it as one of Yahya Beg's disciples who had taken part in her capture and now took his turn guarding her. Nur al-Huda's

knife! That's what it had been for! They exchanged a quick glance, and
the dancer, unembarrassed, arranged the folds of her veil to hide the gory
dagger still in her right hand.

"Let us lose no time," she said in a low voice.

They were in a courtyard planted with dwarf orange trees, among
whose smooth, straight trunks there was not the slightest place to hide.
Luckily, it was empty. They crossed it quickly but without showing any
haste. Through a gate that had been left ajar they reached the main garden of the harem, in full leaf at this time of year: they followed an alley of
fig trees, keeping to the shade of their large, opaque leaves. Despite the
excitement of fleeing, Saba could still hear on the other side of the walls,
beyond invisible courtyards and gardens, the sharp sound of voices and
rumbling noises.

At the threshold of the enclosure they passed a group of eunuchs in
animated discussion who paid no attention to the fugitives. The two
women entered a dark gallery with an ogival vault, which housed the
quarters of the captain of the harem and his soldiers. They saw no sign of
either. At the far end of the hallway they found themselves among the
outer buildings of the palace, where there was normally a bustling crowd
of suppliers, servants, and visitors. They met almost no one there except
for frightened guards who ran about in purposeless disorder. Finally they
reached the great gate of the palace opening onto the Chahar Bagh. Nur
al-Huda squeezed the girl's hand, and Saba understood that a final obstacle confronted them.

The gates were closed. A row of guards protected them. On the other
side surged a crowd they could see only dimly but whose shouts and
threats they could now hear. Carts and wagons full of angry commoners
rumbled over the stones of the avenue. The gates must not have been
closed when Nur al-Huda arrived because she now looked surprised. She
approached a soldier and asked to be let out. He shook his head and pointed at the crowd. She asked another and received the same answer.
Pleading would achieve nothing; the palace was surrounded, and no one
was allowed in or out. Those were the orders. Nur al-Huda looked everywhere for an officer. Hardly any were left since the army's massacre. Men
from the ranks had taken the officers' places as best they could, and they
didn't wear a distinctive uniform. The young woman spied a short soldier
with an enormous black mustache who was shouting out orders, his chin
raised. The others seemed to obey him. She went up to him, still holding
Saba by the hand. The man was full of his tiny importance. He listened to

the woman with disdain while she explained that her friend was very sick. He looked at the invalid out of the corner of his eye, apparently decided that she was not at death's door, and shook his head. The crowd still flowed by with shouts and imprecations. Nur al-Huda raised the tone and supplicated. It was a woman's problem, she said, a crisis taking place under her friend's veil, a question of life or death. Then, transferring the hidden dagger from her right hand to her left, she approached Saba, pretended to slide her hand under the young girl's garment, and shook her bloody fingers under the corporal's mustache.

There is blood, and then there's blood. Men's blood fascinates other men, thus accounting for the allure of battle, and it trickles proudly down the arms of the victorious. The blood of women, drawn from their bodies by mysterious struggles in which the gods very likely play a part, provokes an unspeakable repulsion in men, particularly in Islamic Persia, less from disgust than from holy fear. That blood, which is always hidden, produces as great an effect when it appears in broad daylight as the cataclysms to which it is linked through the moon that governs the tides and eclipses. The little officer backed away two steps at the sight of this gleaming unction. Overcoming his terror, he barked out an order and the two women, with dignity but great speed, passed out through the half-opened gate and melted into the crowd.

42

Jean-Baptiste and Alix, Juremi and George, the four of them seated with dangling legs on the ramparts of conquered Julfa, looked at the cloudless sky with lugubrious faces.

In the Armenian suburb one could hear sounds of celebration, laughter and shouts—less noise, in fact, than a complete victory would have elicited. But the victory was far from being complete. The fall of Julfa had not been, as the Afghans had thought, the fall of Isfahan. This city without an army, breached in one of its suburbs, should have surrendered in its entirety to the assailants. But when the news came that the walls of the Armenian quarter had been broken through, something extraordinary happened. The entire population of the neighborhoods on the far side of the river had armed itself with knives, clubs, shards of glass, and picks and hurried down to the Chahar Bagh. An enormous crowd had gathered at the entrance to the bridge of the thirty-three arches joining Julfa to the city proper. The Afghans, when they reached the bridge, found it in flames, barricaded with the beams and walls of the demolished shops. Thousands of projectiles, thrown by women, children, and civilians, unseated the proud Afghan horsemen, who had thought themselves victorious, but hundreds of whom now found themselves fatally struck down and swept away by the current of the Zayande Rud. Three charges, led by Mahmud himself, had not managed to overcome the Isfahanis' resistance. The bridge offered no room to maneuver: it was a fatal defile for the horsemen, and on the other side the crowd was growing ever larger. At nightfall, the king of Kandahar finally gave the order to establish camp at Julfa. He had forbidden looting, which, though it had already started, was not too extensive. He himself took up quarters in the palace of the patriarch, whom he ordered thrown out.

Alix and Jean-Baptiste had gone within a day from the greatest elation to unutterable despair. George's boldness in opening a path into the city had made them believe that Saba would be saved. Now the third moon had come. They spent the interminable night on a roof terrace at the high point of Julfa, scanning the inaccessible remainder of the city. They watched for the least glow, the least noise, as though their suffering could only truly be triggered by a concrete signal: a cry, fires, some commotion that could give Saba's death the slightest reality. They spoke of her all night and, filling the void with her presence, felt they were protecting her life, forming a rampart around her by means of their huddled, whispering bodies. The third moon rose in the sky, pursued its course, and disappeared at daybreak, the stars still sparkling in the clear sky. Nothing had happened. The night had been perfectly calm toward the city. George, shortly before dawn, decided to reveal in muffled tones his heavy secret. This long childish reticence, ending in tragedy, was worthy of compassion. His revelation brought tears to the eyes of all who took part in the vigil.

But when day was fully upon them, when the troops and crowds started to stir in the town and its hostile suburb, the very idea that Saba was dead seemed impossible, almost absurd. The exceptional events that had convulsed the city the day before must have upset the criminal plans of the king and his magis. A strange confidence returned to them, to which Juremi gave a vigorous baptism by crying out: "She is alive, sacrebleu! It can't be any other way." And at the same time, he shook a threatening fist at the one on whom he kept watch, up there, in the eternal heavens, and whom he never tired of reminding of his duties.

Despondency was useless, grief was premature, perhaps pointless, and in any case almost impossible because of the uncertainty about what had happened. They had to act, to visit the troops in conquered Julfa, to question all who might know something. But despite their efforts, they learned little on that second day. The only sure thing was that, on the Isfahan side, the people were organizing to make a staunch defense of the bridge. The impetus did not appear to come from the king or what remained of the government. Volunteers had sprung up to take the part of officers and direct the miscellaneous militia that had stood up with unexpected strength to the city's assailants. This people's army was led, apparently, by a certain Ahmad. He shouted threatening declarations at the forward Afghan positions, asking for freedom and the lifting of the siege and swearing that the people would fight to the death.

This spontaneous revolt of the populace was interpreted by Jean-Baptiste as a good omen: the king had been outflanked, his authority trampled, and the plans of his magis had certainly been destroyed. They learned nothing, however, that bore directly on Saba. Among all the rumors circulating in Julfa, none mentioned the red virgin.

Juremi decreed that this was a good sign, and none of the others, despite their mounting sorrow and anxiety, wanted to give the signal to abandon hope. The second night was full of amiable talk, but the gaiety was forced. Fatigue and the difficulty of playacting in this way for any length of time made them sink into sleep, where they could confess their fears and their despair.

Juremi and George reported back to their mahouts to tend the elephants, who were now useless and grazed all day on hawthorns under the walls of Julfa, near the breach made by Garou. Mahmud summoned Alix and all the foreign officers and representatives to his court to brief them on upcoming operations.

He did his best to present things in the most favorable light. In the first place, he congratulated himself on the courage of his troops and announced that, in recompense for their courage, the Frankish slaves who had cared for the elephants would be set free, except, naturally, the slave he had given Alix and whom he wanted her to keep. Then the Afghan ruler described the resistance of the people of Isfahan on the Chahar Bagh bridge as a mere incident. He emphasized instead that there existed a second bridge, actually an aqueduct that joined Julfa not to Isfahan but to the country immediately around it and served to irrigate its gardens. Already Afghan horsemen had crossed the aqueduct, thus making up for the lack of a ford and the failure of the elephants to serve as a ferry. Several thousand men were thus scouring the countryside around the city with orders to sow destruction, to annihilate orchards and gardens, to burn the villages, and to seize all convoys reprovisioning the capital.

The crowd could crow all it wanted on its miserable bridge—before long it would know famine. They'd see how long Huseyn could stand such a diet.

Alix returned to Jean-Baptiste the bearer of this ominous news. In the early afternoon, the king's orders took effect: George, Juremi, and Bibichev arrived disencumbered of their chains, which were gone but for the marks of calluses above their ankles. The Bulgar had disappeared wishing them good luck. Jean-Baptiste, whose fate had seemed the most fortunate at first, was now the last captive in the group. But this inconvenience was nothing compared to what those walled up in the city had to endure—Françoise, Alix's father perhaps, and Saba, who might have escaped from immolation, as they continued to believe, only to succumb to famine and epidemics.

The freedmen took up quarters in an ironmonger's shop, which had been looted and left open. They made themselves a practical shelter there, in the midst of metal watering cans and a whole bric-a-brac of pails, ladles, and dustpans that the soldiers had not wanted.

Alix and her personal servant had settled in a wing of the palace Mahmud had improvised for himself in Julfa. They came to the ironmonger's every morning to hold a lugubrious council of war. After the commotion and anxiety of the past days, the new siege tactic brought nothing new and offered no surprises. The Afghans patiently tightened the noose around the city. The population waited. Reserves diminished slowly. The inaction made Jean-Baptiste and his companions bitter and gloomy. Alix, to shatter this painful listlessness, proposed that they visit the patriarch Nerses for news of her father. This idea gave them a little animation. They set off at the end of the afternoon through the maze of Julfa's narrow streets and reached the small door behind which the old man always hid when things turned sour. He came to the peephole himself at the sound of knocking.

"Poncet?" he said with a snicker. "Now who is going to swallow that lie? Go on your way, you thief. Do you think I've forgotten the apothecary's death?"

Jean-Baptiste insisted and gave such convincing proofs of his identity that the old man finally opened the door.

"It is you!" said the patriarch, his eyes wide.

Then, looking at Jean-Baptiste from head to toe and seeing the shackles on his legs, he added:

"Gracious! My poor friend!"

"You recognize my wife," said Jean-Baptiste, pointing with some embarrassment at Alix beside him in the Afghan uniform, a long riding crop in her belt.

"Great God!" wailed the patriarch. "What is the world coming to! Well, each to his own. Come in."

They followed him in with George and Juremi. Bibichev had stayed to watch over the shop. As soon as they were seated Jean-Baptiste gave a summary of all that had happened to explain his accouterment and that of his wife, and to introduce George and Juremi. Then he asked Nerses if he had heard anything at all about a red virgin, abducted in the city to satisfy the crazy superstitions of the Magians. The patriarch was well aware of this business, having followed the king's conversion to Yahya Beg's Zoroastrian delusions with horror. As to the execution of this unfortunate girl, he knew nothing of it at all. The visitors looked at each other silently, making an effort to put all the meager remains of their hope into their glances.

Alix then spoke up, thanking the patriarch for the help he had given her in fleeing. Without mentioning her father's name, she asked Nerses if he had managed to help Cardinal Alberoni's messenger to escape the city.

"Alas, madam, we offered him the chance, but he would hear nothing of it. He is still being detained by the nazir and continues to nurse the absurd—and useless—hope of meeting with the king."

"Which one?"

"Huseyn, who is not much longer for the throne. All we managed to do was to carry a key on his behalf to a man waiting for him in Kashan."

Neither Alix nor Jean-Baptiste could imagine, on hearing a description of the messenger, who it could be.

"Then my poor father is still in the city!" wailed Alix.

"Your father!" said Nerses. "That man is your father?"

"I mean the father of my friend," Alix corrected herself, preferring to give no other explanation.

"Yes," said Nerses. "When last heard of yesterday afternoon, the poor man was still at the nazir's and in good health."

"Yesterday afternoon? Then you receive news from the city despite the siege?" asked Jean-Baptiste.

"Our misfortune is very great," said Nerses modestly, with a trace of a smile, "but we are not utterly without consolation: these Muslims hate each other absolutely, the Afghans being fiercely Sunni, while the Persians believe in Ali and the imams. The upshot is that Christians represent a lesser evil for both camps. They show each other no mercy, but they have accepted a Truce of God toward the Armenians."

"And what does it entail?"

"Well, each day we can send a messenger on foot across the Chahar Bagh bridge. Ahmad, the former eunuch (if the state is one that can in fact be renounced), allows this courier to come and go, and Mahmud does the same. The one condition is that he be searched and carry nothing with him. He leaves in the morning and returns here at night."

"But what function does he serve?" asked Alix.

"Enemies always need a channel by which to exchange messages. It is through this messenger that they preserve a tenuous link between themselves. And it allows me not to abandon our brothers in the city."

This news gave his hearers something to think about. If Nerses had information that came directly from the other side, then it gave all the more weight to what he had said about Saba. Through the patriarch they could pursue their investigation with more efficiency. Jean-Baptiste thought how they might make use of these new possibilities. As the silence drew on, Nerses appeared tempted for a moment to order tea. When he counted the number of people present, however, he decided to wait to slake his thirst until he was alone.

"Monsignor," spoke up Juremi, who had been sitting somewhat in the background, "is there no one you would like to have brought out from the city?"

"Alas, yes!" said the patriarch. "My own son, if you must know, who went there on the day of the tragic events and is now shut in with the besieged."

"Can you not bring him out through this famous Truce of God?" asked Alix.

"That was my plan, as you can well imagine. But it's impossible. The messenger I send each day must start off from here. That way the Afghans are sure that he'll return and won't be used to help someone else flee. If I wanted to bring my son out, I would have to consign one of our brothers to death—here they are oppressed, perhaps, but at least they are well fed and able to move about freely. No one wants to exchange the conditions in Julfa for the certainty of dying of hunger."

"And what if someone did want to?" asked Juremi.

"Oh, that will never happen. But if it did, I would send him, of course, tomorrow morning."

"Well, Monsignor," said the Protestant, looking Nerses straight in the eyes, "send me, and your son will be back with you within a day."

"You, Juremi!" cried out his companions.

The giant rose to his full height and looked at them gravely:

"Sacrebleu! Yes, me, this old carcass afraid neither of life nor of death, me whom you went to the ends of the earth to bring back. Do you think that I would leave Françoise to suffer only a few steps away and not take my place beside her?"

"But, Juremi," murmured Jean-Baptiste, "you'll be going to your death . . ."

"We are all going there, and if I arrive ahead of you, trust me, I'll wait for you there. Goodbye, my friends. Have I your word, Monsignor?"

"Why . . . for the love of my son . . . Oh! It's a terrible choice to make, but I can't make any other. And you suggested it yourself. Well then, all right! I will lead you to the entrance of the bridge tomorrow morning myself."

The friends walked back to the ironmonger's in silence. The Protestant strode somewhat ahead of the group to avoid any questions.

Bibichev greeted them with a pale smile. He was proud of having just sold two tin bowls and a stove. The ironmonger had been wrong to flee: business was picking up. No one paid any attention to him. Annoyed, he sat back down behind the counter, grabbed the notebook he had found in a drawer, and continued to blacken page after page, in the beautiful Cyrillic writing he had won so many prizes for in police school, with the dispatches he had filed away in his mind all during the trip.

The evening passed in pitiful sighs. Alix braided Juremi's hair into a crown around his head in the Armenian style that Jean-Baptiste had worn when he fled the city. The following morning they met up with the patriarch at the lower end of Julfa and accompanied the old Protestant as far as the bridge. All had tears in their eyes, except for Juremi, who stared straight ahead of him.

Crossing the bridge made for a delicate moment. The two facing camps were on the alert for the slightest provocation. The messenger was searched on departure by an Afghan and on arrival by Ahmad himself. Juremi passed this scrutiny without incident and found himself free within the encircled city.

Juremi had never been to Isfahan. He went first toward the bazaar, in the neighborhood of the mausoleum of Harun Velayat, to find Nerses' son and tell him to take his place at nightfall going the opposite way. The patriarch and Jean-Baptiste had described for him many remarkable trees, handsome houses, and public fountains in order that the Protestant might find his way around the city. But he saw nothing in their place but stumps cut off at the ground, facades riddled by shot, and fountains hidden behind clusters of men and beasts who had come there to gather the last drops of drinking water. The Chahar Bagh was devastated. The great trees had served as beams for the barricades, and their branches were fueling cookstoves in private houses. The flower borders had been trampled or else re-planted as kitchen gardens in anticipation of the complete famine expected in the city before long. Having delivered his message, Juremi made his way to Alix and Jean-Baptiste's house. Its garden had been spared, no doubt because of the old doorkeeper who still kept guard at the gate. The Protestant announced himself and was admitted. The cook, deeply affected, explained that Françoise was very weak and asleep at the moment. Juremi insisted on going in to her and contemplated her for a long time in silence in the half darkness. Light is one of the instruments time uses to inflict its sweet rewards and harsh tortures on us. Françoise, in full daylight, would no doubt have exposed her wrinkles, her weariness, her hunger. The blue shadow protected her from such outrages and brought her back, in Juremi's love-filled eyes, to the time of their first meeting and their happiness.

He reached out his big hand to his love's forehead. She opened her eyes, and they both entered the same dream.

43

The eunuch Ahmad had settled his little family at the very top of a house located in the oldest part of the city. Built of wooden sections to the height of three stories, the shack had been carrying two additional stories on its shoulders since the previous century, and it leaned precariously over the nearby alleys. Its occupants, though, were used to it and had even gone so far as to crown its terrace with a lean-to, extended somewhat by a wooden awning. On days when there was a high wind, everything in this shed between earth and sky flapped, vibrated, and pitched as on the deck of a ship. The advantage of the place, which was small and poorly protected from the weather, was that from the first nice days onward the children could run around on the big terrace among the straining sails of the sheets hanging out to dry. Also, and this was not unimportant in troubled times, one could take in the entire city at a glance, from the royal palace to the hill of Julfa. The Mosque of the Imam and the Mosque of Shah Lutfullah startled the beholder by raising the monstrous bulges of their emerald-tiled domes nearby.

Nur al-Huda had taken Saba directly to this landmark on leaving the royal palace. The young girl slept there on a straw pallet in the children's corner. Ahmad's three little boys, boisterous, impudent, but extremely affectionate, were delighted to play with this redheaded foreign girl, no longer quite a child but willing enough to laugh along with them. Their mother had no time to spare for them. The eunuch's wife, small and extremely discreet, had a sad, modest face, expressing how, in every department, she was used to making do with little.

Nur al-Huda and Ahmad ran all day in the streets, each in a different direction, to strengthen the resistance of Isfahan's people. They came back at night with picturesque groups whom the Circassian ordered to be given shelter. The terrace would then be organized for a long night's vigil. Fires were made in the braziers using the scented wood of the orchards; singers, tellers of tales, and dancers took turns trying to make the gathering forget how little there was to eat and drink. Each day there was a little less than the day before. Too bad! They still had dreams to nourish them. The great epic poem of the *Shahnameh* presented the heroic deeds of Alexander the Great and the impossible loves of the Sassanid kings so that they might be chewed for hours on end. Mouths formed the orotund words of Sa'di's mystical poems; bodies forgot their weariness by exhausting themselves in dancing and clapping their hands. From all around the city rose the same sounds of recitation, song, and laughter. Saba, who had been too long alone, became inebriated with these pleasures—the pleasures of those who live so close to danger and death that all fear abandons them.

Nur al-Huda waited two days before approaching Saba. Finally one evening she sat beside her, asking about her health and talking about the night, the dances, and other inconsequential topics. The girl listened to her impassively, then suddenly straightened up and said:

"I have two important things to tell you."

Nur al-Huda continued to clap her hands in time to the music of the zither.

"First," said Saba gravely, "I ask your forgiveness for having badly misjudged you."

"And?" said Nur al-Huda, still entranced by the music.

"And I thank you for saving my life."

The zither player finished his piece. Everyone clapped and ululations erupted.

"Well, that's behind us," said the Circassian, never losing her smile. "Let me in turn confess two things and we'll be even. I like your mother, Saba. She is my dearest friend, whatever she may have said, or done, or thought. It was in the name of our friendship that I came for you."

The zither player had held his four little mallets momentarily motionless in midair. He now began a new melody. It was an old refrain from India, and Nur al-Huda hummed along when she recognized it.

"The other thing," she went on, "is simple and not very creditable: it was the nazir who denounced you. This is something to know and forget. And now you should address yourself to serious things: come sing and dance with us."

The whole audience now joined in with the melody plucked by the musician, clothing in gentle human voices the sharp sounds of the instrument. Nur al-Huda articulated the words exaggeratedly so that Saba could follow along. When the refrain came around again, the young redhead joined in softly at first and was soon laughing with everybody else.

Without undermining this good humor, two pieces of bad news arrived during the following two days. The supply convoys they had been expecting had been attacked by the Afghans one after another, even those that had tried to steal into the city at night. Then Mahmud had ordered the culverins to fire on the city from Julfa to terrorize the population. Luckily, the ordnance was decrepit, eaten away by the salt filtering in during the desert crossings. One of the guns had exploded as its fuse was lit and pierced the camel carrying it like a waterskin. The poor animal was the only casualty of these artillery demonstrations, and the king of Kandahar had wisely decided to forgo them.

Isfahan, being a commercial city, a center of trade and travel, had few reserves. Rationing had spared some for a time, but these were quickly exhausted. Hunger prevailed, inducing a drunkenness comparable to that of the best wines, though it is attained in a less agreeable manner: the evenings grew more spirited than ever. Yet one could tell that the dancers were affected. A musician would sometimes faint. Or a child would cry out baldly "I'm hungry" and the veil of lightheartedness was rent.

One morning Nur al-Huda and Ahmad held council on the terrace. Saba approached them. They didn't ask her to keep her distance, and she listened in on their discussion.

"We must act today," said Nur al-Huda. "We have resisted, but these Afghan dogs have not grown weary. They clearly intend to make us all die. I don't know what miracle we were expecting, but it hasn't happened, and it isn't going to."

"Act?" said the eunuch. "But it's up to the king to do that, with whatever troops he has left."

Ahmad had remained a faithful servant until the downfall of his master the prime minister, even though he had kept a part of his life hidden. In the spiral of his master's fortunes, he had been thrown out into the street and forced to find a way to survive. At heart he remained faithful to his king and continued even now to have confidence in him.

"The king!" exclaimed Nur. "Have you seen him, the pitiful Huseyn? And is he still alive, anyway? Yahya Beg rules in his stead. And that charlatan will let us all die if it means that he can stay in power. No, no, Ahmad, I swear it's up to us to act as long as we are still able to stand."

"What more do you want to do against an entire army?"

Nur al-Huda grabbed the eunuch's arm and pressed against him, speaking all in one go without pausing to draw breath:

"Capture Julfa, Ahmad, I've been thinking of it for three days and three nights, do you understand? It consists of narrow, cobbled, slippery alleys. Their cavalry will be no advantage there, in fact the opposite. Let us cross the bridge, surprise them, throw ourselves by the thousands into this suburb, kill as many as we can, and make the rest flee for their lives. Tomorrow you won't be guarding the bridge anymore but the breach in Julfa's ramparts, which is hardly wider."

She was panting. But the man was still not convinced.

"So we take Julfa, supposing it to be possible," he objected. "What then?"

"That part of town is full of supplies."

"That gives us three days' respite."

"Ten. But I'm counting more on the prisoners."

"The prisoners?"

"Mahmud has taken up residence in Julfa, have you forgotten? If we act fast enough, he will fall into our hands. And if it's not him, it will be his officers, or his relatives. They can be exchanged, they can be sold."

"They can be revenged, you mean," said Ahmad lugubriously.

Saba didn't dare intervene. Yet she felt herself on the Circassian's side with all her being. This wasn't just a debate between two minds, but the simple, frightening face-off between life and death, between resignation and concerted will.

"It's what I want, Ahmad," said Nur al-Huda suddenly, letting go of the eunuch's arm and looking him straight in the eye.

Saba watched this insolence with mounting panic. Would this man not take mortal affront?

On the contrary, these final words, more than any attempt at persuasion, called the servant back into submission. While the ends worried him, she reassured him about the means. He was not to decide but to obey. Saba understood that the strange hierarchy of the harem had survived its dispersal.

An hour later, Ahmad and Nur al-Huda were on their way to arouse the populace. The red virgin received permission to accompany them, on condition that she remain hidden under a veil because the Magians were still looking for her.

Crowds were gathering as they did each morning on the square in front of the palace to hear rumors and, they hoped, announcements. Groups of volunteers, their caftans dirty after spending the night rolled up in them, came up from the Chahar Bagh to be relieved by a miscellaneous brigade. Tall old men in broad turbans, their beards combed, walked beside barely pubescent boys, who wore mean expressions so as to look more virile. Anything would do for a weapon: a bit of rope made a plausible sling, a stake counted for a halberd. The simplest was still a nice sharp-edged rock that filled the palm of your hand.

Nur al-Huda elbowed her way through knots of people talking heatedly, and Ahmad and Saba followed her. At the end of the square toward the bazaar she entered a house whose heavy door stood ajar. It was a building belonging to the king's estate, emptied of its occupants during Yahya Beg's purges. An agent of the nazir's, a half-deaf old soldier, sat under the archway. Nur al-Huda must have visited the place previously; without a glance at the guardian, who showed no inclination to bar their way, she headed straight for a stair and climbed to the second floor. A large room with bare walls gave onto a projecting balcony at the front of the building, closed off by fretwork cedar shutters. She pushed them. They resisted. She shoved harder. They opened with a loud bang. The sound, echoing over the whole square, silenced the many conversations. All heads turned toward the balcony.

"It's up to you now," said Nur al-Huda, pushing Ahmad into the light.

The view from the window was impressive. Standing on either side of the square were two monumental symbols, the pillars of the nation, from which it clearly appeared that only one was still holding firm.

On one side, Religion kept watch in the austere form of the Mosque of the Imam, with its pointed blue-green helmet. The close-ranked mail of its tile garment protected its flanks, and a thousand stone stalactites towered over its monumental entrance like so many daggers to slay the infidel. Facing this powerful reminder of the martial spirit of the jihad was the colonnade known as the High Gate, which served as a monumental entry to the royal palaces and as a setting for certain ceremonies. Deserted, its splendor useless, it only served to emphasize the crushing absence of the Persian royalty.

Nur al-Huda was not afraid. She was perfectly capable of speaking herself, and she held ready in her mind the words that would have swayed the crowd. But she knew that only a man could convince at this moment, a native Persian who could speak to these people in the language of their heart. Ahmad was the most suited to carry the message. Since masterminding the defense of the bridge, the eunuch had been celebrated as a hero. He had set to work busily everywhere since the beginning of the siege, and his orders were immediately followed. Yet he had never up till now made a public proclamation.

Silence fell. Ahmad advanced, hesitated a moment, then began to speak. In his former employment, he had never spoken except in quiet tones, for reasons of protocol and to maintain the voice of a castrato. Now, by contrast, he displayed his power, and his voice surged with remarkable gravity. It was slightly hoarse, warm, persuasive. He used Nur al-Huda's words. As he presented them, they described not a plan but a reality, not a dream but a prophecy. The crowd grew. Word traveled through the bazaars that what they had all been waiting for, though without any premonition or expectation, was finally taking place. An attack, that's what Ahmad was proposing, very simply! Death, but with their boots on! Vengeance carried to the enemy's heart, even if it cost them their lives to deliver it. A vast ovation greeted Ahmad's final words. Every person in the square raised his weapon over his head and gave voice to his energy and joy.

Ahmad, followed by Nur al-Huda and Saba, left the balcony, and they retraced their steps through the building. When they reached the carriage entrance, the mob seized the three of them and swallowed them up. The eunuch held tightly to the two women's hands so as not to be separated from them. They were pushed and pulled. With great pains, they finally reached the far side of the square. Men and women continued to stream in to this rallying ground from all sides. No one wanted to be left behind in the attack. Some were wobbly from hunger, their faces gaunt, their features hollow from privation and sleeplessness. Yet their last reserves of energy had been held back for just such a moment. The very ones who refused to die in the dark were ready to greet death without flinching in the full light of this gory morning.

Ahmad and his companions, still buffeted by the crowd, were finally able to proceed toward the Chahar Bagh. Once inside, the commotion lessened somewhat, as the crowd was able to disperse in the more open space of the garden. But to reach the bridge, they once again had to fight. The militiamen guarding the fortification did not understand what was happening. They held back the insurgents. There were shouts, sounds of scuffles. In the midst of the commotion, a big lanky individual, his hair vaguely gathered in the Armenian style, was elbowing his way through the crowd shouting in various incomprehensible languages. The poor man vainly tried to show by signs that he only wanted to cross the Chahar Bagh and return home. He was protecting a headless chicken, holding it by one wing; it had already lost the other in the melee, along with one leg. Ahmad and the two women approached the place where this unfortunate foreigner was struggling. It is difficult to say if what then occurred was a deliberate act or a clumsy one. At all events, an elderly Persian, probably losing his balance in the press, grabbed Saba's veil and tugged on it. The girl's red hair tumbled out and shone in full sunlight.

A crowd can be ever so tightly packed, yet when a danger arises in its midst a circle forms in an instant as people draw back in shock or fear.

"The red virgin!"

A murmur, a rumbling, a shout swept over the crowd. The Isfahanis had for several weeks been hearing the Magians' preaching and the announcement of the sacrifice of the red virgin, but no one knew what had finally happened to the victim. At the sight of Saba's hair, the crowd immediately and instinctively recognized the girl whose death had been vowed by Yahya Beg.

Never letting go of the girl's hand, Nur al-Huda sought to read the crowd's state of mind in the wake of this discovery.

"The red virgin!" the mob continued to rumble.

Was it surprise? indignation? fear? The Circassian reasoned that the people had probably not decided themselves what to feel. She made Saba climb up next to her on the raised stump of a plane tree and harangued the crowd, staying slightly behind the girl, whose loosened hair shone in the sun like copperware.

"Yes," cried Nur al-Huda, "the red virgin, sacrificed and returned among us to give us guidance. Let us save her! Let us save Isfahan! Hurrah for the red virgin!"

"Hurrah for the red virgin!" a thousand voices joined in, and the sound of this cry carried as far as the upper city.

Saba meanwhile kept her eyes on the ground. A space had cleared in front of her, into which a single man had dared enter. He was only a step away from her. She looked at him. His hair was strangely done up, Armenian-style; he had a European face, lined with wrinkles, and wore a thick, gray, curly beard. The disjointed chicken still dangled from his hand. The girl saw that he was murmuring something. He came closer.

"Saba?" he shouted a little louder.

"Yes," she answered.

He looked at her strangely. She thought he was crying.

"Juremi," he said. "I am Juremi."

She jumped down and threw herself into his arms. It seemed as if she had always known him. Juremi! The man her father had gone to the ends of the earth to find and whom she had never met. She was not surprised that he should be standing in front of her. Everything was strange today.

"Hurrah for the red virgin!" Nur al-Huda continued to shout, at a loss, able to think of nothing but maintaining the crowd's excitement at a high pitch for a last effort.

"What are all these hotheads going to do?" asked Juremi. He held Saba at arm's length by both shoulders and looked at her fondly.

"Why, I don't know . . . Take Julfa, I think."

"Take Julfa!" he exclaimed. "Madness! Your father and mother are there. You'll massacre them first and get yourselves killed next. The Afghans have set traps everywhere. The streets are blocked by barricades. They'll rain death on you from the rooftops."

"Hurrah for the red virgin!" the crowd kept repeating, wavering and turbulent.

"But what else can we do?" asked Saba, turning for a moment toward Nur al-Huda and then looking again at Juremi. "We are dying of hunger, and they say that the Afghans will kill us all if the city falls."

"Is she the one saying that?" asked Juremi, nodding toward the Circassian.

Without waiting for Saba's answer, the Protestant rushed toward Nur al-Huda and signaled to her to come down from the stump. As soon as she was standing next to him he spoke, with Saba translating, never averting his eyes from hers:

"Alix and Jean-Baptiste are at Mahmud's side. I guarantee you that there will be no massacre of this city if it surrenders. It's not Julfa you should be marching on but the royal palace, to make this half king capitulate entirely."

Nur al-Huda thought for a moment. The man's firmness troubled her. She herself was so unsure of her plan that she couldn't produce an opposing argument.

The crowd around them was starting to grumble. With its leaders gone, it found itself at a loss, adrift, pulling in all directions, perhaps already beyond concerted action. Nur al-Huda called Ahmad and spoke two words in his ear. They had a brief discussion, then the eunuch climbed back onto the stump. He raised his arms until the assembled crowd fell silent, and finally shouted out:

"Let's go find the king!"

After a moment's hesitation, the crowd murmured again, repeating:

"To the king, to the king. To the royal palace!"

The cry resounded, rolled through the air, came back as an echo, louder than before, an enormous roar that filled all of the Chahar Bagh: "To the royal palace! To the royal palace!"

"She is alive! She is happy! Oh! yes, I forgive her, good God, yes."

Monsieur de Maillet, alone in the silence of his luxurious prison, repeated these words all day. He had stopped drinking, stopped eating, stopped sleeping, but none of these privations seemed to affect him. He was only a little more parched, a little paler.

"She is happy," he repeated affectionately. "Alix! You are happy!"

From time to time he would feel his legs grow numb and walk about a bit on the lawn. It was thus he noticed that the door was ajar.

"A breath of air, what a good idea!"

He pushed the door open. The guard placed there by the nazir was gone. His chair was empty.

"He's taking a walk, quite rightly, the good man," muttered the consul. "Alix, dear child, how happy I am to know that you are alive!"

The old man continued to advance all alone through the deserted maze of the palace. A distant rumor came from the town, beyond the walls. He pushed open other doors, admired the precious furniture, a lacquered Chinese screen, smiling at everything he saw.

"A beautiful object, truly! The nazir must have great trust in me to leave all this in my care. He is quite right."

A last gate led out into the street. The consul passed through it, waving to a frightened young sentinel who didn't dare stop him. Thus he reached the broad avenue crossing the Chahar Bagh. The gardens looked like a logged clearing in the midst of a wood. There were tree trunks lying about and stumps poking from the ground. In the distance was the commotion of a crowd drawing away.

"Where are all these people going?" asked Monsieur de Maillet. "Probably to the sea, whence they came."

The old man's face wrinkled into a smile. He shrugged and began to walk. The only direction in which he knew to go was toward the French legation. He headed there without thinking and soon arrived at the building.

"No gatekeeper here either. Really, this town is deserted!"

He entered, crossed the courtyard, climbed the entrance stairs. The large French doors were not locked. He pressed the handle down and swung the door open.

"How cool it is! Why, the floors have been waxed. What a pleasant smell!"

He looked toward the inner doors, as though a young girl in a summer dress were about to make her appearance.

"Where are you," he murmured, "since you are alive?"

The great drawing room was empty, and the office door ajar. He entered.

"Good day, Your Majesty," he said respectfully, addressing a shadow he alone could see.

The furniture under its white slipcovers, like a group of courtiers in pajamas, waited for the king's couchée.

"Courtiers in pajamas!"

He allowed himself a little laugh. As soon as he had recovered his gravity, he made a tour of the office, pulled out the desk chair, and sat down in it, settling his forearms on the leather desktop. He was neither hungry nor thirsty, nor tired. He only wanted to think about her.

"Really, they were quite right to let me go. I'm better off here."

44

Huseyn, the king of Persia, was worried. He allowed no one to draw his wine for him in the morning from one of the three full barrels in the cellar. He performed the task himself by candlelight and afterward drew a mark on the wooden rod he used as a gauge. But despite all his precautions, the level of the precious liquid was dropping fast. Was it possible that he had imbibed all that himself? Yet he applied scrupulous, one might almost say cruel, limits on his consumption . . .

The evidence was nonetheless plain to see: he was coming to the end of his supplies. The disappearance of the red virgin had confirmed Huseyn in his dire premonitions: things were taking a bad turn. He had done what he could, though. All the heads that were to roll had been duly chopped off. Yahya Beg could count on his support in all his most brutal and radical undertakings. The Sun could boast no more fervent adorer than his son the king of Persia. Yet the level in his vats was inexorably falling.

The sovereign had reached this stage in his meditations when the nazir was announced for an exceptional audience. Huseyn was quite certain that this rascal of a high chamberlain was still hiding a few casks at his house for his personal use. He had promised himself that he would have them seized the very day he himself ran utterly dry. In the meantime, the nazir was still useful since he kept guard over his own casks. This was a reason not to chop his head off.

Something for a rainy day, thought the king.

"Your Majesty," exclaimed the nazir before he had even reached the center of the room. "The crowd!"

"And what about the crowd?"

"It's on the move."

"Well, well, it won't get very far. Heh, heh."

"A eunuch is exciting them . . ."

"Each to his own," snickered Huseyn, examining his nails.

"All the sentries in my house have disappeared, Your Majesty," added the nazir, who was panting with anxiety. "The cooks, the gardeners, everyone has rushed off to follow the crowd."

"Where are they headed?"

"To the Chahar Bagh first. These shiftless beggars apparently want to attack Julfa."

"Good luck! The Afghans will show them a thing or two."

A rumor came suddenly from the garden. A guard entered trembling all over without even prostrating himself.

"Sire! Sire!"

"Now what?" shouted Huseyn ill-humoredly. "What a day I've had, by the eyes of Ali! Where is Yahya Beg, anyway? He'll put some order into all this."

The nazir and the guard shrugged to show they had no idea.

"But, Your Majesty . . ." the soldier persisted. "They are coming . . ."

"Who is coming?"

The question had hardly been put than the sound of a commotion and shouts echoed to them from the door of the palace. Huseyn took fright and ducked behind his throne. Suddenly, a small group thronged the entrance to the pavilion. In the lead were Ahmad and Nur al-Huda, followed by Juremi and Saba. Seeing her mane, the king called out:

"The red virgin!"

"None other, Your Majesty," said Nur al-Huda, advancing without a tremor to within a few paces of the king.

The silence in the room was troubled only by the noisy confusion of the crowd as it continued to take over the palace. The building where the king sat that morning was one of the most inaccessible of all his palaces. It was called the Pavilion of the Forty Columns, a structure traditionally held as one of the wonders of the world. The crowd that had broken into the sanctuary pushed and shoved for a better look at it. Those among them who had the most schooling had soon counted the columns and realized that they numbered only twenty. The twenty others claimed by tradition were the reflection of the first set in the pool that extended the length of the facade. Far from admiring this poetic doubling, the assembled crowd muttered its disapproval, and the deception only further reduced in their minds the credit of the crown.

Nur al-Huda knew that it was useless at this point to call on Ahmad. The eunuch could stir up a crowd, but he remained frozen with fear and respect before his sovereign.

"Your Majesty," she continued in a strong, confident voice, "your people are hungry. What do you intend to do to feed them, to defend them, to save them?"

"But . . ." stuttered Huseyn.

He was thinking: Where is Yahya Beg? And at the same time: Who is this woman? Then, as if to render him completely vulnerable, the fateful memory returned to him: the level was dropping.

"Your people are listening, Your Majesty. They will obey you, but they await your orders."

"Yah—"

The word was choked off in the king's parched throat.

"Don't cast around for Yahya Beg," cut in Nur al-Huda pitilessly. "We met him on our way here. At a word from the red virgin, the people threw themselves on him and hanged him. It makes no difference anyway. It wasn't to hear Yahya Beg that the crowd came but to hear you, Your Majesty."

Huseyn cautiously came out from behind his royal armchair, sat slowly down, removed his turban, and rubbed his eyes like a man who is exhausted.

"What do you want?" he said in a dull voice.

Nur al-Huda was too far away to see his tears. She preferred all the same to lower her eyes for a moment.

"Freedom, Your Majesty. Life."

"Well then!" he said with a gesture as if to say, Go ahead and take them!

"Mahmud has won this war," declared the Circassian. "The country has been ravaged, your capital is in ruins. There is nothing left but this innocent population, Your Majesty, which has remained faithful to you. Deliver them to the conqueror, on condition that he spare them."

The Gypsy motioned Juremi to her.

"This man arrived from Julfa three days ago. He knows Mahmud. You can send him back among the Afghans. Allow him to negotiate the conditions of your . . . succession."

There was no point in waiting for an answer. Huseyn, devastated, inert, seemed no longer to hear anything, nor to be capable of refusing anything. The way was open to act on his behalf. And there was no time to lose.

Nur al-Huda ordered the palace guard to be evacuated, and in its place Ahmad posted a militia under his orders. A few members of the court, the nazir among them, were detained along with the king until Juremi should return. As to Yahya Beg, Nur al-Huda had lied. The crowd only discovered him on its way out of the palace, and it was actually after this last audience that they hanged him.

Juremi returned to the Afghan camp waving the flag of truce. Alix accompanied him to Mahmud's side. She obtained a promise of clemency from the king of Kandahar all the more readily as the siege had wearied him and he was glad to see it reach a favorable outcome. The profits realized from the looting of Julfa, the soft air of the Persian summer, and a certain pride that they drew from their conquest had mollified the hard hearts of the victors—and of their leader in particular. Cutting throats was losing its appeal, both as a means and as a diversion. The songs and dances carried joyously on the wind to the mournful besiegers each night had inspired them more to join in the celebration than to interrupt it. Mahmud promised clemency, gave strict orders to that effect, then left Julfa for Ferrahabad.

It was there that he awaited Huseyn. The man who was to remain king of Persia a few more hours made his way there on foot the next day, surrounded by a guard composed of his humblest subjects. It was hot; the air would have been of great purity had the acrid smoke of the fires set in the ruins around the countryside not pervaded it. Faint with deprivation and deeply moved, this cortege for an unhorsed king on his way to rejoin the mass of common men arrived on the outskirts of Ferrahabad in the early afternoon. Mahmud, by way of final outrage, made the petitioner wait for nearly an hour, claiming to be asleep and not caring to be disturbed. Finally, he received Huseyn. The poor little king was obliged to cross the entire room by himself, a room he had once presided over from his throne. Mahmud spoke to him sitting and insisted on receiving from the king's own hands the royal aigrette, with which he immediately crowned himself.

"My son," said Huseyn, with some remnant of majesty, "the sovereign ruler of the universe has named the moment when you were to ascend to the throne of Persia. May you reign in peace!"

Mahmud, at that juncture, could think only of Mir Vais, his father. He was moved, and his warrior's face registered an unexpectedly gentle expression.

"God disposes of empires according to His will!" he said. "He takes them away from some and gives them to others. I engage myself nonetheless to consider you as my father and to undertake nothing without demanding your council."

He spoke truly. Mahmud was one of those men who can accomplish a destiny only if it has been traced out for them by an elder. Mir Vais's destiny had been accomplished. He would keep Huseyn for the continuation. The old king was installed in a small palace near the Chahar Bagh. He was allowed to retain five companions in his household and five wives and concubines. This was paring him to the bone. Nonetheless, Huseyn would have given up four of his women to be rid of the nazir, whose head he now regretted having left on his shoulders—the man was part of his remaining retinue. But other than the displeasure this caused him, he lacked for nothing and had never been so happy as with his royalty gone.

In grave silence, the obstacles on the Chahar Bagh bridge were all patiently removed, and the new Afghan rulers made their way, on foot and in awe, into the half-dead city. Alix and Jean-Baptiste went directly home, accompanied by Saba and George. Aside from the withered rosebushes, the cut hedges, and the big mulberry tree that had been chopped down, everything had more or less survived. They each made a tour of the garden, lost in dream, as though to make sure that it was really the place it pretended to be, the haunts that they had carried with them, gilded with nostalgia, through their difficult times. They put off entering the house for a long while and, when they did, examined it with the same deliberateness as the garden. Finally, they arrived silently at the room with the drawn curtains where Françoise, who had survived the siege's deprivations, was resting.

In the half darkness, they could make out the tall silhouette of Juremi, seated next to the bed, holding the invalid's hand in his. Saba ran to the far side of the bed and embraced Françoise tearfully. Alix, Jean-Baptiste, and George gathered around. Under the twin onslaught of exhaustion and joy the poor woman was almost done in. She spoke a word to each, moving her dry, burning lips with difficulty. At the end of the afternoon, she motioned to Saba and George to approach. Then she, who had long known their secret, joined their hands and gave them her blessing.

In the following days, despite the ruin of the city and of the countryside around it, Alix and Saba worked miracles to acquire the best fruits, the tenderest meats, and the finest sweet cakes so that they might give pleasure to their invalid. The invalid was hard put to eat these delicacies, but she brought them close to her lips, and the smells—young, fresh, variegated—paraded before her like actors who walk out on the stage for a last bow before the curtain falls.

Juremi had already recounted a large part of their extraordinary adventures to her. George and Jean-Baptiste completed the tale, and Saba added the story of her own confinement. Françoise had stayed still during these months of pursuits and separations while the world turned around. She had been in the eye of the cyclone, and each of them experienced a strange relief at unburdening himself of the joys and torments of the past months to this font of tenderness, from whom they all seemed to have proceeded.

Laden with these treasures, Françoise, who was growing weaker daily, let them know that she in turn was ready for the crossing. Though she had practiced no particular religion, she felt the need in her last moments to hear speak of God, and the patriarch Nerses came to bring her this consolation. Jean-Baptiste, now familiar with the ways of the church, offered the Armenian a good sum of gold to intercede on her behalf. Nerses accepted with a sigh.

Alix had asked Mahmud to grant her three lives in case of victory. She had been thinking of Françoise, of Saba, and of her father. Monsieur de Maillet was nowhere to be found; Saba had naturally earned the gratitude of the Afghans for her part in Huseyn's surrender; this left only Françoise, but her condition placed her beyond the mercy of any man. When Mahmud asked Alix what she wanted, she could think of only one life that she wished vouchsafed to her: that of Jean-Baptiste. The new king gladly made her a present of it and was informed as of a fortunate coincidence that the slave possessed some knowledge of botany and could even second his mistress usefully in her role of apothecary.

Jean-Baptiste returned to Julfa, to the blacksmiths' quarter, where two great fellows, sweating at their anvil, took two full hours to remove the steel locks that their skillful Khivan colleagues had fastened around the ankles of the former slave.

On his return home, Jean-Baptiste felt a strange sensation, not of freedom, as he was used to doing anything he wanted in his shackles, but of lightness, almost of absence. He barely grazed the surface of the ground, floated rather than walked, and approached others without alarming them with his clanging. Arriving at his house, the impression was even stronger: everything was quiet, and, when he found the family gathered in

Françoise's room, no one paid any attention to his arrival. No one moved. The invalid was stiller than ever, and Jean-Baptiste took a long moment to realize that she too, delivered of her earthly shackles, no longer weighed on the earth and had left it entirely.

After a vigil that lasted a day and a night, Saba proposed to bury Françoise in the hills outside the city, in the very place where they had waited for the scourge of heaven. The young woman remembered how Françoise had told her she would be happy to live there for all eternity. One hovered between heaven and earth with the city nearby, bright and alive. Françoise, who had never owned anything, who had lived free and wandered the world over, could not bear the idea of a city grave, looking like a little house crowded on its mediocre plot of ground. For her eternal stopping place, she needed space, an open view—freedom, in fact. Alix left her faint misgivings unexpressed, and all was done according to Françoise's wishes. Nerses blessed the square of stones and the stela on which her name had been hastily engraved. After the short ceremony, everyone returned to the city. Its jade and emerald domes, in the midst of a ravaged, dry, gray countryside, gave it the appearance of a fairy-tale city, created by sorcery, like those that Saba's nursemaids had long made her see in her dreams.

They went down toward the city silently, bitterly meditating on the cruel magic that, rather than making wonders appear in a deserted place, had this time devastated the area around a treasure.

"Beugrat!" shouted Murad from the depths of his lair. "You took your sweet time. How long did it take you to return from Persia?"

"The roads are bad, Ambassador, and the carriage a little . . ."

The word "heavy" was forbidden in that household.

"Did Monsieur de Maillet give you something for me?"

"This key, Ambassador."

"Well, well, the key to the casket! Leandra!"

The poor woman had just finished putting dye in her braids to hide her graying roots.

"Here I am."

"You saucy wench," exclaimed Murad, titillated by her presence, "dive down under my chair and get the little casket I lent to the consul."

The maid got down on all fours as directly as her rheumatism allowed and looked under the bed. Murad's hand, as heavy as a washhouse bat, groped at what remained of plumpness on Leandra's crupper.

"Hmm! Don't spend too long looking," said Murad, "you're going to put me beside myself . . ."

"Here it is," said Leandra, rising painfully to her feet.

The Armenian took the little iron-banded box, placed it on his stomach, and opened it.

"A letter," he said. "Is that all?"

He turned the casket over.

"Nothing else. And what has he written on the envelope? 'To His Eminence the cardinal Julio Alberoni, Vatican Palace, Rome.' Alberoni! That's just like the consul, always on intimate terms with the great . . ."

He sighed.

"But how will I manage to transmit this missive? There's no question of entrusting these secrets to the Turkish mails, with their spies."

Leandra, along with another Grace, was shaking out the dusty hangings in the room and plumping up the stained cushions. Murad looked at her.

"I've got it!" he exclaimed. "Come here, Leandra."

He took her hand.

"Beugrat will set off again in the carriage. After all, he loves to travel. This time he'll go to Rome and take you. Yes, you, Leandra, don't open your eyes wide like that. You will bring this letter yourself. To Rome, do you hear me? Are those cardinals ever lucky!"

Murad drew the servant to him familiarly, tickling her under the chin.

"I hope you'll behave, my little piglet . . ."

The poor nymph burst into laughter, but took care to keep her hand over her mouth. That very morning she had lost another front tooth, making a nasty gap.

45

After the fall of Isfahan, the Afghans respected their promise to spare the inhabitants of the city. The one consequence of this clemency was to increase the number of people who joined in to celebrate the victory. Both the victors and the vanquished shared the same feeling of relief. Worn out by the long wait and by privations due on the one hand to campaigning and on the other to the hardships of the siege, they broke down the doors to the last granaries, lit bonfires with the wood cut down for battle, and exhausted themselves with singing and dancing. On the third day of this frenzy, Isfahan woke up silent, starved, and morose.

In the countryside, the irrigation system that, at the cost of several centuries of effort, had made the soil of Fars fecund with flowers and fruit was ruined by the war. The earth in these regions can be extremely fertile, but only on condition that man not relax his industry and leave off watering it. The Afghans neither knew nor cared to perform this task. They did nothing to repair the baked clay canals that had been cut by the war, nor to clear the wells that had been poisoned. On the contrary, they mistrusted all who attempted to wander freely through the countryside and preferred to keep the Persians between walls, the better to surveil them. Drought came on little by little, worsened by several rainless months. Isfahan, once lapped around with greenery, became an oasis in the midst of an arid desert. On the morrow of the city's capture, victor and vanquished both discovered their tragic misunderstanding: each believed the other to possess wealth. But there was nothing, either inside or out, but penury and poverty. Trade slowly made up the lack, but prosperity had left the country in the baggage of the foreigners and the wealthy merchants who had fled because of war, taking their goods with them. The city, once flush with superfluity, now found it difficult to gather the bare necessities. The Chahar Bagh gardens were destroyed, the palaces gutted, the riches gone, and Isfahan was no longer a city but its shadow. Once the Afghan victory fêtes were over, no one had the heart or the means to organize celebrations. The country's new rulers possessed nothing but the misery they had caused there. Their main diversions were somber fests where food was scarce and wine forbidden. To escape the depressing reality, the guests sought consolation in the dreams brought on by the smoke of their miraculous resins.

The Persians observed these rejoicings with disgust. Nothing spoke more pointedly of their having been conquered than to be forced to witness such sights. They, who truly knew how to celebrate, and who had even paid for their predilection with their freedom, were now reduced to celebrating its memory in silence. After the early moments of heedlessness following Huseyn's surrender, the city's inhabitants had reverted to a cautiousness appropriate to a humbled people. Even supposing they had ever felt the inclination, they would never have allowed their joy to burst out in song or dance. They were too frightened that the Afghans would take this happiness as evidence of unlawful prosperity and demand their share of it, understandably the lion's share. No longer did one hear the sound of music in the city, nor the noise of banquets, nor see anyone dressed except in plain cloth. After the alacrity of war had come the austerity of peace.

The prohibition on pleasure was acknowledged by all, though never publicly proclaimed. Only someone with the audacity to defy the unspoken order could test whether, in fact, the time for celebration was past.

This audacity came from an unexpected source. The first to exhibit it was Saba.

Since the fall of Isfahan and the return of the travelers who had set off in search of Juremi, Saba and George's secret had become known to all. The two young people were no longer regarded as brother and sister, yet no other way of considering them had yet been hit upon. And they themselves seemed unable to adopt a countenance in public that accorded with the feelings they had avowed in private. Prevented from embracing in the manner of children and too shy to display an adult tenderness, they kept their distance from each other when anyone else was present. This house to which all the old servants had returned, and where Juremi had taken up quarters in Jean-Baptiste's laboratory as discreetly as he could—which was hardly discreet at all— this house that echoed with the sound of visitors, that was crossed by patients coming to get remedies, by Persians, full of bitterness and nostalgia, in a mood to express confidences, and even by Afghans who knew that Alix could intercede for them with the new king, this house, big as it was, afforded no intimacy to the two children who had once known quiet there and tender isolation. They waited until the darkest hour of night to join at the bottom of the garden, on the rose-scented lawn, but almost invariably found themselves startled by other shadows looking in the darkness for the same privacy, making it less discreet there even than during the day.

One morning several weeks after Françoise's death, Saba came to sit by her mother in a small dining room at the back of the house where the morning sun streamed in. They were alone and facing each other across the long table, with two cups of steaming milk between them—a rare food in these times of hardship, but a patient of Jean-Baptiste's had left a jugful for them at dawn.

Since Françoise's wake, mother and daughter had spoken little to each other. Yet in mourning the same friend a new intimacy had sprung up between them. Alix, observing her daughter, sensed that she had changed. Exactly how Alix couldn't tell, and she would have liked to question Nur al-Huda about it.

Saba didn't wait for her mother to finish her cup of milk. Now that they were alone and face to face for once, she jumped at the opportunity. After giving her mother a smile—an expression that now came to her lips often and helped make her unrecognizable—the young woman rested an amused glance on her mother.

"Maman," she asked, "don't you miss all the parties?"

"The parties!" exclaimed Alix.

Here was her daughter, once so severe and full of reproach at the very mention of entertaining, asking her this question! It did not make Alix feel uncomfortable, only a little pitying. She understood her daughter's reference to parties as another instance of the nostalgia that others routinely confided to her and that she herself felt.

"Alas!" she sighed.

A vague shame stole over her for her happy life.

"Why are you sighing?" asked Saba, still smiling.

How unthinking she was, thought Alix, unless this was proof of an unusual cruelty . . .

"Saba, my child," she said emotionally, "don't insist on this sensitive point. Every parent would like to provide the best existence possible for his or her child, and see them live in happy times . . ."

"I had no intention of reproaching you," said Saba gently, reaching across the table for her mother's trembling hand. "Besides, I don't have any idea what happy times would be."

"Saba!" cried Alix, on the verge of tears.

"I don't," said the young girl sharply, her smiling face strong under its crest of flaming hair. "Leave off those thoughts, that melancholy. I don't know what happy times would be because, to me, all times are happy."

Alix was mute with astonishment.

"Let me confess something to you, Maman," said Saba, rising and going to the sunny window. "During the siege of the town, you know we had nothing left to eat. Death was there, coming a little closer every day. To look at its hideous face, you only had to climb to the ramparts in the morning: you could see the fires everywhere in the countryside; the wind carried the smell of carrion . . ."

Alix lowered her eyes. After a moment of silence, her daughter came back to her chair, rested her knee on it, and leaned across the table with a passionate expression.

"Well, we were happy. I've never felt such happiness, do you hear? And why was that? Because we had all of us decided on it. Oh! how can I make anyone understand who didn't live through it? It was the most utter destitution, the end. But our will to joy kept death away and made an ever more copious share of joyousness, of fraternity, burn in our starved bodies."

"Nur al-Huda . . ." murmured Alix.

"Yes," said Saba, resuming her seat. "It's no doubt from Nur al-Huda that I've gotten these ideas. But not only from her. She could never have convinced me of it had there not been all the others."

"All the others?"

"Yes, all the wretched, the poor, the starving, all those around us who had no hope. Oh! Maman, it's true I need to confess to you how much I hated your parties when I was little. I saw in it the most execrable display of wealth, as though the wealthy were making a ritual sacrifice to the god of gold who showered favors on them. And all in the hopes that they would never face poverty."

"What a strange idea . . ."

"I offer it in all honesty as the feeling of a child. I was wrong, perhaps, but that was how I saw things. It was those wonderful weeks of the siege that made me see everything differently. How can I explain it to you? I suddenly understood that joy is not simply an attribute of wealth, a gift from the world, but first and foremost a faculty within ourselves, an aspect of our will. Suddenly, celebrations no longer seemed a luxury but a form of struggle. Well, I think that we have reason to give proof of it today more than ever."

What a strange child! Alix looked at her daughter with a feeling that was neither uneasiness nor reproof, but perhaps a novel admiration, and a sense of what had made them at the same time so different and so deeply similar.

"Then," said Alix sternly, a smile belying her tone and betraying the conviction that had just taken hold in her, "we should celebrate, in this devastated city where we ask ourselves each day whether we will be able to feed ourselves, and where the new rulers know only how to cultivate desolation and to punish disorder?"

"Yes," said Saba bravely.

Astonishment made them keep silent for a moment. Then they both gave in to a long fit of giggles that ended in an embrace.

"I know a zither player," said Saba, when they had recovered their composure, several storytellers, and even a dancer who has not fled . . ."

"Well then, we can start to think about it."

They considered a thousand details and laughingly drew up a list of guests.

"But come to think of it," said Alix with sudden gravity, "what reason will we give for these rejoicings?"

Saba had patiently waited for this moment, preferring that her mother raise the question. Still smiling broadly, she suggested:

"It could be . . . for your engagement."

For all its surprise, the idea was not a bad one. Ever since she had returned to town as the mistress of a former slave, Alix had been living in a highly irregular situation. The Persians had all recognized Jean-Baptiste, naturally, but being a subject people, they had fallen into complicity with a lie whose only dupe was the occupier. Not one had betrayed the apothecary, and Mahmud continued to believe in the fable of the widow who had taken up with a freed slave. The fiction could not be expected to hold up forever, and as it was too late to confess everything, the best thing was to sink a little deeper into illusion.

"Excellent idea," said Alix, amused. "That's it, we'll say it's for my engagement."

Saba, truly admirable in her patience, finally experienced a sense of relief. She felt a pang of tenderness for George and judged that the moment had come to say what she had come to say.

"For your engagement," said Saba, smiling. "And also," she added gravely, "for mine."

Thus Alix and Jean-Baptiste, and Saba and George, the parents and the children, celebrated their engagements on the same day, in early spring. The party given to mark these unions was the first seen in Isfahan since the fall of the Persian royal dynasty.

Alix presented the news of the upcoming ceremony to Mahmud herself, and he did not object. For a moment she even thought that he had decided to attend. But a lingering shyness in the mountaineer made him fear that the gesture might be inappropriate. He wished the betrothed luck and lavished handsome presents on them. So that Alix might feed her former elephant keeper fittingly, the king gave her a garden near the river, where the moisture from the riverbank still made it possible to plant vegetables and harvest excellent fruit.

The double engagement was announced for a Sunday, and following two weeks of preparations, the great day finally came. If one were to consider only the food and the decorations, it was a very meager ceremony in comparison with the splendor and fantasy that were once seen in this city and particularly in this house. But if past festivities had all fused in memory into a bright and indistinct glow, this one was to remain in the minds of all as an incomparable night. Despite Mahmud's consent, no one was entirely sure that the Afghans would not decide to brutally disrupt the proceedings. This small barb of fear gave a further irritation to minds that were already on edge and made them register everything with delicious intensity. At the cost of untold effort, which included intercepting an eastbound caravan two days from town, Alix and Saba managed to purchase spices, raisins, and all the thousand little things necessary for everything just to seem normal, without attaining to luxury—yet luxury came of itself because of the very rarity of such occasions.

Many rich Isfahanis had fled when Julfa fell and even before, during the temporary evacuation of the city. Those who remained had sold off their clothing and their plate piece by piece in order to have the means to survive. If this misfortune served any useful purpose, it was to make the rich and the poor practically alike in appearance and allow them to be invited together. Their former repugnance toward mingling notwithstanding, they all marched to the same beat, wearing the uniform of poverty. Some former officials still had remnants of handsome cloth and fur, and heavy turbans of fine silk, but thought it foolhardy to display them. The Persians all came to the party adorned in the incomparable dignity native to this people, but wearing dull-colored smocks. Alix had sounded the call to arms in every house to assemble brilliant tableware. Small candles, scattered everywhere in pots, lit the garden and the house, making the silver platters and fruit bowls sparkle. The guests, swaddled in heavy cloth, seemed to absorb this outburst of luxury the way a black body absorbs the light of the sun. Only their eyes shone with pleasure, exalted by a sudden and secret revenge.

The diplomats, the associates of trading companies, the money changers, and the majority of the religious functionaries had disappeared at the time of the invasion. Few were the foreigners who had not fled, and those who remained had entirely adapted their habits to penury: first the penury of the siege, then of the bankruptcy that followed. A short Polish Jesuit named Kruzinsky started to appear in people's houses. He could be seen at times standing apart and jotting down notes. He had resolved to write the recent history of the country and gathered these twigs intending to toss them one day into the blaze of a great narrative that would enlighten mankind.

A few foreigners had been sent to attend on Mahmud in Ferrahabad even before Huseyn's abdication, but these plenipotentiaries and traders had been discouraged by the anarchy that ruled the country ever since the Afghans' arrival, and by the Afghans' hostility toward all their neighbors. The only one to have immediately set to work without the least show of impatience was Bibichev.

After he finished writing his notebook of dispatches in the Julfa ironmonger's shop, the spy had finally found a way to transmit it to Moscow. This meticulous work of the informer's art, conveyed by an agent who was thought to be dead, had elicited the admiration of connoisseurs in all the Russian bureaus. Everything was luminously demonstrated: how the formidable Cardinal Alberoni, thanks to the buried gold of the Urals, had managed to overthrow the Persian monarchy and place his henchmen in the entourage of the new king. An express order, sent by return mail, instructed Bibichev to remain in Isfahan and accredited him as the new Russian ambassador. He was proud to serve the tsar in a capacity consonant with his worth and the devotion he had always shown. But he was also relieved that his analyses could no longer be proved wrong: now if the plot he had described came to nothing, no one could blame his overactive imagination but would instead praise his unrelaxing vigilance.

Bibichev had abandoned his breeches and put away his otter tails in

favor of a severe costume, tailored for him in the bazaar, which restored
the undertaker's look he preferred. The new ambassador was one of the
first to arrive at the party, determined to put to good use anything he
might see there. He informed Alix that his wife was traveling down from
Moscow and was expected in Isfahan from one day to the next. Bibichev
hoped that the poor woman would arrive safely and without losing any of
their eight offspring along the way, as he had reached the more reflective
and less fertile age at which one no longer feels oneself to have the strength
to repair such losses.

The party started slowly: people stepped with apprehension onto this
exposed stage. Saba was everywhere: in the kitchens, the drawing room,
and back and forth from the house to the garden. As the guests discovered
the steaming bowls filled with delicate meats, which had been all the more
carefully prepared for having few ingredients, they gave their joy scope.
The zither player, whom Saba had somehow unearthed, took over one of
the terraces and was surrounded by a circle of rapt faces. Two poets, one
in the garden and the other by a fireplace in the drawing room, began to
tell the deeds sonorously represented in the great and venerable epics.

When the evening was well along, the two betrothed couples walked
out onto the entry steps, and everyone gathered around them calling for
silence. The patriarch Nerses came forward as a friend and made a touching little speech bringing the fiancés together. There was no question of an
actual sacrament: one of the couples was preparing for the future sacrament of marriage, while the other had already received it in the past. The
blessing showered on them was one of mixed tenderness and mockery, as
no one present ignored that among the fiancés were a husband and wife;
laughter was directed at the Afghans who were incapable of knowing this
or, had anyone revealed it to them, believing it.

Although the ritual was pared down, its sacred anointment was not
forgotten. Servant girls filled the cups, and the guests—terrified and
delighted—toasted with an excellent wine from Georgia, expressly
brought up from a friendly cellar where it had lain protected from the
war. Saba had talked her mother into this final act of audacity. She
claimed that the Sunni Afghans considered the Persians heretics in any
case and took little interest in the manner of their attaining perdition.
While the wine continued to slake the guests' thirst, dancers appeared in
the garden, the lower part of their faces covered with a modest veil,
though it did not go so far as to hide their naked stomachs.

From this point on, the party took a different turn. The last vestiges

of caution were flung aside. Once the first mortal sin has been irremedia-
bly committed, just as well to commit them all, so as not to be convicted
for too little. The Chahar Bagh and the surrounding neighborhoods rang
with the sound of songs and ululations as in the finest days of the siege.

Jean-Baptiste and Alix wandered away from the joyous mêlée hand in
hand to find a seat on a stump along the border of the avenue. They who
had been threatened by the humdrum of daily life and had separated to
escape it were now together and at home but confronted with all the
uncertainty of life, its danger, its beauty.

In the end, the Afghans may not have been wrong to consider them
foreigners who had recently been brought together. The somewhat world-
ly, settled, and contented apothecary of Isfahan was truly gone, and Jean-
Baptiste often amused himself by looking at his grave in the garden.
Another man had returned, his spirit rounded like a pebble washed in
every storm, saturated with hardships, drunk with the beauty of the
world, and filled with a love that now owed nothing to circumstances and
everything to dreams and to freedom. As to the young, too-happy girl who
had persisted in the one transgression that had delivered her still a child
into the arms of the man of her life, she too was no more. The woman who
succeeded her was free of the regretful sentiment of having loved insufficiently. She no longer feared the end of happy times. She felt strong
enough to bring happiness into existence anywhere and no longer depended on anything to create it.

There they were, somewhat apart from the festive throng, the former
elephant driver and the woman who had chosen him, entwined, moved,
renewed, when suddenly the rumbling of a carriage clattering down the
Chahar Bagh avenue made them start and turn pale.

46

The four dashing horses stopped with neighs of fright and a great saw-ing of their heads when they reached Alix and Jean-Baptiste. Though har-nessed higgledy-piggledy, their rich trappings and the vestiges of rickety plumes rising from their shaved forelocks unmistakably spoke of the hors-es' noble station. The avenue was no longer lit since the war, and it was only when the vehicle's emblazoned door opened did Jean-Baptiste recog-nize it.

"Huseyn's carriage!" he exclaimed, squeezing his companion's arm.

It was unmistakably the luxurious equipage of the former king. Yet instead of the sumptuous slaves in gold-embroidered livery that had once attended it, the carriage was driven by two bearded, ragged Afghan guards. Three other mountaineers with even fiercer mugs jumped from the foot-man's bench and arrayed themselves around the vehicle with truculent miens.

"Did Mahmud take it for his own?" whispered Alix.

She trembled at the prospect of seeing the new sovereign materialize. She was still afraid, despite having given his consent to this entertainment, that he might take it into his head to ruin it by showing up in person. But the man who extracted himself painfully from the carriage, groping with his foot for the step, was not the nervous figure of the ruler of Kandahar. He was slowed by his bulk, clumsy, and groaned with the pain of setting his massive body on firm ground. A voluminous cloak wrapped him around and hid the lower part of his face in a thick fur collar. Finally he was standing, walking toward them, and they recognized him.

"The nazir!" said Alix, as though hypnotized.

The old Persian, on hearing his title, came nearer and in turn recog-nized the two strollers.

"It looks as though you were waiting for me," he said, smiling, and without giving them time to answer, he dragged them toward the house. "Come," he went on, "let's not stay out here. I haven't much time. Let me see a bit of this party that I almost missed."

Alix and Jean-Baptiste, each held by one of the sturdy old man's pincers, entered their garden and crossed the threshold into the house, where the guests, absorbed in clapping to the rhythms of the music, paid them no attention.

The colored candles had burned down entirely: their wicks floated in little puddles of liquid wax, which they sputteringly set ablaze. Saba, wreathed in laughter, her red hair billowing, walked from room to room feeding the little braziers of joy into which the storytellers, the drummers, and the guests tossed all their griefs and troubles to melt them into ingots of gaiety and hope.

The nazir roared with pleasure at the sight of this animated scene.

"And what are all these people drinking?" he asked, bearing down on a serving girl carrying a stoneware pitcher.

He grabbed it by the handle and, treating it like a cup, emptied it in a single draft.

"Thunder and lightning but that's good!"

Handing the jug back to the astonished girl, he asked her to bring him another on the double.

Observing him in the candlelight, Jean-Baptiste finally realized what had made the elderly Persian unrecognizable: he had cut off his mustache. The endless hairs that had once twisted in long curls to the middle of his cheeks had disappeared. Where these ropes had hung was now a bare lip, motionless and overlong, where there still glistened two little drops of the wine that the nazir had greedily drunk.

"Come," said Alix, pressing her new guest, "you've been standing too long. Let's find a place to sit on the terrace."

The nazir, delighted at the sights and sounds around him, allowed himself to be led to a sofa, collapsing at its foot and resting his elbows on its cushions. At a sign from their mistress, serving girls brought out dishes of food, which sought by their number and bright colors to distract one's attention from the monotony of their contents. But Saba was right, and the happiness ordained by man had become incorporated into things: though it was gray and cold, the rice eaten by the nazir penetrated him more deeply with pleasure than ever did the rich pilaus from the days of plenty.

When he was restored and refreshed by two new flasks of wine, the nazir stretched lazily and with a satiated glance indicated his willingness to talk.

"I had heard that you were . . . with King Huseyn?" hazarded Alix, picking her words.

"You might more accurately say that I am a prisoner. As to Huseyn, there is no point in calling him king. But yes, I spend my days face to face with this monster."

"And . . . you are free to wander about town?" asked Jean-Baptiste.

"Rarely, all too rarely. But yes, I have that pleasure. The Afghans who watch over us allow one of the five souls who form this wretched man's company to venture out on his business and send his messages. I have that task today."

"Then Huseyn has charged you with a message for us?" asked Alix somewhat fearfully.

"Not in the least," said the nazir, heaving a great sigh. "A chance remark, overheard on one of my rare outings, informed me two days ago that you were giving this party. I took good care to say nothing of it to that dog. He would never have let me go. If he can ever dream up something to antagonize me, you can be sure he'll do it. He hates me. Fortunately he no longer has the power, or he would have cut my head off long ago—the Afghans have stripped him of the privilege. But you've noticed that in revenge he chopped off my mustache."

Tears came to the poor man's eyes.

"How then do you spend your days," offered Jean-Baptiste, "in captivity?"

"Do you know, we are shut up in a palace that would not be at all unpleasant if one could find a moment's privacy there. Alas, it's impossible. No sooner do we wake up than we gather in the audience hall to listen to the maunderings of that madman. At first, life was not too bad. We had five women and gladly left them to the king for his personal use, hoping it would make him less mad. But Huseyn is no more a vigorous man than he was ever a wise king. And captivity seems to have taken away his remaining strength for such games. He finally sent all the women away, unable to bear for us to share their favors. The result is that everyone is unhappy: the women, because they are locked away in a little courtyard; us, because we no longer have the balm of this pleasant intercourse; and Huseyn himself, more unhinged than ever and with no other distraction than to inflict vexations on us. At first he received visitors. Mahmud himself came to consult him. But it didn't take the Afghan long to realize that he would learn nothing from a person who became king only by chance and did not have the wits to remain one."

Describing the daily routine made the nazir so gloomy that Jean-Baptiste thought it best to proceed no further on this topic. There was a long pause. The sprightly rhythm of the tambourines filled the darkness, coursing from the shadows of the garden into the depths of their hearts.

"We haven't seen each other since . . . since my death," said Jean-Baptiste finally.

"Ah, yes! Your death! Heh, heh. It worked out quite fortunately for you."

"I am no longer the same, you know."

"That's what I've heard. My compliments. Your new fiancée is even more charming than your former wife."

They all laughed. The nazir continued:

"Do you know, I made the excuse that I had a stomachache in order to come here tonight for medicine." He mimicked pain by rolling his flat upper lip back, like an old dog that is being antagonized. "Huseyn must have suspected something. He kept me with him as long as he could. It was after eight o'clock when he took the notion of challenging me to a game of chess. He plays very poorly and I can beat him in six moves, but then he becomes violent. Tonight the torture lasted two hours. I very nearly missed your party altogether. That would have been a great shame!"

The former lord high chamberlain was now quite relaxed. The wine, which he was not used to—the Afghans supplied their royal prisoner with very little and he left nothing at all for the others—filled the grief-stricken heart of the nazir with melancholy torpor. Deprived of all his schemes, bankrupt, beyond hope, the former intriguer allowed the depths of his soul to appear, showing himself surprisingly indulgent and philosophical.

"A wonderful lie, your death," he went on dreamily, addressing Jean-Baptiste. "And all the rest—Alberoni . . . was that all an invention too?"

"Yes," said Jean-Baptiste, lowering his eyes.

"My compliments."

Poncet assumed a modest, somewhat embarrassed expression.

"No, no, truly. I am sincere. Believe me when I say it's something one finds all too rarely among Westerners. Their lies are little needy things. They say yes when you ask them a question to which the answer is no, and their art extends no further. That's hardly what we call a lie in these parts."

Alix had slipped away to join her daughter in another group. The nazir motioned to Jean-Baptiste to come closer. He once again became animated, his outsize hand with its graying hairs describing large circles in the air.

"Creating a good lie," he went on in the tone of a gourmet, "is for us the invention of a beautiful story that succeeds in duping the listener. What we get in consequence for duping him is no more than the wages owed the artist for allowing another to share in his illusion. And if the illusion is to be shared it must be beautiful, it must be told with talent, and the teller must know how to use the thousand little elements that derive from the real and that make up the false . . ."

"No, really," said Jean-Baptiste weakly, "calling it an art . . ."

"You see? You yourself undervalue the discipline of which you are a master. For you are a master, believe me. You had me gulled completely. Yet I have to confess: I doubted you beforehand, Poncet. That way you had of always keeping your word quite distressed me. Do you remember? I said to you one day: 'Do you take yourself for the Prophet, that your word should be sacred?'"

Jean-Baptiste, still unsure whether the nazir was speaking seriously, apologized:

"You mustn't hold the Alberoni affair against me. I couldn't tell you the truth, otherwise—"

"The truth!" interrupted the nazir, with an air of absolute indignation. "Do you think I give it a moment's thought? Nothing is more boring, more disappointing, in a word, more useless. Do you see, Poncet, truth is not for men. Even when they pretend to come across it or to preserve it, it never belongs to them. They will never be more than its slave. They suffer it, repeat it, are pained by it, and finally resign themselves to it. Whereas a lie! Ah! Poncet, a great, a true lie, now there's what can make each of us equal to the gods. We create worlds through lies, we give life to what doesn't exist. Without this faculty there would be neither genius nor conquest, nor religion, nor love."

A poet in the neighboring room had begun to recite an epic poem, his words falling on respectful silence.

"Why do you think that we Persians confer such honor on our storytellers and poets?" said the nazir, raising a fat finger into the air as though to trace in the smoke of the candles the diaphanous trajectory of the poet's words. "We are halfway between India and the West, don't forget. To one side, the cycle of reincarnation, and to the other, the stifling reign of a single truth, whereas we have chosen a path between them: we create ephemeral worlds, dreams, tales, lies, if you like. The wind disperses them. They augment our lives without giving us more than one life."

"But only until the Afghans arrive . . ." said Jean-Baptiste, immediately regretting the harshness of his remark.

"Yes," the nazir admitted simply. "Perhaps our dreams were no longer strong enough and that explains it. But believe me, when the Afghans have destroyed everything, which won't be long now, our dreams will be strong again. Then one of us will arise and set the world on its ear."

A leaden melancholy settled over the old man. Jean-Baptiste thought for a moment that he had gone to sleep. He jumped when the nazir suddenly asked him in a loud voice:

"By the way, if it was all a lie, why did Alberoni send an emissary here?"

"I don't know."

"You see! Lies, truth, just try and figure it all out. Did you at least meet this odd stick?"

"No. But I'll confess something else: he's Alix's father."

"The consul?"

"Yes, the former consul of Cairo, whom I affronted in the old days by abducting his daughter."

"Did he know about your fabrication?"

"I don't think so. My guess is that his arrival was a distant repercussion of my first lie to you, which then had a life of its own."

"Astonishing! And . . . where is he now?"

"We never found him again. The entire city has been searched."

"Have you visited my former palace?"

"He was no longer there. No one knows what became of him."

"Really? The extraordinary thing about lying is that its consequences never end. Oh, while I'm thinking of it, did you look for him in the French legation? That's where he was staying when he first arrived."

"No," said Jean-Baptiste, "but I suppose we would have heard if he were still there."

"No doubt," said the nazir thoughtfully.

He drifted off again, this time for longer. Jean-Baptiste left him to doze and rejoined Alix.

At the first light of dawn, just as the last of the delighted guests were leaving, the nazir awoke with a start, looked with terror at the time, and, bowing briefly to his hosts, beat a hasty retreat. His Afghan jailers were in fact on the point of coming to fetch him themselves and bring him back to prison before the morning inspection. The carriage, whipped up to a frenzy, jolted back up the avenue with a clatter of axles and shafts.

The day after the party, Jean-Baptiste went to visit the French legation. Hasan, the gatekeeper, had disappeared during the capture of the city. He must have been one of the few casualties of those turbulent days. His nephew, a very young boy, was still waiting for him at his post by the embassy gate. He hadn't dared enter the building himself.

Jean-Baptiste persuaded him to let him pass. The front door was unlocked. He entered the front hall, searched the drawing rooms, then came to the office. The consul was seated, arrested in his dreams, desiccated, intact, under the portrait of Louis XIV. A weight at his neck tipped him slightly forward. Jean-Baptiste discovered on approaching him that it was a bag of gold coins. Death had rigidified the consul in this solemn position. A coffin was made for him in the shape of a throne. Alix came to pay her respects once he was installed. She stifled the tears that she had longed to shed, finding this formal audience from beyond the grave inhibiting. Saba and George first saw their ancestor in this posture of majesty.

A deep hole was excavated on the grounds of the embassy. At nightfall, attended by the small knot of mourners, who were more frightened than moved, the peculiar coffin was lowered into the earth. Thus was the consul buried upright, his gold at his neck, like a Scythian.

Persia, after being conquered by the Afghans, sank gradually into anarchy and lost everything except its spirit of gaiety, which engendered many celebrations after the conquerors' severity had been breached by Alix and Jean-Baptiste's engagement party.

The former elephant keeper, whom the Afghans gradually discovered to be a skillful apothecary, had no trouble exercising his art, and there was regrettably no lack of clients in this ruined country.

To the audacious George, who had charged the walls of Julfa alone, and to the much discussed red virgin, Mahmud gave one of the residences in the crown's possession that was now his to dispose of as he pleased. The buildings consisted of two main pavilions separated by a long garden. On learning this, the two young people decided to offer one to Juremi. The old Protestant would install a laboratory in it and live on the upper floor in a vast attic room lit by dormer windows that opened onto the roofs of Isfahan. Juremi accepted all the more readily as he and George had become inseparable. They worked together in Jean-Baptiste's laboratory, where the old preparer of philters taught the young scientist all his tricks. They still argued often about the question of faith and reason. The one claimed that the greatest power man had was to create gods and sacred realms, while the other countered that only reason and law could prevent the excesses that followed naturally from faith and the will to impose one's faith on the world. Their travels had provided each with a great quantity of evidence for his own position; they were convinced that this dialogue would have no clear winner and last as long as man himself. Notwithstanding, they hashed it out passionately, often exchanging sides. Despite his former prejudice against the chimera of science, Juremi came to take an interest in the arid disciplines of reason, and he even read Leibniz with pleasure. And as to George, while he maintained his faith in progress, mathematics, and the rational method, he avoided taking them too seriously. He even published, in a very austere English journal, a learned article describing a new animal species. Only a single specimen was known, discovered in Persia by the young naturalist: it was a hybrid of the elephant and the rhinoceros, with a bump on its forehead almost resembling a horn. The monograph was accompanied by a handsome engraving of Garou, who was happily living out his days on an island in the river that was thickly overgrown with willows and bamboos.

Alix looked everywhere for Nur al-Huda, but she had disappeared from sight after the fall of Isfahan. The Afghans' harshness, moderated by their promises to the general population, was nonetheless given full license in their treatment of dancers and prostitutes, and it was likely that the young Circassian had sensibly feared she might be taken for one of their number. Alix eventually became convinced that her friend must have fled the city during the time that King Huseyn was abdicating. Ahmad, whom the new ruler had not forgiven for leading the city's resistance, had fled with Nur al-Huda, taking his wife and children with him. By questioning the Gypsies who came through Isfahan, Alix gathered bits of information suggesting that Nur and her little band had gone far to the west, to the country along the Euphrates and even beyond. She consoled herself for her friend's absence by reflecting that the future always reunites what has been separated as long as love survives, and she kept the picture of Nur al-Huda bright in her memory.

A few months after these events Alix, who had returned to wearing her Persian and Western wardrobe, was obliged to visit the seamstress to have her clothes let out at the waist. But despite her ample veils, there was soon no hiding it: she was pregnant, in fact she was remarkably, impressively round. And as it had been decreed that the children of Alix and Jean-Baptiste would come in pairs, she gave birth to twins.

Epilogue

"*Is that all,* Pozzi?"

"Yes," said the secretary unctuously. "Your Eminence may leave with full peace of mind. All the mail has been answered and all the business has been taken care of."

"Well then, everything's perfect!" breathed Cardinal Alberoni, looking perhaps for the last time at the fresco by Raphael.

"I almost forgot," Pozzi interjected, looking more disgusted even than usual. "This letter was left for you by a . . . singular . . . person."

He extended a slip of cheap paper toward the cardinal, its seal cracked.

"Singular . . . in what way?" asked the cardinal, snatching the message.

"Your Eminence would spare me from impropriety by not obliging me to describe the person. Suffice it to say that the person would never have penetrated into these courtyards without the intriguing of the Swiss coachman, who found complicity among the guards. Fortunately, eviction was swift."

The prelate read over the letter quickly.

"What a good fellow!" he exclaimed. "And here I was on the point of forgetting him altogether."

Pozzi discreetly rose to his tiptoes to make out the writing.

"Do you remember Maillet?" asked the cardinal, "the former consul? You insisted that I see him."

Pozzi tilted his head, indicating repentance for an ill-considered act.

"Did he prove an ingrate?" asked Alberoni with a nasty smile, revealing that he was not unaware of his secretary's doings.

Pozzi sniffed.

"In any case," the prelate went on, "the poor man has done me loyal service. Listen to how he closes: 'If Your Eminence receives this letter, it will be that I have laid bare the imposture leveled against you. Unhappy circumstances have alas kept me from reporting the full story personally. But I will expend my last dram of energy to unmask the villains who have tried to take advantage of your sacred self.' Poor wretch! He seems to have met with evil circumstances all because of me. In any case, I am reassured that this business won't leap out again just as the pontiff is conferring another archbishopric on me."

Through the open window, the autumn sky, studded with small round clouds, filled the high-ceilinged room with its peace.

"While I'm thinking of it," said the new archbishop sharply, "have you already returned the Holy Father's seals?"

"No, Eminence. I am to take them back to the secretariat later."

"Well then, quickly write me up a memorandum rehabilitating this good man's book. What was it called already?"

He opened the letter again and found the reference:

"Ah! that's right. *Telliamed,* published in Holland and sold in Paris at Duchesne's, a bookseller on the rue Saint-Jacques, below the Saint-Benoît fountain.

The secretary disappeared from view.

Trotting over to his large combination safe, the cardinal opened the door and emptied its contents into a fat leather briefcase, which he placed on his desk. He made a last inspection of the room, ran his carefully tended fingers over the back of his chair, and took in, for the last time, the scene painted on the ceiling and the large Adoration of the Shepherds by Raphael. He came back to the mantelpiece, set the pendulum of the porcelain clock in motion, and straightened the wick of a candle.

The secretary reentered with the sheet of paper bearing the few lines rescuing *Telliamed.* Alberoni signed it with a flourish.

"Take this right away to the records office for publication."

"Yes, Eminence."

"I am happy that my last act on leaving is to send a man to heaven," said the prelate, "unless he is there already."

He extended his ring to the clerk to be kissed, picked up his briefcase, and went out.

The carriage was waiting for him in the courtyard of the great galleries, glowing at that hour under sunlit greenery. A spring squeaked as he put his weight on the step plate. The two horses drew him away at a fast trot, the most dancelike and joyous of a horse's paces. They left behind the court of Saint Peter and threaded their way through narrow streets as far as the Tiber. The cardinal rested his arms, as was his wont, on the gutter of his bulging stomach.

Passing in front of a palace by the Sant' Angelo Bridge, he noticed a young woman making the same gesture on the rounded form of her expectant belly. With tears of joy in her eyes, she reread the letter in her hand: "Marcellina, my love . . ."

Even the violet of the priests' cassocks looked joyous in the October light. The ocher facades filed slowly by, delightful almost to monotony. In places the black upright of a cypress intervened, awakening the eye to further beauty. A pleasant humor stole over the cardinal's heart and stayed with him the entire way, as far as Parma.

A Note on the Sources of
The Abyssinian *and* The Siege of Isfahan

A historical novel reconstructs the hills of History, that is, it restages what actually happened. An adventure novel takes place more in History's valleys. It fills in the unknown and provides a reality (among others) where we have no knowledge at all.

It is to this second category that *The Abyssinian* and *The Siege of Isfahan* belong. Not that History is entirely absent: on the contrary, it is there to establish bounds and fixed landmarks, in whose vicinity the imagination can be given free rein.

This accounts for the reader's troubling impression of not knowing what is "true." As a novelist, my tendency when queried on this point is to say that the highest truth is that of the imagination. It is not based on any authority and derives its power only from the conviction it gives rise to in the reader. But this novelistic truth does not satisfy everyone. Some feel they have been duped and want to suspend their disbelief in full knowledge of what is "historical" and what is not.

The disclosure is often a disappointment and always a surprise. For what appears most novelistic in *The Abyssinian,* for example, is often authentic: Le Noir du Roule and his distorting mirrors, the moldering elephant ears, the Armenian cook who is appointed ambassador . . .

By contrast, Poncet is a hybrid being, in part real (an apothecary sent to Abyssinia in the company of a Jesuit, tried in Paris for confabulation . . .) and in part imaginary (which explains that he has retained his family name but received a new first name, the old one being "Charles-Jacques"). The real Poncet did not break with the Jesuits but became their tool. The idea of a sunny, sovereign character, who protects and closes behind him the country he has discovered, belongs to *The Abyssinian* as a novel and not to history.

Alix, for her part, did not exist. In writing this, I have the impression of uttering a falsehood, so alive, so necessarily alive, does this character appear, to the point where putting her reality in doubt seems a lie, not to say a crime. But the idea of Alix belongs entirely to this novelist, and my confession, disagreeable as it may be, remains true: Alix never existed.

Monsieur de Maillet, her father, had no children. It is this detail alone that distinguishes the character in the novel from the one in real life. For the rest, Benoist de Maillet was very much as he has been represented. He is known in History from two sources: on the one hand from diplomatic archives, which relate his activity in service to the king of France, and on the other by his philosophical works, which were published almost clandestinely and cost him much criticism. *The Abyssinian* describes Maillet as he appears in his consular dispatches. *The Siege of Isfahan* shows rather the author of *Telliamed.* The work in point of fact appeared in 1725, preceded by a poetic dedication to none other than Cyrano de Bergerac! I am grateful to Dr. Maurice Châtillon for having brought the work to my attention and allowed me to consult a copy. Maillet's essay is of such importance that, in works treating the history of ideas, he is cited as the European precursor of evolutionary thinking. Before Buffon, before Darwin, Maillet posited the idea of species mutation in a philosophical dialogue so bold that it initially had to be printed in Amsterdam to avoid censorship. The "second" Maillet, as he appears in *The Siege of Isfahan,* though the description of his actions is very free, is faithful to this little-known facet of this singular character's destiny.

The Siege of Isfahan, which no doubt gives a greater impression of freedom with respect to History, is every bit as informed by it as *The Abyssinian.* Cardinal Alberoni, the king of Persia and his nazir, the Swedes deported to the Urals, and the selling of slaves in Khiva are directly taken from historical accounts. The fall of Isfahan, including the surprising attack by Garou the elephant, is drawn from, among other accounts, the chronicles of Father Kruzinsky, whom we meet in the penultimate chapter wandering through the drawing room of Alix and Jean-Baptiste. A number of dates have been transposed, as in placing Israël Orii in Isfahan slightly after the time when he was Russian ambassador to the king of Persia.

In the case of each of the two books that compose the Abyssinian cycle I have drawn widely on the magnificent travel literature of the sixteenth and seventeenth centuries: Bruce, Chardin, Tournefort, Lady Montagu, Tavernier, Potocki, Arminius Vamberi, and so many others.

To revisit this period literature, animate it with contemporary passions, and endow it with romantic plots provides the author a twofold pleasure: that of wayfaring with these astonishing travelers, and the perhaps greater pleasure of causing these buried sources, which run always fresh for being fed by the virgin worlds that now exist only in their pages, to be reborn in the present.